9/7/13

for Readers —

Enjoy! with aloha,

Jo Ann Lordahl

PRINCESS RUTH

Love and Tragedy in Hawaii

A NOVEL

JO ANN LORDAHL

This is a work of fiction and fact. Facts are usually end noted and opinions express the author's viewpoints.

Jo Ann Lordahl books may be ordered through www.joannlordahl.com, Kindle, Amazon, booksellers or by contacting

Jo Ann Lordahl
2363 Puu Road, #3C
Kalaheo, HI 96741
www.joannlordahl.com

ISBN: 1461180627
ISBN-13: 9781461180623

Library of Congress Cataloging-in-Publication Data
Jo Ann Lordahl
Princess Ruth: Love And Betrayal in Hawaii
p. cm.
Includes bibliographical references.
1. Hawaii—History—19th century—20th century
2. Royalty—Hawaiian—Princess Ruth—Ruth Keelikolani
3. Niihau—Gay & Robinson—Sinclair
4. Hawaii—GMOs—land—pesticides
5. Hawaii—Immigration—Race relations
6. Hawaiian—Fiction

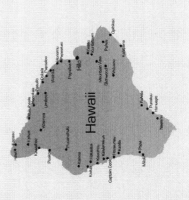

Hawaii

Hilo

Maui
Kaupo
Hana
Kipahulu

Molokai

Lanai

Kahoolawe

Oahu
Waimanalo
Kailua
Honolulu

HAWAII

Kauai

Niihau

INTRODUCTION

PRINCESS RUTH HAD MY HEART as soon as I saw her on the cover of *The High Chiefess: Ruth Keelikolani*. This is the story of Princess Ruth and how Samantha, a haole newcomer, settles into Hawaii. Other major themes are GMOs, Hawaiian history and women's special stories with Kauai's beauty and places and the *forbidden* island of Niihau close behind.

This book records a change in consciousness—from ignorance to a deeper knowledge of *what really happened*. My views of Hawaii, Native Hawaiians and U.S. governmental behavior have changed 180 degrees.

At first my interest in Hawaii was purely personal and pragmatic, getting along in a new place. Slowly, as a writer becoming more engrossed, a sense of justice stirred to life and the desire to tell my Hawaiian story.

Soon I was writing snippets of novel and Hawaiian history, a mishmash of fact and fiction. I love research and reading and taking notes. With a computer to indulge my extravagance, well you can imagine, I ended with reams of research that I could not bear to pitch.

The only aim that kept me afloat was the intense desire, almost a compulsion, to share what I was learning. *If I was so uninformed then so were others*. History is conflicting and leaves out a lot. This new-to-me Hawaiian history was so richly detailed and informative, that I was convinced readers also would be fascinated.

Doing something I don't know how to do, without guidelines, is difficult. Would my book be fact or fiction? When I felt discouraged an acquaintance would answer an unspoken question, or Princess Ruth would whisper at midnight. Yet as friends encouraged and stacks of writing grew, I still dangled at the end of my rope—how to respectfully illuminate fact and fiction?

Answers appeared: Separate sections (the reader can choose to skip forward through factual subjects) and endnotes (the reader can skip the endnote entirely or follow my sources and comments if they choose).

Many people contributed to this book. At crucial early stages Lisette Langlois read pages and kept me going. Charee Watters contributed her university-honed editing skills. Mi-ki encouraged and monitored GMO information. Linda Pascatore made gentle suggestions as did Maureen Martin, Levon Ohai, Janos Samu, Diane Moore, Vickie Sullivan, June Langhoff, David Kure, Bill Salm and Petra Sundheim among others. Tony Lydgate added some organization and editing. The LaBedz's, Jimmy, Janos, Kelly, my hula Kumu, Dee, Amber, Allen, Karin, Sondra, Aletha, Kimo, my daughter Lynn and so many others patiently suggested and corrected. Thanks also to Rick Hanna and Bob Nishek and the National Tropical Botanical Garden and to Hawaii libraries especially Karen Ikemoto, Lisa Nambu, Aimee Inouye and the staff at Hanapepe library who are amazingly vigilant in providing resources and friendliness.

Please forgive mistakes of fact and opinion. I never intend to be ungrateful to Hawaii and its gracious people. Encouragement and love, assistance and information like beautiful lei stacked around the necks of graduating seniors have heaped upon me in full measure. My heart is filled with gratitude.

For comments and corrections, please contact Facebook, Linkedin, www.joannlordahl/blog or email jlordahl@mindspring.com.

With the glare and heat of the lava upon her, the old Chiefess moved majestically, approaching step by step, slowly and alone, walking up to her goddess. Within the twenty onlookers surged a mighty feeling. This woman, who had been rocked on the knee of Kamehameha the Great, was making her supreme test to prove her gods more potent than the sightless God who lived in a book. [She chanted, threw tribute to Goddess Pele, and slept all night in her bed next to the lava.] The ground became silent, and at dawn, Oliver Stillman sped to Hilo to tell the people that their city was safe. The woman was beautiful, beautiful as their goddess Pele; and some even whispered: "She is Pele."

Eugene Burns, The Last King of Paradise

CHAPTER ONE

I PICK UP MY LIFE. When I consider events as they happened, my decision is simple. After life shatters—if we still draw breath, and sometimes that is in doubt—the choices are two.

Become bitter. Blame others. Blame fate. Seek revenge. Accuse whatever gods you've trusted for letting you down.

Or, gather what's left of your intelligent self and go on.

Long ago I understood with a friend in trouble that at bottom-crisis we choose life or death. In my simplistic mind I get it. If it's death you choose, then you might as well commence: the long suicide of self-destruction or short, immediate and final. If life, then open your mind, your heart, your soul. Let go the past. Absolve yourself of grief. But most of all release your guilt as quickly as you gain strength.

Bitterness is negativity and negativity never gets you anything but more unhappiness. Waste is a heavy dislike of mine. I suppose that's what finally reached me—the waste of life. First his life irretrievably gone and then the unnerving experience of watching myself disintegrate. Six months since my beloved husband Thomas died in a senseless accident. Six months of shrinking into myself, of everything around me collapsing.

Finally, a spark of life catches my attention. At a deep unconscious level, choices are made and we find out later what they mean. Somehow, in the depths of my despair, while the conscious me has no idea what fate holds in store, a tiny sense of purpose takes birth. Weak and broken in spirit, this is my turning point. More light appears. A summons, however faint, a calling. Purpose that doesn't yet have a name. Then suddenly I know: this new job that's offered in Kauai. I must accept. I'll leave the old and trust the unknown. In the space of a microsecond I'm no longer running away but being pulled, moving forward.

I don't think well on my feet. Even with my training as a scientist, things fly away, get scattered. Writing is a calming discipline as it lets me choose a place to begin and to keep track of events, even to feel an illusionary control that comes from naming.

My name is Samantha. A few people call me Sam, which pleases me if it's the right person. But call me *Sammie* once, and you're blacklisted. I'm five feet two inches tall, 100 pounds dripping wet, as they say, with blue eyes and flyaway reddish-blonde hair. Getting what I wanted was always easy enough with my philosophy of make your best choice of what's available and get moving. Simplistic times in a simpler world. And I lived then with protection—the will of someone who loved me shielding me from harsh reality.

Or perhaps my old life only feels protected now that I endure ice in my bones.

Getting from there to here, Southern California to my little rented house in Kekaha, Kauai, the oldest in the Hawaiian chain of islands, is the usual frantic mess. Every possession I pick up is a decision: pack, leave or pitch. It's exhausting. Once moved, it's turning on electricity, locating a grocery store and settling after a fashion at work. I go through the motions of ordinary days while a question whispers just outside of my understanding: *why?*

But the new landscapes intrigue me, the beaches and beauty of nature, and the nagging questions—*why* and *have you a clue what you're doing*—begin to fade. When I look inside there's still a hole in my soul where a meaningful life used to be. So mostly I don't look.

Confirmation that I'm in the right place doing what I'm supposed to be doing quietly dawns. Ineffable fate gives current reality a nudge.

Casually drawn to her picture on the cover, I check Princess Ruth out of Hanapepe library. Princess Ruth, as the missionaries call her, was born in 1826 into old Hawaii. She's ugly as sin on the cover of *The High Chiefess: Ruth Keelikolani*—her heart doesn't show.

Tall, imposing, imperial: she's a big woman dressed to the teeth in Victorian finery. Her strong face shouts, "This is wrong!" How could I know how quickly I'd come to love and respect her?

I wish I could understand what's happening. Why me? It was so odd, deep in the night in a strange house, to hear words in my head, and to know they weren't mine. From the mists of time Princess Ruth spoke:

> *Some fool haole white woman asked where I got my dress? I didn't answer. Because I refuse to speak English, she thought me stupid.*
>
> *I'm pleased you've come. Try and get my story right. Stay pono and I'll help you.*
>
> *Don't get scattered. Collect mana. Remain strong.*

Shaking my head against my downy pillow, I wonder if I'm going haywire? When the foreign thoughts come again I lie still as a little mouse chased in from pineapple fields.

> *Tell my tale of old Hawaii, of our free land and people. We didn't write things down. We kept them collected in memory. In chants. Told our*

stories in hula and spoken genealogy taking hours to recite. We were precise and magical. We took time for true aloha.

So many times my highest hopes crushed. You haoles take everything. My world collapsing. Destroyed.

As the voice in my head fades, I'm puzzled but not frightened. Princess Ruth sounds friendly. I need a friend. Yet I can't help but wonder if I can become what she seems to expect, almost demand: A vessel to manifest her story.

This sudden move to Kauai is a reward for my breakthrough discovery; we work on genetically modified organisms, GMOs. And this job, I think, is my boss Kevin's, attempted consolation for the loss of everything I loved. Kevin Broadman, I've known him forever. He wants to shield me. He thinks I am delicate. And probably he wants to keep me working at top capacity. I need this job; need the money. But I'm not ready yet to examine motives.

Nor am I comfortable talking about a Hawaiian High Chiefess' voice or thoughts in my head. Or whatever my experience is. So where does that leave us? I keep trying to puzzle what Princess Ruth is doing in my life. I feel an upsetting empathy for her. A connection.

Perhaps some history would be calming: My history. Or the history of the islands, about which I don't know much, but even that little, I'm quickly learning, is not what I thought. The romantic tropical islands with affluent tourists seeing only happy, carefree sarong-clad natives delighted to fulfill every desire. How pleasantly exotic.

I'd always assumed Hawaii was part of the United States, a state like any other, only located way out in the immense Pacific. The most remote land mass in the world, two thousand miles from anything. How pleased Hawaiians must feel at being a part of the great United States. Little did I know.

The United States actually stole the Hawaiian Islands. We took away their sovereignty as a nation, changed everything. I can't help but be horrified, and fascinated, as more and more true facts come to life.

I promised myself I wouldn't get shrill. A frantically grasping-for-a-cause woman is not who I want to be. Truth to tell I want my life as it was. As I was.

Skipping grimy details, the accident is so out of the blue. One day my husband Thomas and I live our dream life in a dream home. After a chaotic childhood with no surviving relatives, I can relax. Everything is perfect. It's difficult now to think of that time, even six months later. My husband dead. My dream home being foreclosed and debts that Thomas left for me to pay. Part of me still expects Thomas to walk in the door and explain everything. I get lost and I can't think. I have trouble believing in death and sleep is a nightmare. I still can't face sorting that last Chinese box of his childhood things.

A drunk driver—repeated offender it came out later. He got two years for hitting Thomas head-on, driving the wrong way down the expressway after his drunken Saturday night party.

Handsome is the word for men but to me Thomas was beautiful. A football star who played the violin. Strong and sensitive. I loved to look at him—that open Greek-modeled face, blond hair and Paul Newman-piercing blue eyes. Thomas said he loved me.

My life is gone. Perhaps that's why I resonate with long-ago Hawaiian High Chiefess Ruth. Feel sad for her. Her babies die, her beloved husband of six years dies. Her homeland culture falls into ruins around her. How did she remain strong? Princess Ruth, as haoles call her, has lessons for me. Haole used to be the Hawaiian word for foreigners; today it means any white person. I have to laugh—haole literally means *no breath*. Hawaiians couldn't believe how shallowly the missionaries breathed and so they called them *no-breathers*. Breath is key to mana, I'm learning, meditation breath, prayerful breath. Breath that rests in the *is*-ness of creation, in the connection of all things, in nature living without end.

At first I envied Thomas being dead. Even now in bitter moments I think that by dying he didn't have to deal with the chaos of his death. Yet I shouldn't complain. Timothy Brown, our long-time lawyer in California, said he'd help with my finances. But even so, money and death and everything changed; it was too much. I was drowning. Yet I am a survivor. Kevin was right to offer me Kauai. The Garden Island. This lush Hawaiian land slowly brings me back to life. I feel it happening. Nature—the life-force here—is strong.

Once in South Miami, where we lived before California, I took a pick-axe to the below-the-surface coral in our backyard and peeled back the bark from blood-red hibiscus cuttings I'd gathered from next door. After I planted and faithfully watered, those cut-off small limbs became blooming plants. It's faint in me but here on Kauai that same indomitable life-force begins moving.

The other day I understood why coming here felt like returning home. How could I feel I was coming home to Hawaii when I grew up on a farm in Alabama? I was sixteen before I ever saw an ocean, and then it was the placid Gulf. It gnawed at me, how Kauai felt welcoming, familiar.

Tears come as I write: Home, wanted, safe, accepted, understood, cherished. What we all desire in our hearts, what I've missed so dreadfully. A companion, a lover, a fellow traveler through time. Continuity. Someone who knows you. Not a day goes by that I don't miss Thomas. Thomas wasn't perfect, but love has eyes larger than perfection. There's a black hole where he was. He took care of me. I took care of him. Like that Taoist symbol, we were a magical yin-yang circle. At least I thought we were. With Thomas I lost the present and now my trust in any future is shaky indeed.

I keep losing my place. What was I talking about—how Kauai feels like coming home. Then one morning, a couple of weeks later, while I was driving to work at Purity Corporation in Waimea the answer just settled in my mind. I jotted the ideas down on a shopping list I'm making.

This red dirt of Kauai is exactly like my old red hills of Alabama. And the energetic greens of the pines and hickories, oaks and magnolias of my childhood find eucalyptus here, koa, African tulip and candlenut trees.

Sitting alone in a pine tree in Alabama or breaking open a warm watermelon to eat only the heart, where no seeds grow—to my young sensibility these were magic. Kauai is nature grown large: Magical, the sparkle and mystery of childhood come home again. This life-force searches to heal. Its tranquil touch reaches out like clouds over Kahili mountain luring me to accept its generosity.

Princess Ruth, oddly enough, feels part of this caring aloha; in the depths of my despair, she found me. I won't shut her out. High Chiefess Ruth wants to be heard. Somehow I'm understanding that once again her homeland of Hawaii is severely threatened.

Old beliefs tell of *Nightmarchers*, ancient spirits come back to right wrongs from their lifetime. Their spirits cannot find peace until they make those transgressions right, or pono. Princess Ruth, powerful with mana power, insists on reaching her people. Why shouldn't she extend across space and time? After all she faced fire Goddess Pele and stopped a volcano cold in its tracks outside Hilo on the Big Island of Hawaii.

Strange to say but I do feel Princess Ruth helping me. Last night the Princess came in a dream. Young and beautiful, dark hair pulled up and back from her face with its extra-long length from eye to mouth, large dark eyes, she is almost wistful. *Look at me.* Her voice is low and thrilling. *Look at what I was.*

Then flashing for an instant in dream fashion, Princess Ruth is hugely fat with an ugly flat nose. *Look at what I became.*

Take warning, the returned young Princess Ruth intones like a chant. *Take heed. Things are not what they seem.* Dream drums sound and Hawaiian chanting. In the far background hundreds of feet march in ominous rhythm.

Yet oddly I'm not afraid when I awake in the night. Easily closing my eyes I simply fall back into my dream-state hearing Princess Ruth's voice whisper in the night and then fade away:

> *I felt you looking at my picture on the cover of that book,[1] she says. Felt your compassion and understanding. You searched for me, young and beautiful, and found that later picture at my second marriage to Isaac Davis. Evil, ignorant, easily led. There's a story I will tell you later … way beyond anything you'll find elsewhere. Ignorant haoles. Perfect name for them. No breathers. No breath. No understanding.*

Ha, breath, is how you grow and collect mana. How you connect with the land, aina, with spirit, soul, with your ancestral beginnings, your aumakua.

We are all accidents waiting to happen. So few of us own the capacity to appreciate what we have when we have it. We can admit to possessing heaven in the past but how often do we stop time and say to ourselves: *I look at this rainbow, at this beloved face, a moonrise, at this rocky wave-dashed shoreline and say: Now, this moment—this is beauty to the height of my capacity to receive. Joy permeates everything. This is paradise.* We have it and we don't know. Don't appreciate. I had my paradise and I lost it.

Dreams are odd—real and unreal at once. My young dream-Princess has materialized from a picture in my book showing her second marriage to Isaac Davis[2]. The newlyweds stare straight at us. Isaac looks older, determined, handsomely dressed, seated with his hands on his thighs. Is it me, or is that look really on his face, saying to Princess Ruth, like a cat to a canary, *I've got you now. I've won.*

High Chiefess Ruth is six feet tall, ruling alii blood to her toes, the great-granddaughter of Kamehameha the Great who created the united Kingdom of Hawaii by 1810. She is no helpless canary. The Princess knew love, real love, with her first Hawaiian husband, and I think that saved her from Isaac's lies. Isaac could have loved her but I don't think he did. Princess Ruth knew what true love was; Isaac wanted only her money and power. And her land, the aina, the incredibly valuable land. Somewhere I came across a book detailing a plan by missionary businessmen of that time to deliberately marry Hawaiian royal women to gain control of their Hawaiian land.

The young Princess Ruth stands, bending slightly forward in the posed picture, both hands on the table between her and Isaac. An arresting face. What goes on behind those watchful eyes? Was she Governess yet of the Island of Hawaii? I have to learn more. High Chiefess Ruth comes to warn and inform, I suddenly realize.

It's no wonder I feel Princess Ruth likes me—I searched out that picture of her when she was young and beautiful, before Isaac broke her nose and she, understandably, acquired many extra pounds. A big woman, not just tall but well filled out, was considered desirable back then. Besides, high-born women of Princess Ruth's time faced difficult choices: keep the old Gods or join with the new missionaries. And, from the missionary's point of view, get civilized.

Following missionary influence, everything Hawaiian was looked upon as inferior. High-born women rushed to wear Victorian fashions of high-necked, long-sleeved dresses of brocade and silk. Uncomfortable to say the least in our summer Hawaiian humidity and heat. Many Royal Hawaiians adopted Western dress, seeking to belong and by emulating show that they, too, were civilized. And traders made plenty of money by selling fancy goods.

Does wanting make it so? Where is your heart? It's high noon at Salt Pond beach. With incredible beauty and peace, this is a day full of grace. More and more my heart expands into this aina, this land. Manao, or meaning, latches onto me. Manao (what a thing means to you) comes clearer. I embrace boundless blue skies at Salt Pond; my spirit escapes into those fluffy cotton clouds dotting and emphasizing the blue. Constrained bits of me loosen. Love of land and place free me. I am welcomed.

Putting the past to rest is nasty business. I don't know how people resolve the regrets, the if-onlys, and find answers to why we made those bad decisions.

After the accident I was numb and couldn't bear to think. I should have gone with Thomas that night, sprained ankle or no sprained ankle. I didn't want to hold Thomas back from enjoying his friends at the hometown football game. I could have used the crutches in the basement. Bad decision heaped upon bad decision.

Hard pressure came from work. Work was all that mattered to Purity Corporation. Not, "What have you done for the company," but "What have you done yesterday, this morning?" My weekly report was overdue but without the bad ankle I'd have gone with Thomas. Now it's too late.

The treacherous mind says changing the past should be easy. Steer it differently into a different outcome. Make the drunk man sober and presto, no accident. Allow me to travel along on the fatal trip and presto, no accident, for my presence would change the equation. Only think of how many incidentals, each nothing in itself, must come together to allow a fatal accident. It's enough to make you believe in fate.

I think that is one result of death, of the finality. You realize in your gut and heart that you deal with immutable facts. Nothing will change these facts. Nothing brings the dead back to life. Part of you is cut off, forever gone. Only memories and you are left. Only time layers over damaging pain.

It's like I came into a sea of chaos and sorrow. Only a few threads kept me alive, the faint idea that I must live well for Thomas, that now I live in part for a dead loved one. And that life itself is precious beyond belief. And that all unknown to us, fate, life-purpose, hidden machinations of ordinary reality are always happening. It's true: this day is the first day of the rest of your life. What you do matters and I've found—even if I don't understand it—that there is help when you ask and accept. I guess this is how I explain to myself Princess Ruth's role in my life.

But, how do you live your life, when you're not living the life you want to be living? That is the question.

Hawaiians of old knocked out their front teeth when a beloved partner died. I read of one dying woman who made her handsome husband promise not to do it, but he knocked out his teeth anyway. How graphic, how symbolic, how fitting. The reminder of the love of your life is carved into your physical body as its loss is tattooed into your heart. We carry the scars inside, why not let them show?

Kauai has numerous special places. They reach out and I am captured. Today, anticipating the comfort of this place, I slip a small glass jar of red wine in my shoulder bag. Late evening, just as the sun begins to retreat, is my favorite time to visit the tidy hidden-away Japanese Garden at Kukuiolono Park in Kalaheo. I'm awkward, but I'm learning to pronounce some Hawaiian. It's Koo-koo-ee-o-Lo-no Park.

A friend at work gave me a one-minute talk on Hawaiian pronunciation of place names:

> To begin with, the Hawaiian alphabet has the same five vowels as in English, but only seven consonants, so many of the names appear to be similar. Two consonants are never together.
>
> As opposed to English, each vowel has only one way to be pronounced—that is: ah eh ee oh and ooh. That makes it easy!
>
> When two vowels are together, each is pronounced separately, although they are often slurred together, as in Hawaii. Two of the same vowel together are separated with a glottal stop, such as two i's in Hawai'i or ali'i. Or two o's, as in Kuamo'o Road.

My friend says that's all there is to it. But for me it's not that easy; I'm simplifying by leaving out glottal stops and macrons—those lines above the vowels to indicate they should be spoken long.

At the park I'll follow my usual pattern: Japanese garden, Hawaiian stones, then a token visit to sugar planter Walter McBryde's grave. There are always flowers on his gravestone. Since he died in 1931, I wonder who still puts them there? And I love the pair of standing stone lions, which look so British and charming. The lions tell a story, perhaps I'll learn it. Kalaheo is the only mountain town on Kauai, and it exists because Walter McBryde encouraged his Portuguese sugar plantation workers to homestead—which meant they could eventually own their company houses and land. McBryde envisioned a community of small farmers, and fought to help real agriculturists own farm land—as opposed to big plantations or land speculators. This was not a popular position in 1906.

Creating an irrevocable trust to hold his 346 acres of land and considerable money, he left this golf course and park in perpetuity to benefit the public. As I later learned, McBryde was one of the few missionary descendants who freely gave back land wealth they'd amassed. (Or stolen, even if the actions taken weren't always so named.) This hill was called Kukuiolono, 'the light of the god Lono,' a major Hawaiian deity. The house McBryde built on this hill was famous for his country hospitality. As with other of the old plantation homes, it was taken over by the military in World War II, was not treated properly, and was later torn down.

After the lions and the grave with its red ginger and heliconia flowers, I usually take the asphalt path through the golf course to the hidden pavilion. My goal today is an ancient wall of lava rocks in front of the pavilion. The entire long wall is constructed without mortar. The trained eyes of these ancient artisans automatically sized their volcanic stones and they laid them unerringly so they fit together for centuries, unless thoughtlessly destroyed by the ignorant or greedy.

I've found a favorite spot on the ancient wall before the simple pavilion. The rough stones on the low wall rise on my right—perfect for sitting on my sweater. Spread out far below me, from this high elevation point, are astounding views of the island and the Pacific Ocean.

This is the site of an ancient heiau or place of the gods. From below a sweep of healing energy flows over me like the breath of heaven. For additional healing uplift, fat cotton clouds float almost at eye level. Repairs to the pavilion behind me and to its surrounding planting area have gone on during the working day; bright orange webbing cuts off the area. But the grass around the end of the orange webbing is trampled, so I trample also on my journey to the wall. I'm rewarded with solitude except for a jeans-clad man and his running dog, who scramble below in the scrubby pili grass and soon disappear. Far out at sea one small sailing ship heads south toward the tourists in Poipu.

As time slows to an ancient rhythm my gaze sweeps the placid sea, green fields, few houses far below, and skies so open and close above me. I take another sip of Merlot and wonder at myself in this high place on a delicate island in the vast reaches of the Pacific Ocean. How interesting of fate to bring me here. I stop my thoughts before pondering again if fate, all unknown to me, has reasons, and what my purpose is. This is time out of mind. I will enjoy this present to its fullest. Yesterday is gone and tomorrow's worries can wait for tomorrow, or forever. Lost in thought, I take another little sip of wine and come perilously close to spilling it. Kevin Broadman is supposed to meet me and I've forgotten about him.

"I thought I'd find you here, Samantha." Kevin's voice is low and strong with a hint of possessiveness that puts me on guard. "You look a million miles away. Is it okay if I join you?" By the time his words arrive, he's stepped close. After so much time alone, I'm not used to people.

"Free riding," he explained, "involved taking the benefit of collective action without contributing in return."... It was unadulterated selfishness, she thought, an example of the individualistic posturing that had once been so fashionable and had encouraged both greed and economic disaster. It was not rational to look after oneself at the expense of others, for the simple reason that we sank or swam together.

Alexander McCall Smith, The Lost Art of Gratitude

CHAPTER TWO

KEVIN'S VOICE STRETCHES OUT slower and deeper. "Samantha," he muses, "always doing what she says she will." Before I quite return to the present time, Kevin moves closer to cup my face in his hands. "You look so fragile," he says, sweeping his hazel eyes over me. "I always forget how delicate and tiny you are. Yet so strong."

Concentrating on keeping my wine from spilling, I instinctively raise the glass jar like a shield. Kevin has hurt me before.

He stares at my mouth before he drops his arms and seats himself beside me on the rock fence. "Anything I can help you with? How are you settling into Kauai?" He pauses. "I've waited, you know, to see you. To give you time."

Kevin's presence is disturbing. I feel fluttery, my safe bubble of solitude invaded.

"Kevin, somebody at work put an article about GMO's on my desk. Under some critical papers. It's written by a Doctor Pang. He's the Public Health Administrator on Maui."

"Don't say another word." Kevin's face springs into anger. "That man is a menace."

He breathes audibly, dragging air. His efforts at control—slowed breathing and expression without a hint of emotion—are fairly obvious. I've seen them before. Then I wonder, *Why am I picking a fight with a lover from so long ago I've blotted him out?*

"Samantha," he sounds almost stern. "I came here to talk about us. It's time."

"Dr. Pang thinks Purity Corporation's field testing of experimental crops puts workers and neighboring communities at risk. Not to mention people who eat GMO's. And he says …"

"Pang is an alarmist. Naïve about realities." Kevin waves a dismissing hand. "We're a worldwide company. With an international reputation. Our scientists, you …" Taking the wine he places the jar on the grassy ground. "You," he continues, "do great work. Our seeds increase farm production; we feed more people. We help farmers.

"You know all that." Dismissing and impatient, Kevin stomps a foot on the grass, almost knocking over my wine.

A slow breeze moves up from the sea far below. Clouds dot the horizon and the light takes on a pale yellow clarity. Kevin's words are slower now, the impatience gone, "Have we a chance?"

My eyes linger on the width of his shoulders, their strength, his full passionate lips. *It's been a long time*, flits across my mind.

"Kevin, it's too soon … way too soon."

I eat Sunday lunch in my old black bathing suit alarmingly loose in vital spots top and bottom. The blowing wind changes direction in an instant. One second it blows from my back toward the off-shore island of Niihau. About fifty feet down Salt Pond beach a red kite on a short leash also flies over the water toward the island.

One instant the kona south wind is comfortably at my back. Then suddenly the heavy breeze shifts and comes from my front, blowing loose hair off my face. The low kite also reverses direction, fluttering over sand not water. The cool wind upsets the sea previously so quiet with long intermittent waves. Now the waves come closer together—higher and louder.

From a wide open sky that was deep blue with layered high thin clouds, grey skies close in. The moving air is much cooler. Still Niihau crouches low and straight ahead on the sea horizon, easy to miss if you don't know it is there.

This morning's dream-impressions of Princess Ruth return as suddenly as the wind. In my low bed on the floor I am caught in that strange hollow space between sleep, dream and waking, slow molasses running in my brain—not my usual clear waking orientation. Click me on or off. No usual piddling around for me, no slow dreams. I used to be one who was awake or asleep. Nothing in between. But this morning is different. Every contact with Princess Ruth is different. Now, memories of the morning come swiftly back with the wind. I am neither awake nor asleep but am caught in the middle, unsubstantial, a dream myself. As I am to learn, this is Princess Ruth's territory. She owns it.

In my dream state, gradually aware of a presence, I am not afraid, merely curious. It's odd to say but feelings of love, home, acceptance steal into my being, like fingers of wind bringing ease from pain. Heart pain has become such a companion I don't even know I have it, so accustomed am I to its presence.

High Chiefess Ruth fills my awareness. Maternal love, caring. She wants me whole and healed. Princess Ruth wants an equal, I sense, someone capable of truly hearing, understanding and sharing the feelings and information she has to impart.

Power comes from the immaterial figure of Princess Ruth, huge in a purple muumuu with white flower leis down her vast front. Oleander leis probably, for as I learn later, she wears them a lot. Princess Ruth is glad to see me; I feel her welcome. I know without words that it is me she has come to find. She yearns to tell me something. This is crucial; I should know it now, whatever it is.

In my dream-impression, I grow more alert, tensing in my sleep, closer to waking. This is important. I try to reach out, move closer. Her presence is like a huge energy field. I remember that Hawaiians believe energy is the food of being. I want to join this warm strong power, become one with it. Princess Ruth speaks:

The Hawaiian people and this land are the important things. Know, you must understand, how we love our land. Our place, each rock, tree, bend in the road, the waves, the look of a river—they all mean something.

We get messages from wind, rain, a flower, a rock, a fish swimming, sunrise, clouds.

Understand this: No words existed in our language for what was happening—the non-caring, the irresponsibility of the new hordes of people. Haoles brought killing disease, foreign ways of seeing the world and events. You haoles are separate. You wall yourself off. Try to control. Run everything. Make life fit you.

My people need the strength of the old ways, the mana, the power. The merging of self and nature. Being nature. True aloha and caring and sharing.

We join. We flow. We listen. We hear. We purify. We ask. We are.

But something is wrong, a divide, a separation. Without words I know a melting on my part is required, an empathy. An understanding, more knowledge that I don't have, is needed. Princess Ruth wants to give—whatever it is—but I can't take. Sadness strikes so suddenly it jars me from sleep.

I awake to loss. A familiar emptiness fills my arms, fills the bedroom, fills the world, is all there is and ever will be. I cry for myself, for Princess Ruth, for Hawaii, for all innocent victims, all that is loved and betrayed and lost. I cry until there are no tears. And know, as I dry my eyes and blow my nose, that these tears finish off forever the deepest sorrow of my past. I am done feeling sorry for myself. Yes, I need to understand the past—but I don't live there any more. My heart makes this decision. All the events of my life, good and bad, were required to get me to this island. I like Kauai. I have settled without words into knowing that I belong here. For better or worse, this is my home now.

Then my thoughts fasten back on Princess Ruth. There is a faint thread I can grasp—an instruction, a way to proceed.

What is it? Finally, like mist over Kahili mountain, words and feelings come trailing: *Learn more. Become one with this place. You belong to this time. Join with nature. Become one—merge with this air, sea, sky, people, land. You are its caretaker. Fill your heart with this island. With true Hawaiians. Fall in love with this beautiful, nani Kauai.*

I'm deep into another book about Hawaiians. The Hawaiian people are so battered and unfairly treated. It's all there in the right books, easy to read. Fascinated and protected by history's distance, I want to cry— *how could they?* How could these newcomers to the Islands just come in and take over? How could they treat the indigenous Hawaiian people so badly?

Tragedies start early. Betrayal began with first contact in December, 1777 and January, 1778. England's famous explorer, Captain James Cook, set out with two ships to search for the mythical Northwest Passage, a link between the Pacific and Atlantic oceans. Instead of a link, Captain Cook stumbled upon the Hawaiian Islands, a pristine place with a functioning culture and without diseases. The people were healthy and beautiful. All of the islands were populated and people lived well. Things were about to change for the unsuspecting Hawaiians.

Captain Cook kept a detailed journal. On January 30th of 1778, Lieutenant John Gore went ashore in command of three armed boats to get a closer look at a landing place. Dangerous surf kept the men on the island of Niihau (off the coast of Kauai) for two days and three nights. It was on Niihau that venereal disease first spread to the Hawaiians. "Regrettably," Cook wrote in his journal, "the very thing happened that I had above all others wished to prevent."

Cook is writing about his infected sailors having unprotected sex, the only kind ordinary people had back then, with innocent and healthy Hawaiian women, and the inevitable passing of sexually-transmitted diseases.

Thousands of Hawaiians would die and suffer from Western diseases. After living alone on their pristine islands for isolated healthy centuries,

Hawaiians had no immunities to European diseases. Ordinary childhood diseases such as chicken pox, measles, mumps killed these healthy people. Young, old, mothers, fathers, ordinary people, even the ruling alii: tens of thousands sickened and died.

Cook found independent sovereign island kingdoms with tenured land management by customary chiefs on the separate islands with the people growing taro and bananas, fishing and playing games, happy and doing well. This system, in place for centuries, lasted only a generation, or about twenty-five years, after Hawaiian contact with Westerners.

It's early this morning, before work, as I walk Kekaha beach, a 20-mile curving stretch of sand. The bright full moon is going down. As I pause to absorb the scene, I feel at peace. On the edges of thought, I'm experiencing this beauty, and myself, as fragile creations in the making, not yet complete. Yearnings arise to believe in something: Divine essence, magic, nature, an all-seeing intelligence who creates this majesty and watches over it.

The moon is full, huge, and glowing yellow. The sky brightens in soft shades of pale rose against a bluing background where the sun will rise. Fresh breezes blow. The running sea spreads out before me while mountain shadows crouch behind and become more visible as I turn to look. The ocean is deep blue, patient and calm; water laps in rhythm, sound expanding in my consciousness.

So much beauty. How can any heart remain unchanged by this fresh perfection? A world creating itself with you as witness. An impulse to homage arises. Gratitude and thanks to whatever forces bring me as witness. The world as divine playground. Paradise. My heart settles into a kinder rhythm. Old burdens lift as light as this air. Joyous and accepting, I walk the sand while the magic moon sets. As full daylight comes with light traffic and two or three swimmers in the distance, I walk home.

My rented house is practically empty. A mattress on the floor in the bedroom, a lamp beside it. Some pillows. I read, study, work, and there's plenty of room to spread out papers. I like the view from the floor. With my lap-top and printer, I can communicate with specialists all over the world.

The kitchen has a refrigerator, an electric stove, a counter, and one stool. Many purple and some white orchids bloom off the open garage beside the kitchen door I use as a front door. Someone at work told me people here don't lock their doors. I wonder if it's true?

I work long hours, get fascinated with a project and can't stop. It takes all my concentration to solve the problem I'm working on. I got used to intense effort and precision instruments working on my degrees in biochemistry, knocking around test tubes for years. I cut my teeth working for companies developing the chemistry and tests that give blood panel results. You obtain a blood sample, test it and out come the results. Easy and affordable and I had a part in making that happen. I can't help taking pride in improving people's lives. While doing good, I'm privileged to be on the cutting edge of discovery. I've liked being out where the wild things are, being among the first people to uncover secrets of science. Only here at Purity Corporation, I work in a black box using numbers and working with DNA and RNA, the building blocks of life itself.

Perhaps you'll understand better if I explain my job before Purity Corporation. Then I helped develop a product making comparative analysis of the gene expression between normal and different types of tumor tissues. And, using this product, doctors and experts can determine whether the patient is at high risk or low risk for potential life-threatening cancer and treat their patients accordingly.

What I do is to make the product and not concern myself with what is done with my research work. I design computer programs for checking out complicated chemical and biochemical relationships. To me, my laboratory, or my place of work wherever it is, is clean and white and pure—a refuge where I can work on special projects. My mind isn't cluttered with anything except the problem I'm given. Since losing my husband I've retreated even more into my work where isolation creates a safe bubble. Kevin feels like a nuisance. I wish he weren't my boss. He distracts me from my growing fascination with Princess Ruth and Hawaii.

I read about living on an island. How you don't behave badly and move on to a new place where nobody knows your name or what you've done. On an island everybody who counts knows—your deeds, who you are, follow you like soft whispers. You must be careful not to antagonize a person because you'll see them again and again.

Barbara Jackson—I met her at work, she's lived on this island for 30 years—told me how, when she first arrived it would take her three hours to go to a nearby store to buy milk. Not to be labeled rude, she needed to *talk story* with everyone she met—on the way there, with those she saw at the store and on the way home. People here always say they're *talking story*. Makes me think of the Indian talking stick, where everyone is paid attention and respectfully allowed to speak their truth and whatever they need to say.

Barbara has a farm in Kilauea, the North side. People talk about *sides* of the island so I'm learning them. Barbara is tall, with painfully straight long dark hair she usually wears down, not like my flyaway strawberry red hair and blue eyes. Her eyes are brown and she's lean with a healthy outdoor glow. She comes to work part-time here on the West Side only to augment her income. An openness about Barbara, an acceptance, a quality of 'meeting you where you are' attracts me. I yet haven't told her my complete story, only that my husband Thomas recently died. Only that most of my salary goes to pay off debt. When she invited me to an expensive benefit for the local Hospice, Barbara understood instantly why I couldn't join her. I like that about her. There's an additional element I can't describe, except to say that she's easy to be with. We laugh about where we work and the people sometimes—they take themselves so seriously.

Barbara knows many things, has always wanted to earn her place in the world. Flying from Australia, she was grounded on Kauai when President Reagan fired all the air traffic controllers, and she never left. She lived through hurricanes Iwa and Iniki. "All we had was each other," she tells me. "People looked after each other. Not like now," she says with scorn. "Did you know 90 percent of the food on this island is imported? It's a disgrace. We could feed ourselves. Just thirty years ago Kauai was completely sustainable. We can do it again. Hawaiians of old were totally self-sustaining."

This land reaches out. It wants to speak, wants you to know its true story. Without formal writing these incredible people have history, connections, know their place in their world—while we haoles, with our writing and get-ahead linear skills, our 'only take care of yourself' values, we've lost a heart–to-heart, spirit-to-spirit knowing, a vital connection with land and life itself.

A door opens for me. I sense I'm invited into mystery, into knowledge. I'm so alone but somewhere there's a place for me. I keep educating myself, learning from people I meet. I sense that Princess Ruth, especially, holds life lessons.

Princess Ruth was Governess of the Big Island for twenty years, and the richest woman in the Hawaiian Islands. Regardless of what Americans have written, High Chiefess Ruth Keelikolani was an intelligent and competent woman. She understood and spoke English quite well—when it suited her.

Something else I've just realized: and here's the place to clear up this common misconception. When most people hear *Hawaii*, they think *Honolulu*. But Honolulu is on the island of Oahu. We have a state named Hawaii, and also a separate island called Hawaii or, as the locals say, *the Big Island*. The identical names (the State of Hawaii and the separate Island of Hawaii) and the fact that the Island of Hawaii was the home of King Kamehameha, the great chief who first united the islands, contribute to the confusion. New arrivals are constantly surprised to learn that Honolulu is on Oahu. I'm learning to call the Island of Hawaii, *the Big Island*, which reduces confusion.

All the Hawaiian islands are the tops of volcanoes and as they erupted, lava slowly built up above sea level to form them. The state is made up of eight major islands plus 124 minor islands, reefs and shoals. Most of the minor islands are small, lie to the north of Kauai, and are uninhabited, barely above sea level.[3]

In slow motion time, visualize a crawling undersea volcano, first spitting out Kauai, then pausing before creating Niihau, seventeen miles across the treacherous Kaulakahi channel. Then, sixty miles away, the eons-slow moving volcano, over millions of years, creates Oahu (900,000 people now in Honolulu, around 1.3 million statewide.) Then comes Maui with nearby Kahoolawe, Lanai and Molokai. Eons ago, these four were one land mass. For years the U.S. military used Kahoolawe, visible from Maui, as target practice until brave Hawaiians took back their island.[4] Apparently no one lives there now although this island was sacred to the Old Ones.

At the end of the Hawaiian chain of islands, four hundred miles east of Kauai, lies the Big Island, where Goddess Pele—she lives in volcanoes—is now creating new land. Raw lava flows in varying degrees from the only two volcanoes still active in Hawaii, Kilauea and Mauna Loa. Kilauea has been erupting continuously since 1983, sometimes spectacularly into the sea. I'd love to see lava flowing hot and boiling into the ocean, especially at night. A new Hawaiian island, now being created grows slowly, still underwater. Nineteen miles off the coast, it already has a name: *Loihi*.

Niihau hangs in the back of my mind (Pronounced Nee-ee-how in Hawaiian; Nee-how in English). The *Forbidden Island*. Forbidden is such a capture of the imagination. Today, if you don't drown in information, world-wide web reveals all, including information you'd better check. One website says Kauai was formed first, the next that Niihau came first. Barbara at work told me, I don't know where she gets her information, that we're living in a time of human history when secrets will out, hidden things will be revealed. I think of that every time another duplicitous U.S. politician sleeps around on his wife, gets caught and lies.

Always I look for the off shore island of Niihau, always low on the horizon, but sometimes its shape is sharp and clear like dark glass against the sea. *Forbidden* comes up so often. With my inquiring mind I can't help wondering if it is forbidden because the unfortunate islanders first infected by Captain Cook's sex-starved sailors lived there?

Niihau was purchased from King Kamehameha Five by Elizabeth Sinclair in 1864 for $10,000 in gold, a lot of money at the time. Originally from New Zealand, Elizabeth Sinclair settled in Hawaii and ever since her descendants, now the Robinsons, have owned the island, using most of it for cattle ranching and recently leasing tracking station space to the navy's Pacific Missile Range at Barking Sands for cash income. But that's another story.

Niihau is the only Hawaiian island where its 150 plus residents still speak Hawaiian as their dominant language. Many work for the Robinsons, and the island is generally off limits to all but relatives of the island's owners, U.S. Navy personnel, government officials, and invited guests. A few paying tours are also allowed.

I create little puzzles for myself and then they are solved, at least for a time. I find one form of *forbidden* came about because of measles and in 1915 Aubrey Robinson, grandfather of present owners Bruce and Keith Robinson, closed the island to keep the native Hawaiians safe. Safe and protected? Or exploited? How can one tell?

I appreciate Aubrey Robinson as I learn he planted 10,000 trees per year during much of his ownership. The Robinsons seem devoted to keeping the island as a living preserve of Hawaii's ancient ways.

However, I'm learning Hawaii frequently has an exception, or another way of seeing things. Wikipedia says, "Residents are not allowed to own radios, televisions or cell phones, and visitors are not allowed to bring a cell phone to the island, even for personal use."

If you owned an island, wouldn't you set the rules?

I've seen Niihau up close from a snorkel trip to the Na Pali coast, when we crossed the strait and passed miles of deserted low Niihau beach before anchoring in brilliant fish-filled waters off the small bird sanctuary island of Lehua. After snorkeling and a plentiful lunch, we begin circling the volcanic rock that's Lehua. First the boat pauses before *the key*. This hundred and forty foot tall key-shaped opening hooks together an almost broken off bit of crescent-shaped Lehua. *The key* exists in the middle of the ocean in the middle of nowhere. I'm awed as I absorb the monstrous power that created this quiet spectacle.

The full majestic beauty of Lehua, with Niihau in the close distance, comes into focus as we round Lehua into a picture that belongs on a postcard, only this is impressively real. A glorious bluish crescent of volcanic rock holds the sparkling blue sea. The entire scene is like a dream. I watch as long as I can.

Dolphin, green turtles and forbidden islands swim in memory. Like Bali Ha'i, or Shangri La, the Forbidden Island becomes a mystical dream, forever out of reach.

Except maybe I'll save my pennies and actually take a tour of the island.

The more I learn, the more privileged I feel. Princess Ruth, a bastion of old Hawaiian ways, refusing even to speak English—she chooses me, an unaware haole, to educate and to tell her story. Why me? Such an unlikely choice.

But then, what is the motivation of the Princess? This powerful spiritual woman fears for her Hawaiian people. She knows these fragile islands in the Pacific, indeed the entire world, can be destroyed by technology gone mad with its sharp divorce of science and responsibility, and with unintended consequences thrown in for good measure. We have an exploding military with more money than it knows what to do with. We have GMO international companies interested only in bottom-line gains, and how much immediate profit can be extracted. We all know that just because you *can* do something doesn't mean you *should*. Princess Ruth, knowing the nexus of these problems, seeks straight lines of communication and change.

History is on her side. The American Indians are finally getting some sort of justice, at least some people are finally paying attention. The American people—past our greedy government, big internationals, and powerful military—are a basically decent and good people—with a democracy that wants all lives better in a fairer world which has liberty and justice for all.

Of course, in the long run history will win; Hawaiians will obtain justice. We—the U.S. invaders—will have to leave their islands, or pay them fairly for our aggression. History always wins.[5]

After long thought, it becomes clear to me: Princess Ruth sees an epicenter here. She sees powerful CEOs who regard our beautiful islands as disposable. Run any dangerous experiment you like. This is an island. Risk is contained. If everyone dies in an experiment gone crazy, if the whole thing explodes, who on the mainland will know or care? Tell any lie you want. Use your gigantic power to roll over people. Hire lawyers. Crush those who bring truth to your lies. Princess Ruth has been in this space before. Understanding the dangers to her islands, she wants to use me and my story to reach ordinary people, to use me as a bridge of information.

That's my explanation. Responsibility falls heavy. I did not ask for this task that grows burdensome. Perhaps if I see telling Princess Ruth's story as an avenue back to life, as a task I'm called to, that will help.

Strange how when I attempt to see the whole picture, I get caught up in details. My perceptions keep changing as I learn more and experience more. Sensibilities get honed into sharp awareness. Little things grow huge in implication. For example, there is Anne Landgraf's[6] book of interviews with Kupuna (wise elders). *Aloha* is discussed, a word hitting close to home as I've developed a habit of closing emails with *aloha*, meaning to me *love, I greet you heart to heart, I want only the best for both of us*—something like that. I've read a hundred definitions of *aloha*, but I don't really know what I'm doing. Except I want to pay respect, and deep down, borrow a little aloha for myself?

As an aside, speaking of truth, only truth will free us.

Hawaiian wise elder speaking: "*Aloha* is being abused. Its true meaning is lost.… Aloha is an action word between two persons and it must come from within…. Aloha means respect. Aloha is the spiritual essence of the tangible self that gave you and me the breath of life." Anne Landgraf's Kupuna tells of standing up, pointing his finger and saying to a professor of Hawaiian at the University of Hawaii, "You may have a degree, but I'm pedigree."

This Kupuna asks, "How can a Haole know the Hawaiian language? There is the kaona inside. That is the most important, the hidden meaning.

The Haole people learn plenty things about Hawaiian people and then write a book. They make a profit off the Hawaiian people. The misuse and abuse of the Hawaiian people never stops."

This is when I realize—to stay on my path of truth—I'll need to share a fourth of profits (assuming there are any) of Princess Ruth's book with Hawaiian causes. This Kupuna is correct. The Princess, and my conscience, won't let me take part in "the misuse and abuse."

We haoles arrive ignorant to the Hawaiian Islands. We ordinary U.S. citizens don't know that we (our ancestors) are the invaders, the intruders, the oppressors. We don't realize our people stole this land and that many of our people remain stealing and oppressing today. Nobody told us. We're whistling along oblivious and happy. We love it here. We're tourists bringing good money and good cheer to *their* beaches.

Do you see the problem? Have solutions?

The degree of psychic injury this rape of culture and language produced down through the generations cannot be underestimated.

The death of a culture, like the death of a star, lasts longer than anyone can possibly imagine. The sadness, the echoes and ambiguities, persist for hundreds of years.

Victoria Nelson, My Time in Hawaii: A Polynesian Memoir

It is a story of how colonialism worked in Hawaii not through the naked seizure of lands and governments but through a slow, insinuating invasion of people, ideas, and institutions. It is also a story of how our people fought this colonial insinuation with perplexity and courage. But ultimately, this is a story of violence, in which that colonialism literally and figuratively dismembered the lahui (the people) from their traditions, their lands, and ultimately their government. The mutilations were not physical only, but also psychological and spiritual. Death came not only through infection and disease, but through racial and legal discourse that crippled the will, confidence, and trust of the Kanaka Maoli as surely as leprosy and smallpox claimed their limb and lives.

Jonathan Kay Kamakawiwoole Osorio, Dismembering Lahui: A Hitory of the Hawaiian Nation to 1887

CHAPTER THREE

WHERE TO START? I just found out that ninety percent of GMO's are controlled by one company: mine. Stunned, I'm thinking about this as I drive to a dinner party with local people, some from work that I don't know very well. If Kevin is at the party, should I ask him how much he knows about home-office Purity Corporation? I decide I'd better wait and see.

Our hostess Karin Flanagan, and her two enthusiastic mixed-breed dogs, welcome me to her spacious lanai. Open on three sides, her lanai is covered and comfortable with three sofas and lots of room for conversation groups. Kevin isn't here, only seven other people.

"Pretty soon the entire island will be GMO corn." Charlotte is emphatically gruff in contrast to her abundant curly hair held back on one side by two red hibiscus flowers.

"We're rats in a nasty experiment," adds her partner, a graceful athletic-looking island man named Akita wearing the male island uniform of casual tan shorts and a festive Hawaiian-print green shirt.

"We don't know the half of it," Charlotte breaks in, cutting off her hostess. "Way back when I was still married to Deck, we were out camping at Polihale. Coming back after dark, I saw a blue glow in those Purity Corporation fields along the road. At first we couldn't imagine what in the world. Finally we realized the light came from corn plants that actually had a blue glow—like fluorescence in the dark.

"You could see armed guards around those fields in the daytime. Men wore goggles and white outfits like space suits. I heard Purity Corporation was growing pharmaceuticals." Charlotte is upset.

"That's right," Karin our hostess, breaks in. "They're putting genes from jellyfish into corn plants. That's where the blue glow comes from."

Blue glow, I think, *like man-o-war jellyfish. Beautiful as they sail along in the ocean, all those tentacles floating about. But poisonous. Why would scientists put poison in corn?* This is a good time to keep my mouth shut. These local people are not happy. Nor am I. I'm worried.

"Remember that last flood?" asks Karin, "How high the Hanapepe river was? A Purity Corporation barge broke loose. Nobody knows what was in that barge. Think about this barge sunk out there in our waters, and just waiting to rust through. Release who knows what poisons."[7]

"Yes," agrees Akita. "And you should've seen what came down that river. Black tubing, plastic pipes for water and fertilizer. Pesticides. Red soil. The whole river was red. Made me think of blood. All pouring out into the ocean. They used to catch fish right out there. Plenty fish. But not any more."

"We're brainwashed by biotech industries," Charlotte says. "I bet you didn't know that between 1994 and 2001 food related illness in the United States doubled. That's the same time GMOs flooded the market. Something is going on besides giant corporations making tons of money.

"Realize this," Charlotte continues, "once GMO's are let loose into the environment you can't get them back. GMO's contaminate our regular plants and they spread and destroy in unforeseeable and uncontrollable ways. And nobody can get them back once they're out there. Soon the U.S. is likely to be the only country in the world that doesn't label those blasted things."

"Yeah," laughs Akita, "big companies fight tooth and nail to keep labeling away. Those companies know that if people understood what they were eating, they would boycott GMOs. And those irradiated things they call food that last forever—who knows about them?"

"Yes," adds Charlotte, "but here's a ray of hope. Just yesterday I got an email[8] that a couple of rice farmers in Missouri sued big giant Bayer and won."

"What happened?" Akita leans forward eagerly.

"The subject line in the email puts it clearly: *Bayer Loses in Court—Admits GMO Contamination is Out of Control.*[9] I'll forward the email if you like. I remember Bayer admitted that even using best practices, it couldn't control the spread of its genetically-engineered outdoor field trials."

"Exactly what we're facing here on the West side," Akita throws in, "open field trials. We probably lead the world in outdoor GMO field trials."

"And the best part, you'll like this," Charlotte grins, "is that Bayer has to pay two million U.S. dollars to two Missouri farmers after their rice crop was contaminated with an experimental variety of rice that Bayer tested in 2006."

"The GMO companies gotta love us in Hawaii—we don't seem to care what they do. And don't you wonder," Akita asks fiercely, "with all the court stuff we've seen before, if those farmers, and their lawyers who'll probably take ninety percent of the money, will ever see a dime of that two million?"

"Don't you know it," agrees Charlotte.

"And did you see that picture in the paper today? *Huitlacoche*, (weet-la-ko-chee) Mexicans call it, corn smut, to us." Akita throws back his head in a long peal of laughter. "Plain old corn smut that the U.S. has spent millions trying to eradicate turns out to be packed with special proteins, minerals and other nutritional goodies. The joke's on us; the so-called ignorant Mexican peasants turn out to be right all along. Corn smut, that gnarly, gray-black corn fungus is long-savored in Mexico for good reason: It's good for you! And guess what—huitlacohe only grows on corn that has not been sprayed with a fungicide. There go Monsanto profits."

"I saw that picture," adds Karin, "a woman's hand holds what looks like a small grey brain. Like an oyster—makes you wonder who first ate that corn smut?"

"If only we were as smart as we think we are." Akita speaks quickly. "Common knowledge was the corn smut had nutritional values like the corn it grew on. But nobody knew until finally scientists actually tested and reported in the *Journal of Food Chemistry*. Makes you wonder doesn't it—we look down on the Mexicans, the true inventers of corn, sacred to them—without any idea what we're really doing?"

"You know," Akita confides as the other six people take off on best local places to go surfing, "that GMOs are expanding exponentially on this island?"

"Where does your interest in GMOs come from?" I am curious. "And how do you know so much?"

"Oh, I'm a long time closet activist. Got some early training at Berkeley. I grew up with sustainability. When you're poor on an island you learn to make do. Hawaiians have strong traditions of giving back what you take, like gathering limu or seaweed. At Molowa[10] we'd pick limu kohu by placing our fingers in between the limu, shake it, and then pull it up. The roots were always placed back in the sea to grow again. Limu is good for you, has lots of iron. Fresh seaweed is becoming a luxury. When I was little my mother took me to the ocean. We picked only what we needed. Limu ligeepee is my favorite"

His face becomes solemn, his features softening. I see nostalgia and yearning as if he wishes those times back.

"We didn't know we were poor and so as children we had lots of fun. But young and old, we all loved a hukilau. Hukilau," he explains, "is an old Hawaiian way of fishing. When a spotter finds the schools of fish, we cast a long net from shore and gather friends to help pull the fish-filled net to the beach. We line the net with *ti* leaves, which help scare fish toward the middle of the net, and us kids would get to pick the leaves. Children's share was less but everyone else got an equal share of fish—all kinds."

Then Akita startles me with an intimate question he asks hesitantly, "What do you do when someone you trust lies to you?" He pauses as if gathering his thoughts. "Even if you have to pull their motives out of the air … and you begin to understand their arrogant goals go something like this: *'Let's patent life and take over the world. Everyone will have to buy our seeds and our pesticides.'*" Akita reaches for his Heineken and takes a big gulp. "It's hard to get your mind around evil … around this unthinking arrogance … and the ignorance of how our aina really works.

"Actually," Akita takes a deep breath as if committing himself even further, "Purity Corporation is coming pretty close. Did you realize that right now the biotech giants make farmers pay for the privilege of using these human-made organisms? Greenpeace says that farmers in North America and Latin America, which is where most of the world's GMOs, or genetically engineered agriculture is—these farmers have to sign contracts that specify that if they save the seeds to plant again the following year, or use any herbicide other than the corporation's own, they can be prosecuted. I'm trying to learn about these things." Akita confides, "I thought Monsanto's plants were sterile, make no viable seeds."

"Time to eat," Charlotte calls loudly. I don't know whether or not to be glad for the interruption. "Come, Akita, and slice this wheat bread," she demands with a sideways look at me as if I'd been monopolizing Akita.

A day after the dinner party, still upset, I am in a wild rush to get to work. I'd finally dropped off to sleep around 3 a.m. and couldn't wake up. My Ford Ranger pickup is running on empty. My credit card won't work at the local, and only, gas station. Finally the card works but the gas still won't pump. The calm Hawaiian woman sitting behind the cash desk is weaving a lei of white plumeria (we called this plant frangipani in Florida) that smells like heaven. A baby sleeps in a cradle at her side. She remains impassive as I began losing it. Her sereneness increases with my frustration, and my frustration with her self-possession. Finally I yank out some money, move to a second pump, get gas, and storm to work.

As I calm down, shame at my behavior begins percolating in my thoughts. Hawaii is a foreign country. It's taking a while but I'm getting it. This culture has rules of behavior and I'd violated them. Local people are nice to each other. All the time. I'd been rude, arrogant, out of line. Why had I selfishly expected her to drop everything and join my hurry-hurry hysterics? This island isn't going anywhere. The world will still be here if I am late to work. I am wrong.

At lunch I buy her a bunch of pink ginger and mixed heliconia flowers, and go to apologize. I'm a guest in this special land. Without fully understanding, I take a step toward realizing this. Already I learn Kauai holds the charm of the unexpected, and the mystery of different values and ways of being.

I've stumbled across another file that I wish I hadn't on my work computer. Now I'm wondering who has access to my computer? How *did* this file get here? Should I talk with Kevin? *Shut your eyes*, I tell myself, *forget it and it'll go away*. But those inconvenient facts aren't likely to disappear and I don't know what to do. *Whistle-blowers*, they call them. I don't need this. Odd how that file just showed up.

I'll think later about what to do. Deciphering Princess Ruth's life and times in old Hawaii is safer. Yet, parts of that file are blasted into my mind: evidence that Purity knew the runaway barge during the flooding in Hanapepe held huge amounts of experimental pesticides and GMO seeds. And that the company did nothing except lie about the facts. An idea jumps into my thoughts. There's a disconnect between administration and what happens in fields thousands of miles away, where plants are actually grown. I'd love to print out that entire file, take it home to study. But I'm frightened. Better delete it.

I should be more practical. Put getting a life somewhere on my to-do list—to-do's I haven't been doing. An old friend advises: "Make a new list," she says, "What will cost you the most not to do. Choose the most critical thing and focus your resolve there." With my life gone I still have to live. No whining allowed. I see whiners always complaining that something is wrong. The excusers saying, *not my responsibility*. The putters-off saying, *next month, next year, next forever I'll stop smoking, or eating or drinking too much*.

I'm scared to drink beyond a glass or two of wine. I could dive into a bottle and never get out.

Barbara has invited me to a community meeting to hear Dr. Pang from Maui—and to meet a new man she wants to introduce. The meeting is fine, but I don't want to know anyone new. I'll smile politely and back away. That's my usual style when I don't want to get involved. Too much now on my plate. Things dripping over like Salvador Dali limp watches, falling off. I must keep resolves I've already made.

Speaking of which, I've promised myself that once a week, no matter what, I'll visit one of the island's premier places. Today it's historic Queen Emma's beach. A minor player in this beautiful perfection of sea and beach, I ache for Thomas and my old safe life. I come here looking for healing and respite from work.

Events heat up. Pressure builds and I don't want to face what's coming. How much can I absorb at one time? Or accept things that turn out not to be what I expected and would have bet my life on? Thomas treads across my thoughts. I know we had savings – both of us with good jobs and no unusual expenses. What happened to the money?

A light veil of vog shades my view, blown over these 300 plus miles from an erupting Kilauea on the Big Island. Vog is a mixture of escaping volcanic gases and fog. The sea is grey and rather loud as waves crash against rocks. The air is warm with a hint of coolness. I sit on a fallen log about ten feet from surf working its way through low beach stones and surging high on side rocks. The sound never stops its constant heartbeat of the earth. Alive, moving, I have a world to myself with heavy strong mana from the earth on my way here to Queen Emma's Beach through National Botanical Gardens near Kalaheo. Recent rain brings more lush greens of ten thousand shades from palest yellow-green to a throbbing almost black-green.

The sea falling and rising is soothing. A queen's bay is before me. *Rest,* it says, *stay with me.* This was Queen Emma's refuge on Kauai and where she came from her home in Honolulu to mitigate heartache. Queen Emma's deaths were first her young, heir-apparent son, and then her husband, King Alexander Liholiho (Kamehameha Four). He died at 29 and left her a childless widow at twenty-seven. Queen Emma's house is a small quiet cottage behind me. In Queen Emma's time the cottage was on the pali (cliff) above but was later lowered to its present location. Behind the cottage is a blaze of fuchsia bougainvillea. An enthusiastic gardener, Queen Emma planted bougainvillea here, and rose apple, pikake (her favorite flower, a jasmine that smells wonderful), white spider lily, tamarind, and thorn-less kiawe.

The sea snakes over rocks within four feet of me. And that lulling sound never stops. One small boat is a dot on the horizon and four young Hawaiian men are here with surfboards. A queen's refuge. I wonder if it was? I settle into Queen Emma's beach thinking this might be a place to reach peace, to come to better terms with the past. Perhaps I have a rather desperate hope that peace will fall like leaves covering the path I took through the gardens. Under its blanket of quiet stillness I'll return to happier times.

Today my dead Thomas hangs in my mind, stopping ongoing action like a barrier reef. Queen Emma's bay and beach are places of memories, of accepting and readjusting the past so a person can go on living. This beauty holds an element of sadness, of loss.

I need to understand how Thomas could be so different from what I thought. Perhaps it's disloyal but a large part of me wants to move on.

And my boss Kevin. Before Thomas there was Kevin. Once someone betrays you, can you ever trust them again? Akita's words echo with his questions of truth and lies.

I cross the curved bridge over Lawai stream and around the corner of the beach, passing among high pili grass and old graves huddled among flowers. I wonder whose they are as I write down names to look up. I sit now, writing at a picnic table under fragrant kiawe that looks and smells like mesquite. Ponds of pale pink lotus rise straight ahead as I breathe in tranquility.

There's a strength in pono, in making things right, that I never understood. When someone commits a wrong against you, what do you do? What do you do when you think they've committed a wrong and they don't agree they were wrong? Or they are simply ignorant and don't know any better?

You can go for 'an eye for an eye.' And we all see what that gets us: More of the same and war without end. Like Iraq and Afghanistan, I want to say as visions of all that destruction and billions upon billions of wasted money and destroyed lives and irreplaceable resources blur in my thoughts.

What will our descendants think of us—that is if we don't kill off our world?

You forgive the wrongdoers. But do you really? Forgive them totally and trust them again? Are humans made like that?

I'm not, I'm afraid. That largeness of heart has been beyond me.

Is my history repeating itself? All that time ago and that event still hides in crevices. Years before I learned to love and trust Thomas, there was Kevin. I arrive unexpectedly at my apartment to find my then beloved fiancé, Kevin, in my bed with another woman. Kevin apologizes. Of course he apologizes. After a time lasting forever I said that I forgive him. "Let's be friends," I say, struggling to keep my heart from flying in all directions.

But my heart closed then to Kevin and it has never opened to him again. I could leave that town, that man, and I did. Taking the geographic cure, I layered ongoing events and time over Kevin. Whenever my mind went to Kevin, I deliberately turned away my thoughts. Sealed Kevin tight in a 'never go there' bubble. I forgot, but did I forget? I moved on to love, trust, and marry Thomas. But have I moved on?

No, actually not. When I pay attention I *feel* that old knot, that hurt, that wrong. Hawaiians use the same word for *feel* and *think*, I'm surprised to read. Fitting really but I wonder if it's true? More things to look up.

Pono, making things right, clearing away past concerns and problems. Can it be done?

Can we assign monetary value to non-monetary things? Well yes, you can. Once in the depths of an everlasting Canadian winter, I figured how much cash I would deal out for four hours on a warm Florida beach. It was a lot and if I'd had the money I'd have paid it and happily.

Pono. Kevin wants to make his old sin disappear. He desires to make it right. He wants me back. Kevin wants us to try old time Hawaiian hooponopono, an Hawaiian process for settling old wrongs and forgiveness. I lift my book from my canvas bag and begin reading.

"Today the way they do hooponopono is really different. During our time it was just family, a family circle, *midi auk* or *midi main*. You sinned against me and you have to do right. You have to do away with ill feelings. Whoever was the head of the house conducted the ohana. No outsiders were present to break the family circle. The family would unite in ohana or meaning to have family worship together. It was a time of *ohana kazoo*, pray time," quotes Anne Kaplan Landgrave[11]. Today I've brought along her collection of interviews with old time Hawaiians to examine further in peace and quiet.

What do I want? To forget, to forgive old history? To live today on this incredibly beautiful island, alone on this sand touched by royalty? Perhaps it's enough to wander again to Queen Emma's beach, past the bridge, and turn left along high, craggy red rock where lookout fisherman of old kept watch for schools of fish. Hawaiians on shore would net the shiny fish for luau. This is the hukilau process Akita told me about. I can just see it here—huge nets laid in the ocean and everyone gathering to help pull the fish-filled nets to shore. Pictures in my books show laughing people, some getting wet at the edge of the sea as they gather live food for the coming luau. I stroll over piles of small wooden debris and out on the beach again where a light salt-sea breeze penetrates my skin. Healing.

So interesting how I'm doing my bit of drama today. Earlier I lost my computer glasses—put them down and absolutely could not find them. Took the place apart, checked all floor covering, closet, every pile of stuff I'm sorting for work, everything. And then, as I'm explaining to Barbara who is visiting for coffee, what a bad habit I've formed of placing my glasses on surfaces and then having to locate them. I move the shower curtain in the bathroom. There's a clatter and of course there are my glasses. I'd placed them on the tub ledge, pulled the curtain over them (clever of me wasn't it?), and then, oddly enough, could not find my glasses.

Oh how I weave troubles for myself. But I did not panic. Like yesterday, looking for my lingerie (lurking behind the door in a bag where I'd carefully stashed them until I buy a chest), I kept my cool and lo and behold, finally, finally the lost shows up.

Things scurry in my mind—Princess Ruth is a big deal. I yearn to know more about this intriguing woman. But my best choice, I think for now, is to back off.

Kevin Broadman. An ex-lover. My spiritual partner, I used to think. My long, last love. An obsession, an addiction—that I got over. Or at least I think I've gotten over.

Perhaps I have to lose my glasses every so often so I can slow myself down?

What don't I understand about Kevin? What don't I accept? What must I change about myself? And, it may well be, I've done it: Gotten him out of my mind, heart, body, thoughts. *Possibility* was always my intrigue. What we could be and do together. Except we didn't. Except, I somehow become at fault for my expectations of faithfulness. Expectations that became seen as demands. Okay, this is like my insight that when I keep feeling WE need to talk—that in truth it is I who need to talk. Everyone else is just fine with status quo. Only I am unsatisfied. And I don't even know what I want. Except of course I do: I want my life back. Or maybe it's even the dream life I thought I had with Thomas. I don't know anymore.

So what I may be telling myself is that when I am unhappy, it is myself who needs examining! And changing.

Perhaps I give myself little clues: lost glasses, lost lingerie, a broken tooth? What has Kevin left to teach me?

Well, I may have done a better job getting rid of Kevin than I wanted. Basically, at the moment, admittedly busy, he is mostly gone. I've opened up my life. Layered over the personal and immediate obsession until Kevin is not real. Was he ever real? Yes, I have such clear wonderful memories. But I now know the outcome and so memory is tainted. Perhaps I have to come against a barrier to learn that I don't choose to have that particular bit of behavior in my life. I've always disliked stupidity, especially in myself.

Much too much is happening too fast. Events run away with me. I've got to stop writing for now. Barbara's invited me to a GMO public meeting for the community. I'm leery and feeling disloyal but going to the meeting is the right thing. I'm not telling Kevin. He'd try to stop me. I need to check out things for myself. Dr. Pang is speaking at the meeting and his scientific credentials are impressive. The man is not a crackpot. Barbara admires him too.

"I was on a long visit to Maui," Barbara tells me, "when dengue fever struck the island. Another name for dengue is breakbone fever and from what I've heard that's exactly what it feels like: your bones breaking because the ache is so deep. I was on Maui because a friend in Haiku asked me to house-sit."

"How do you like Maui?" I ask. "I've heard it's touristy and over-crowded."

"Like here or any of the Islands, depends on where you go," Barbara answers. "Stay at fancy hotels and you can travel the world and never leave mainland U.S.A." Barbara smiles happily, "Or go with the locals. I've always found that's a lot more fun and way cheaper. Anyway Haiku town was a delightful change—still rural but more people, green and cool and a mile or so from the sea.

"I practically lived on avocadoes: huge ones like butter. Every morning one or two would fall from Peggy's tree. And she had a garden with cherry tomatoes, bok choy, beets, and assorted salad greens."

"Must be really nice to inherit a garden in full production. I want a garden, but can't seem to find time to start the actual work of making one," I say.

"Definitely a problem," Barbara agrees. "I'm always digging and planting. Nice to have things in place already; all I had to do was water. I ate like a queen and traveled like a tourist. Sunrise at Haleakala crater was so different from our Waialeale volcano crater and quaint shops in Makawao. And to break my avocado diet, duck sandwiches at Café Mambo in Paia. I was lucky to take the fabulous drive to Hana before dengue fever hit."

"I've always wanted to go to Hana," I say. "I hear it's quite a trip: narrow roads, steep drop-offs and one-lane bridges."

"A couple of people started getting ill," Barbara says. "At the post office we talked of how sick the ailing were. Dengue fever was mentioned and how entire islands in the South Pacific were infected. How tourists would stay away from Hawaii in droves."

"I've heard how dangerous dengue fever is."

"Yes," agrees Barbara. "It's a crafty disease with four different closely related varieties of illness. Being immune to one didn't keep you from getting another strain. And once you'd had the disease, you were doubly vulnerable to the other strains. It was rare but the virus could become hemorrhagic. People bled and died even in these modern times. Mosquitoes carry the virus which fortunately is not contagious. We were told we shouldn't get bitten."

"Mosquitoes don't like me," I interject. "I seldom get a bite."

"You're lucky. Rumors had us all frightened. Next thing you know, Dr. Pang quarantined sick people and their houses. Placed signs on the doors. Newspapers, radio, TV carried information about dengue fever. What to do like eliminate places of stagnant water where mosquitoes could breed: old tires, open water-filled pots in gardens. Information was relentless."

"Sounds scary."

"I'm convinced Dr. Pang's quick and thorough action saved Maui from dengue fever. Probably saved all the islands. You know how quickly invasive species spread. Think of the mongoose brought here to control rats in the pineapple and sugar cane fields. It doesn't seem like rocket science but nobody noticed in time that rats came out in night time while the mongoose was a daytime animal—eating rare native Hawaiian bird eggs.

"Birds that had no natural defenses. Quite destructive to Hawaii. Now the mongoose is on all the islands except Kauai." She adds with a wry laugh, "And if our people had let the Superferry[12] dock here, we'd have mongoose too."

Another book gives me another view of Hawaiian history. This fascinating personally-written story[13] took place over a century ago. It is Hawaii through a Korean woman's immigrant eyes; her view helped me form a larger picture and see connections from Hawaii's past to present time. Here the immigrant woman will join native Hawaiians to greet the disposed last Queen of Hawaii, Queen Liliuokalani. The scene takes place in early 1900s:

> The man explained to me how Hawai'i had for centuries been a kingdom, ruled by the *ali'i*, the royalty. For most of its history each island was ruled by separate chieftains, until united by Kamehameha I more than a century ago. Then in 1892 a thousand years of autonomous rule came to an end when a cabal of greedy businessmen—aided by the collusion of the American ambassador—seized control of the government, and under the implicit threat of American military might, forced Queen Lili'uokalani to abdicate. Twenty-five years later, the "haole elite" of businessmen still ruled Hawai'i, now a territory of the United States. They were known as the "Big Five" companies—sometimes called "the Invisible Government," owing to their power behind the scenes of the Republican Party that dominated Hawaiian government and politics.[14]

Curious, I look up *Big Five* in Wikipedia:

> The Big Five was the name given to a group of what started as sugarcane processing corporations that wielded considerable political power in the Territory of Hawaii during the early 20th century and leaned heavily towards the Hawaii Republican Party. The Big Five were Castle & Cooke, Alexander & Baldwin, C. Brewer & Co., American Factors (now Amfac) and Theo H. Davies & Co. The extent of the power that the Big Five had was considered by some as equivalent to an oligarchy. Attorney General of Hawaii Edmund Pearson Dole, referring to the Big Five said in 1903, 'There is a government in this Territory which is centralized to an extent unknown in the United States, and probably almost as centralized as it was in France under Louis XIV.'

Another chance to learn to do it right! Just threw away a half hour's computer work by not carefully saving before being carried away by competing interests. I can't recreate the lost writing but the following quote is what I was thinking about.

But first I should say that I'm *feeling* Princess Ruth pushing me—throwing things in my path to help me—this time with noticing parallels between the history of U.S. treatment of Hawaii and how our society treats (used to treat?) women:

> Excluded from the center of male-created culture with its power politics, wars, and great "art," women unselfconsciously weave the threads of an alternative cultural vision. Though in the past women's works served only to humanize the periphery of male culture but not to transform it—to bind the wounds but not to stop the war—Rich[15] recognizes women's traditional work as the creation of an alternative cultural vision. The threads of nurturing, emotional sensitivity, and simple beauty may be woven by women of today into a new culture. In recognizing a continuity between herself and the numberless women whose names were never in history books, Rich finds strength to believe that it is possible to weave a new culture—not from scratch, but from threads our foremothers have left us.[16]

These words make such good sense. I *see* Barbara in the foregoing quote, and this Hawaiian culture, of course. Is this what conscious present-day Hawaiians are doing—weaving, discovering, reowning their past so they create a brand new blended Hawaiian culture?

Our own U.S. culture may be entering a time when it's safe to advocate openly for one's beliefs. This ties in with my strong feelings that our women's culture is again on track. We can come out of hiding. A quick idea is that the big fight over Obama's health care program is the last gasps of a dying, totally patriarchal way of dealing with the world—power over, control over, money over. I win—you lose. People are sick of this attitude. Most want a win-win for everybody with everyone cared for and especially the land which nourishes us all. Old time Hawaiian values for sure.

Voicing your concern is no longer a futile waste of energy. Like-minded people can prevail. We join support groups where we can but don't give our full heart to places that don't support and cherish us.

I'm scrambling about 'looking for a permanent home'. Looking for new rules of behavior, schedules, routines, things to try, places to put my heart.

What I've left out so far is the compassion with which I learn to view my own addictive behavior (concerning Kevin), and that of others. They can't help it and I haven't been able to change myself either. But with new insight surely I can mitigate my behavior with Kevin. I won't fall under his spell again or go back to him.

Name it: *This is addictive behavior.* I do the same thing over and over without changed results. I expect something different but I get the same thing. I must recognize choice. Do I wish to waste my energy and life, being unhappy with others? Kevin brought deep unhappiness. Do I want to stick myself in a fixed pattern with someone who is incapable of change?

If I choose *no change*—the status quo—I must recognize that life keeps rolling along and I'm wasting mine!

If I choose *change*, I need to look into myself and admit what I can and cannot live with.

At work, I am scared to look at my inbox this morning. Sure enough, another file shows up on my computer that's supposed to be private. The originating source is a Dr. Mercola. Puzzled—this is nothing I recognize—I decide to delete the file.

"Read it!" a stern voice intones. Of course the voice in my head is Princess Ruth. Her urgency pulls like a rip tide. Here is the file—cut drastically:

Expert Jeffrey M. Smith, author of **Seeds of Deception** *and* **Genetic Roulette**, reveals shocking facts about genetically modified organisms (GMOs). Smith links GMOs to toxins, allergies, infertility, infant mortality, immune dysfunction, stunted growth, and death.

Dr. Mercola's Comments:

The distance between our food source and us is, I believe, an alarming problem! And it has allowed giant corporations to essentially hijack your health for profit.

Returning to natural eating habits is a must if you want to thrive in today's modern world, and banishing genetically modified (GMO) food products is an essential step of this process.... you've been led to believe you can live on synthetic chemicals. But you can't! ....

The problem we face here in the US is the fact that GMO products are not labeled.... After some 14 years of fighting for GMO labeling in the US, it's time to realize that we can't wait for government to listen. Instead, we must educate each other, which is exactly what Smith's organization, Institute for ResponsibleTechnology.Org is all about. Their slogan, "Healthy Eating Starts with NO GMO," is worthy of being pasted on your refrigerator as a constant reminder.

For an in-depth education on the many dangers of GM foods, I highly recommend reading Jeffrey Smith's books, *Seeds of Deception* and *Genetic Roulette*.

Smith documents at least 65 serious health risks from GMO products of all kinds, including: Soy allergies have skyrocketed after the introduction of GMO soy; Genes from GMO crops transfer to human gut bacteria, which might transform your intestinal flora into a *living pesticide factory*; No one knows the full extent of what happens to the end product when you splice in new genes, and then eat that product for several generations. The only thing that is guaranteed is that it will create surprise side effects.

"Samantha," **the gruff tone** is a command. "Come to the conference room, please? As soon as convenient?" Kevin's voice is strong with puzzling undertones. He does not sound friendly. Guilty as sin, my heart thuds alarmingly as I give thanks that my computer monitor faces away from him. Anyway, what am I guilty about—I'm just reading information, aren't I, facts available to anybody?

"Sure." Above my racing heart, I am casual as can be. "Will ten minutes be okay? To finish here?" Needing to catch my breath, I search his closed face to no avail. His features tell me nothing. Am I being fired? Does he know about these GMO emails?

"See you in ten." Kevin is noncommittal. I can read nothing in his features past my own agitation, so I return to my reading. Ten minutes isn't long and I need this file off my computer.

Moratorium Called on GMO Foods

On May 19th, 2009, The American Academy Of Environmental Medicine (AAEM) sent out a press advisory calling for Immediate Moratorium On Genetically Modified Foods" and for physicians to "educate their patients, the medical community, and the public to avoid GMO (genetically modified organisms) foods when possible, and provide educational materials concerning GMO foods and health risks." They also advised that physicians should "consider the role of GMO foods in their patients' disease processes." …. "There is more than a casual association between GMO foods and adverse health effects. There is causation, as defined by recognized scientific criteria. The strength of association and consistency between GMO foods and disease is confirmed in several animal studies."

Playing with Technology We Don't Fully Comprehend

Dr. Mae-Wan Ho of the Institute of Science in Society (ISIS) explains the heart of why GMO foods are so dangerous: "The rogue genes inserted into a genome to make a GMO could land anywhere; typically in a rearranged or defective form, scrambling and mutating the host genome, and have the tendency to move or rearrange further once inserted, basically because they do not know the dance of life. That's ultimately why genetic modification doesn't work and is also dangerous." ….

If your diet consists largely of processed foods, you can be sure you're eating about 70 percent GMO foods.... In conclusion, remember to appreciate the power of your pocketbook! If more of us begin to refuse GMO foods, food manufacturers will have no choice but to listen.

My brain is running away with itself. Thought is a crazy jungle. This is *my* company, and I don't want to know bad stuff. I need this job. It's too soon to look for another. What does Kevin want?

Then I wonder, *What would Kevin say about this email?* Easy to guess. He'd say, *forget it*. Can I? Deep inside I know what's happening is more than craziness or intuition. Princess Ruth reaches a long presence, gains force in my awareness. She's touching a hidden part of me that I don't usually pay attention to. As best I can understand, nature here, Kauai's beauty and spirit, if I can think such a thing, brings growth to me like a plant grows in proper soil, sun, rain and conditions. As long as I've been aware, I've had a plan for my life. First this, then that. Order. Control. These slip away and, now, I barely notice.

Could Kevin know of these anti-GMO emails? My heart sinks. It's time to find out what Kevin wants.

A few of these cloaks are still in existence; the best collection is locked in a vault in the Bishop Museum, Honolulu. These cloaks are valued in excess of one million dollars. It took fifty of the tiny red and gold feathers to cover a thumbnail and but two such feathers came from each tiny bird, now extinct. Most cloaks took more than four generations to make. The color yellow was reserved for Hawaii's royalty.

Eugene Burns, The Last King of Paradise
– published in 1952

Chapter Four

THE GMO MEETING BARBARA invited me to, passes in a blur. I am simply not paying attention. Perhaps it is avoidance, or the fact that my capacity to take in anything new is exceeded. My body is at the meeting, but not my mind. The seats are so hard I feel like I'm sitting on volcanic rocks. After squirming endlessly, and with some embarrassment, I make my escape. Barbara, seeming to understand, invites me to a Hawaiian musical event the next evening. My intuition tells me I should accept. When the next night arrives, I'm quite glad I did.

Barbara is to meet me. I've been searching for familiar faces but she hasn't yet arrived. My eyes fall upon an intriguing man and suddenly I am observing a secret life in the midst of people, watching a man alone and comfortable with himself and his tools of work. Caught in a curious time warp, I see past the usual façade. Swinging in his own time, this vibrant musician is alone, just him and the guitar he is tuning in a corner of the noisy room.

What alerts you to one person and not another? I have no idea. This man's contained power grabs me. I don't know him but I've always known him. He is the romantic dream of sixteen and the reality you embrace to forget that dream as soon as your heart gains some sense about men. Still unable to take my eyes off the strange bronze man, I am instantly on guard. *Don't be juvenile*, I tell myself. *This is ridiculous.* Facts, though, are inescapable. No matter what I say to myself, I still look. Male beauty. Sculptured features with extra full lips, dark hair a little past his chin, high forehead, deep-set dark eyes with hints of sadness.

As if there are only two of us, I feel alone with the man I watch. Slight tinges of ownership trickle in, the way that being in a high place in a landscape makes you feel you possess what you see. What your eyes take in becomes part of you. As if sight, seeing, makes you a crucial partner. *I want to know more* pushes at the edge of thought. *Who is he?*

Barbara touches my back. "Here," she orders, "Try this laulau. It's great." She hands me a plate of traditionally wrapped ti leaf that contains steamed pork, wrapped in taro leaf. I savor the almost tart taste of taro leaves combined with sweeter pork or fish. Traces of old Hawaii warm me and welcome me. That acceptance. That non-judgment. A living and breathing aloha. *Be happy for this moment. This moment is your life.*

This Hawaiian culture, when I can get local, knocks me out. The freely given generosity and unquestioning acceptance thaw frozen bits of me, set them struggling for life. A box of avocadoes set by the side of the road, free for anyone to take. Oranges in season, grapefruit, pomelos, even lychees offered free to whoever wants. I yearn to imitate, to become what I witness. To be kinder and more generous. To give as I receive. Seduced by nature's beauty everywhere I look, I am changing. Is my attraction now to this man—completely unaware of my existence—simply part of my longing to belong? Some days, I yearn to just to cram everything to myself. I want it all.

While Barbara and I stand around talking, eating our laulau with the usual rice and macaroni salad, greeting friends with kisses on each side of the face and hugs as is the custom here, I keep an inside awareness focused on my unknown musician. I could have questioned Barbara, who probably knows him, but that seems like breaking a privacy.

I notice that his air of containment follows him when he joins his fellow players as the group disappears through a left side door off stage. Musicians play and sing and Barbara talks about them. She has favorites, is excited to hear them. I sit not knowing what the hell I'm doing but glad to be here anyway. Electricity in the audience grows as the next group is announced, an anticipatory charge. Three men sit with slack key guitars. Contrary to what has gone before, their sound is soft. You want to bend forward to hear better. Soothing tones. Calmed nerves. Creeping into my awareness I know there is nowhere I have to be and nothing I have to do. The music is so present, the sound brings me along, carrying me into a timelessness that is new. I think later that my heart beats in the rhythm they play. Calm. Beautiful. Like taking your heart in its musical hands and petting it quiet like a fractious child. I am enchanted.

I keep dodging and trying not to think about Kevin's important talk with me. Things were truly odd. Kevin sounded so stern when he demanded to see me that being fired looms large in my mind.

But instead, the big surprise. Kevin has a new job for me, paying more. They want me to give talks for the company: publicity and public relations. I didn't sign on for this. My scientific output and reputation are rock solid. Am I being set up for something fishy? Is Kevin behind this?

I think the company wants to use me for propaganda. Or am I just being paranoid? Purity Corporation gave me a sizeable raise while also implying—or at least Kevin did—that these extra assignments will be fun.

After my husband's death, this life I'm composing in Kauai is turning upside down so quickly. In my need for steadying influences and continuity, Princess Ruth's presence and influence become more real, especially as I follow her instructions to learn more about Hawaii. My fascination grows but encountering new facts is not always easy. Also, way out of sight, stray thoughts of the handsome Hawaiian slack key musician work their way to consciousness. Learning more about his Hawaii could bring me closer to him.

Hawaii land, while biologically rich and beautiful, is complicated; important things happened long ago that yet litter the landscape. I'll never understand about land in Hawaii without writing down facts. And even then I'm unsure. This history was written by the winners, and they don't want us to know.

From a distance, the United States are stealers and thus winners; Hawaiians, taken advantage of by force, are, so far, the losers. One history book paints rosy pictures which are flatly contradicted in the next book. Still, some things show the lay of the land. Ninety-eight[17] percent of native Hawaiians signed the 556 page *1897 Petition Against the Annexation of Hawaii*[18], which protested their country's takeover by the United States. I've heard rumors but lack details that these petitions were buried in the Library of Congress and only came to light when a woman graduate student in the 1990s, searched for something else entirely.

Here is a true story on the petitions, related by Sally-jo Keala-o-Anuenue in her excellent *The Heart of Being Hawaiian*:

> A few months later, while on a personal visit to Washington, D.C. Silva [Noenoe] went to the National Archives and asked to see the petition. She expected a few sheets of paper with a few hundred signatures. But in a tidy archival box was filed more than a ream of paper---556 pages signed in 1897 by 21,269 Hawaiians opposing U.S. annexation of Hawaii. With the signatures on a separate petition, the total came to nearly 40,000—more than 80 percent of the kingdom's citizens.
>
> The edges of some of the yellowed sheets crumbled in her hands, the bottom signatures falling to dust. On one page of the women's petition she recognized a name: Kauhi Lehuloa, age 58. She was Silva's great-great-great-grandmother, from Kalapana on the Big Island,

where 101 women of the tiny village belonged to the Hui Aloha 'Aina, the patriotic league that circulated the petition.

"I come from some serious women," Silva said. "Why would I want to forget them?"

Silva [Noenoe] suggested the well-echoed theory that most American immigrants came from elsewhere to start a better life. It's important for them—and their descendants—to forget where they came from.

"But we Hawaiians didn't leave our homeland," Silva said. "America came and got us. We have no reason to forget ourselves. We have a continuity of relationship with this place."

The idea of follow-the-money didn't start in the U.S. It's been in Hawaii a long time. Only here it's 'follow the land'. Follow who owns the land. Or who controls the aina as ancient Hawaiians had an interesting method of land control. The ruling chief controlled his territory, was boss of that land, and its people. When the chief (alii) changed (was killed in war, or died), all the land and wives and property of the former chief now went to the new chief, and his rewarded followers. As I understand it, the common folk, the maka ainana mostly went with the land—now they just paid their ordinary Chief's portion of their work and produce to the new Chief.[19]

The land was not *owned*. The land wasn't the chief's to do with as he wished. No, the chief was caretaker of the land and his people.

All of a sudden I'm taking off on a theme like wailing the blues. No one person owned the land, but the land belonged to everyone. And everyone was responsible for caretaking it. And living in supreme transparency for the chief lived on an island. Everybody not only knew his name, they knew everything. And wrote songs (mele) and made risqué jokes if they chose. A modern mele hula tells of a chief's sexual equipment. Last year's Merrie Monarch festival had a hula that was wickedly funny.

Land ownership as in *I own this land, this field, this tree; my wish alone commands its fate* was not part of Hawaiian culture. Hawaiians loved the land, their aina. This paradise, this aina, this land was *owned* and governed with principles of the good-of-all and sustainability. Remember, ancient Hawaiians were isolated; all they had was the land, the sea, and each other. Nobody was going any place. You, your Hawaiian group of people, were responsible for supplying your needs and creating and maintaining what you needed and wanted. Sustainability to the max. And ultimately, of course, you were responsible for the society you'd live in.

In most early societies feeding the population was hard and took most of everybody's time and energy. Think of our own Pilgrims who would have starved to death but for the Indians and that first Thanksgiving we still celebrate. And for that matter, think of how we repaid the Indians.

In contrast, food here in Hawaii, with ingenious cultivation, soon grew plentiful. An estimate is that ample food production required only four hours of work a day, leaving plenty of time for cultivation of the arts of singing (mele), dancing (hula), making leis of beautiful flowers, or feathers, learning how to heal, how to best deal with others, and with time for games, play, sex. And war, of course for just like ours, their society hadn't yet evolved; some conflicts were only settled with physical fighting.

When you follow the land, the behind the scenes machinations begin to show. King Kamehameha I was the first chief to unite the major islands under one rule. He won the islands one by one in fierce battle—himself at the forefront of his warriors. On his way to ultimate power Kamehameha I proved himself both extremely smart and brave. As a young man, living on the Big Island, Kamehameha met Captain Cook, who in 1778 commanded the first English ships to land in the islands. Kamehameha saw and understood the power of the guns (remember Hawaiians had no metal and hence no knives or guns. Before Cook's arrival, their weapons were made of wood and stone, sharks teeth and other natural materials.)

Kamehameha was quick to grasp the new rules: get some guns; corral some foreigners to help you plan new tactics, and win all your battles. When Captain Cook was stabbed at Kealakekua Bay, ironically, with one of the very knives he'd brought to the islands, the young leader was there to strongly suggest that two Englishmen join him to advise and help him unify the islands. These were Isaac Davis and John Young who both married

Hawaiian Chiefesses and were rewarded by the King with land and power. (Later the grandson of Isaac Davis marries Princess Ruth.)

Kamehameha lost his first home battles on the Big Island but he learned fast and kept at it, not only winning the Big Island, but reaching out to conquer other islands.

Kamehameha had a vision of the islands united. This brilliant chief realized right away that without unification of the islands, all was lost to this invading rush of new English and American civilizations. First, Kamehameha took nearby Maui and then Oahu. Barbara recently told me she'd actually seen a Kamehameha plaque on the Big Island commemorating his capture of Maui using two U.S. warships! Although nature helped scuttle Kamehameha's two major attempts at taking Kauai, duplicity and diplomacy later won the day.

King Kaumualii (King K, the last King of Kauai) promised allegiance to Kamehameha at an 1810 meeting in Honolulu. Two stories diverge: First is that King K is tricked into handing over Kauai to Kamehameha's rule. The second is that he voluntary surrendered control. (Which would you believe?) In any case, in 1821 Kauai's King K is whisked off, or kidnapped, to become a husband of Queen Kaahumanu (Queen K) who was appointed by Kamehameha I as spiritual advisor to Kamehameha II and later III (this is the one who kidnapped King K). And so Kauai comes under Kamehameha rule, last of all of the islands. (Queen K is also an early foster mother of Princess Ruth, dying when the Princess was six or seven.)

Ironically, as soon as Kamehameha has all the islands under his control, he outlaws war throughout Hawaii. It's enough to make you believe that Kamehameha read the future, and knew Hawaiians would have to use every drop of their strength against the invaders and shouldn't waste any more life energy fighting each other.

I've been feeling into the heart of Kauai, seeking to establish contact with I know not what. Motives aren't clear but somehow Princess Ruth more than intrigues me. I want to get into her frame of mind, the forces that made her, to understand her territory of power and mana. Or rather, more accurately, make definite and give words to something I know is there but am not sensitive enough to make clear, even to myself. Attempting to nail nebulous feelings, I've even revived childhood bedtime prayer, which seems to bring me closer, but doesn't completely satisfy. Sitting quietly writing the feelings in a poem might help, or watching clouds or trembling leaves, letting everything move at its own tempo.

Most fulfilling are simple things like sparkles of light off early evening taro leaves. The shimmering leaves are mesmerizing, drawing me into some essence of taro nature. Besides being peaceful, this quiet time helps me feel into a companionship with Princess Ruth, who lived in intimate harmony with the aina and the bounty the land provided.

Hawaiian life is linked closely with the taro plant. According to the creation chant *Kumulipo*, taro grew from the first-born son of *Wakea* (sky father) and *Papa* (earth mother). The child was stillborn but when buried his body grew into the plant *taro*, which means everlasting breath. The second son became the original ancestor of the Hawaiian people, so taro and Hawaiians are family. Taro is the beloved elder brother who feeds all of us and so we must take care of taro.[20]

Hawaiians believe that taro has the greatest life force of all foods. The word, ohana which means family, comes from the way taro grows in a cluster. The largest stem is considered to be the mother, and the little stems around it are keiki, children. Taken away from the mother plant at the appropriate age, these keiki then grow a new circle of life, a new ohana.[21]

Main staple of the Polynesian diet, taro's large purple bulb or corm is steamed and pounded into *poi*, an *ono* (delicious) paste that goes well with raw fish. The ancient Hawaiians on Kauai used their own version of the traditional poi pounder, a large heavy stone with a hole at the top, used as a handle. The women on Kauai were the only ones in the Hawaiian Islands allowed to pound poi and the handle was to make pounding easier for them. My intuition suggests that Kauai women enjoyed more equality with their men while the scientist in me yearns for empirical studies to prove it.

I love boiled taro, sliced and then slow-fried in coconut oil with garlic, but I'm still working on developing a fondness for poi. Taro leaves are tasty, like spinach only better, and it's easy for me now to remember to cook them for a long time. (Taro has needle-like calcium oxalate crystals in the leaves, stem and corm. As I discovered the first time I tasted a raw leaf, these are extremely irritating to the throat, causing a stinging sensation.) Fortunately I ate only a small amount that wasn't cooked enough. But enough to remember not to undercook taro again.

From early times, taro was the primary food of the Hawaii people, supplemented by breadfruit (*ulu*), sweet potato (*uala*), yams, greens, ferns, fruit, fish and seaweed (*limu*). The first Polynesian settlers brought taro with them in their canoes, and it has been cultivated as a staple and staff of life from ancient times. In the early days there were more than 300 varieties of taro but today only around 87[22] survive. A taro farmer exemplifies self-sufficient stewardship of natural resources through hard work.

When scientists at the University of Hawaii tried to patent a form of GMO taro, farmers and activist protested, gained control of the taro patents and burned them. Genetic modifications of taro (kalo) are now forbidden in Hawaii until 2013.

Kauai has room for the unexplained and happenings purely of the moment. Nature is powerful here, not yet entirely paved over. The beauty opens your mind.

Yesterday at Salt Pond (Hawaiians continue to make salt here) I'm watching the sky, the day creating itself. It's fairly early on a Sunday morning—no one else is on this curving section of beach—when, snorkel in hand, I stop short in the sand. Three feet before me in the shallow clear ocean is an oblong dark shape. A monk seal lazes as relaxed as cane syrup, a creature totally at home in its world. The seal is so still, relaxed, completely moved by the sea water, I fear it is dead.

For ten minutes I watch as the barely moving seal lifts its face, nibbles the bottom, is alive. What a privilege. Then the seal slowly drifts, sometimes moving a flipper and swims down the beach, slithers itself up onto the sand, and goes to sleep for its labors. I enter the sea.

In Princess Ruth's time the ancient four main Gods were: Lono, Kane, Ku and Kanaloa.[23]

More personal to Princess Ruth was Pele, the volcano Goddess, who was a special protector of the Princess, her aumakua, her ancestor. Some have it that Pele's full name is Ikiikiikapoliopele.[24] The Princess always refused to travel out of the Hawaiian islands as if she always knew she gained special powers here.

No account of Ruth's life could be complete without at least some telling of her best-known and incredible achievement: how she stopped Mauna Loa's lava flow from destroying the town of Hilo [on the Big Island] in 1881.

Mauna Loa had begun erupting the previous year on November 5, 1880, and by August of 1881, the lava that had formed into three rivers of molten fire had reached the outskirts of Hilo, about sixty miles away.

Prayers were offered at all the Christian churches in Hilo. Even the future Queen Liliuokalani prayed there, but to no avail. The lava kept moving ever closer towards Hilo, and when local kahunas [priests] performed their rites and still could not appease the Volcano Goddess, Pele. Anxious Hawaiians begged Ruth to sail over to Hilo from Honolulu and intercede with Pele to stop the lava from wiping out Hilo.

Ruth went to the edge of the flow in the darkness of the evening of August 9, 1881. With her were assorted kahunas and retainers, sacrificial pigs and pigeons, red handkerchiefs, a bottle of brandy, and her bed.

While standing near the lava flow and its great heat, she chanted to Pele, sometimes loudly and at other times softly. She then threw about thirty red silk handkerchiefs one-by-one into the fire, followed by the bottle of brandy, which she smashed on the lava, yet no pigs or pigeons were sacrificed.

Ruth then spent the night close by the flow in her bed (which had been hauled to the flow) – a most dangerous venture, since no one knew the rate of advance of the flow.

By the following morning and to the amazement of all, the lava flow had miraculously stopped and had begun to cool. Ruth Keelikolani had saved Hilo.[25]

How did she do it? The old Gods live as Princess Ruth stops a volcano. One woman creates a miraculous event that no one can deny. How did she do it? The great-granddaughter of Kamehameha, she is full of mana, of power. She cares for her people, loves them, feels responsible for them and she returned to Honolulu to great acclaim from her rejoicing people. But, how did she halt the flow of lava?

My mind worries away. Like a washing machine I tumble names and emotions: my dead husband, my boss and long ago lover, Kevin, and now a slack-key Hawaiian musician—something new in my tired repertoire of relationships.

It's so upsetting learning about these GMOs. It's hard to maintain focus and keep working. My new job is surely a respite, as it helps me put aside these GMO concerns. Like that helicopter ride yesterday over Kauai. Kevin said people at mainland Purity headquarters, want me to know more about this island, become familiar with local people. Still there was something off-putting about the way Kevin approached me and this new job, as if he knows something I don't.

I traveled on Safari Helicopters with six passengers, including the pilot. I didn't make conversation with anyone, only the necessary, and soon lost myself in a quick progression of tourist view after view. Stunning close-ups of sharp mountain tops were followed by lots of red earth, green valleys, and the ocean always out one window or the other. Cool blues, so many greens, the sea suddenly turquoise with scalloped white beaches. There was mist and it rained as we traversed The Grand Canyon of the Pacific. Waimea Canyon is 10 miles long and 2, 857 feet deep with exquisite shadings of color, mist, waterfalls, land, and shadow. Just as I felt scared by storm clouds, a rainbow appeared.

Along the Na Pali coast we flew into valleys, then came up abruptly over the tops of high-ridged mountains. The pilot said people used to live here, that in these long green valleys voyaging Hawaiians first learned to be Hawaiian.

I'd heard of Mt. Waialeale, the ancient volcano at the center of Kauai, now collapsed, inaccessible except by helicopter. Mt. Waialeale holds the world's rainfall record, 460 inches per year. Every day, that's around an inch and half of rain. At the top only a few days are ever entirely clear of heavy rain and fog. Highest elevation is 5,066 feet. These summits and remote mountain tops are the edges of land and sky, places beyond human intellect and devising. Places where, beyond rationality and what is easily conceived, we see that everything is connected. From the summit, all is small compared to what *is*, to the experience itself.

I'd pictured flying into a huge dead volcano like Haleakala on Maui.

Instead the helicopter comes into an opening in the side of the long dormant volcano. My breath catches at the sacred beauty, at what I witness. A full rainbow, in glorious color is flung from one side to the other: red, orange, yellow, green, blue, indigo and violet. Behind the rainbow is gigantic ribbed-grey basalt, or granite like a monstrous grey elephant. Solid. Eternal. The rock and the rainbow. Eternal rock, ephemeral rainbow.

Water flows in waterfalls, with greenery on either side, as my eyes focus high on the background of rising grey stone. I've a sudden sense of awe, of spirit. Humility floods me. Who am I to gain this privilege of seeing into the beating heart of Kauai? All trails to this place are lost they say. *Yes,* Princess Ruth whispers in my ear, *the trails are lost to the ignorant, the greedy, the unworthy. Yet even to this day special kahuna come to this sacred place to worship, connect, gain power, put things right.*

In that instant of bright rainbow and ancient grey rock, something moves in my heart. Princess Ruth has prepared me for what is to come. My world view changes. This magic land reaches out to capture the essence of me. A curious giving and taking. A part, missing since the accident, or perhaps missing forever, regains a place, a home. In this moment, a blessing, I gain loyalty and respect for ancient wisdom, an appreciation and deep connection to Kauai.

Rainbows are paths from terrestrial to celestial. Symbols of good luck, rainbows join heaven and earth. Ancients believed Gods slid down rainbows when they had earthly business. Amazing how that rainbow, with the rock behind it, stays imprinted on my mind.

I've read that more heiaus (ancient sites of worship) are built on the slopes of Mt. Waialeale than anywhere in the Hawaiian Islands. Hawaiians used to perform sacred hulas at some heiaus. Suddenly, I'm struck with the desire to visit a functioning heiau for myself.

This island of beautiful Kauai asks something of me. Privileged beyond belief, I'm entrusted with a task, although I don't yet know what it is. I grow calm and waiting. In time, in Hawaiian aloha time, I will learn what it is.

It crosses my mind that in some ways, we—our collective U.S. presence—is reminiscent of ignorant children playing with something of great value, without the slightest notion of what they have. Or might carelessly destroy.

Imagine setting out in a small sailing ship, the Mary Frazer, in 1836 from Martha's Vineyard, Massachusetts, going around fearsome Cape Horn in South America and then San Francisco and on to the Sandwich Islands (Hawaii's name at the time). With fire in your heart, leaving behind everything you know, you set sail for mysterious islands of heathens. You and your mate occupy a 6 x 5 foot cabin and the average age of your 16 missionary friends is 26 years, one and one-half months.

Your God-given missionary task: Civilize the savages. Teach them to read and write, to follow the *Lord*, and to learn to do right as model Christians:

One of the first tasks facing the missionaries was to translate the Bible into Hawaiian. But the Hawaiian language had no system of writing. Before they could translate the Bible, the missionaries had to devise a Hawaiian alphabet. Once this was done, they had to teach the Hawaiians to read and write.

Within a few years, the missionaries had opened schools on Hawaii, Oahu, and several other islands. By 1824, about 2,000 Hawaiian students were enrolled. That number zoomed to 52,000 by 1831. Almost two-fifths of the islanders were in school.

The Hawaiians enjoyed learning from the visiting missionaries. They turned it into a game and eagerly competed with one another. Reuben Tinker, a missionary in the port town of Honolulu, writes that exam day was a kind of festival. 'About 2,000 scholars were present,' he recalled, 'some wrapped in a large quantity of native cloth, with wreaths of evergreen about their heads and hanging toward their feet—others dressed in calico and silk with large necklaces of braided hair and wreaths of red and yellow and green feathers very beautiful and expensive.'

Another task the missionaries set for themselves was to change the way Hawaiian women dressed. The wives of the missionaries designed long, loose-fitting dresses that covered the women from neck to ankles. [Muumuus and Holyoke or Mother Hubbards were patterned, they say, after missionary women's nightgowns.] The Hawaiian women soon came to accept the new clothing style.[26]

When I read about early missionary women covering up Hawaiian women, I bristle. Here we go again, imposing our rules of behavior. Yet, Hawaiian values of the time were designed for life in pristine Hawaii, and not what life in the islands was becoming. Strange diseases were rampant. Diseased whaling sailors were taking advantage of the women. The Hawaiians, used to sharing everything, now shared terrible killing diseases they had no knowledge of, or immunities against. These terrible diseases caused infertility and much suffering and dying. The very existence of the Hawaiian people was threatened. With more sympathy for the covering-up missionary women, I can't help but dislike the exploiting men willing to take advantage of innocence and ignorance.

Speaking of sexual disease transmission, Hawaiian sexual practices didn't diminish disease, but to my feminist sensibilities the Hawaiians sound more advanced: "In Hawaii there is no such word or thought as adultery. It was a common practice and such conjugal flirtations were known as mischievous sleepings. However, there was this difference: the female usually selected her mate for the occasion. And so, even the missionaries who translated the Bible into Hawaiian had to content themselves by rephrasing a commandment into: *Thou shalt not commit mischievous sleeping!*"[27]

My future was a causality of the accident. Pure loss and blackness was all I could see. Without purpose does one even have a life? Certainly I didn't.

I've gone back to bedrock life at its simplest. It's easy to see now that with my life as I knew it stripped away I was simply an automaton. Friends, people I knew were cut off as surely as if I'd taken a knife. Their kindnesses were salt in my wounds, reminders of loss with no hopes for the future.

As beauty and sheer charm of place wake me from the dead past, this consciousness I find myself with is new. There's an inclusive connection I never noticed, probably didn't even have. Somehow, it's as if I've lost my tidy small world and in return have gained a world-view connecting me to a universe beyond my imagining. *We are one*, makes new sense. We are connected: each person is vital in an endless evolving chain of life. Previous rules for living are revealed as meaningless. The *certainties* I built my life and dreams upon fade, and old ways of being become ephemeral as mist.

Late yesterday afternoon I sat quietly beside the water of a shallow calm branch of the Wailua river on the East side. Across the wide river was a dense stand of hau,[28] a kind of hibiscus. These common hau bushes grow by water, their yellow blooms fading into orange blossoms as day goes on. I settle into the hypnotism of moist warm air and gentle water. Small sounds wash through me; a leaf and then an orange hau blossom slowly drift on dawdling water. I watch a picture postcard of beauty. Kauai has a lot of them. I know I've been as empty and purposeless as the floating leaf and flower. For so long I haven't cared about anything.

Now I start to care.

Kauai draws me into its orbit and I'm assimilating its startling beauty and soft vibrations in heart and bones. Yearning to understand, I want to know more and experience deeper. But how do I capture new feelings, own, and give them names?

To break the log-jam of 'This topic too big, and I can't handle it,' I resort to an old trick: just do my best at my task for thirty minutes, and then I can do whatever I want.

Okay. Where to begin?

I need to nail down bare facts about Princess Ruth (or at least one version of them), so again, I check out the library book[29] that first fired my interest. I look at the pictures. Only eight or nine photographs of High Chiefess Ruth are known to exist. My new favorite shows a sitting Princess Ruth dressed in Victorian finery. You can tell that this woman is running the show, and looking pleased with herself. As well she might, for two handsome young men stand at attention, holding *kahili,* long ivory-handled feathered poles at an angle to meet over her head. (The longer the poles, the higher the rank.) One man is Sam Parker; for $80,000 she sold him the land that later became the largest ranch on the Big Island. I've read somewhere that the Princess actually hired Parker to teach her land negotiations after the Great Mahele. which enabled foreigners to own Hawaiian land. And so Princess Ruth held on to ownership of her land—she merely leased her vast holdings, seldom selling outright.[30]

That mischievous look in her eyes helps me believe that quite lascivious story[31] that Princess Ruth traveled with a troop of young men! More on Hawaiians sex practices as I learn more!

Later, when fading memories of Thomas and Kevin weave across my mind, I think, *Kauai heals me. I'm returning to my old self.* But that old self didn't worry about money. Suddenly it occurs to me that perhaps I'm whining. Princess Ruth, suffering loss after loss, change and more change in her Hawaii, also managed to keep tight control of her business affairs. I need to check with my lawyer in California, see how he is doing with settling my affairs.

"Have dinner with me at Waimea Plantation and let's go to Art Night in Hanapepe? Kevin had asked earlier. "We'll celebrate Friday night and the end of the working week."

"Can't," I said. "Something I have to do." I hate myself when I lie to Kevin, and yet I keep doing it. Kevin was not happy. Nor was I with his heavy frown. But my sense of urgency prodded me, curiosity close behind. I want to continue my study of Princess Ruth.

Princess Ruth Luka Keanolani Kauanahoahoa Keelikolani was born in 1826 and died in 1883. Princess Ruth married Leleiohoku, a love match; he was the same age as Princess Ruth. Reports vary; they were fifteen or sixteen. They had two sons, first William Pitt Kinau (Kinau for Ruth's step-mother—mother of Kamehamehas Two and Three, Princess Ruth's kingly half-brothers). Princess Ruth's second son died in infancy. Her young husband then died at twenty-two. The Princess took over her husband's vast estates and soon afterwards, the Governorship of Hawaii (the Big Island) and was entertaining people from all over the world.

Princess Ruth and the High Chiefs enjoyed great hopes for her son William Pitt Kinau's future as he grew older. Kinau was highly intelligent and self-possessed with leadership qualities. This was the young man the elders had looked for, showing lineage of great chiefs in the genealogy of both his parents.

In his photo, her son Kinau has a strong face and looks older and more mature than 17; Princess Ruth is raising him in the old ways while she makes sure he also gets the best contemporary education possible. Her son, Kinau, will be an enlightened ruler of all Hawaii.

"Great was their shock and dismay, and dismal their sense of loss when William Pitt Kinau died in an accident on the Big Island at the age of 17."[32] Princess Ruth's pain—another great loss on top of all the others—can only be imagined. Her son—a future ruler of Hawaii—is now dead, a lost dream.

I wonder that Princess Ruth at that wretched time didn't drown in grief and 'if-onlys.' Remember her mother died at her birth, her beloved guardian Queen K when she was six and her loving step-mother Kinau near the time she first married. Then her child and beloved husband. Grieving one sorrow, she'd be hit by another. All those early losses must have made later ones even more horrifying.

In 1856 Princess Ruth remarries; she's around twenty-seven and beautiful. Isaac Young Davis is the grandson of famed Isaac Davis who with John Young had been captured from their ship by Kamehameha the Great in 1790. Both Davis and Young served as Confidential Advisers and Companions-in-Arms and took Hawaiian Chiefesses as wives. "Davis and Young were the first white men known to remain in the Hawaiian Islands."

In one report, the ladies around Princess Ruth dressed exactly alike in lilac cotton. Princess Ruth wears a double necklace of feathers like the chiefs cloaks—"yellow, crimson and green; this of course shows her high rank, none but the *High Chiefs* having the right to wear these feathers."….

"U.S. Minister Henry A. Pierce made no secret of the fact that he disliked [Princess] Ruth intensely. He described her as having '…no intelligence or ability.'

(Much more later about cousin Bernice Bishop, married to Charles.)[33]

Princess Ruth gave away her birth son with Isaac Davis as a *hanai* or adoption to Bernice Bishop. Hanai is an old Hawaiian custom in which one family gives a child to another family. When a child was given in hanai to a chiefly or royal family the child gained rank from the new family. This practice helped keep the chiefs closely bonded and not fighting each other.

Isaac Young Davis, the husband and father of Princess Ruth's child, was furious at her actions as was her step-brother King Lot. King Lot (Kamehameha Five) then made Princess Ruth legally adopt his own younger brother, who she renamed Leleiohoku in honor of her first husband. (Hawaiian names can drive you crazy if you let them.)

"Although she persisted in speaking only Hawaiian, Ruth saw that Prince Leleiohoku had the best broad education that money could provide." She spared nothing in grooming this boy whom she idolized … someday he would be King of Hawaii, and she wanted him to rank in manners, education and wealth with any of the crowned heads of Europe.

But Ruth's dreams for the gifted young Prince were never fulfilled." Sent to California as part of his schooling, the Prince contracted pneumonia and died on April 10, 1877 at age 23. Ruth had lost her second Leleiohoku (the first was her young Hawaiian husband).

And isn't it odd that Princess Ruth, famed for keeping to the ways of the old Gods and practices, should be entrusted with raising these future Kings—her own first son dying at 17, and her beloved adopted son now dying at 23?

Heartbroken, Princess Ruth carried on. Three years later, she made a deal to sell her part of the Crown Lands to Sugar Baron Claus Spreckels for way below market value of $10,000 cash money. Speculation was that Princess Ruth had a hidden motive of desiring a court ruling on her own 'rights' to Crown lands. (More later about Crown lands.) Common knowledge was that Princess Ruth had put one over on Spreckels, who was not pleased.

Princess Ruth's new mansion in Honolulu was called Keoua Hale; she had a huge luau to cerebrate her splendid new palace—a palace that just happened to eclipse King David's own 'Iolani palace. (King David Kalakaua, and later his sister Queen Liliuokalani, are the first rulers of all Hawaii outside of the Kamehameha lineage.) This account says Princess Ruth fell immediately ill and went home to Hilo to die. (Another account puts her death several months later.)

After Princess Ruth died her palatial house was occupied by Charles and Bernice Bishop; then Charles alone after Bernice died, then the house was made into Honolulu High School and was razed by the end of 1925. "Her one page will dated Jan 24, 1883 had only one sentence," according to Wikipedia "'I bequeath to Princess Puaahi (Cousin Bernice Bishop) my elaborate mansion, Keoua Hale on Emma Street in Honolulu, as well as approximately 353,000 acres of Kamehameha lands.' This totaled nearly nine percent of the land in the Hawaiian Islands." Some land she left to others was only for their lifetimes. All her other vast Kamehameha holdings that she inherited, and kept largely intact, will revert to the Bernice Bishop estate, soon falling under Charles Bishop's control.

A personal remembrance said that Princess Ruth "liked to sleep on the floor and her bed was a cushion of fragrant maile vines, over which was placed a velvet blanket. After she reclined, her attendants placed many small cushions about her as she directed."

What goes around comes *around. What you put out is what you get back,* are attitudes I've come across more than once. I thought of that today with a wry, almost disbelieving laugh, as I read this paragraph in a contemporary Hawaiian novel,[34] describing descendants of missionaries, living today on early-stolen Hawaiian land.

> To their credit, the cousins [the writer's cousins] are not greedy or gaudy or ostentatious. Their sole purpose in life is to have fun. They jet ski, motorcross, surf, paddle, run triathlons, rent islands in Tahiti. Indeed, some of the most powerful people in Hawaii look like bums or stuntmen. I think of our bloodline's progression. Our missionary ancestors came to the islands and told the Hawaiians to put on some clothes, work hard, and stop hula dancing. They make some business deals on the way, buying an island for ten grand, or marrying a princess and inheriting her land, and now their descendants don't work. They have stripped down to running shorts or bikinis and play beach volleyball and take up hula dancing.

I think this pretty much says it: the missionaries, our military people, Japanese, Tahitians, tourists, traders, Chinese, Portuguese, Filipinos, and GMO workers like me, we all come to paradise—like the Hawaiians before us, except they got here a couple of thousand years earlier—and we want to stay in Hawaii. Thousands of new arrivals do stay and continue staying.

The problem is that some of us find ourselves coming to consciousness at this moment in time. The reality now is that the Hawaiian people are pushed off their land and their way of life stolen. We can't give them back their decimated population or restore the innocence of a pre-contact people.

Nobody turns back time. The best we can do is restoration, beginning with a full-hearted, truthful confession of our sins—our country's sins—with greed and lying, hypocrisy and ignorance heading the list. We can at least treat Hawaiians and their ancient customs with respect.

We can fix the environmental messes we've made as best we can. We can bless a 'not yet killed' healing spirit of this special land. We can stop our military occupation, or at least cut it drastically.[35]

Sex and how people live. Sex and the Hawaiians. Sex and the missionaries. I've been reading stories and I'm sick of the missionaries and their hard-nosed, superior viewpoints. So many and so hypercritical and self-righteous.

The missionaries wrote from their time in history and of course their viewpoint about what they found. *We'll civilize the heathen savages*, seems their prevailing attitude. The Hawaiian's didn't write and so whose version of reality do we have? Too bad Margaret Mead wasn't alive and studying Hawaiian sex and culture before Western contact, and for that matter, studying our own at that time.

However, to go into the bare heart of ancient Hawaiian sex practices, I fortuitously came across surprising views in the fascinating *The Last King of Paradise* published in 1952. Eugene Burns came to Hawaii in the late 1940s as a park ranger and says he spent four years reading old manuscripts and newspapers to get at true facts about old Hawaii, truths he felt were being glossed over and rapidly disappearing.

"Almost unconsciously I knew that I must describe the culture which grew naturally out of land, and sea and sky," Burns wrote, "and how it met the white man's civilization head on, and lost; and that I could find a native leader who tried to hold off the inevitable as best he could and lead his people back. I found him in David Kalakaua, the last king of the Hawaiian Islands. *The Last King of Paradise* is a product of original sources."

Here, we quickly learn, that along with Dorothy in *The Wizard of Oz*, we're not in Kansas anymore. The birth of future King David Kalakaua is described and his baby penis gets a name, *Halala*. And a hula is performed in its honor. And when King David Kalakaua marries: "Last [in the festivities] there came a rarely done *ki'i* hula, a marionette dance, which recited the history of the bridegroom's private parts with the aid of a puppet two-thirds life size. From the naming of the mai, Halala, through the ceremony of circumcision, the first intercourse with Tutu, the conquests and a final paean to the bliss of this, the wedding night." No, this is not Kansas but it sure is interesting! And it's an awful lot of detail to be totally made up.

It's bothered me not quite remembering some unsavory history of Charles Bishop marrying the young high-born schoolgirl, Bernice, Princess Ruth's cousin. I find good reason for my unease:

> Actually, however, he [Foreign Minister Judd with missionary connections] wanted to get Prince Lot Kamehameha out of the way and thereby help to bring about the marriage of his dollar-a-day customs clerk, Charles Reed Bishop, to the fabulously wealthy Princess Bernice and thereby get the first solid hold upon Hawaii's royalty. So far, both the Kamehameha and Aikanaka dynasties had steadfastly resisted white intrusion. The princess, at birth, had been promised to Lot. With the prince in Europe and with the Cooke's support, Judd thought the marriage might be consummated. [The Cookes run the Chief's School where Bernice is a boarding student.] To promote Bishop's ardor, he promised the young man the lucrative position of Collector of Customs, should his suit be successful.[36]

And more interesting detail: "Gossip carried news of the courtship to Bernice's father and mother, who called at the school at once and give explicit directions that the wooing should cease and that Bernice was to marry no one but Lot Kamehameha [V]. But Bishop was always about and Lot was in Europe or Washington. Bernice decided to marry Bishop."

I've been so intent on Princess Ruth, my Hawaiian research, new job and all the GMO stuff I'm learning that it's easy to forget that making a new life for myself needs attention. Uncharacteristically, I've accepted an invitation to come 'look at his wood carvings' and visit the attractive musician I met at the music festival with Barbara.

I'm at Kaimana's place in Waimea valley. I feel the calmness, the at-homeness in his skin, the belonging. This merging of male and environment is subtle. I'm made part of the whole before I even know it. Imagine a complete *now*, a moment so real that all time *is* now and there is nothing that is not *now*.

Comfort permeates every atom. No matter how I arrived or what others may feel, I *belong* here. If I could think I'd wonder how Kaimana does it, making me a gift of time and comfort as if they were ordinary, nothing special. Yet even his name is special. *Kai*—the sea. *Mana*—personal power and strength. I went up to talk with Kaimana after the musical event Barbara had invited me to, and somehow—he urges me—I've ended up at his place deep in Waimea valley.

The result is bliss. Joyousness I've done nothing to achieve. But the question of *deserve*, or method for attainment never gains a foothold. I do not own the bliss; bliss owns me. Joy expands and expands. Does the sky have a limit? This universe and all universes known and unknown? Without words I feel everything—bliss beyond compare. Combining old and new, his home is a marvelous blend. I sit now on a low couch before a gleaming koa wood coffee table. Wooden pieces that Kaimana has fashioned from old and new hardwood are all around. While I struggle to keep my cool, to behave as if the top of my head and heart are not blown off, Kaimana quietly places a cup of hot chocolate before me. The cup and saucer are delicate English china covered with pink roses and a dab or two of gold. His hands take up the space of two or three of these small cups.

My hands are big but his are huge—long tapering fingers, wide palms. His hands should appear clumsy but don't. These are kind hands, competent and skilled. My breath catches. I don't know what to do or where to look. Words are beyond me. A new language is required with syllables I've never heard.

Rebirth appears like a headline in my thoughts. Rebirth, like being born again, starting over. Innocence. Is this what I've wanted and missed? To leave the old behind, the limitations, mistakes, blunders, the undone, unthought-of, and not yet known. All of the old. Simply leave it. Just walk away from tired rules, the old me. Surprise myself. Why not?

"Try it," Kaimana invites. "Home-made chocolate like the ancients made it. Chocolate wasn't in Hawaii until recently, but Aztec kings and Mayan rulers drank chocolate every day. Ambrosia from the Gods—they knew these secrets."

After a long time of silence and no movement, I hear him again. "Drink," he suggests, his voice low and seductive as the delicious chocolate when I taste it. Ambrosia.

That night alone in my narrow bed on the floor, I pull a book from my seed library[37] (all that is left from the severe pruning that moving had required) to reread a marked passage:

> … from the dry dock of mute old men
> bring back the miracle of a tear.
> from the delta of good intentions
> bring back a seed that will change a life.
>
> From the fields of the dispossessed bring me a donkey
> with Byzantine eyes, from the wells of the mad
> bring the bell and lantern of heaven

From the bay of forgetfulness come back with my name,
from the cave of despair come to me empty-handed,
from the strait of narrow escapes come back, come back.

My awakened heart smiles over Lisel Mueller's poem. Byzantine eyes. Enchantment. A special magic that is mine. Smiling, I sleep as if I'll never wake to any reality that isn't wonderfully special.

They took all the trees, put 'em in a tree museum, and they charged the people a dollar and a half just to see 'em. Don't it always seem to go that you don't know what you've got till it's gone.
They paved paradise and put up a parking lot.

Joni Mitchell

"The environment has to be balanced against the economy"…. Environmental messes cost us huge sums of money both in the short run and in the long run; cleaning up or preventing those messes saves us huge sums in the long run, and often in the short run as well. In caring for the health of our surroundings, just as of our bodies, it is cheaper and preferable to avoid getting sick.

Jared Diamond

CHAPTER FIVE

THE VERY SOIL of this land is underwater in lies, greed, treachery, betrayal. When I awaken from my dreams of the night before and Kaimana, it's only a few hours before I find myself in a very different reality. Agatha from work shares her story. *Hapa* means half and Agatha is hapa-haole: father white, as she expressed it, mother pure Hawaiian.

The day outside is bright sunshine. Barbara and I sit at a four-person chrome table on white plastic chairs drinking decaf coffee, the only hot thing available, with fake creamer and counterfeit sugar.

"Most Americans live in a fake world," Barbara observes as she motions Agatha to join us. The room is empty except for us. "And leaving you with that happy thought," Barbara stands up, "I've got to go. A minor emergency of the land. An overbalance of longans to cut and get ready for Farmers Market tomorrow in Kapaa. Longans," she adds to me, "are poor cousins to lychees but still very tasty."

Barbara's words about fake lives dance in my head.

Agatha pulls a pint jar of water from her canvas bag and a red-topped glass container of sliced mangoes, two forks and two yellow cloth napkins. Handing me a fork and a napkin, she indicates the mangoes. "These grow by my house. Try some?" As her voice rises with the question, there is a wariness about her, a manner of being on guard yet also wanting to connect. My losses have made me more sensitive; either I've been alone too long or this is a kindred spirit. I see the deep sadness in her chocolate-brown eyes. We are both reaching out.

Feeling awkward, I need something to say, so I comment on the printed pages she has carefully placed on the table. "A new problem for work?"

"Not work. Personal. I'm studying genealogy," she says with soft pride and an intriguing shrug of self-depreciation.

I move closer to look at the top printed page.

"Not like the Mormons do genealogy, I'm doing my mother's line of ancestors first and then my father's."

As she turns a couple of pages I see one long Hawaiian name followed by the English words *great-great-grandmother*. "How totally incredible," I say, "You know the name of your great-great grandmother. And who she married and how many children she had." Ancestors. Known roots. My mind mulls over what I'm hearing. Few on the mainland even know the names of both their grandmothers. This is awesome.

"Hawaiians of old used only one name." Accepting my admiration, she pushes the sliced mangoes forward.

"These are wonderful. Thank you," I say. "And how clever to serve them like this." I can't resist. "Did you know?" I ask, "the only way to eat a mango, beside this," I gesture toward the slices, "is in a bathtub? Lets you wash all the juice off immediately."

As we laugh together more tension flies out the door.

"You grew up on this island?" I ask.

"Yes, eight children. I'm the seventh. I was a rebel. My mother was strict. We never got along. My father was a farmer, but an only child. Privileged background. I was twelve when the war came. The Japanese bombed Pearl Harbor and we instantly had World War II." Agatha's voice goes higher as disbelief and anger creep in. "One day the U.S. army showed up here on Kauai. Told my father he had to get rid of all his horses, cows, pigs: all the animals that fed and supported us. The army knocked down all our buildings, leveled the ground, put up barracks, and more soldiers came."

"Did the army pay your father," I ask, horrified.

"No. The army just takes what it wants."[38]

"That's awful. How could they do that?"

"Wartime. The military takes anything they want. I was twelve. Rebellious. But I like to learn, to know things. We had *Books of Knowledge* and I read them all. My mother was scared with all the soldiers around, so I was sent to Honolulu, to Kamehameha boarding school."

"I'm so sorry," I say, my thoughts ablaze with being a twelve year old girl and having your life torn apart.

"After they took our land, my father got work on Oahu. It wasn't so bad. On weekends we'd return to Kauai together. We took the old-time ferry boat. Once my father told me about when he was twelve years old." Agatha unscrews the lid and takes a long drink from her pint jar of clear water.

"My father was close to my mother's grandmother. My great-grandmother was trained as a *Kumu*, spiritual leader and was training my father. He was twelve when his beloved Kumu was dying. She told him— he never forgot—that he must side with the foreigners, the missionaries."

I stop breathing as I think of ancient knowledge that is dying with his special teacher. Agatha's father will not be blessed with his *Kumu's* traditional last breath, her final knowledge passed on. His sacred Hawaiian heritage is stolen away.

The grandmother knew that life, living, and staying alive overrode everything. With life you could come back. With death you were done, your tribe, your people, you were finished.

Hobson's choice. The Hawaiian grandmother and the twelve year old boy. My very bones soften with sorrow. All I can do is blink away tears, and say again my useless, "I'm so sorry."

I'm still reeling from Agatha's story when another strange file shows up on my computer at work. Now used to this, I simply print out the pages and put them into my briefcase before deleting the file. When I get home and take them out again, I find the article,[39] set in Kauai, offers the unexpected pleasure of reading about a familiar place. The article doesn't pussyfoot around:

> The West side of this tiny island is home to the U.S. military's Pacific Missile Range and testing grounds, part of the longstanding military occupation of the Hawaiian islands, and to the headquarters of giant agrochemical corporations Syngenta and Dupont. These corporations test and produce genetically modified crops on former sugar plantation lands here and throughout Hawaii, along with toxic herbicides, insecticides, and fertilizers. It is the very worst of America's "agrochemical military industrial complex," imposed on the ancient homelands of a rich traditional farming and fishing culture, in the midst of some of the world's most precious biodiversity.

As the article continues what upsets me most is reading how the plantation owners used the U.S. military to force the monarchy of Hawaii out of power. And "the imposition of plantation agriculture on Hawaii's traditional system and the conversion of the Hawaiian people to a Western lifestyle." I am shocked and growing angry. As I document what I've been learning, this wealth of information is hard to take. *What do we think we're doing*, runs like a mantra through my mind.

The food being imported into Hawaii is produced, processed, packaged, and transported using enormous amounts of fossil fuels. By one measure, the current U.S. food system uses 10 times more energy than it produces in the form of food calories.... When oil production peaks, and prices rise again, as they inevitably must, food in Hawaii will become unaffordable. What will happen when the gas pumps and grocery store shelves are empty? .... American commodity agriculture has become a bloated industrial machine dependent on chemical inputs and government subsidies to survive. Commodity farming is not about food for people. It's an extractive industry, often compared to mining. It mines the soil and pollutes the water and creates mountains and rivers of waste. Soil regenerates on a slow natural timescale, about one inch of topsoil in every 500 years.... There are no brakes on this runaway technology train. The continual expansion of corporate power poses even greater looming dangers.... biotechnology cannot feed the world.[40]

Stunned with more shocking facts, I start reading everything I can find relating to farming, seeds, and GMOs, using all my training to synthesize as I go.

Here's how traditional farming works. Each year the farmer (he or she) plants seeds saved from last year. Of course he saves the best to plant, or he buys the best new seed he can afford. Seeds are a critical phase for the farmer. These seeds will determine the new crop that is grown; they watch seeds very carefully. Farmers have saved and traded seeds for millennia, developing crops uniquely suited to their individual circumstances of soil, weather, and water.

Modern agricultural colleges and the government developed programs intended to help farmers make better use of their land, and grow larger crops to feed more people. Individual farmers mostly prospered, made a living for their families, and passed on the land to a next generation of farmers. Farmers prized their independence and ability to *make do* and to endure the bad years. They knew theirs was a valuable service; they fed people, kept them alive. Farmers were basic to human life, even if they weren't always appreciated as they should be. For many, farming wasn't a business; it was an unarticulated spiritual discipline.

Farming and farming practices in the U.S. rocked along. With help from land grant colleges American farmers fed our people and a lot of the world. American food prices went down. Fewer people were required to be farmers and farmers shared in a general rise in prosperity. Clouds on the horizon included farms getting bigger and farms being bought up and consolidated into ever larger farms with an ever-increasing trend toward mono-crops—acres and acres of corn, soy beans, pineapple or sugar cane. These farms required more capital and more and bigger machines, and soon some farms were immense businesses making tons of money for somebody. That somebody was increasingly a corporation—out for bottomline profits. Greedy for profits and figuring new ways to get them, became routine for many corporations, like manipulating farm subsidies to their own advantage. Farm subsidies were meant to give aid to family farms, not help corporations make more profits, grow even larger and be even more competition for family farmers.

Individual farmers found it harder and harder to compete. Farmers are a hardy lot and some, seeing the handwriting on the fields, chose to become specialist farmers: concentrating on growing flowers, growing organically, or becoming truck farmers. Too many farmers were caught in the middle of greedy banks, unfair competition and simply perished; their farms of many generations were foreclosed. Untold misery, bitterness, broken families and hearts, and loss of land and livelihood soon followed.

Still, some independent farmers trudged on, clever, lucky, working harder and smarter and doing what they had to do to keep farming: to keep feeding their neighbors in town, the U.S. and the world. They continued to save seeds and bought better varieties.

Then along came something brand new under the sun: Seeds that would grow corn whose corn plants could be dusted with an insecticide that would kill the corn beetle, and even pesky weeds, while allowing the farmers' corn plants to live!

How could a farmer not be entranced? Plant these newly-developed seeds and come weeding time, just run through your crops spraying Roundup, at significant savings in labor and time. Presto, no more weeds! You, the farmer, make more money for less work. Hallelujah! Of course you'll sign those papers that let you buy and plant the new seeds. Problem solved. Everybody happy.

But wait a minute. Let's look at these corn seeds in more detail. Let's fully understand what it means to plant and grow these new seeds. A seed is a seed is a seed. Everybody knows: You plant a seed and you grow a plant. What's different about these seeds?

Plenty! Enough to change life as we know it on this planet. Perhaps end all human life in gruesome ways.

The new seeds were first made in a laboratory; they are genetically modified organisms, a life form brand new in the world. In 1980, the U.S. patent office, in its wisdom, granted the first patents on a life form,[41] a genetically engineered bacterium able to digest oil spills. (As I later learn this bacterium was never used, as it not only digested oil spills but also swallowed everything in sight.)[42]

Having read more than I can absorb, I am tired from my efforts to put facts together. I turn off my computer and bed lamp only to lie awake in the dark. What have I gotten into? I am torn. My sensibilities tell me I must resign from Purity. My reality cries that I can't afford this emotionally, or financially. I'll have to stay where I am—work covertly from the inside to change things.

The sea is calm. Sound magnifies. Distant, fifty feet or so, surf rumbles against the coral reef, flaring up periodically into breaking foam. Close to my feet where I lounge in my beach chair, baby waves move in counterpoint against the sand. This particular sand a dirty yellow with underlying rocks piercing through. I've brought my lunch to the beach. I need to think about last night and all the new information I'm learning.

As I raise my head, straight ahead is the forbidden island of Niihau. Low lying against the blue sea, the island blends in a mist with the blue of the sky. If you didn't know it was there, would you see the island? Last week, David, a visiting fellow scientist from the mainland, was annoyed when I pointed out Niihau. David asked why he hadn't seen it before. Laughing with him, I began to understand so-called primitives who didn't *see* big boats until after Westerner's ships became more commonplace. Their inexperienced eyes had never beheld these shapes on the sea.

We look but we don't see. David didn't *see* because he didn't expect to see. I can't help wondering what other things we don't *see*? And I remember my first moonlit view of the Great Pyramids of Giza, how I felt new shapes being imprinted on my eyes, creating a new order of seeing.

To my right, where the crescent rocky land meets the ocean, I see a sailing mast from a vessel put into near-shore on this picture-perfect day for snorkelers. Rising from dark rocks further right is the vibrant green of left-over sugar cane, a deeper green against paler patches of uncultivated fields of grass. Then around the crescent of Salt Pond beach, tall coconut palms protect low red-roofed picnic and bathroom buildings. Behind them rise brilliant green fields of more young sugar cane and an orange life-guard tower. A few people are scattered along the sand with parked cars behind.

Overhead are intermittent and noisy low-flying single-engine, single-person aircraft that look like toys and probably are. Perhaps, some brave day, I'll fly in one.

To my left are higher old coral rocks. In front on the beach is a family with three dogs. The smallest dog, white with one black ear standing straight up, digs a branch out of the sand. Then, he puts the limb down and wallows on his back in the sand. I can feel the dog grinning in freedom and pleasure.

Far to the left white surf sprinkles the sea. Beauty, peace. Who could harm such innocent beauty? Who are those who put money ahead of people's lives and health? I don't want to know them.

Princess Ruth came to me last night in a dream I can't recall in the cold light of day. I remember only that she was encouraging. *Stay pono,* she warns me. I want to say I am being truthful and honest, but with my feelings so adulterated by unpleasant facts I'm learning, it's hard to stay real and present.

I am coming to understand that I *get* Kauai in levels, like something I'm growing into. Right now I understand on a current-vision level: this beauty before me is what I grow to love as home—beyond skin, into heart. Some people don't ever get beyond the surface: most tourists probably, and developers who look at gorgeous beaches like the long curving stretch of Kekaha and see condos and shopping malls instead of rippling sand and sea that is free for everyone.

I found a novel[43] that explains how those developers built over so much Kauai land—with the help of local politicians. This book also contrasts a New Age guru with a get-ahead schemer and tells great stories, like this one about Sleeping Giant, a landmark hill on the island's Eastside.

Budama swept an arm toward the ridge of the Sleeping Giant, now lying coolly in the shade because of a passing cloud.

"Ah, the giant sleeps, but be not deceived. Though he lies fixed in stone, his sleep is not eternal. According to the legends of the Menehunes, those little people who labored through the nights of long ago, the giant wakes slowly beginning with the quarter-moon, when his penis hardens and slowly rises. At the half-moon, his proud member springs fully erect, and many times in the half-moons of autumn, I'm told, one can see the giant's mighty phallus trembling beneath the stars, reaching for the great black womb of the Hawaiian night sky".... The obese woman tourist in a pink polyester pants suit coughed nervously. Her husband, who wore khaki shorts and limp black socks, sheathed his camera. After a swift exchange of privately coded glances, they turned and began picking their way carefully down the path like two swollen bugs on pipe-cleaner legs.[44]

I puzzle over my feelings. How can I become more connected with Kauai, as Princess Ruth suggests? How do I get past feelings, put names and then go deeper? Inside myself I unfold in response to this excess of splendid creation, this paradise where peace, joy and beauty gain a spirit, a presence. Is this mana? Am I sensing the energy, life spirit, and just don't have words for it?

Clues come from glimpses of my backdoor neighbor over the fence. The yard was an unplanned mess when this fiftyish, grayish woman moved in with her dog, Sherry. I've been in Hawaii long enough to know that she's probably not Hawaiian because she's living alone. When I mention all the yard work she's doing, she tells me, "I feel I have to pay back, to care for the land. If we each took care of our own, think what a difference. We can all do something toward feeding ourselves. Make this island more sustainable, then we don't have to import so much."

I come away from our conversation thinking that here's someone who is walking her talk. I vow, once again, to visit more Farmers Markets and to spend more time on my own garden beyond watering the rosemary and basil, two herbs I use in my scant cooking. I've noticed how different cooking is when you're the woman in the family, and when you live alone not paying much attention to what you eat.

Kaimana wanders into my thoughts. He's asked me on a real date. I haven't been on a date in forever—what to wear? This is exciting. More music. More meeting his friends. Kaimana said it was a casual meet and sing and play and hang out on the beach. Something new for me—hang out time. A most romantic island in the world and I've been alone. Still I've needed this solitude. I've required this time to get back to myself and over my husband's accident, if anyone ever entirely gets over the death of someone they love. The loved one is so much a part of you, memories come floating when you least expect. And Kevin being my boss makes me jumpy. Yet as this island is different so is Kaimana and my life now. Pushing away thoughts of Kaimana, I get back to current research.[45]

The day is beautiful in its grayness. Directly in front of me, silver-grey drops of rain hang from baby avocado limbs. High-growing new leaves are pale crimson, while below them green mature leaves flutter in a light breeze.

My old interest in growing herbs stirs to renewed life. A garden raising healthy food is suddenly a next project. I want to do my part toward caring for the land. I think of getting my hands in dirt, and remember how proud I am to open my morning door to find a new overnight orchid. It is a single-blossom dream orchid: huge and white with a deep purple center. All I've done is to be in the right place to appreciate the orchid, but I feel like I created it myself.

Or perhaps I'll volunteer at the National Tropical Botanical Garden in Kalaheo, help to support their mission of saving endangered plant species. I remember a guide explaining that Hawaii has 170 species of plants that have fewer than 50 wild individuals remaining in their natural habitat. Hawaii has the dubious honor of being the extinction and endangered plant capital of the world.

As the guide pointed at the low branching tree by the old nursery, laden with hundreds of white blossoms, he said, "This is a male tree. It takes two to tango. This tree is the last known one of its kind. Our scientists tried everything to propagate this plant," he added ruefully. "And nothing worked. Our plant people searched for a female tree in the wild but so far, nothing. If we don't find a female tree, that's the end. Another plant gone to extinction."

It's one thing to read of plants and animals on endangered lists. But quite another to stand before a beautiful blooming plant and learn it's the very last one of its kind. A male blooming profusely for a, so-far, nonexistent female. So lonely and sad. And somehow I find myself thinking of Kaimana. What would he say about this plant? How would he feel?

It's after singing and hang-out time with friends on the beach. Kaimana and I are alone and pleasantly tired. *I'm so lucky* runs like an anthem in my thoughts. The yellow half-moon beams in a dimming blue sky that's turning pale rose. The hushed low-tide sea swells in quiet waterfalls over coral reefs at deserted Baby Beach on the far side of Salt Pond. We sit in the sand on a brown towel Kaimana spread for us. The magic of two souls in tune enfolds us.

There's tenderness, a closeness, surrender of a kind. A sweet trusting of spirit that snuggles nearer—Kaimana ventures an arm around my shoulders. *Here I am.* I've been so lonely and this is respite; I can worry later whether it's real or not. Beyond words I sense him yearning to be closer as he implicitly trusts me, knowing that I too have surrendered to the magic of our immediate time, to destiny, to fate, when *now* is all there is and time disappears. I'm not fighting any more and he knows it.

Kaimana's head in my lap is the next thing I realize. My heart swells as I lean over to kiss his dark curly hair. A full heart: now I know what that means. Love swirls and rises above everything except love. I'm surely being an idiot again, but Kaimana goes right past my defenses as if they never existed. Puzzled but rather contentedly, I think, *it's all true about love.*

Scales drop from my eyes reading about King Kaumualii (King K),[46] the last King of Kauai. (The earlier *Last King of Paradise* was King of all Hawaii and lived about a hundred years later.)[47][48]

I've felt a disconnect between how common Hawaiians were reputed to relate to the land back then and how this relationship might play out in their real lives. The land, a place, a home is so crucial to us all. What really happened back then? How did Hawaiian ownership of land evolve? Especially for the common people? Here's a recollection and easy explanation by a Hawaiian friend in a remote valley near Honolulu written in the early 1940s:

> His father had told him that when the foreigners first came to Hawaii all the land of the Islands was owned by the King, but each Hawaiian family was assigned a homestead called a *kuleana*, which meant a piece of land in the mountains for growing kalo (taro) and fishing rights at the seashore. Thus each family was assured of a place to live and food to eat.
>
> But under the pressure of the foreigners, King Kamehameha III had relinquished his control of the land and divided it among the people. Many loyal friends of the Hawaiians foresaw the inevitable

tragic consequences of such a plan, but their protests were over-ruled. The King believed sincerely that he was doing a great and noble thing for his beloved people. And so the lands were divided.

A third of the land was assigned to the Chiefs, a third to the commoners, and a third retained by the Crown. The Chiefs got their allotments, the Crown lands were retained, but few of the commoners secured theirs. For in order to get his *kuleana* each person had to make application for it to the government, a procedure far too complicated for most of them to understand. In addition, they knew nothing about private ownership of land. The land was there; it would always be there; it had always been theirs to live upon; there would always be some place to live.

And so, for a few years, the commoners continued to live upon the land wherever they found it, until they were suddenly and cruelly faced with the fact that land was no longer free—no longer theirs for the asking. They learned that they had no place to call their own.[49]

I'm having problems with the huge amount of research and reading I'm doing on Kauai and Hawaiian history and culture and GMOs. With so much material, I cannot keep track of it. Most frustrating is when I remember facts, but can't locate corroborating evidence. I could give up but decide I'll go ahead with remembered facts, while keeping my eyes open for the exact evidence. For example, I have a pamphlet of women's stories (which I will eventually find of course). A woman eye-witness tells of living in a Hawaiian community that became *Ala Moana* shopping center in Honolulu.

One ordinary day, all the people were warned a tsunami was coming. They must leave immediately. Everybody cleared out, taking what they could and their animals and livestock. The tsunami never arrived and the Hawaiians eventually returned to their houses. Only to discover there was nothing to return to. Bulldozers had destroyed their homes and property. The people were told to go elsewhere and nothing was ever done to right the injustice. I sort of remember that a wealthy Dillingham, not a good name in some parts of Hawaii, was involved.

This is fun. I hope. I've invited Kaimana for dinner! This is a big deal for me. So far, only Barbara has been inside my new home, and cooking in this inadequate kitchen is a challenge. I don't even know if the oven works as I haven't prepared a real full meal in forever. I'm raising the ante by deciding to use island-grown ingredients. And I'm not really examining my motives for inviting Kaimana. I just sort of skate over that part; this dinner feels like a next step in our relationship, and I take it.

First I'll buy salad ingredients from the Farmers Market.[50] Then choose my meat from the butcher in Kalaheo who sells local-grown beef.

I'll pick up some arugula, lovely baby tomatoes with taste, and a ripe avocado. I'll throw on excellent goat cheese from the local goat dairy and extra-virgin olive oil with a dash of balsamic vinegar, and there's our salad.

Living on Kauai is fascinating, like living in a small town which I am, come to think of it, a small town with only about sixty-five thousand inhabitants.[51]

Later, driving up the hill on Papalina Street, on the right, is Medeiros Farms. After asking her advice I talk story with Natalie, and learn that her father, coming over from Portugal, started Medeiros Farms. Now she and her sister Carol and daughter Carla run the place. Carla is pretty; they're all attractive with dark hair and flashing eyes. When the brother who was the butcher fell ill, the women took over his work and they seem to thrive. They're always so helpful; thanks to Carla now I know which cuts to use for soup, a staple that lasts for days when I don't want to cook or eat out.

Today, it's a fresh-cut pot roast I buy. I don't know why pot roast. Pot roast is what I want and used to know how to cook. Gathering this meal feels familiar but also exciting. Now I'll need fresh carrots, onions and those local, dense purple potatoes. Fresh fruit for desert, maybe cheese, as I don't want to push my culinary luck.

"You're wonderful," Kaimana is relaxed sopping a last morsel of beef and gravy before sipping the wine he brought. "This is so special." As we look around my garden with its candles, floor-length patterned tablecloth and ginger flowers, low light so the moon shines overhead, it's hard to recognize the place. I'm contented, satisfied, complete, basking in the glow of being with Kaimana. Plus, I planned something and it turned out perfectly.

Life condenses to simplicity. Kaimana and I drink our wine, decide to forget any dessert as we enjoy the night and talk and talk of books and places and ourselves while the candles flicker in the light breeze. At last, wordlessly in unison, as if we've done this a thousand times, Kaimana carries dishes to the sink as I put leftovers away.

We turn together and our mouths and arms reach for each other as we've been yearning to do. But have held ourselves in a space of waiting, of anticipation. Like eating dinner, like this entire evening we take our time. After kissing and savoring faces and lips and bodies a long while, we hold hands as we walk into my bedroom. We lie down on my bed on the floor and I forget how to think, only feel.

These winds on Kauai are incredible. I've stepped out in hurricane winds in Florida less than these. My plan this morning is to take a long slow walk, wake up, and think (well dream) of Kaimana and last night. It was late when he left and we didn't get a lot of sleep.

Today, there is hard wind in a clear sky. It's unsettling. I find no walkers but me as I lean into the wind. Then, on deserted Puu Road, the wind stops. The silence is almost loud. Next, I hear a low sound and think, *perhaps it's a car or truck.* The sound comes again, low, behind me with a menacing quality.

I know there is nothing there, but feel impelled to turn anyway. The roadway is empty. Rustling wind sweeps through the green and red pepper trees bordering the road. Sound with no cause. Nightmarchers came to mind.

I almost run to the shelter of my pick-up truck. I drive faster than usual to work.

I'm working on my home computer and it's late at night. Can't sleep. Greenpeace seems a good place to dig for life-giving, community-oriented facts about GMOs. Interesting that when it's something you don't want to know, it's very hard to learn it! I guess I must admit difficulty and keep going as best I can. Repetition always helps with learning. Princess Ruth is a prod and a model as she kept going when life handed her pain and more pain.

What's wrong with genetic engineering? asks Greenpeace as they tell me some things I already know:

The products of genetic engineering are living organisms that could never have evolved naturally and do not have a natural habitat.

These genetically modified organisms (GMOs) can spread and interbreed with natural organisms, thereby contaminating non 'GMO' environments and future generations in an unforeseeable and uncontrollable way. This 'genetic pollution' is a major threat because GMOs cannot be recalled once released into the environment.

Because of commercial interests, the public is being denied the right to know about GMO ingredients, thereby losing the right to avoid them despite labeling laws in certain countries....[52]

Farmers in North America and Latin America, where most of the world's GMO agriculture is, must sign a contract that specifies that if they save the seeds to plant again the following year or use any herbicide other than the corporation's own, they are likely to be prosecuted. *I've read this before. Wonder if it's true?*

We oppose all patents on plants, animals and humans, as well as patents on their genes. Life is not an industrial commodity.[53]

Catching sight of a by-now familiar name, I hold my nose at all this negativity and continue reading. Yet all the time I'm wondering, where have I been while all this life-transforming change is going on? Am I the only one who doesn't know this stuff? "Genetically modified organisms (GMOs) entered our food supply in 1996. During the next nine years the number of Americans battling three or more chronic diseases nearly doubled—from 7% to 13%. Are GMO ingredients, now in about 70% of our foods, contributing to this dramatic increase? Have they promoted obesity, diabetes, asthma, allergies, or the doubling of food-related illnesses from 1994 to 2001?" asks Jeffrey Smith.[54]

Jeffrey Smith goes on to tell us that in supermarkets here's what you should look for:
   * A four-digit number means that produce is conventionally grown
   * A five-digit number beginning with 9 means it's organic
   * A five-digit number beginning with 8 means it's GMO

I need to study more about Princess Ruth and stopping the volcano. As far as I can see her incredible feat didn't receive proper attention. I'll go back to Burns:

> From a fiery eruption of Mauna Loa, billions of tons of white-hot lava slithered down the snow-capped mountain's massive shoulders and advanced in a broad river of fire upon Hilo, Hawaii's second largest city. Like a giant dragon, the lava flow consumed lehua forests, damned up streams, and coiled across valleys. Roaring filled the air and the ground shook. At night, hundred-foot fountains played fiery jets, making the heavens glow.[55]

The town of Hilo on the Big Island is in severe danger. And there's also a face-off in Hilo: It's the old Gods (Pele) against the missionary God in 1881. Unlike Princess Ruth, Princess Regent Liliuokalani[56] comes down on the missionary side exhorting Hawaiian people to pray and to *get right with the Christian God*. By confessing their sins, she proclaims, they'll be forgiven and the missionary God will stop the lava flow and save Hilo.

But the Christian prayers don't work even when entire church congregations give prayer a good try. The lava keeps moving on Hilo. So Queen Liliuokalani follows scientific advice (was it missionary?) to use dynamite to divert the lava stream.

Dynamite blasts fail. Nothing works. The lava keeps flowing. Straight to Hilo.

> Days passed and with each twenty-four hours, the thirty-foot lava wall rumbled forward forty or more feet. Yet [Princess] Ruth refused to budge from her Hilo home…. When the withering hot blasts, blowing over the twenty-five mile lava furnace, carried the acrid smell and heat into her darkened room, she did nothing, sitting silently, hour after hour.[57]

As clearly as if Princess Ruth appears before me and tells me herself, I know the Princess, silent in her dark room, is communing and praying to her Goddess Pele, gathering mana —incalculable to us today—spiritual and personal power. One lone woman is to stop a volcano. This powerful almost-beyond-belief woman is gathering raw forces of the universe to her entreaty, her command, her duty, for she herself—the living embodiment of all her chiefly Hawaiian ancestors—Princess Ruth is the intersection, the interceder between her beloved people and the Gods.[58]

Princess Ruth remains in her dark room, praying, meditating, collecting mana, spiritual power. She's following, unknown to us now, rules for how to do this: change huge chunks of physical reality, that is, stop a volcano. This knowledge she surely took to her grave, leaving us all diminished. How did she stop the volcano—for stop it she did. After praying and offerings to Goddess Pele, Princess Ruth sleeps all night, alone in her bed she had brought to the fiery edge of the lava.

In the morning the volcano is quiet, the lava flow has stopped.

Destiny and a task worthy of that destiny. Sacrilege or not, the only similar thing that comes to mind is Jesus and his forty days of wandering in the wilderness. Or Buddha under that sacred tree in India. Jesus raised the dead (two thousand years ago) but we've got a woman, in almost our time, who halts a volcano.

As an aside, you'll remember Jesus saying to his disciples about his powers that anyone of us could do them; what if Princess Ruth simply had another way of tapping into the source of what we proclaim as *miracles?*

When I return to surfing the internet—another sleepless night—various bits about GMO sugar beets, Monsanto, Roundup and the glyphosate molecule cry for my attention.[59]

Today's paper has more sugar beet news: sugar beet farmers are having tantrums because they can't keep planting GMO sugar beet seeds, the judge saying the USDA had plenty of time to scientifically test the new sugar beet seeds and didn't do the proper testing. The judge's ruling is to put a hold on the new sugar beet planting until a proper environmental impact study is done. Now it's coming out that "the USDA hasn't properly overseen genetically modified crops."

But I also read that the U.S. Supreme Court is lifting "a ban on the planting of genetically modified alfalfa seeds?"[60] What is going on? Give with one hand, take with the other?

"Once it's deregulated and out there, it's not easy to do a challenge," Neil Carman, clean air director of the Sierra Club, says. "The problem is that with some of those crops, the horse got out of the barn before we were ready to file legal cases."

I suppose that says it for now. Wait and see. Still I have to laugh when the head of an association that uses GMO beet seeds says that unless the GMO seeds are approved they won't be able to produce enough sugar. *Well,* I want to say, *that's great! People are eating way too much sugar anyway!* A view not likely to win me friends in pro-GMO camps. Or, here at work. I'm getting sad feelings that I'm researching myself out of a job.

After logging off my computer, I sit quietly. I have a problem.

It is told that Buddha, going out to look on life, was greatly daunted by death. "They all eat one another!" he cried, and called it evil. This process I examined, changed the verb, said, "They all feed one another," and called it good.

Charlotte Perkins Gilman[61]

Chapter Six

"Turn left," Barbara, my farmer friend from work, directs. "There just beyond that palm tree."

The dirt and gravel roadway is narrow with overhanging palm trees. I slow almost to a stop before I can see where to turn.

"This is beach access for *The Cottages*," Barbara continues. "All the big developments have to reserve space for the public. We can bless Hawaiian tradition and law for making our beaches free to everyone. Nobody can stop anybody from walking any beach in Hawaii up to the high-water mark. It is all public property. Go over there." Barbara points to an empty parking lot covered with dry grass.

"I was so surprised at all the available beaches in Kauai," I say, noticing how the open surfing sea is shining as if you can own all you can see. "I remember driving forever one time in South Florida. I needed so bad to put my feet in some sand. For miles all I saw were houses and gates and private access signs. No people or beaches at all, just closed off private space. It was frustrating. After a while the deadness was almost scary. I felt so insignificant. Not like here."

A sense of peace blows from the ocean as we come nearer the sea searching for a shady spot under hanging palms. On our right are several large and strange-looking Pandanus trees, *hala* to Hawaiians with their multiple uses.[62] Not a soul is in sight except for a lone man in red trunks standing by the outdoor pool. A couple of palms over, a wide rope hammock, large enough for two, flops empty. I set up my striped beach chair and Barbara unfolds her Navaho blanket.

"This is one of my favorite places. Blake and I come here often." Blake is Barbara's long time, on again, off again, now off, boyfriend. Just as we avoid discussing my dead husband, so we've skirted the topic of Blake. *She must be missing him*, I think. Already seated on her blanket, Barbara takes out of her basket an intriguingly curved bit of dark wood, probably mahogany or koa, and peers closely before scraping delicately with a razor blade. Scraping again, she wipes the wood with her finger.

As I watch Barbara I think, a bit enviously, of how she's blended so seamlessly into Kauai.

"Where did you get that one?" I indicate her piece of wood.

"On the beach of course," she replies. "Just a salt-washed ordinary piece of driftwood. But I liked its shape and its weight was solid. It's turning out nice."

"Truth and lies. How have you sorted it, Barbara—when someone tells you lies?"

"Lies break trust. Paint a false picture of the world. We believe the person who lies to us and we are hurt. And then we feel foolish because we were so easily misled."

"I've been puzzling ancient Hawaiians," I say. "How they had all these rules in place. *Kapu*. Taboo. Forbidden. Men did all the cooking, for example, pounding taro for poi. Except, I've read, on Kauai women also pounded poi. All these rules around food. Men and women didn't eat together. Women's diets were prescribed. Of the 25 or so varieties of bananas, women were allowed to eat only three—that seems so strange to our modern sensibilities. If it were me, I'd sneak a few bananas. I wonder if women did?"

"Food rules were a form of control," Barbara says. "Of showing who was boss."

"Yes," I stumble over my words as I hurry to agree. "Touch the alii or chief, and you die. Even his shadow. Rules. Laws. The men and women had to live in a certain amount of pure fear. Proscribed behavior. Protocol. Expected ways the world is constructed. Which God to worship and which God to ask for what. Your place in society is drummed into you and your punishment known, certain, and sure if you transgress the rules."

"Reminds me of serfdom in Europe or the segregated South," Barbara adds. "People knew their place and kept to it."

"Most disturbing to me is how badly Hawaiian people could be treated. Missionaries stealing land and telling lies—you just don't expect that," I said.

"Part of it was the times," Barbara comments. "Life was cheap. Might made right. Whites were the superior race and all others were inferior: Chinese, Japanese, and any people that could be called *Black*. We forget what segregation was like. My mother told me about seeing Harry Belafonte in a segregated movie house in Alabama. Whites were on the main floor, Blacks (the nice word then was Negroes) sitting upstairs in the balcony. The balcony even had a separate entrance. How weird is that? We've all come so far. We can hardly believe that segregated behavior now." Barbara takes a heavy swipe at her wood.

"Deep inside I still expect life to be fair," I confess. "To hold justice for all. That belief is sort of crazy. And speaking of injustice my mother told me about discrimination she faced as a divorced woman working to support me." I scoot lower in my beach chair. *This is such a beautiful place,* I think. *I'm so lucky to be here.*

"My mother had worked herself into a top level job. Except for me, that job was her life. Even back then she had an expense account taking clients out for dinner, paid parking, and a lot of responsibility. She was in line for promotion to the home office, which she'd earned, when she married my step-father. Partly to give me a proper home I learned later.

"Then my mother found out, after she resigned, that the company promoted a man to replace her. Paid him twice what she earned because, *he had children to support.* I was invisible I suppose and we lived on air."

"That's terrible," Barbara bursts out. "So unfair."

"Anyway my mother always used to laugh when she told the story—her revenge. The replacement guy couldn't do her work. They had to fire him."

"How many lives we all live." Barbara smoothes her wood. "Amazing. It's enough to make you believe in past lives."

"I always laugh thinking about past lives." I add, "How often Queen Nefertiti and Cleopatra come up. Nobody's ever a slave in their past lives." I laugh. "And Mother got more of her own back by being quite successful in her second career. Up until she died we had a lot of fun. I miss her. Sometimes really bad."

Unexpectedly Princess Ruth grows in my thoughts with a new perspective I'm not yet ready to deal with. Then suddenly my invisible censor slaps down: *Don't open that Princess Ruth can of lives and past lives and how our influence passes down the long generations. Some things just are.*

Pale thin winter rain, cool and dark. It's a quiet morning with space to think as I snuggle warm in my bed on the floor. Facts, and purported facts, churn in my mind. History from this point of view, that biased or ignorant way of seeing, and nobody knows what really happened anyway, it was so long ago. Bits and pieces. Garbage and gold. The more I study and read, the less I know. I'd walk away fast, but on an island, where will I go? And with a life I'm determined to live with meaning, there is no place to hide.

Stay, I remind myself, in the place of struggle. That uncarved block of the ancient Chinese Taoist is a pure potential of creation, of past, present, and future.

Still when I try to understand Hawaii, to get at the real meat and bones, I'm stopped cold every time. Immeasurable wrongs were perpetuated against an innocent people. And those wrongs were repeated and reinforced again and again. How does the mind hold such horrors, and how can we get beyond them?

The only thing that works for me is to lay out facts, and the *knowings*, as I call unassailable information that arrives full blown from I know not where.

My solution is simple: I'll borrow a clear outline from an interesting self-published novel by a University of Hawaii teacher and add facts from my own study. (See Backpiece on page 331)

Princess Ruth senses how restless and impatient I am, so she helps me. *Go to Hanapepe library.* The Princess' voice in my head is relentless, *Get to the library.*

To gain some peace, I finally rationalize, *I'll have lunch at Salt Pond. Then I'll visit the library before going home.*

Past the bright blue bicycle racks, the waist-high bins of free books and magazines and the friendly librarians, I go straight to the Hawaiian video section. I put out my right hand and pull out *Then There Were None.*[63] I take it straight home and play it.

Impossible to express the impact of this video, which speaks from the viewpoint of the conquered. Tears cram my eyes. I feel Princess Ruth's satisfaction. *Now you know*, she whispers, her words melting barriers.

Population figures say it all.

1778 - Over 500,000 Hawaiians

1893 - 40,000 pure Hawaiians

1993 - 8,711 pure Hawaiians

2044 - Demographers predict there will be not one pure Hawaiian.

The video box text summarizes some of what I find so distressing:

A compelling story of a race displaced and now on the verge of extinction is brilliantly told in this award-winning documentary created by the great-granddaughter of Hawaiian high chiefs and English seafarers, Elizabeth Kapuuwailane Lindsey.

To millions of travelers the world over, Hawaii is an alluring picture postcard paradise. But to its indigenous people, the Native Hawaiians, nothing could be further from the truth.[64]

This morning is totally gorgeous with bright sunshine, chirping birds, and the repeated but pleasing calls of mourning doves. I've taken my coffee outside for quiet time before my trip into work. On the surface things go right for me: a raise, even a monstrous worry off my shoulders as Timothy Brown, my long-time lawyer in California, assures me he's consolidated my remaining debts into a package I can handle. I'll even be free of debt much sooner than I'd hoped. I just have to keep this job. I can do that, can't I? A job is a job. Work is work. They call it work for a good reason: it's *work*. You trade your life energy for wages. Someone hires you, and you do what they tell you. Or what you somehow intuit they want you to do. You're loyal. And you do your work well if you expect to get ahead.

You take company money, you owe them. I guess my question becomes: How much do I owe? Where does loyalty stop? Or maybe even how much sand can I bury my head in before I suffocate?

I'm cringing inside realizing again how my husband Thomas was a shelter. How even my ignorance was a shelter from fully realizing I'm dependant now on a job, on wages Purity Corporation pays me.

If worse comes to worst, surely with my qualifications I could get another job. But in this job market ... how long would it take? And would the people I owe wait while I get a new act together? I don't think so. And the hassle. Another move. Another uprooting myself yet again. Leaving beautiful Kauai. I'm just making friends here and there's Kaimana. I want to see where this relationship evolves. Beside where would I go? I love it here. I shudder in mind and body at the prospect of a move.

In the meantime, back on the missionary front in my Hawaiian research, the first U.S. missionaries land in 1820 to be greeted by the news that King Kamehameha One is recently dead. A first act of the missionaries, under the leadership of Hiram Bingham, is to gather on the deck of the brig *Thaddeus* and thank the Lord that Kamehameha is dead—surely a terrible thank you for a religious person. Now their job of converting the savages (this is what they thought of the Hawaiians) would be a lot easier. A popular local saying is: *The missionaries came to do good and ended by doing well.* Then the locals (locals here, meaning those in the know) laugh as they mean, of course, that the missionaries did very well indeed. For themselves.

On his deathbed, King Kamehameha One appointed his son Liholiho, age 22, to be his heir; Liholiho will be popularly called King Kamehameha Two. And the king also named his favorite Queen Kaahumanu (Queen K) to be the new King's spiritual leader and advisor. Without biological children of her own, Queen K is supposed to be the young King's advisor and helper. In reality Queen K is the de facto ruler of Hawaii.

There's a revealing bit in Wikipedia: "When Liholiho sailed toward the shores of Kailua Kona [on the Big Island and the capital at the time], she [Queen K] greeted him wearing Kamehameha's royal red cape, and she announced to the people on shore and to the surprised Liholiho, 'We two shall rule the land.'"

Liholiho, young and inexperienced, had no other choice. Queen K became the first Kuhina Nui (co-regent) of Hawaii. Liholiho was forced to take on merely a ceremonial role; administrative power was to be vested in Kaahumanu (Queen K). He took the title "King Kamehameha Two", but preferred to be called *Iolani*, which means "heavenly (or royal) hawk".

Remember also that until the Princess was six or seven, Queen K was Princess Ruth's beloved guardian. I see the child Princess Ruth like a sponge absorbing wiles, shrewdness and wisdom: traits that would later stand her in good stead.

This decision by Kamehameha One to appoint Queen K as spiritual advisor, (or her seizure of power) also let ownership of the land (remember the land) stay exactly where it is—owned by the new Kamehameha Two. But in reality the land and power remained under the control of Queen K, who knew exactly what was going on. Avarice and love of power are not confined to Westerners. She liked being the most powerful person around.

But Kamehameha Two died. Remember when there's a new chief all the land is redistributed—everything to the new King: Land, power, women. Queen K enjoyed the power and control she had cleverly increased, and had no intention of stepping aside. She continued on her merry way by influencing the appointing of King Kamehameha Third—grandson of Kamehameha One. And guess what, the new King is eleven years old, no problem here, and so Queen K keeps power. She's the de facto ruler of

Hawaii, owning or controlling thousands of acres of Kamehameha land distributed throughout the islands. (Kamehameha land, we know now, that comes down to Princess Ruth.)

Kevin has captured me for lunch at Kalaheo Steak House. I want to excuse myself but there is no mistaking his 'I'm the boss' look. The more Kevin chases, the faster I want to run.

Determined to be annoying—and to take my mind off the brown devastated soil of former sugar cane fields, now open-field GMO-planted crops from Hanapepe to Waimea—I recite for Kevin a memorized roster of Hawaiian birds, resident and migratory: "Honeycreepers, aki (Hawaii's woodpecker), great frigate birds, boobies, terns, shearwaters, albatross, osprey, quail, mockingbird, common pigeons, Pacific golden-plover (they are here for the winter, I tell Kevin), myna, zebra and spotted dove, bulbul, Japanese white-eye, yellow-fronted canary, java sparrow, finches, cardinals, cattle egret, jungle fowl or chickens, wild turkey, partridges, peafowl, owls, hawk, ricebird, waxbills, pheasant, crow.

"And I can't remember the name," I say finally, "of a wonderful bird with a long tail and a beautiful song. That bird and the honeycreepers are my favorites."

Kevin ignores me but his indifference only prods me on.[65] When I pause to allow him to speak and he doesn't, I continue, "Once there was even a mamo bird they used to get feathers from. Two feathers from each little bird. It makes me cry; the Hawaiians were careful to capture and release each little bird so there'd be more birds. The Hawaiians are natural sustainers with one foot in the future. Living on a small isolated island did that, I suppose. The mamo is extinct now," I inform Kevin. "Many of the native birds had disappeared by mid-1980s. Guess what happened to them?"

Kevin keeps on driving and ignoring me.

"You don't even care." Looking at the destruction around me I try harder. "Listen, one-third of the nation's endangered birds are in Hawaii.[66] Right now we've got thirty-one endangered, more than anywhere else in the country. We're a disaster and all you have to do is look out there and you see why."

"Don't you get it?" Kevin almost snarls. "We're an international, world-wide company. We do what we have to do."

A couple of days later, I run across a Hawaiian historical novel *Amelia*[67] by a missionary granddaughter.

Amelia reminds me of *Gone With the Wind* before the Civil war. All that idyllic outdoor healthy life, and the kind, cheerful, loving natives, who live in grass huts, love their masters and are delighted to do all the work of being servants to the masters and keeping up the place. The missionary granddaughter, I surmise, tells of her grandfather:

> He was not the only Englishman to seek haven in this distant group of islands cradled in the Pacific Ocean. There were already fellow countrymen living with their families on Kauai, the island of his choice.... It was virgin lands. No beast had as yet grazed its grassy acres, no plow turned a furrow there. What few native Hawaiians lived in the vicinity were in thatched villages down by the seashore, their taro patches terracing the lower valleys which mountain streams, through ages of erosion, had cut seaward."[68]

And later, her heroine's mother dies at her birth and she's raised by Hawaiian Hina and her family. "My child was happy in this aboriginal Eden," Elisabeth remembers. At age eight her father sends Elisabeth to Hanalei to be civilized living with an English family.

Where does it come from? This knowledge that something is way out of kilter when we find an uneducated servant class and then those with money and power who live off their labor? Do the invaders, the occupiers, the users, the ones who gain from other people's labor ever have any idea about what they are doing? Is innocence a justified excuse? Do any of the oppressors ever care? Ever, in fact, even know they're being oppressors? I'm reminded of early Kamehameha schools educating young Hawaiians to keep their subservient places! And not even letting them speak their native language.

Sometimes I'm too smart for my own good; I wish I didn't see, intuit or make up stories I write in my head to explain what I think I'm seeing. Here's where my imagination can work overtime as I consider *Reminiscences of a Life in the Islands*.[69] It's a lovely book of colonial privilege and of an energetic, exemplary life. Beautiful photographs of lovely healthy happy people. All the right ingredients even to spear-heading our Humane Society Shelter on Kauai. Homes for the dogs and cats, not that I have anything against animals.

For me, these privileged lives contrast sharply with a fact that keeps beating me over the head.[70] The fact: *fourteen young people in Anahola committed suicide in the last couple of years.*

"Why?" I ask.

"Hopelessness. They could see no future for themselves."

Young Hawaiians, not yet out of high school, and no future on this beautiful island! No place for them in their homeland?

I'm sure I'm being unkind about these 'looks back at idyllic Hawaii' memoirs. We all get to chose our causes, our lives and to what degree we wish to become conscious and involved with the people around us. (Well some of us do.) And some are luckier than others. A lesson I take away about privilege is to carefully examine how I'm living, and spending, mine.

The further back I go in Hawaiian history, the more wrongs creep from the platitudes and pretty coverings put over early, nasty and unfair treatment of Native Hawaiians. I learn about Kamehameha Schools, Charles Bishop and the Bishop Estate.[71]

A standout fact for me is that five-sixths of the Bishop land-wealth came from Princess Ruth.

Books, newspapers, public information all seem to delight in, even emphasize how large and ugly Princess Ruth was. Every account I've seen is quick to add that she was the richest woman in Hawaii. Some note that Princess Ruth was a good businesswoman and others that she had a good and kind heart.

Last of the old-time Kamehameha rulers, except for Cousin Bernice, the Princess left everything to Bernice Bishop (Mrs. Charles) who lived about six months longer. It's fascinating how I gain these ideas of Hawaiian history. Then I go to more original or truer reports and my opinion reverses 180 degrees.

Beauty and grace and presence (mana) of older Hawaiian women is attractive. Many women are so-called *large* size. They dance with flowing bodies and happy smiling faces as they perform difficult hulas while making it look easy. The first time I saw a halau of older women perform in Hana, on Maui, I knew I wanted a slice of what these women created for themselves: Joy, friendship, skill, beauty. What they owned couldn't be bought. You had to earn it to possess it. And what size you were mattered not an iota; it was your heart, your mana, your skill and grace. Your knowledge, your spiritual advancement, who you were.

U.S. women now earn 79 cents for a man's equal work. No matter how you slice it, this inequality is weird.[72] I despised patriarchy growing up on our farm in Alabama, long before I had names for the privileged practices of white patriarchy. The patriarchy had the power; they made the rules. Underwater rules. Hidden rules running my world. Almost the air I breathed and certainly the climate of my mind was affected. What aspirations, my worth as a human being, my *proper* place in society were all subtly controlled. Here's the end of a "coming-to-consciousness poem" I once wrote about my oppression by the patriarchy; certainly not a tragedy but mighty hard to live through. Yet I feel those experiences fueling my sympathy for native Hawaiians. You (the oppressed) know something is wrong but you have no names for this wrongness. No validation. And frequently no one else seems to experience what you see and feel.

From my place on the floor
    I'm learning those codes behind their eyes,
    the claw of a cat sheathed in a superiority
    even their own minds don't compute.

But mine does. I learn. I live.
I probe:

Never in my life, until now, have I said
   a calm:
   No, you ask too much.[73]

Here on the farm was born my fierce sense of justice. And now an ever increasing sympathy for the Hawaiians and their ill-treatment by the U.S. government.

This is a thing I learned about oppression: When you finally get it together you can be in better shape than the oppressors; you know them from the inside out. But they don't know you. Nor do they have your advantage of seeing from both sides.

"Finally the Hawaiians are dancing for themselves. Not just for the gods, not just for the alii, not just for the tourists but finally for themselves."[74]

Injustice and Betrayal. I feel like asking where I've been all my life as I watch this other face of myself being peeled into view. Perhaps it is the solitude where the center of my life is myself only. And, too, Princess Ruth is a strong suspect, for my intuition senses her guidance. As I come to know her, the Princess is a wise-grandmother influence, infinitely loving but stern, too, for my own good.

The face, facet, whatever of myself that charges into my current life is critical and judgmental. And with an almost missionary zeal for right and wrong. I'm sizing up betrayal and injustice before I know it. And, sharing my opinion before I know it.

Look behind injustice and you'll find betrayal, pops into my thoughts. Is this true? I know that my new face is actually taking on the hurts and wrongs of others where previously I saw little but my own concerns. (I hate to say this about my partially unaware, spiritually unawakened self but I think it's truth.) Maybe true also that we live in a safe seed-bubble until cracked open to grow by death, traumatizing events, beauty, luck, who knows where the portals are?

So I've concluded that I'll need, occasionally, to allow voice to this editorial viewpoint. How will I know what I really think and feel, if I don't express myself!

I could play a game: name the injustices or wrongs as I see them. Then hunt for an underlying betrayal. I used to love games. But, somehow, as a grown-up woman, I've stopped playing.

My journeys into special Kauai places continues. Excited, I've been looking forward to this one. A hula sister, Susan, now dancing with a halau in California, will show me a heiau—ancient Hawaiian place of worship.

It is early morning before dawn and then pale light. A full moon sets into the water. On an island, sun and full moon always rise from water (if you're at the right shore) and set into the ocean or mountain. It's hard to see to drive. We'll go the back way and then take the narrow road over one-lane bridges down to Hanalei. On the drive we catch a view to the bay with mist rising off the ocean. From here the moon looks pure yellow. We go through deserted Hanalei town and then over one-lane bridges. My truck hits a hard rock and is difficult to control. Heavy seas roil and tight waves come in fast. Then our drive takes us inland through Australian pines.

Past Haena State Park, at the very end of the road at Kee Beach, I pull into the Kalalau side close to the lifeguard station but it's way too early for a guard. The air is cool; I pull my red sweater close. We see the trail heading from the edge of the light-brown beach sand over rocks to our left. **Keep out**, the sign says as we pick our way over tree roots and rocks.

"Let me ask permission." Susan moves ahead eight or ten steps to the water's edge facing forward to the sea. I wait hearing her low chant and watch ocean foam spewing off the tops of waves four feet high.

The moon dims as day comes.

"It's okay." Susan sets a brisk pace forward but then the trail is blocked by a door carrying another warning, **Keep Out**. Susan climbs around the rocks that hold the door directly barring the trail. I scramble over jutting rocks and follow. The air is cool, quiet, expectant.

The path isn't easy, only rocks and more rocks to climb over. I place my flip-flop feet carefully on top of stones, in cracks, on ledges, picking my way. It's high tide. Water splashes nearby. The roar of the ocean is loud and close. Susan has moved ahead as the rock trail gives way to low wet grass. My feet in the flip flops slither around even more as the rocks force my feet into sharp angles. Then the trail becomes grassy, faint but discernable. Rocks and grass alternate as encroaching shrubs and vines twine close.

"This is not right," Susan exclaims. "I missed the turn." She stands very still and chants before she reverses, passing me on the way back. I hurry but can't keep up. My feet slip and I go slower, keenly aware that I don't want to fall, or twist an ankle or my awkward knee. At the back of my mind those **Keep Out** signs loom large.

"Here," my guide says and plunges up a faint trail, mauka, or toward the mountain, and she is soon far ahead. We climb through stones that shift under my feet and bending tree limbs that I crawl under and more wet grass. My feet slip and I find myself bent over my hands, seeking purchase on volcanic rocks that rise and rise. The jungle is deep about us as if trying to hold us prisoner, the sea a roaring background. But when I take a breather to look back, the ocean is glorious. In full light now, the sun hits the tops of breaking white waves with foam spewing behind, clouds with a pink glow, full moon dimmer but still shining.

The power of nature is so strong here that a second wind comes to me easily as I turn back to climb higher. I scramble over and around boulders, pulling myself forward by grabbing roots and dew-wet branches, breathing faster from exertion. Susan is even farther ahead. *How much longer?* I'm determined to make it as my feet slide hard against the thin strips holding thongs on my feet. *If the plastic breaks I'll have to go barefoot.*

Ahead my companion slows and then climbs out of sight. I'm aware that I approach sacred, even forbidden ground. I'm privileged to be here and I know it.

With a spurt of energy I climb to the grassy plateau guarded by huge boulders. This flat open space is carved into the side of a mountain. We face a stone altar with flower offerings laid right and left. Susan goes closer to the altar, chanting; her voice is clear; silence all around, a heavy stillness, except for her chant and the everlasting sea.

Power rises like breath.

I look to the mountain crowned by tall slim trees, to the altar cut so long ago from volcanic rock, to the ocean—all in alignment, beautiful and perfect. Nature endlessly creating itself. I'm flooded by an awareness of being a part of something infinitely greater than humans. Gratitude and appreciation rise in my consciousness like strong sea currents. For a time I don't think or feel, I relax into being.

Bordering this open grassy plateau are massive stones, and I sit timidly on one as Susan finishes her chant and then joins me.

"That was a special chant? I ask softly.

O Laka, me ka 'ano'ai aloha e, e ola e! O Laka, we greet you with love, live on! Susan translates for me and then adds, "Laka was the goddess of the dance, but also Laka meant abundant growth and hulas were done in her honor at planting times." Then aware of how impressed I am, she continues, "Here's another very old prayer to Laka." She recites softly in English.

A cluster of herbs, O Laka,
An offering of growing things is here.
Calling upon you, O Laka, we stand here.
The prayer to Laka has power,
The maile of Laka grows now anew.
A freeing, grant us a freeing,
A two-fold freeing.
Free us, we ask, free us.
A kapu profound is yours to keep.
A freedom complete we ask for us.
The goddess is Kapu still.
Now we who ask are freed![75]

Again we are silent, and I think about Hawaiian people first carving this space from the mountain, then constructing the altar. This grass is freshly mowed. For how many generations have dedicated people worshiped and groomed this place? History hovers close. Past, future, present blend. Time is timeless.

"My halau visited here in September. Auntie Harriet is in a wheelchair. It takes six men to carry her up the trail." Susan points off to our left. "When she got here we were all crying. She asked us why? She's so brave. Used to be a great dancer. She dances now with us in her wheelchair."

"What happened?" My mind is caught on dancing the hula from a wheelchair. "She had a stroke. Now she can stand a little. She says she'll dance hula again. She probably will."

I could understand the tears. A dancer who can't dance. A former dancer who stays sweet-tempered, participating as best she can, teaching forbearance, patience, love, and aloha to all who can learn her life lessons. Suddenly I understand the rightness of the trail's difficulty in getting here. Reaching a place of homage is not supposed to be easy. I think of the contrast between getting here and being here.

"This heiau. Has it a name?" I ask quietly.

"Oh, I thought you knew. This is Laka's Heiau. She's the Goddess of Hula. Those leis on the altar are maile which is sacred to Laka. And the red jacket you're wearing—red is sacred to the gods and to those who love them. Did you know," Susan is so still, a part of the elements of this place, "that the ancient name for hula was haa?"

"Haa," I repeat. "Haa."

I puzzle reality again. Feelings. This was a busy 24 hours beginning with joining Susan at her fancy Princeville time-share. Yesterday we drove to Hanalei and walked out on the pier and then I treated us to yummy $28 pupus (Hawaiian appetizers) at the newly redone St. Regis. Really good food and a really small amount. But later the hot tub and more food back at Susan's. Lousy couch bed but I made up my mind to sleep and I did. (Still I won't leave home again without my eye shades as light interferes with my sleep.) Early, early to rise, and over to Kee Beach and the climb up to Laka's Heiau. Nice walk later on Kee beach with views back over the Na Pali cliffs down to the sea.

Heiau. A filling of senses. I had on flip flops, not a smart move. Home to breakfast at the time-share where I get to eat facing a picture post card view of palms and flaming hibiscus flowers and a couple of proud chickens—Kauai's national bird. Simply gorgeous.

Later, as I drive home alone—Susan is staying on in her time-share—rain clouds roll over the mountains, dark obscuring the blue. Cooler breezes blow harder. Drove home and just now looked at the final two parts of a DVD series I'm watching. A therapist and four patients and the therapist himself as patient to another therapist. I'm thinking how real this TV series seems, and what is reality? And how the media plays with us now. Seeing the therapist, Paul, on the DVD, I could reach out and touch his hand. I know him. But he knows nothing and less than nothing of me.

The pretend therapy is intense. I get involved. I have feelings. I identify. And I remember and re-experience my rush of emotion at my husband's death. It's unexpected and almost too much to have these feelings again. So strange and yet leading me to understand that there are things I think I've got under control, and I don't!

Some things I'm better off backing away from for a while. Feelings rise up to the surface and are raw. Clearly, over the holidays (an emotional time), I won't see Kevin except at work. I need time to deal with Kevin. Not now. My heart says Kaimana has shoved Kevin right out of my life. But my head says Kevin is my boss, controls my job, and the money that supports me. No burning of bridges at least until after the holidays.

During my time at the heiau I could feel into the power. Susan said she'd stood on a stone at the heiau and felt power rise from her feet. Go through her like an electric shock. I was aware of latent power at the heiau. Powerful mana as in Princess Ruth's presence.

Dare I go back to the heiau by myself now I know where the path is?

Susan asked for permission. I could do that. Later, when I was driving back alone from the North shore and being stopped for construction on a bridge I felt a disconnect, a shifting of reality, another world possible, another way of looking at things.

That intensity, that closeness, that realness, that's what I've looked for. Kevin and I had that merging of selves so long ago but his broken trust, lies, killed our chances. My wanting to get close, being drawn in—sort of what

Kevin keeps trying to do now when it's too late. It's mutual fascination, which you're not even sure is happening. Only for me, my contribution is continuing the interaction, a continuing to remain engaged. Not running away. Thoughts of Kaimana come flooding. When will I see him again?

I push away thoughts of Kaimana. He scares me. I'm attracted like crazy. Last time Kaimana held me backed against the kitchen sink, pushing into my body, blood rushing. Sex rising wild alive from frozen bones. So good to be held. I keep forgetting. I thrust him away but my body remembers, reaches to take more.

Thinking later I realize a man's desire is the biggest turn-on of all. *I want you. Here and now. You fascinate me. You and this aware moment are all there is.* Where's the defense against that?

Princess Ruth continues to intrigue. I need something besides Kaimana, and Kevin, my dead husband Thomas, and the mysteries at Purity Corporation to think about. Ancient Hawaiian history baffles and horrifies. I keep replaying facts. Casual statistics are tossed about. By one account, before contact, one million Hawaiians lived in the islands, thriving and happy. In 1778 the British Captain Cook showed up in Waimea on Kauai followed by more ships, sailors, outsiders bringing disease to Islanders living healthily in their paradise. A mere 100 years after Captain Cook there were 40,000 Hawaiians left, only one out of twenty-five Hawaiians still alive. Whole families were wiped out. Men, women and especially children died from measles, mumps, small pox, pneumonia, venereal disease, cholera and I'm sure broken hearts. Hanging over everything was a gargantuan battle: the old ways versus the new ways; good versus evil, the old Gods and the way of Kapu, versus Calvinistic Christianity.

Warped Christianity. It's the kind of Southern Baptist, too often hypocritical, nonsense I grew up with. Heaven or purgatory. Sin, and you're thrust in fiery hell for eternity and there's no escape. Such a cruel God, unforgiving.

Or perhaps it is this God's so-called servants: Calvinistic missionaries like Amos Cooke and his wife Juliette who ran the Chief's Children's

School in Honolulu, which was a boarding school for Hawaiian high-born alii children. The Cookes, I've read, were interested in saving heathen souls; the chiefs were interested in saving their own kingdom on earth. The Cookes told the royal children that it was the will of God that the Hawaiian race was dying out and that the land would be taken over by a more civilized race. Those poor royalty children. My heart breaks for them and for the sovereign islands of Hawaii. How history hangs on some events. One thing happens and life is changed. The automobile accident that killed my husband. We don't know these outcomes as Hawaiians couldn't know the effect of that school.

Untangling Hawaiian genealogy can keep me occupied for a long time. No sooner do I place young Princess Ruth with her second, or 3rd or 4th step-mother—with three new half brothers and one half sister—than off go the brothers and sister to the High Chief's boarding school. These weren't ordinary brothers. Alexander and Lot would later be Kings Kamehameha Four and Five.

But Princess Ruth didn't go to the boarding school says the reference I'm reading. Another thing to check. This neglect, if it was neglect, is her salvation. Where the others were indoctrinated with warped Western ways, Princess Ruth is not. But why wasn't she sent to school with the rest? Discrimination? I'll have to dig deeper. I'm already discovering too much. To modern eyes, and any sort of sensibilities, Amos Cooke and the Chief's Children's School is a horror.[76]

The man actually kept track in his diary of beatings he administered, boasting that his only goal was salvation, conversion from Hawaiian Gods to Christianity.[77] Princess Ruth's half brother, Moses, first in line to inherit the throne, ahead of Alexander and Lot, was beaten 22 times in one school semester, according to Cooke's diary. We're talking about tied down and whipped so hard the doctor warned Amos Cooke to be more careful.

Half-brother Moses died at nineteen.[78]

When his rules were broken, Amos Cooke devised a brilliant system of beating all the children until the real culprit of the latest sin confessed and could be properly punished—with another beating. Amos Cooke usually began with the most vulnerable. Eight year-old-kids used to nothing but kindness and love would break easily, he thought. I cry for the children. And I'm sad too for King Kamehameha III who set up this school and reportedly chose the students. He wanted to train young royalty to thrive and care for their people in these unprecedented times in Hawaii.

I can just imagine the shock, humiliation and anger these children must have felt. These were young alii. Alii rulers sanctioned from antiquity by their ancient Hawaiian Gods. In the not-distant olden times, ordinary people were put to death for touching them, or even their shadow. Touching would steal mana, their power. Mana is an awesome life force living everywhere in nature: in the animals, trees, fruit, stones, mountains, the sea and all its creatures.

"Mana was the miraculous power which motivated the universe and all things in it. Leadership, charisma, courage, intelligence, talents, birth status, strength and good fortune were evidences of personal mana. A fishhook which caught fish had more mana than one which did not, and a seaworthy canoe had more mana than one which was poorly designed."[79]

In bodies and spirits like Princess Ruth's, mana could stop volcanoes. The missionaries hated mana almost as much as they despised hula.

Just mailed off *Hotel Honolulu*[80] to a friend caught in bed while her leg heals. Linda needs diverting and this intriguing, modern and irreverent picture of a displaced writer living one of Waikiki's many lives will do the job. "I was resident manager of the Hotel Honolulu, eighty rooms nibbled by rats…. Hawaii was paradise with heavy traffic." I picked up *Hotel Honolulu* at an early morning garage sale. Hard cover, in good shape for an entire fifty cents. Now I'll keep my eye out for every copy I can find.

I'm charmed and beguiled not only with pleasing my friend (she'll love it) and to begin a new tradition for myself, but most to recognize and deliberately start this tradition. One of those tiny cogs in living a life that used to delight me and now my refound ability to pay attention to a friend's need is quite pleasing. Kauai is healing in a personal way I've never gotten from a locale before. Can you fall in love with a place? I think I have!

Amazing how things you need or should see fall into your lap. Hanapepe library has waist-high bins outside the entrance where staff and patrons place used books, free for the taking. Many books of course are trash or written in languages foreign to me: Korean, Japanese, fundamental religion. But treasures pop up. I'm now happily devouring *Ancient Hawaiian Civilization*.[81] These lectures, begin in the 1930s by experts in Ancient Hawaiian practices, aimed to bring back pride and knowledge of their rich Hawaiian heritage to native-blood K through 12 Kamehameha students.

Native culture was looked down on and Western business ways were in full ascendance. Missionaries did their best to squash Hawaiian culture to death. Native Hawaiian language was forbidden in schools. "Using the Hawaiian language as a medium of education was outlawed in 1896, and legal constraints against its use were maintained by territorial and U.S. state governments until 1986 ... ninety years."[82]

Hawaiians of old used only one name. Under penalty of law, actual jail sentences, Hawaiians were forbidden to give their children a first name in the Hawaiian language. First names had to be English. In 1860 Kamehameha Four signed the Act to Regulate Names. Hawaiians were to take their father's given name as a surname, and all children born henceforth were to receive a Christian, that is, English, given name. Hawaiian names were transferred into middle names. The law was not repealed until 1967.

The best and brightest Hawaiian students were trained as policemen, teachers, nurses, workers. These occupations were necessary but subservient service workers. And not scientists, doctors, engineers or top government officials who would challenge the plantation mentality imposed since the illegal overthrow of sovereign Hawaii.

The plantation mentality is "You: white haole boss. Me: hard-working, obedient, non-educated, low-paid imported Chinese, Japanese, Korean, Filipino, Portuguese pineapple, and sugar cane plantation workers who live in segregated camps working dawn to dust, earning pennies a day. Local Hawaiians were loyal and hard working paniolos (cowboys) or house servants and a surprisingly large number of them worked the plantations fields.

Since I've become so engrossed with Princess Ruth and her powers, I keep a sharp eye out for the unexplained, for magic. First-hand accounts fascinate and grab our attention. This happened and let me tell you about it. Glen Grant, one of the experts (*Ancient Hawaiian Civilization,* my recent free find) with an interest in Hawaiian supernaturalism, tells how in the 1980s, as a young university professor, he was invited to Waianae Valley to meet Theodore Kelsey, a living Hawaiian treasure.

Kelsey's own story is interesting enough. Brought to the Islands at four from the mainland, Theodore Kelsey developed a life-long passion for the Hawaiian language and culture. By the time Glen Grant met him, Kelsey only communicated in Hawaiian—because Kelsey felt the native language offered him the only true door into the deeper cultural worldview of Hawaii's indigenous people.

After meeting Kelsey, conversation shifted to a friend (not named) who had grown up in Indonesia as the son of a Dutch Catholic missionary and he shared his story about his father. Paraphrased, the missionary father was gung-ho, pushing and pushing a local shaman, challenging, "If you've got any powers, let's see them." Finally the shaman told the father to walk down a path into the near-by jungle, take the right turn and stare into the jungle.

When the missionary father did this, he found himself looking into a room in his old home—a kitchen where his mother was making bread. After staring at his real-life-looking mother, he ran out of the jungle, ran out of his missionary stance, and his old life. The story teller relates further how later his father received a concerned letter from his mother asking if he was all right as she'd had the strangest happening. Recently, looking out her kitchen window in Holland, she'd seen him clear as day in the jungle. But he'd seemed upset and had run away.

It's crazy how things fall into your mind: insights, understandings, knowings. Suddenly I got it that some happenings don't have a thing to do with whether you believe in them or not. They simply are and there goes your world-view about reality shot to hell.

Do I even have a current world-view anymore? I wonder. Yet into my world of mystery I sense movement. Concrete things begin to happen.

Before sleep last night I read of Kamehameha rage. Kamehameha One, who united the Hawaiian islands, was the first of the Kamehameha lineage noted for losing his temper: throwing things, raging and yelling with his distinctive powerful voice. Later I dreamed of Princess Ruth pitching a pillow at an attendant, while violently pushing away food in a calabash.

In the dream I'm in a grass hut identical to the one Princess Ruth preferred to live in on the Big Island. The Princess alternately leans against small yellow pillows and heaves herself about.

"Can't you see," she glares in my direction. "Don't you get it? It's the land, the aina." Her sorrow, her conflict, her rage, and frustration reach me. Princess Ruth wants something, but despairs of getting it.

"My rage has no limit," she booms on, throwing another pillow. "I'm tied in struggles. I hate haoles. Beneath contempt. Ill-mannered, no-mannered louts. No patience. Disrespectful. No understanding of protocol. Greedy. Me. Me. All to myself is all they want. Hypocrites, preaching how we, all of us ignorant undeserving natives, should give haoles everything. While you look down on us."

Another yellow pillow hits the wall while low-bending attendants scurry to replace them. "Go home haoles. Take your pestilence and death. Go home. Leave us alone."

Princess Ruth's body swells with sorrow. "Death is your aumakua, your ancestor. Go back where you came from."

Caught in the dream, I feel myself becoming smaller and smaller.

"The night has taken them one by one," she intones. "Death to one child. One mother. One father. Death, one after another. Thousands of my dying people. Night falls like shadows. Death stalks our islands. The aina you desecrate falls silent. Death. Red earth you color black. Plants die. Death. Poisonous taro. Disease-bringing food. Death."

My heart aches. Breathing stops. The extermination of a people fills my consciousness until there is nothing else. I wake crying.

I've had to turn away from these dream implications. I can't absorb living souls who watch themselves destroyed by the thoughtless, heedless, greedy, and ignorant. Sorrow and pain to the marrow and beyond. No wonder the Hawaiians, dying like flies, lost all hope and died even faster. Is there a way to keep your sanity past this?

Once, long ago when I dreamed of writing books, a writing guru appeared. His name was Jones, a loving and special man. I dreamed of him later last night as I still do sometimes although our time together was short and long ago. I dreamed of Jones and me and a little girl. Jones entrusted me to take care of the child. We were in an outdoor picnic place with lots of light. Not bright light but luminous. In the dream I was happy. My dreams of Jones are usually happy. In dream language I know Jones represents the optimistic, innocent, pure part of me, mostly missing since Thomas died.

I wake enough to recognize that Jones is entrusting this pure-self little girl to me to care for. Fully awake I recognize this is dream encouragement I've allowed myself to receive. And I also recognize how much uneasiness lies in not continuing to tell my story of Princess Ruth. Lately I haven't worked as hard as I should.

And the Princess pulls unseen triggers. I'm confused. How would I proceed if Kevin were not my boss? His desires seem all too clear. Whose reality rules? Please don't tell me I'm silly enough to forget that I work for him, and on an isolated small island where jobs are hard to find. Kevin can fire me—he asked me to dinner again last night. Tried to hold and kiss me. I believe I've learned my lesson. I politely turned him down. He didn't like my standing up for myself. I feel his anger building.

The Congress apologizes to Native Hawaiians on behalf of the people of the United States for the overthrow of the Kingdom of Hawai'i on January 17, 1893 ... and the deprivation of the rights of Native Hawai'ians to self-determination.

United States Public Law 103-150, signed by President Clinton on November 23, 1993.

CHAPTER SEVEN

WHAT IS AN APOLOGY without some concrete action to make up, to pay back for what you have done? *What are you doing to make up for your ancestor's mistakes?* is a question I can't get around.

What am I doing to make up for my ancestor's mistakes?[83] This question has flat nailed me. Even, what am I doing to make up for patriarchy's discrimination against me as a woman? Other than reveling in the freedom I now enjoy? Feeling my appreciation and gratitude brim over?

Maybe, for now, writing Princess Ruth's story is my payback, my way of changing deep-set ideas about how this bit of the world works. And especially how the land works.

On April 15, 1920, Kuhio's[84] argument in Congress was that the common people had been omitted in the Great Mahele of 1848. He explained to his colleagues, that after the king and chiefs acquired 1,619,000 acres of land, the local government received 1,505,460 acres. The remaining 948,000 acres that should have been conveyed to the common people, reverted to the crown instead.

[What's not made clear here is that *the crown* is really the government—effectively our U.S. controlled government.]

Kuhio was extremely critical of this injustice to the commoners. His criticism carried on to the gaining of the land by the missionaries. Cupid (Kuhio) related that <u>33 missionary families received 41,000 acres, while at the same time, 3,000 Hawaiian families obtained only 28,000 acres</u>.... Today the great majority of the Hawaiian people own no land. [Underlining mine][85]

Why isn't this Hawaiian land information readily available? Or I guess I don't need to ask: If you're in power, if you run everything and have all the money, won't you naturally hide the dirty tricks that got you your high status? And won't your high status act as a protecting shield? And keep others from looking too closely or asking embarrassing questions about how you and your ancestors are acting?[86] Or have acted?

I guess I'm back where I started: *What am I doing to make up for my ancestor's mistakes?* The real question is: What is my individual responsibility?

Quickly realizing that I've done about all the hard thinking I can stand for this night, I grab the next book off my research stack.

"Take an early lunch with me?" Barbara is suddenly in my office. "Let's run down to Candy's place for an espresso, grab a sandwich, and eat in Captain Cook's park in Waimea."

Something is up with Barbara. Except for being clean she could have walked right off her farm dressed today in her usual blue jeans and T-shirt, this one bright yellow. The air around her is light and electric.

"Sure. Let me turn off this computer and I'm ready."

Past the old Russian Fort with its wide areas of red dirt, over calm Waimea River, right turn immediately after the bridge, three long blocks, and there, a block or so down on the left, is *Aloha-in-Paradise*. Candy's place, as we call it, sells only contemporary Hawaiian art. Huge bright flowers grace the walls, and pictures of koi fish, mountains, sea, graceful waterfalls and depictions of nearby Waimea Canyon jockey for wall space. Tucked into an imitation grass-hut on the right side of the main display room, coffee and food are new additions.

"Have you heard the latest?" Barbara bursts out almost before we sit on a bench in the park with our picnic fare. "I've been a local too long." She tears into her sandwich as if she yearns for something more solid.

Unable to decide if her face holds fear or anger, I can't contain my curiosity any longer. "Tell me," I say. "What is it?"

"Purity Corporation is importing Mexicans in here to do the field jobs. I just learned about it." Barbara is indignant. "They're suiting them up like astronauts from Mars, I heard, and sending them out to the corn and experimental fields. I ask you—what is going on? It's shocking and morally wrong. Local people need the work. Why aren't they hiring locals? The company doesn't want us to know what's going on. Money and greed."

Barbara barely pauses for breath. "These Mexicans are living twenty to a room, someone told me. Running extension cords here and there, inside and outside. Creating fire hazards." Outrage fills her features and rings in her voice. This isn't right.

"And the thing is," Barbara laughs wryly, "More immigrants. Immigrants come and these won't want to leave either, when their contracts are over. No one wants to leave. It is the history of the Hawaiian Islands all over again." Sighing deeply, she stays very still.

"Yea," I agree. "More people." Thoughts crowd of long years of indigenous Hawaiians being pushed farther and farther off their ancient homelands. Would evil dressed in its clothes of ignorance and greed never end?

"Remember when Syngenta sprayed those pesticides next to the Waimea Canyon Grammar school? Teachers and kids got sick and the company said it was stinkweed? Yeah, stinkweed all right but stinkweed wasn't in the fields, it was in the people who ordered pesticides sprayed that close to schools. People here on the Westside are too passive."

Barbara is sad now and imploring, "I bet this wouldn't happen in Hanalei. The Eastside won't let them get away with destroying the environment; they're too aware. Corporations get away with anything here on the Westside. It's that leftover plantation mentality. *Don't rock the boat. Do what the boss says. Get along or you'll get in trouble.* And this horrible economic climate isn't helping a thing. Everybody's worried about their jobs." Barbara sighs again before smiling slightly. "Guess I should apologize," she says slowly, "blowing off steam like this."

"No, it's all right." My thoughts chase each other. "What are friends for? Mexicans. How many Mexicans?" I ask.

Looking for a better life, I think. We all want a better life, and for our children. These undying hopes live in our hearts. Seeking. Striving. Wanting more, more. Encoded in human genes—or is it? The more I learn about Hawaiians. the more I get it that they've had to be carefully taught American values. And not everyone accepts them.

The next time I have ten free years with nothing to do, I've promised myself I'll read all three volumes (and the index) of Abraham Fornander's *An Account of the Polynesian Race.*[87] Fornander's breadth of knowledge is simply amazing. He came to Hawaii immediately following the first missionaries and "... soon realized that the missionaries were succeeding all too well in replacing the Hawaiian culture with their own."[88]

Princess Ruth is in Fornander's book with a genealogy lasting forever and also King K, the last king of Kauai. I can only observe that a book like this helps you confront your ignorance. And be extremely grateful for this legacy of sincere information.

Missionaries are writ large in Hawaii's story. Contradictions swirl around them: truth and lies. Duplicity and incredible selfless labor for others. When I come across *Grapes of Canaan*, a 1951 book by Albertine Loomis that is based on actual journals and letters of an original missionary couple, Elisha and Maria Loomis, I feel I've hit pay dirt. These original sources record opinions and facts between 1819 and 1827. Elisha and Maria Loomis are among the pioneer group of missionaries. Albertine Loomis, their great-grandchild has done a terrific job—with her day-to-day details you feel like you're in old Hawaii arriving with the missionaries, seeing with their eyes and sensibilities.[89] "In Kamehameha's day all the land was the king's." Loomis tells how the king would give or loan the land to others for as long as they lived or the king found them loyal. And how taxes were paid and commerce conducted.

Always we see events through the prism of our time, place and circumstances. And of course after almost 200 years we must take missionary stories with several grains of salt—as they are told through the missionary viewpoint (they think Hawaiians are savages) and through the missionaries' own, normal at-the-time, straight-jacketed, self-righteous, religious attitudes (whether they knew they had them or not).

Yet most of the original missionaries tried to do right, to teach and to provide a written language; they wrote and printed the books that provided literacy for an entire people.[90] Hawaiians are now putting back words and culture the missionaries left out.

What I see from my perspective is strong-beliefed, rigid missionaries arriving to an Hawaiian culture that was primitive by some standards. Yet, was totally beyond their missionary comprehension in terms of complex sophisticated human relationships and, while not religious by Christian standards, in actuality Native Hawaiians possessed a much truer spirituality. And with an evolved sustainability they were sufficient unto themselves. Certainly, by contemporary standards, much more appropriate to an island culture and sustainability than what's been imposed. (And now I'll climb down from this missionary editorial.)

And back on the GMO front a local man calls it as he sees it in *The Garden Island*, Letters to the Editor

Toxic Village

On Aug.6, [2010] *The Garden Island* ran a front-page article on the drought showing a color picture of former Gay & Robinson plantation sugar fields up to Kaumakani all dried up.

Then on Aug. 9 on page A6, *TGI* ran another color picture of Kauai Coffee plantation on the other side of Hanapepe River lush and green.

The difference is not caused by the drought but the GMO corn companies.

Fred Dente in his two *TGI* op-ed articles has been right: "Kauai has long been the Petri dish for planet Earth," with a laundry list of chemical soil washing. When they (the GMO companies) prepare a field for planting, they kill everything in the ground, on the ground, above the ground, and anything around or near the site. Notice in the picture no koa growing, only at Hanapepe Heights, Salt Pond and Kaumakani Village.

This defoliation is caused by spraying of herbicide, insecticide, fungicide and rodenticide. Gone are the nematodes, ants, grasshoppers, bees, songbirds, hummingbirds, chickens, doves, rats, cats, bats, dogs, etc. Drive along the highway between Hanapepe and Waimea and notice you will not see any bugs on your windshield or birds on the lines. Only in the oasis of Kaumakani village and Pakala....[91]

We sure have had many deaths, cancers, birth defects, and a list of health horrors since GMO came our way in the last two years. I hope Kaumakani doesn't become Toxic Village, Hawaii

Bobby Ritch, Kaumakani

Hawaii is unique: astounding physical beauty and native Hawaiian reverence for land, nature, beauty, ancestors. Hawaiian history goes back to myths and some myths still take living form. Like nested Russian dolls with new history written every day within and on top of the old.

At first glance history is, of course, written by the conquerors—as if history (the Sureness of God) was inevitably always supposed to be this way and will remain so forever. No one much cares or minds or thinks about old history. In this polite version of history, rough edges are smoothed and inconvenient facts forgotten along with their implications and inevitable results in current life. Each today slides into the past: History is made pretty. And remote. The writers of this history are probably nice people but the uneasiness of lies strikes and I sort of want to throw up.

Shelby Foote, our great civil war historian, tells of writing from inside the past, of empathically gathering facts and then writing from within that past time. Or how about some history written by the conquered? The ones who lose? We all know that provides a different story!

The *pretty* past has its appeal and I've read a lot of it. Simplistic. Makes Hawaii a state like any other, even a model, only a little more complicated. "In two centuries time these peoples of diverse cultures have gathered within the confines of an island group and have lived in tolerance and understanding of each other. This, perhaps, is Hawaii's unique contribution to the twentieth century."[92]

True, but not all of the truth as I grow to believe this *happy model history* is built on the backs of indigenous Hawaiians. What culture is this: bringing aloha, generosity, love of flowers and beauty, and the precious land, the aina? Whether overtly or simply as facts of being—try, as invaders, oppressors and immigrants might, indignities piled upon atrocities—native Hawaiian influences refuse to die.

Some rules for the newcomer to the islands are easy: Take your shoes off before entering homes. The newcomer gets it quickly. Island life is easy (when you've got the money and resources) and soothes the soul. Why do you think people come and don't leave?

Another silent rule is that it's rude to be rude. Only haole newcomers hang on your bumper, or push ahead, me first, resolutely refusing to allow the car or truck ahead to ease into traffic.

Paradox abounds in these *pretty* histories: Hawaiians are ignorant and lazy and then in almost the next words tell of hula students coming to hula school at Kee at Haena, Kauai, renowned as the ancient site of a *halau hula* and shrine to Laka (where I visited) where expert *kumu hula* (teachers) train dancers from all the Hawaiian Islands. Ignorant and lazy? Just try hula if you want to change your mind fast!

It's too bad I didn't stop reading with my pretty history. But I quickly got corrupted, as some would say, learning unpleasant truths. Haunani-Kay Trask and her unequivocal book will do that:

> Because of the overthrow and annexation, Hawaiian control and Hawaiian citizenship were replaced with American control and American citizenship. We suffered a unilateral redefinition of our homeland and our people, a displacement and a dispossession in our own country.... As a result of these actions, Hawaiians became

a conquered people, our lands and culture subordinated to another nation. Made to feel and survive as inferiors when our sovereignty as a nation was forcibly ended, we were rendered politically and economically powerless by the turn of the century. Cultural imperialism had taken hold with conversion to Christianity in the middle of the 19th century, but it continued with the closing of all Hawaiian language schools and the elevation of English as the only official language in 1896. Once the Republic of Hawaii declared itself on July 4, 1894, the "Americanization" of Hawaii was sealed like a coffin.... Fully one-fifth of our resident population is military, causing intense friction between locals who suffer from Hawaii's astronomically high cost of housing and land, and the military who enjoy housing and beaches for their exclusive use.[93]

It's impossible to read Trask, keeping an open mind, without realizing most people haven't been getting the whole story. Our so-called U.S. history has been drastically prettied up.

Haunani-Kay Trask is upsetting. I have to keep reading and rereading because I can only absorb so much at a time. Repetition is needed for things to sink in. Time for contemplation is also required to get meaning and connect implications.

"Each day, we all face a peculiar problem. We must validate our past, face our present, plan for the future."[94] This morning reading my daily bit from *365 Tao*, I'm struck by how Hawaiians might cope and how hard this must be. Validate the past. Face the present. Plan for the future.

Validate. Where did we come from? Who are our people? What are our legends and myths?

On record anyway, the Hawaiian past is findable, and more and more this past is admirable, sustainable, and holds particular genius in intricacies of relationship. Validate. Yes, say the *kama aina* (locals), I am a proud Hawaiian, grounded in my past, feeling my ancestors, my kinship with race, solidarity with family, and at home in my world—when I can find it natural and free.

Face the present. Face killing loss. Face a frequent grinding poverty, no decent jobs or housing or suitable schools. Face indignity. Face having your land stolen. Face rage at oceans of injustice and dead indifference from those with power. On all sides, face attitudes of *Why can't you just go away and be happy. Get out of my face. It was so long ago, who cares?* And galling, galling in your blood must be the on-going making of decisions affecting you and your aina by people who don't even belong in Hawaii in the first place! The stealers of your land (the Big Five for example) their descendants and the descendants of those brought here to toil plantation land who now hand down legal judgments as if they had that right.

The imposters choose to forget. But you cannot. Love of the aina and those murmuring ancestral voices will not let you rest or forget that your generation holds the legacy for the children, and possibly the world.

Face the present. What is the reality in which I find myself when I wake up enough to open my eyes and ask the question? As a Hawaiian: What are my personal assets and liabilities, possibilities and dreams?

Where did I read of an Indian elder explaining to a young adult of this generation: "All the land gone, all the old ways gone. Makes him feel helpless, 'cause he can't do anything about it. Festers inside him, eating him alive. I told him, Grandson, you gotta let it go. The people had to let it go. We gotta go on and live. Everything that killed us in the past, it'll keep on killing us if we don't let it go. Step out ahead of it, I told him. Get on with your life."

And the Indian grandfather who tells his grandson of two fighting wolves living inside him. One who rages, kills, destroys. The other wolf who is peaceful, builds, enjoys life.

"Which will win?" asks the boy.

"The one you feed," answers the grandfather.

"It boiled down to this," says poet Pablo Neruda,[95] "You had to pick the road you would take. That is what I did and I have never had reason to regret the choice I made between darkness and hope in that tragic time." Neruda chose to deeply involve himself in the beginning war in Spain in the 1930s.

Will you take on in all earnestness the task of your evolution of self? Define chosen duties to yourself and to your world?

How do you convey that we each hold our lives like delicate crystal? The decisions, what we do matters. We take on the task of holding on to our dreams (which means working toward them) and training ourselves each day to walk more fully in paths we have chosen. We dedicate and rededicate ourselves to being our most true self.

Face the present: tough for each of us, tougher for contemporary Hawaiians.

Plan for the future. How will I change aspects of my present I don't like? Increase those I do? How will I spend my life?

Where do you go as you graduate from your individual chains of lack of knowledge? Or opening your eyes to the truth? Is it simply happier and happier, more useful to yourself and to your world? Or do you go crazy with facing injustices? Be unforgiving?

Well I've definitely got to climb down from this editorial before I fall off from exhaustion! Where is a magic wand when I need it to wave and make everything right? Holding myself in a somewhat neutral area of learning about old Hawaii, difficult to say the least, offers the advantage of letting me run from my own troubles.

"As a haole, let me give you some advice about living on Kauai," says my next door neighbor in Kekaha. "Number One: If you get in trouble, don't call the police. Number Two: If you get in trouble, don't call the police department. Number Three: If you get in trouble, don't call the police."

I take her advice with several large grains of salt. Fortunately I'd vacationed on Maui and accompanied a haole friend who, after she moved to Maui, charged heavily into business as usual: licenses, trying to get information, dealing with the locals. It didn't take me many times through the cycle to get it—this was *their* island and the locals (as I remember there were not that many Hawaiian ancestry among them) were going to run *their* island *their* way. Any form of being rude, screaming and yelling, being indignant, being in a hurry, and especially, 'In the states we do it ….' was a lousy idea. I slowly begin getting a clue. Being pleasant and open, allowing lots of time moved your personal agenda along. Seething and any form of rude jammed up the works.

And there is my "getting gas" lesson in my first weeks here on Kauai where I'd lost it with an innocent attendant and had to apologize for my rudeness.

Were the clear politics of the Kauai police only examples of the old *divide and conquer,* or just our local Big Five running their version of the usual show? Or just another millionth example of Native Hawaiians not included in decision making and being marginalized in their own country? I can't help but wonder, where are representative native Hawaiians in this story as *KPD Blue*[96] tells of racism. But it's men: Japanese and Portuguese mainly who are fighting to the death, hiring lawyers and making wrong use of our tax money to keep out a Chinese man, to hold progress at bay, and to cover over past mistakes with huge settlements to hide wrong-doings.[97]

This back story with a vengeance is written by a local-at-the-time newspaper reporter with tons of applicable experience. So many things are explained that I never got before. And a whole lot that's distasteful at best. I don't know how true *KPD Blue* is but I certainly don't know enough to dispute it.[98]

Meanwhile back to my advice of 1, 2, 3—don't call the police: "Kauai is one of very few places in the United States where the citizens—with good reason—fear their government. Retaliation is essential for the government to keep the peasants in line."[99]

Scary. Is it true? I wonder if I should worry? Do I have to delete this part?

Am I a peasant? Of course! I'm not happy about being called a peasant. But to my way of thinking, if you owe your soul to the company store, if you're a wage slave, you for sure ain't free. The Native Hawaiians had the right idea: sustainability, living within your means, being pono in all ways. It's the only way to go.

I tell myself: *When you see the same old names in our local politics voting the same old way, then get a clue: it is business as usual, same old, same old.* Then it occurs to me that perhaps problems are built into the way government is set up to run: top down, few if any women in seats of power. Large questions I wish I had answers to.

Any great change must expect opposition because it shakes the very foundation of privilege.
Lucretia Coffin Mott, 1793-1880[100]

Chapter Eight

KAIMANA HAS DISAPPEARED. Not a word since he said he was leaving for a music tour including the Big Island and Honolulu. Something is wrong and I don't know what. Or maybe it's just that Kaimana needs all his energy to go into his music. Being a musician in the Islands can't be easy. I'm pretty sure that what's required from me is simply pulling back, allowing space.

Yesterday, I was thinking about us as I was driving. John Cruse came on KKCR, our community radio station, singing *Come to Me Gently*. My eyes moistened at the sheer beauty of the music; Cruse played and sang while Kaimana played in my emotions. *Come to Me Gently* is so evocative of Kaimana and our lovemaking. Such a sweet song. Such a sweet man.

Sometimes I get a bad feeling. Perhaps now it's abandonment I feel. First Kaimana and—while I'm following Princess Ruth's instructions to learn more about Hawaii, reading and studying history every spare minute—the Princess has also disappeared. I miss her contact and guidance, something that keeps me on track while my job and GMOs hover.

As I probe, my feeling is not of black doom; I've had those before and they must be given immediate heed. I'm appreciative of my Black Dooms as they've saved my life. But this current feeling is of depression and knowing nothing good will come of what's coming up in my life.

In the past, barely aware, I've sort of noted the feeling, then gone ahead with the coming event as I become more and more reluctant, only to have my premonitions fully confirmed.

At least I've learned a few things. Now I slow way down on preparations. I stop perfecting a speech I have to give at work, stop expecting things to go as I wish. But, so far, however grudgingly, I've carried on. For example, this last Friday night, in the rain, I moved slower and slower, reluctantly. And sure enough, I was correct to be apprehensive for I soon wished I'd followed my feeling and stayed home. More aware now, next time I'll give my intuition more respect.

The question: Do I fulfill my own prophesy? Do I *cause* the bad outcome by believing it's coming? Or am I simply *reading* approaching events—while not taking warning, or exercising what control is possible.

What I will attempt next time *negative* feelings come over me, is, I will search the event for a positive outcome. Example: I could say to myself: *This is practice, I will do the best I can with what develops. I will take the* bad *feeling and deal with it at the source, that is as soon as I become aware of it.*

I could simply stop. Be in the moment. And then choose how I wish to use and learn from the event.

Maybe the only purpose of my *dark* feeling is warning—to tell me to calm down, to work less and think more, to change, to pay attention. I think of seeing Hunani-Kay Trask[101] on a PBS show admitting, "I've got some bad habits; I've got to address them." How I admire reform that begins with oneself!

The dinner tonight is hosted by Vanessa Kamoku, a friend of Barbara's who lives way in the middle of the island, up above Kapaa. It will probably take me an entire 40 minutes to drive. This is a distance I'd never give a thought to back on the mainland but which, oddly, here on the island has stretched longer and longer. Smiling, I see I'm becoming more anchored in place—a common island happening, my friends tell me.

I'll leave early to allow plenty of time to get lost. Every street seems to begin with the letter *K* and some defective wiring in my head mixes up right and left. Once found, retracing my path is always easy. But getting it right the first time can be a pain. Also, I'm allowing time for a perusal of the sacred Wailua area. I've read about this Wailua center of Hawaiian Kings and Queens but only taken quick looks in passing.

Barbara prepared me earlier for Wailua by handing me a guide book, internet pages and a sheet of paper:

> The Wailua River is the largest (and only navigable) river in the Hawaiian Islands, and its mouth faces the rising sun. Nobody in her right mind could fail to grasp the divinity of this location. The Hawaiians constructed a succession of heiau, beginning at the river mouth (now Lydgate Park) and ascending Kuamoo Road to the summit, across from the parking lot where now tourists gawk at Opaekaa Falls. (Kua means spine or backbone, moo a legendary lizard.) At the summit is the remains of "hikini a ka la", "la" of course being sun, a large enclosure where traditional rituals (including human sacrifice some say) took place. This is possibly the second most sacred place to the Hawaiian people in the entire archipelago, after Kau on the Big Island. There's also an even larger enclosure down by the river mouth, on the mauka (to the mountain) side of the road across from the Aloha Beach Hotel. Word has it that after the abandonment of the kapu system and traditional Hawaiian religion in the mid-1800's, haole planters used the enclosure to corral cattle, as a special reminder to the remaining Hawaiians that their gods were dead.[102]

With all information in hand, I look forward to leisurely exploration of this Wailua valley area. A gorgeous Saturday afternoon, the first driving is easy over old cane-haul Wailua Bridge—no construction on weekends and little traffic. Left turn by pathetic looking Coco Palms, a once brilliant hotel. But since Hurricane Iniki in1992, a disgrace to the beauty of Kauai, and a pitiful monument to the inadequacies of local government.[103]

I pull in at the first park-looking left turn and gather my information, more complex than I expected. Breathing deeply the air becomes still and sacred. Princess Ruth hovers close. I consult guidebooks. Too much to see. Too little time. I note places I'll return to like kayaking or taking the 40 minute cruise up the river to the Fern Grotto.

Tantalizingly nearby now are special petroglyphs and bellstones used to calibrate summer and winter solstices and *rung* or struck to announce major events like royal births. When directions to Kamokila Hawaiian Village show up, I know I must return armed with clearness of mind and adequate time to explore these riches.

I've raced this road before but today I wind up curving Kuamoo road awed by how open, still and green this valley feels. Inside gears shift, I'm entering sacred space and suddenly I have all the time in the world. Near the crest I swing left into a parking area and am drawn to the edge of this high pali (cliff) looking down into Wailua river far below. Two tiny yellow kayaks ply the curving brown stream. Green fields banking the river are dotted with toy cows, some grazing, others lying down and white cattle egrets flutter. In this bucolic scene, tranquility rises like air.

As I glance around, a huge heiau on my right is the largest I've seen. Closer, individual stones are huge, and the precision of construction fills my thoughts. The immensity of this place of worship, each of these thousands of rocks and stones were carried manually up from the valley below. How many generations of Hawaiians labored and worshiped to create this temple-space? In awe, feeling the heiau's powerful mana, I walk around it except for the side bordering the cliff where dense trash bushes grow—probably to keep folks like me from falling over the edge. Imagine seeing this heiau in full majesty.

Suddenly Princess Ruth helps me realize that missionaries and early visitors to the islands were probably frightened by native Hawaiians into needing to tear down this kind of power—instead of seeking to understand the Hawaiians culture that produced it, let alone learn and benefit from what they had to offer. So much knowledge lost and destroyed.

Then thoughts of being late for dinner prompt me to get going. I drive almost directly across the highway and park in front of Opaekaa Falls.[104] In full glory today, three streams of powerful splashing waterfalls glitter in the afternoon light. The magnificent power of nature saturates every atom. Sacred ground.

After a time, living in a sort of grace, I follow directions perfectly to my dinner engagement at Vanessa's. The last narrow road goes almost straight up before I park and look behind me and out and over to rippling green mountains. This view after Wailua is almost too much. Being in a place of the Gods is how I feel. Like at Mount Alban near Oaxaca, Mexico, a lightness, a joy, a lifting toward heaven.

Amazing, I learn later, I'm actually in the Waialeale (rippling water or overflowing water) volcanic cauldron. Those far peaks are Waialeale itself at 5,148 and to the right along the same ridgeline, Kawaikini is slightly higher. The mountains are a green velvet patchwork quilt from here, but up close it's strong winds, fog, heavy rain, steep drop-offs and faint trails if any at all. Hikers who dare the summits tend to need rescuing by helicopter.

This expanse of farming land and houses below, when I lower my eyes, is the floor of the volcano so incredibly old now that it has become green and fertile land. In millions of years this is what the volcanic cauldron, Haleakala on Maui, dry and barren now like a moonscape, could become. Except for the water, the life-giving rain. What a difference a few million years can make, and water! Suddenly I feel so privileged to be here, marveling at the wondrous work of the Gods—who even cares which gods.

People want to climb Waialeale peaks. This is where all that rain comes down, 460 inches a year. Clouds hang low and even by helicopter you rarely see actual land. Today is beautiful, only small wispy clouds in front of Mount Waialeale like a Chinese painting. Like a dream you can easily walk into—except this is twenty miles in the distance.

When I stay still, I feel the mana of this entire area, especially here and back at Wailua Falls and out walking the eroded river's edge. Mana rising, the vistas so open, so free, the power of beauty clear and strong. The land, the aina is the crucial thing, I know, via Princess Ruth. People just get in the way!

I walk up to the house where old and new friends greet me and I'm soon engrossed in island politics with Akita, an acquaintance I'm glad to see again.

"What a close call on governor," he comments. "We could have had Duke Aiona and Christian values … I quote, "into all aspects of Hawaii society, including government.'"

I've been amazed by the layers of points of view and double dealing, treachery and depth of Hawaiian information that's available. But only in the right places, for information is frequently unclear and messages are mixed. You've got to keep your ears and heart open and be willing to listen. Being a know-it-all and telling the Natives and *kama aina* how to run things is the kiss of death.

Karin is now speaking, "Yes, we could be more Christian by taking still more from Native Hawaiians. I want some people in government with a good heart. I have hopes for Governor Abercrombie. So many people are upset now. Disheartened. And they're afraid. Too many factors spiral out of our control."

"Speaking of control," our hostess interjects, "you heard about that Kekaha shrimp farm wanting to dump up to 30 millions gallons of wastewater a day into the pristine blue waters of the Westside. Sunrise Capital says there will be no impact on water quality. You believe that? 660,000 gallons a year of contaminated, untreated wastewater into our ocean."

"You know I remember catching shrimp—old style," Akita muses to me as general conversation veers off on contamination. "My grandfather used to take me up the Hanalei River. He showed me how to catch fish and prawns with bare hands. Not intrusive. Grab 'em with your hands and if they get away, they still have a chance to live. What a time. We used to paddle down to the Na Pali Coast on surfboards."

Abruptly, Akita changes the subject: "Remember the forty days and forty nights of rain back in 2006? March has always been the wettest month on Kauai. Blu Dux even wrote a song about it. Remember when that earthen dam at Kaloko reservoir broke and several million gallons of water took everything in its path to the ocean, including three buildings and seven people swept away to death?"

"That was Pflueger, wasn't it?" I ask. "Rich Auto King on Oahu and egotistical skunk here. It's all in court. I heard that Pflueger ordered the spillway on the dam covered over."

"Yea, there were warnings beforehand. Nobody paid any attention. A friend, Michael Dyer, sent faxes to Pflueger about the need for spillways, pictures and how to fix the problem. When Pflueger didn't respond, he tried again, then notified and also sent pictures to state officials at the Department of Natural Resources. Nothing was done to change the unsafe situation. I was driving the highway." Akita looks concerned and angry. "I knew as soon as I saw water pouring over the road that Michael was right. That spillway didn't get fixed."

"Well at least it's made them check out our other dams … try to keep it from happening again."

"Yes, but I'm still not sure I'd want to live in the path of the water," Akita says.

"That situation at Salt Pond with the feral cats is a big mess," Karin observes quietly as we've moved off into a corner.

"I thought Krystal and Sheena were taking food out there every morning," I say.

"That's the trouble. People with the salt ponds don't want those cats there … feces and messes and sick cats right near the water where they're making salt. You know don't you, that this is about the last working salt pond in Hawaii?" Karin asks.

"Krystal and Sheena are passionate about those homeless cats. People dump kittens and unwanted dogs and don't get their animals spayed," I say.

"The old men at Salt Pond have a point," Karin says, "someplace else for the cats would be better. Say, do you remember when Salt Pond Park was going to close at 9 p.m.? Be locked up with the rest rooms closed and dark?"

"I heard rumors."

"That's when our Mayor was going around gathering community opinion. Those old men … they're self-appointed park caretakers, told the mayor that everybody used the park. That Salt Pond was like an extended living-room for graduation parties, luaus, birthdays, celebrations, you name it. That closing the park to decent families would open Salt Pond to druggies and alcoholics. Nasty people wouldn't care if the park was closed at night. They'd come anyway and do their business, spoil it for everyone else. Those old men keeping order out there knew what they were talking about. And the mayor had sense enough to listen and keep Salt Pond open," Karin observes with a smile.

Into Karin's sympathetic manner, I give expression to worries: "Some days it seems the world is falling apart ... over four dollars at the gas pump. That horrible earthquake and tsunami in Japan. All those people dead. Atomic reactors blowing up. Lives in chaos that will never be the same again. We're an island 2, 000 miles from anything. I'm finding out just how unsustainable our GMO agriculture is: oil for pesticides, oil for airplanes, barges, oil to move everything. It's enough to get you down."

"I know." Karin is understanding. "But here are some thoughts to cheer you. Soane Lagmay, a concerned, knowledgeable man—I'll introduce you at the next Seed Exchange in Hanapepe—was telling me that he figures the future this way ... that those military people and technicians out at the Navy base are smart, educated people. They've got their families here. And so are the GMO people educated and aware. Amazingly, Soane thinks a lot of the GMO people are already growing their own food, eating organic. They don't believe their own hype. Anyway, he feels everybody's going to get down to survival, to basics and realize that, as an island we've got to feed ourselves at the very least. And find decent renewable energy. Soane says when all us Islanders get on the same side and focused, there'll be incredible changes. We've already got so much: Great climate, you can grow all year around, plenty good water and just about anything you put in the ground grows."

"Thanks, Karin. You've cheered me up considerably. And I'm rejoicing over KipuKai Kualii making it onto our County Council, a native Hawaiian. This has to make a difference."

On the drive home, sustainability plays in my thoughts and how we can make it work on our island.

Truth to tell I'm becoming really down on missionaries. I want them to do right. Barbara laughs ironically when I read aloud, "*The churches have a moral obligation and responsibility to raise awareness in their congregations and in the State of Hawaii about tourism's negative impacts and consequences* *on native Hawaiians. The churches are called upon to* 'wrestle against the principalities and powers' *that exploit people."*[105]

"Well," Barbara comments, "I see you've found my favorite activist. Did you know that Hunani-Kay Trask also writes poetry? And, if you harbor any belief, as I was once propagandized to do, that you're doing the Native Hawaiians any favors by coming here as a tourist, listen to this:

Tourist

The flourishing hand
   of greed, a predatory

      face without dreams,
         In the marketplace,

            glittering knives of money,
               murdering the trees.[106]

"Nice imagery isn't it—*glittering knives of money.* Hunani-Kay was the first Director of Hawaiian Studies at the University of Hawaii and is still there. She doesn't pull many punches."

"Yes," I agree. "Her book cuts to the marrow." I search Barbara's face for clues. What does she know that I don't? Is she trying to tell me something? "Barbara," I confess, "I'm struggling to deal with Hawaiian history that turns out so different from what I've always thought or been taught."

"Yes," agrees Barbara, "and this book may help. Or raise more questions." With an odd, almost secretive look, she hands me a deep purple volume, adding, "It's a short history of missionary churches in Kauai."

"Just what I need," I enthuse. "Missionaries are a stumbling block. I read that when missionaries promised "life everlasting," the Hawaiians, starving, desperate and dying of strange diseases all over the place, thought the missionaries were promising life right now!"

"Yes," agrees Barbara. "When I was around twenty-five I had my tonsils out. The general practitioner botched the job. I couldn't eat for over a week. I'd never felt actual hunger before. As the starving days passed, I amused myself by figuring what I'd do to get food I could actually eat. Food for my then husband. And food for my child. My values and morals took on decided shades of grey. The experience was like peeling an onion. There were questionable things I'd do without a qualm for food for myself. A lot more I'd do for my daughter. And not much I'd do for my husband." Barbara laughs, adding, "Since I quickly realized I didn't love or respect him, that marriage was soon over."

"What an experience," I exclaim, "you were getting down to the bedrock of your values, of what's truly important to you."

"Well," Barbara says dismissively as if she's shared more than is comfortable, "at least I learned more appreciation of what hunger and want can do to people. And mine was a light experience … not real hunger … not starvation by a long shot."

Later, when I discover Barbara's book is put together by the State Council of Hawaiian Congregational Churches as recently as 2008, I figure this is trustworthy Hawaiian history.[107]

Wouldn't you love to have been a fly on the wall—knowing what we do now of course—as the missionaries "established 24 churches and 50 mission stations.… and a Seminary on Maui in 1831 to train Hawaiian as teachers and assistant ministers." But didn't get around to ordaining any Hawaiians as ministers until 1849 sending many Hawaiian ministers to foreign missions in other countries.

There's a lot of ambiguity between *protecting* Hawaiians from negative influences—mostly by negative Westerners—and the *missionary role* as a Christianizing society, and then moving on to allow Hawaiians to put their own interpretation on how this played out. "It is better for the islanders, and essential to the continuance of their institutions as a nation, that the offices be filled by natives….," said Rev. Rufus Anderson from the U.S. home office of the Missionaries in 1846. (My feeling is that home-office

Anderson is urging missionaries in Hawaii to *do right* and voluntarily hand over some power to native Hawaiians.)

You can observe the missionaries are saying one thing while doing another. Missionaries resigned right and left from being missionaries to go into politics and business and by 1845, "only one fourth of men in cabinet posts had any Hawaiian blood."

We get a clue as to missionary status when the Maka ainana (people)[108] petitioned for the removal of the ABCFM (missionary) dominated cabinet in 1845. The Hawaiian people wanted those missionaries out of there! The alii (Kings) had learned to trust the missionaries but the people knew better. Worse was to come.

I live on an interesting tropical island. Tired last night, I go to sleep quite early. Woke wide awake in the night, turned on my bedside lamp, thank goodness, (sometimes I pad about barefoot in the dark) ready to climb from my little bed on the floor against the wall. As movement catches my eye, I glance down to a four or five inch long crawling dark centipede on the floor. I yelp, but there's no one to hear. It was always Thomas's job to take care of the bugs, and creatures. Now there's no one and I'm scared. One of these centipedes bit me before, smaller, and the bite hurt like fire.

Getting my broom and sweeping this thing out crosses my scared thoughts. But what if the creature crawls under my bed while I'm gone and I can't find it? Or into my bed covers now flung helter shelter? What to do with the evil crawling thing now waving antler-like protrusions? It's all I can do not to scream.

One minute asleep. The next confronted by this thousand-legged insect with poisonous jaws. Suppose I hadn't waked up? And it crawled … I, for sure, don't want to think about this. My solution hits suddenly and completely. A wonderful small thick oriental rug Thomas bought me as a gift lies to one side of my room. Grabbing the edge of the blue patterned rug, I thrust it over the creature and stomp on it. This is terrific. I can almost breathe easy.

I lift the rug. But the insect still wiggles. Quickly replacing my rug I stomp as hard as I can like stomping grapes for wine. When I lift the blue rug this time the creature is mush and so am I. Holding my breath, as fast as I can, I seize old newspaper. With my hands full length away from my body, I gather centipede remains and deposit them outside. As I pull the rug back in place, I try to remove the crawly creature from my mind.

Things happen, I philosophize to myself. Wonderful to dig in the garden, carry trash and leaves in my arms with nary a worry of snakes. No snakes in Hawaii. I can put my feet and hands in piles of limbs and discarded garden clippings. Never a worry. (I'll be a lot more careful now.) Except for centipedes and they only tend to come in the house in the rain my next door neighbor tells me.[109]

I take action. Closing my eyes, taking deep breaths, I focus mental powers and broadcast in all directions: *Extreme Danger. All bugs and crawly creatures: roaches, spiders, ants, centipedes, geckos. This is hazardous territory. Off-limits. You will die. Do not venture into this house. Off limits. Death.*

Then I search out my trusty *Harris Famous Roach Tablets*, clean and simple tablets of mostly borax which quietly desiccates creatures who eat them, and I put out new tablets, especially around my bed. And I don't remind the creatures that I capture geckos and granddaddy spiders in small kitchen towels before releasing them outside. I've always hated bugs in the house and seldom find them.

Some of the new GMO fertility studies in animals would curl your straight hair. And we're eating that stuff! Would we, if we had a choice? I don't think so. Remember that Obama promised mandatory labeling of GMO's in his campaign? Where is this labeling? I went to a couple of websites for more information and education. Amazing treasures on the web but sometimes I get so angry and disheartened.[110]

A Look At Prejudice and Hawaiian History at a Critical Time. Unspoken during this time of early missionaries is the terrible prejudice, a covert total belief in so-called *white* superiority, along with its unthinking claims to privilege. Haole Hawaiian businessmen, convinced they and their ways are superexcellent, have no problem taking what they can get anyway they can get it.

Slaves were literally owned in the U.S. at this time—mid 1850s. Our Civil War was still in the future. As was a plaque in 2010 placed in Congress commemorating U.S. slaves who built the place—a small recent attempt at some restitution.

"The Great Mahele of 1848—the great partitioning of lands—was adopted during Kamehameha Three's time and forever changed Hawaii's traditional land tenure system, and the social landscape of the islands."[111]

Rapid growth of the sugar industry (mostly U.S.) in the 1870s put the plantation owners (mostly missionary connected) front and center. When Hawaiians refused that terrible work in the sugar fields (Just wait till you see later enlightening immigration statistics from *The Peopling of Hawai'i*), the sugar planters started importing contract laborers by the tens of thousands—which radically changes the population. The foreign laborers were single men; many married Hawaiian women. Although you can't say it was exactly planned for this outcome, it is another way of stealing the land. And Hawaiian heritage—bring in a bunch of new people and dilute the native Hawaiian population.

In 1887, foreigners and missionaries presented King Kalakaua with a new constitution and demanded he sign, *The Bayonet Constitution*. The monarch was reduced to a ceremonial leader.

By 1890, the 40,623 Hawaiians were a bare plurality of the total of 89,900. Remember when Captain Cook came Hawaiians numbered approximately 500,000 or more. "The alliance between the Hawaiian ruling class and the mission families began to come apart."

"In 1893, a small group made up primarily of American businessmen and some Christian missionary descendants conspired to overthrow the Hawaiian monarchy."[112]

By now Queen Liliuokalani (sister of the deceased King Kalkaua) is determined to replace the Bayonet Constitution. But the U.S. Minister John Stevens landed U.S. troops, positioned them alongside the Government

Building on January 16th, and "on January 17, 1893, the revolutionists read their proclamation establishing the provisional government and imposed martial law."

Now there's much going back and forth with Hawaiians on the losing side: Queen Liliuokalani is imprisoned in her own Iolani Palace and forced to abdicate her throne. The U.S. President Grover Cleveland declared a "substantial wrong has thus been done which a due regard for our national character as well as the rights of the injured people requires we should endeavor to repair." Cleveland was calling for a restoration of Hawaiian monarchy. Petitions notwithstanding, and the Spanish-American war of 1898, "the U.S. moved to annex the islands by a Joint Resolution of Congress"—which remains controversial among Hawaiian groups."[113]

My thoughts are set on fire by the substance of *Celebrating Advocacy*. Here's an institution (the church) admitting it did wrong (supporting the overthrow of the legal Hawaiian government), and now, years later, attempting to make some restitution. *Way too little, way too late*, I'm thinking.

In my dream I'm married—husband not clear, but definitely not Thomas. Or Kevin. Perhaps an Americanized Kaimana? One child. My dream husband and I always wanted children. We come home to live. My father (or father-in-law, not clear) is a university professor having a seminar in the house and I am attending. I had a place on a couch, but I'd left and when I return someone else has taken it. I am fine with that. In the meantime, before the seminar starts, I decide to clean up and to take care of things nobody else has had time to do. The car, a really nice expensive one, has its manual, its spare tire and tools missing and, to help the family, I decide to get them replaced. My father (father-in-law) is a nice man. Professor. He likes me. I drive the car to a neighbor's with my mother-in-law; I have warm feelings for her also and she approves of me. I look into the open lighted living-room and like the house. Full of books, lights, happy. At the house we drive to, I will call the mechanic, a rather difficult man to deal with. This is when I wake up.

But at some point in the dream, I'm back where I now live and even talk with my dream daughter that I like this move—that it's nice being around family. I won't be lonely. I count up the people. The house is arranged for several generations and when I'm there I'm happy and useful and approved of—loved. I'm loved! I gave myself a nice family, a happy circumstance. Pleasant. Wish fulfillment. Like the Hawaiians, aloha, accepting everyone. I choose to put things in order, but no huge deal over doing it immediately. I looked forward to and was delighted to be attending the seminar. Asking who all would be there. I was happy. Pleased. This was a good move.

The dream was quite detailed. My yearning and need for companionship was satisfied. I wasn't lonely any more. An ideal family for me. I fitted in. I was wanted and loved and was not self-conscious.

I can give myself any feelings, anything I like or need! There's my in-the-past-not-being-okay on the one side—or of sufficiency, competence and completeness on the other side. This is my dream message. I have warm happy, fulfilled feelings. I am not lacking. I have, already, whatever I need. I am enough. I am capable, strong, sufficient. I can do whatever I want. I have support while I do my present work of writing about Princess Ruth.

This is another chance to start over with renewed enthusiasm and vigor and hope. I am what I think and do. I define myself and keep on defining myself. Another variety of *If no one else gives me value, then I give it to myself!* Something I told myself long ago when I was having an especially hard time.

So I don't need to hassle with my overburdened, too-much-to-do-life. But instead I can get my thinking, feeling and evolving self busy living this one as I like. Fulfilling my best self while doing work I was meant to do. Action. Action.

And, while I'm soul searching, I can admit how I've been running, refusing any but necessary contacts with my present boss and old lover, Kevin. How I haven't returned a phone call from Kaimana. That's dumb. I don't need to run away, or have any divided loyalties. How fascinating to have one part of yourself (dreams from the unconscious) giving reassuring information to your consciousness (your daily life and hopes and goals).

Making Pono: Wrongs and Restoration. What does it mean to do the right thing, and to clear old wrongs? Restoration, redress, doing the right thing concerning old wrongs, inevitably involves making sacrifices. Will we make the sacrifices ourselves and actually take part individually in the restorative solution of making things pono? Or will we simply calculate what others *should* do?

A first step in this process of clearing means admitting wrong was done and that *we're* responsible. I guess it also means admitting that we are our government and then taking responsibility for the actions of our government.

This is a large rock to swallow. We are small cogs; too many of us don't even bother to vote or to inform ourselves politically. And then too often, unless it's in our own backyard, something that directly affects our self-interest, we haven't a clue, even about local government. *They*, the government, and the people who actually run things, are out there in the foggy distance somewhere doing their thing, while we go about our oblivious, self-centered lives.

To right ancient wrongs means we tilt at windmills—a futile even silly activity.

But wait just a minute.

Suppose you are one of the wronged, the discriminated against, the battered wife or child or husband. Suppose you are the Indian living on a reservation, locked in the evils of poverty while *your* government steals your oil and mineral money—looting your legal birthright for years.

Suppose, closer to home, you are the native Hawaiian caught in the unfair and horribly frustrating discrimination of being marginalized in your own *stolen* nation? How galling is that, and maybe you don't even consciously know your own outstanding history?

Suppose that you are one to whom injustice, large and small, rankles. *Might* does not make *right* to you. You never enjoy sticking your head in the sand or calling a spade anything but a very definite spade. Suppose, with John Donne that no man or woman is an island but that all deserve to enjoy the same rights to life, liberty, and the pursuit of happiness that you have.

Suppose you vaguely understand your motivation for justice, barely getting it that wrongs and injustices hold you personally in negativity—that something in you rebels against accepting gain on the backs of the wronged—such wrongs and injustices make you feel ashamed and diminished. You get it that old wrongs are burdens, shackles, guilty threads around your heart that yearns to be free —whether or not you actually did those particular wrongs, for, of course, you probably did not.

Are you your Brother's and Sister's keeper?

Suppose you do actually feel diminished when others are mistreated and gravely wronged. Suppose you fiercely love your way of life for the personal freedom it has afforded you, and that equally forcefully you want your government to live up to its highest ideals. For after all what is government but a collection of us? And when your government has done wrong—stolen, cheated, lied, taken unfair advantage, spends your taxes in wrong ways—you want our government to stop the erroneous behavior, and to apologize for past transgressions. And, further, to make restoration, redress, to make right, to make pono, the unfortunate situation as it has now come to exist.

"Impossible," you cry, "too complicated. No one could ever bring righteousness to this situation." *This situation* being the historical unfair treatment of the Hawaiian people and stealing their nation.

"When the missionaries arrived, they were emphatic that traditional Hawaiian religion, dance, chants, dress, customs were incompatible with Christian beliefs.... Hawaiian church members quietly grieved, not only over the loss of Hawaiian life, land, culture, and self-governance, but also over the conference's [church's] betrayal of Hawaiian trust," says Sheldon Ito. Ito adds that Queen Liliuokalani, near the end of her reign, felt so betrayed she vowed never to go to church again.

Sheldon Ito's *Yes* article about the Hawaiian church's restoration, says that in 1997 (process started in 1991) Dr. Paul Sherry (President of the 1.7 million member United Church of Christ) made an Apology to the Hawaiian people; a service of Apology, confession, forgiveness, reconciliation, and commitment to redress was held and money and property has changed hands.[114]

Taking a break for hot Earl Grey Lavender tea, I sit at my kitchen counter. It's late but I couldn't be more wide awake. Somewhere I read that the cultivation of appreciation for the smallest things in your life will give you the greatest results. The lavender scent from my tea is pleasantly refreshing.

As I've watched my emotions run from bliss to sorrow and back again, the stability of my old married life is appealing. But values change and what I used to admire is no longer alluring. Lately I'm seeing choices as pearls on a gold string. Better choices, better life. In this state of mind it's simple and easy. Choices brought me here; choices will take me where I want to go.

And I'm also giving myself an out by deciding that the only one who really needs to see you is you. Or, better said, the only one who really needs to see me is me which means that I don't have to tell everything to everybody. And that not only can I practice discernment, if I want to keep my job, I'd probably better! Still I know that nothing else matters except what you do with your very being.

Lately, whenever it occurs to me I repeat a new mantra: *I shower myself with bliss, growth, and gratitude.* Somehow I'm quite sure of Princess Ruth's approval.

Yet constant struggle leaves us tired and empty. Our struggle for reform needs to be tempered and balanced with a capacity for celebration. When we lose sight of beauty our struggle becomes tired and functional. When we expect and engage the Beautiful, a new fluency is set free within us and between us. The heart becomes rekindled and our lives brighten with unexpected courage. It is courage that restores hope to the heart.... Courage is amazing because it can tap into the heart of fear, taking that frightened energy and turning it towards initiative, creativity, action and hope.... There are secret sources of courage inside every human heart.

John O'Donohue, Beauty: The Invisible Embrace

CHAPTER NINE

"OUR TIME IS PAST."

"What do you mean? We've got our whole lives ahead." Moving his arm in a hard gesture, Kevin is incredulous.

I sigh. This conversation is inevitable. I might as well have it and be over, hope I still have a job.

"All right, Kevin." The breath I take goes all the way to my toes. "I want more."

"More? More? What the Devil are you talking about? Marriage? A stable and secure future? My solemn promise to be faithful forever? This isn't enough for you?" He covers my right hand with his. "I'm getting a promotion to the home office in St. Louis. In charge of all GMO field trials worldwide. I've waited to tell you until I was sure." His nose and chin seem to come to a point; his voice turns petulant. "I thought we'd celebrate."

As he struggles seeking more words, I pull my hand free. "You wouldn't have to work," he adds.

As I remain silent, just wanting this conversation to be over, he bestows his fond look, and says with pride, "I'll take care of everything."

"Kevin, that's just it," I break in. "I don't want you taking care of everything." Looking into tall palms blowing gently into a light breeze, it's my turn to search for sincere words. "I'm not expedient," I say slowly thinking it out as I go. "Out to make the best deal for myself. I appreciate what you offer. And you're right in a way. The American dream. Onward and upward. More and more. I've lived that dream as blindly faithful as anyone. Not asking questions. And even when I did question, not believing I could do anything to change the status quo.

"Well, Kevin," I lean forward. Fiercely, I want him to understand. "I don't believe that way anymore. That companies and individuals have the right to use killing chemicals any way they choose. Poison the land for generations to come. I don't think that nature, the land is ours to dominate. We humans are here to learn to live in harmony with nature. The Hawaiians had the right idea."

I pause, thinking my way as I go along, "Somewhere along the line I'm learning to use my energy for myself. In service to things that matter to me like environment and sustainability. Caring about people. About this blessed island of Kauai. Each person does make a difference. We must."

Suddenly the strong presence of Princess Ruth is almost palpable. Her mana is empowering. Her presence is as huge as her spirit. "Kevin," I burst out, "I'm not leaving Kauai. My home is here now."

"You've found someone else! The coconut wireless is correct for once. You're seeing a musician. A local," he adds scornfully. "That's what is going on. You've fallen for fake charm. I heard stories. But I didn't believe such a thing about you." His pause stretches out like time gone bad. "It's okay," he adds almost as an afterthought to himself. "We'll move to St. Louis. Forget the past. Leave it behind. Both of us. Begin fresh in a new place."

"Kevin." I pause for long seconds to get his full attention. "No."

"I know you. You'll come to your senses. You're just confused." He grabs both my hands as I struggle to free myself.

"Kevin. Listen to me. I have spoiled things in the past by not speaking when I should. You—for your part—wrecked us with your betrayal and lies."

I've pulled my hands free and moved back a step. His eyes are eager. "So that's it. You're still harping on that old mistake." He is quiet for a moment and then pounces. "You can't forget."

"Kevin," I hear the patience in my voice and wonder if he does, "ever notice, when someone is dishonest in a relationship, how they can't simply say, *I was wrong. Please tell me how I can fix it?*"

"I was stupid. And wrong. How can I make it right?"

"Here's where we came in, Kevin. It's too late. We're over." In that moment I am a free butterfly emerging from a too tight cocoon. I can afford to be kind. "But a new job, Kevin. A promotion. Hey, that's great. I wish you nothing but the best."

The world so often chooses a dark hour to give us a blessing. Today, when I need it so badly, I find exactly what I require—heart words, and the thrill of another expressing my own feelings.

> Many of us find ourselves being powerfully drawn to Kauai, sometimes without reasonable explanation and sometimes for a variety of known reasons. We may come on vacation to rest and replenish ourselves, swim and surf, bask in the sun and listen to the language of the sea, walk in blessing rain, fish, hike and kayak. We may move here to establish a safe, happy and passionate way of life, whether to start a new business venture or in retirement. We may come to clarify ourselves, to shed stressful layers of fast-paced living by immersing ourselves in nature and natural things. We may come to embrace our spiritual selves, or to give ourselves—our interests and knowledge and talents—to the island…. What better place than an island of such dramatic beauty and friendly people?[115]

This early Friday morning rises like an accusation. In the company lot before work, Barbara drives up and parks beside me. She looks preoccupied.

Getting out quickly she hands me a package and says, "Throw this in your truck." A worried look crosses her face. "Better not open it until tonight when you're home."

"Wow, it's heavy." Taking her gift and instructions, I toss the object on my empty truck seat. "What is it, lead or another book?"

"You'll see," is Barbara's cryptic reply.

As we enter the main Purity building, before separating for our places of employment, Barbara heads outside to the seed-sorting shed. Today, I'm in the office where I need to write a speech. This necessary task thrills me about as much as you can imagine. I hate it and the thought of actually giving a speech turns my bones into soft jelly. But, I think, *money is a powerful motivator*, as I gather up written materials praising Purity and GMO companies. *I can't wait to stop worrying so much about finances.*

By the time I get home that night I'm in a fine mood, ready to eat nails for dinner and old flip-flops for dessert. Thinking about flip-flops, I remind myself to call them *slippers* as the locals do. Grabbing a glass of my current Merlot (Ménage a Trois and why the name makes me smile I don't know) and Barbara's package I head for a garden-sitting area I've begun putting together. I relax a bit feeling the chair's comfort fold about me. I sip the wine, put my feet on the low table and admire my blooming green-with-red-center orchids. I might as well live, at least until tomorrow.

Sighing—was this what life would be like from now on—I wonder, why am I being such an idiot about Kaimana? Why haven't I been able to return his phone calls?

I open Barbara's package. Draw a sharp breath. The book is bright red with standout white lettering: *Genetic Roulette: The Documented Health Risks of Genetically Engineered Foods*, by Jeffrey M. Smith. *What's this?* I think, my blood running a little cold. I've seen some of this material before on the internet. But not this book. *Barbara is telling me something. Do I want to hear it?*

Well, no. At the moment I don't wish to pay attention to anything that requires brain cells, anything I'll have to think about. After rewrapping the book and placing it face down on the grass, I take several swallows of wine. I admire my orchids some more, deciding I really do love these plants—without doubt, orchids are my favorite flowers. When my glass is empty, I get another, and while I'm at it, the rest of the bottle, some Irish white cheddar and wheat crackers. I take my treasures back outside, where *Genetic Roulette* stares accusingly through its wrappings.

As the red wine disappears and the evening languishes into darkness, I relax further into my chair scooting down and resting my head against the chair's high back.

Well, says the voice in my head, a bit sarcastically, I think—*fading out already, are we? Can't take reality?*

Give it a rest, I tell Princess Ruth, sitting up straight as a board. I am downhearted, belligerent and half drunk, not a good combination for anyone.

I can see the Princess plain as day. She wears her purple muumuu with white oleander leis. She sits across from me overflowing the sides of her chair.

No. I can't rest, the Princess says. A wild grin I'd never have believed possible splits her face as she adds in a commanding voice that booms in my ears, *Keep it up. You will have success.*

Awestruck, but it seems natural at the time, I humbly ask, *What can I do? I'm only one person.* I know I've had too much to drink. The Princess is probably a huge figment of my imagination.

Princess Ruth looks at me, peers straight into my eyes—and deeper. The wisdom of the universe is in her face and her truth is expanding. Love, certainly. Forgiveness possibly. A scatter of retribution. Oceans of care for her people and Hawaii, but more than anything, the depth of her love and forgiveness are almost beyond my comprehension.

I sense a vortex of power with a center of diamond purpose honed laser-sharp over the eons. Moving so slowly I am mesmerized, Princess Ruth raises both hands—now holding out flowers—in a benediction. *Find your truth. Tell our Hawaiian truth.*

Next thing I know I am alone in my back yard saying like a mantra: *Find my truth. Tell our truth.*

I stare in wonder at my left hand—holding one oleander blossom— slowly, slowly fading as I watch in amazement.

Begin where you are. Where I am is hung over on a Saturday morning, drinking coffee and nibbling wheat toast until my stomach settles. I don't feel too good. It helps not at all that I have only myself to blame. I decide not to beat myself over the head but to get on with the next task in front of me: taking a searching look at last night's *Genetic Roulette*. Princess Ruth wants me to look for truth, well here's a good place to explore. With coffee and toast, I pick up the book and settle in my garden chair.

Later, quotes from the book hang in my mind: "The gene-manipulators claim they can foresee the evolutionary results of their artificial transposing of human genes into sheep, bovine genes into tomatoes, altered bacterial genes into eggplant, etc. But such claims are a reflection more of arrogance than of scientific analysis."[116]

"While the public was fed a steady barrage of revised, updated, and reworked regulatory guidelines, giving the appearance of rigorous scientific oversight, the insurance industry quietly let it be known that it would not insure the release of genetically engineered organisms into the environment against the possibility of catastrophic environmental damage."[117]

Talk about learning more than you want to know. I've got to get out of here. No doubt about it: resign my job at Purity. My head is pounding like ten drums gone crazy. No matter how small, I can't, with any kind of conscience at all, continue to be a part of these lies perpetuated upon the public. This is disaster waiting to happen. Or already happening. *What is fueling our obesity epidemic?* runs through my jumbled thoughts. It's so scary to think that GMOs are at the bottom of it. And that all Purity cares about is bottom line profits. I don't want to be here. But I am. I feel so helpless. So alone.

Still making my skin crawl, "Glufosinate-tolerant crops may produce herbicide "inside" our intestines …. the data obtained strongly suggest that the balance of gut bacteria will be affected, that the wellbeing of the feeding host will be affected."[118] The *feeding host* is me. My stomach being turned into a pesticide factory! No wonder I feel queasy. My friends and I and the people of the world are eating this stuff.

Only heaven knows what these artificially constructed GMOs do to our bodies. Doesn't anybody care?

Princess Ruth and Hawaiian history offer refuge from mind-numbing GMO information. "It is impossible," I read, "to take seriously the candidacy of Princess Ruth, one of the richest and fattest women in the kingdom. Her Gargantuan frame and coarse features, as depicted in various old prints, leave an impression of overwhelming and immovable mass. She could neither speak nor understand English. Her accession to the throne undoubtedly would have led to political madness."[119]

My outrage builds slowly. *Yeah,* I think, *the Princess was smart enough to see through your missionary self-serving lies. No wonder you wanted her kept out of ruling power.*

Do you really think Princess Ruth didn't read and understand English as she, reportedly, not only attended the Chief's Children's School,[120] but she held on to, and added to, her vast land holdings—and was Governor of Hawaii's largest island for twenty years?

I'm in Honolulu to attend a Quaker camping retreat and I've stayed an extra day to experience Princess Ruth's place of burial. First is the long bus ride from Waikiki in Honolulu to the Royal Mausoleum on Nuuanu's Mauna Ala (Fragrant Mountain) where all the Kamehamehas are buried, except for two: Kamehameha One, ("His bones were buried secretly, according to ancient custom, and are concealed to this day.")[121] and the last Kamehameha, King Lunalilo, buried, at his request, in a Christian churchyard.

On his deathbed, he requested a burial at Kawaiahao Church, with his mother on the church's ground. He wanted, he said, to be "entombed among (my) people, rather than the kings and chiefs" at the Royal Mausoleum in Nuuanu Valley. This was due to a feud between Lunalilo and the Kamehameha family over his mother Miriam Auhea Kekauluohi's exclusion from the list of royalty to be buried there. Thus, in 1875, he was taken from the Mausoleum to the church. During this procession, eyewitness reports stated that a sudden storm arose, and that twenty-one rapid thunderclaps echoed across Honolulu which came to be known as the "21-gun salute." [122]

High and windy and still powerful, greatness hangs in the air over this hill. Loneliness is an underlying motif; I feel the sadness. The main Chapel closed, I turn right and walk past slow workmen. The above-ground tomb says: *Charles Bishop.* Immediately, I want to ask, *What's he doing here?* As far as I'm concerned Charles Bishop's main accomplishment was marrying High Chiefess Bernice Pauahi and inheriting her vast wealth, most of which came from Princess Ruth. Bishop with a tomb of his own in this sacred place of the Kamehamehas? Why, except for ambition, vanity, money and power? All of which took him mighty high, so who am I to scoff?

Where are the last physical remains of Princess Ruth? She is the reason I'm here. I've read of the funeral possession of Princess Ruth's casket, with hordes of mourning people. The richest woman in Hawaii, beloved by the common folk, she was the last woman admitted to the House of Nobles before American businessmen shut Hawaiian Chiefesses (and the Hawaiians) out of power simply because they were women and the businessmen wanted their power. Or were Black (Negro) to the white men of power. Remember this is before our Civil War. Black people were slaves. Women couldn't vote. White moneyed men ran the world.

Hugely tall royal palms blow gracefully in the ever-present almost mournful wind. Deep in my mind I'm calling out to the Princess as I retrace my path to the side of the mausoleum. Steps lead down to a locked grill through which gold embellishments shine. Straining against the grillwork, over to the side, I see Princess Ruth's name. She's here with many minor players of Hawaiian royalty but this is the closest I can get to her. The Chapel is closed for repairs.

The gold inside the locked crypt shines brightly but something is not right. I sit on the bottom step in what feels like dampness but isn't. I close my eyes and my next task arrives like an obsession: *Go to the Bishop Museum.*

Several bus rides and an hour or two later, I'm at the Bishop Museum. The young male Hawaiian ticket taker is friendly and pleasant with almost black eyes and dreadlocks. "I want to see the Princess Ruth Keelikolani artifacts."

"Third floor of the red brick main Museum," he smiles and tells me, "third floor on the right."

There's a hanging whale in the open middle of the Hawaiian exhibit and a complete outrigger canoe. Then, over to the side, skimped in a small exhibit are an astonishingly few treasures attributed to Ruth or Luka Keelikolani. And again one of the few dreadful pictures of her. Nothing when she was young and beautiful, and not much of her real accomplishments except being Governor of the Big Island of Hawaii for twenty years.

My outrage increases as I look around. Princess Ruth's wealth surely built this place. And she's over in a small corner with practically nothing written or exhibited here to show how great she was? History is unfair. All through the ages—I'm ready to scream— and it's the same here, another powerful woman's accomplishments diminished and forgotten.

That night as I close my eyes, I call on Princess Ruth to help me. A night bird cries and I feel time and space fade between us. Something intangible connects across the years as I thank her and ask her to continue to help me ferret out and tell her true story. Then I again thank Princess Ruth for guarding her precious islands of Hawaii, her people, and for extending her blessings to me.

Midnight, back on Kauai and I'm roaming the internet again. Important research coming out of Hawaii? Here I am as prejudiced as anyone but proud too that we make it into the *Scientific American*.[123]

Read it and weep, I think realizing that here is real evidence to back up my gut feelings about fast foods.

Headlines are: *By tracing the unique chemical signature of corn, scientists have shown that most of the meat in fast food is raised on corn.* And: *As much as 93 percent of the carbon in a fast food hamburger can be traced back to corn, with its attendant environmental impacts.*[124]

In this easy-to-read article, the long and short is that looking at the "chemical composition of more than 480 fast-food burgers from across the nation," the researchers were able to track a signature marker of corn" and deduce that while we poor suckers trying to save money and time by eating what we think is healthy fast-food meat we are really eating corn! Mostly GMO corn and so we get a double dose of toxins.[125]

Our fast food hamburgers are 93 percent corn. How bizarre is this?

Ghost, apparition, what? Occasionally it dawns on me that our English language, being patriarchal, has entire areas, so far mostly female-spiritual, that simply aren't named very well. As I look up *apparition* I find spirit, specter, phantom, ghoul, vision. *Ghoul* is out right away—sounds scary; this was not. *Specter*, maybe as I did feel a participation from the *spirit?* Yet *specter* also sounds a bit scary. *Ghost* is too Haloweenish. *Phantom* is sort of *Phantom of the Opera* and no way did I feel that. I'm left with neutral *apparition* or *spirit* and I think spirit. The figure felt friendly; I'd like to meet it again actually. Ask it some questions! *Has it a message? What does it want?*

Here's what happened. Just at the door of my bedroom—looking in at me—in bed, which directly faces the door, was a male figure. It was facing left but seemed to be drifting right. No, the more I think, the figure looked straight at me and then drifted or faded out of sight to my right. He was dressed in a luminous red and yellow shirt hanging out over white pants and I think his hair was blond. I didn't recognize him. I felt no hint of scared but almost startled. He faded quickly but I never had any doubt that he wasn't solid matter. Light was shining through and from him as if each cell held a separate life force.

A guardian? I wondered who he could be: someone who died here? Or am I inventing a companion because I'm lonely? It bothers me to be on-the-outs with Kaimana. I badly wanted to see where we could go as a couple.

This is the first time in my adult life anything like this spirit has ever appeared to me. Perhaps as a child. I don't remember. I've a notion that Princess Ruth is changing my perception of reality. What is reality anyway? This experience was real to me while it was happening.

Genetically Modified Hawaii catches my attention, another *Scientific American* article—*New varieties of genetically engineered crops thrive in the world's most isolated landmass:*[126]

Just beyond the defunct Koloa Sugar Mill on the Hawaiian island of Kauai's south shore are acres of cornfields that have sprouted over the past decade in a state made famous by its pineapples, bananas and sugarcane crops. Slightly out of place in the Aloha State, they otherwise look quite conventional, although in fact they are not: The crop is among a bounty of others in the state that are grown from seeds that have been genetically engineered or modified (GMO) to produce sturdier plants able to withstand weather and disease as well as thrive in the face of insects and chemicals sprayed on them to kill destructive weeds.

In front of one plot of corn stalks is a red and white sign warning, "Danger: pesticides. Keep out." Tacked to it is a list containing 15 chemicals that may have been applied to the crop. In this case, the chemicals circled are the herbicides pendimethalin (brand name: Prowl), dicamba (Banvel) and atrazine, the latter of which is banned in the European Union (E.U.) because of its link to birth defects in frogs that live in groundwater contaminated with it....[127]

The extraordinary biodiversity (and, so, native plants competing for space and nutrients), along with the intractable problem of invasive species would seem to make Hawaii the least likely place to grow controversial crops, risking their uncontrollable spread. But seed companies and some scientists believe the benefits outweigh the risks of damage to the fragile ecosystem, most notably Hawaii's crop-friendly moderate year-round climate—an average of 75 degrees Fahrenheit (24 degrees Celsius)—and its open acreage. And over the past 10 years, Hawaii has become the locus for genetically modified crop field trials and a microcosm for the controversies over the safety of growing and eating transgenic food.

To date, Hawaii's fertile soil has nourished more than 2,230 field trials of genetically modified (GM) crops, including corn, soybeans, cotton, potatoes, wheat, alfalfa, beets, rice, safflower, and sorghum—more than any other state. A total of 4,800 acres [much higher figures now] (1,940 hectares) of such crops now grow throughout the state, some 3,500 (1,415) of which are corn and soybeans, 1,000 acres (405 hectares) of which yield genetically engineered papaya, and the remaining 10 percent are field trials for new potential GM crops. "Hawaii is ideally suited for field trials and seed production, because of the climate and the ability to grow corn and soybeans 52 weeks a year," says Cindy Goldstein, a spokesperson for Johnston, Ia.–based Pioneer Hi-Bred International (a subsidiary of DuPont Chemical) in Waimea, Kauai. Her company has been producing GM corn and soybeans in Hawaii since the mid-1990's, when the FDA approved the crops for commercial sale.[128]

Such an odd happening. At midnight I'm crying in my back yard—lately, I seem to live out here. Not loud, but tears slide down my cheeks as I half-heartedly work to banish feeling sorry for myself. I've got it so much better than so many. Who am I to moan?

Yet I'm not living the life I want—not that I know exactly what that life is. Thoughts of Kaimana try to break through but I'm too depressed. Tonight the weight of a treacherous and betraying world crouches on my shoulders, troubles my heart. I feel deep-down sorrow, the *I'm Helpless In A Technological World Gone Mad* kind of pain. The *I Can't Effect Any Change* brand of hopelessness. I'm tempted to resign from life, to try a different living in kinder times or in a more caring universe.

Just when I can't sink into any more doom and gloom, vague thoughts in my head become clear. *I understand,* agrees Princess Ruth. *I'll send you help.*

"I can't sleep either." It's my next door neighbor who ignores my tears as she puts her tray on the table and hands me a tiny cup of hot tea she's poured from a darling glass teapot. "It's chocolate tea," she says, "and it's wonderful. Made from the bark of the chocolate tree, if you can believe. Expensive. Ten dollars for two tea bags but I've found a place in Hanapepe that's much cheaper." Sighing, I smell the chocolate tea—a world that holds a new angel and hot chocolate tea at midnight can't be all bad.

"You know," she says, "I work with the mentally distressed. We have a house where they live together under supervision. I've been trying something new lately. Not officially. They'd replace me in a New York minute with a normal person if they knew. But," she leans confidentially forward, "do you know of Hawaiian hooponopono?[129] Where you go to the root and fix old wrongs and concerns?"

"Sort of," I say as I kick GMOs, evil corporations, greed-heads (as a friend calls them) and Kevin out of my thoughts. Since our last conversation and really since I met Kaimana, whatever else is going on, Kevin is emotional toast. I think instead of the newspaper story I'd read of the Hawaiian therapist who made the decision to try this hooponopono method all by himself on his entire ward of mentally ill criminals. The story went that Dr. Hew Len, concentrating on one prisoner after another, doing hooponopono by himself, had emptied his prison ward. A happening you only wish were true—an urban legend, probably. Except later on the internet Dr. Hew Len's[130] story checks out.

"Sometimes my clients are bloody pains to deal with," my neighbor says, "I have to center back in myself." In the half light from my house, she glances at my cup and pours more tea. The tiny cup feels kind in my hands, delicate. Elegance strolls into our space with our impromptu tea party. My mood reverses its downward spiral. I am vaguely interested as she adds in a soft voice, "The version of hooponopono that came to me has five simple steps:

     1. Forgive me.

     2. I'm sorry.

     3. I surrender

4. I love you.

5. Thank you.

"For each of the first three steps, I tap three times on three points on my face. I go in a circle like this." She demonstrates by tapping between her eyes (the third eye) and saying three times, "Forgive me." Then tapping the outside corner of her left eye, she intones, "I'm sorry." Then tapping the bottom center of her left eye, she says, "I surrender," three times. Next she taps three times on her center chest saying, "I love you. I love you. I love you." Last, holding her hands finger-tip to finger-tip three or four inches in front of her chin, she says, "Thank you. Thank you. Thank you." Pausing, she urges, "Try it. Think of a situation or a person causing you pain."

"That's no problem," I say visualizing my dead husband, Thomas, and tapping between my eyes. "I forgive you. I forgive you. I forgive you," I say quickly remembering how with death, Thomas had turned out so differently from what I'd expected. What secrets did he carry to his untimely death? A quick thought crosses my mind of Tomas's Chinese box of childhood treasures. I have yet to bring myself to go through this box. Soon.

"Not, *I forgive you*, but, *Forgive me*." My midnight neighbor laughs. "Move past the blame game," she suggests. "*Forgive me*. You're asking forgiveness for your part in your shared story."

"Forgive me. Forgive me. Forgive me." Tapping along with my words I'm almost lighthearted. *Forgive me*. Well, nobody is perfect. I could possibly have done one or two things in our married relationship that weren't perfection. Moving my hand to my left eye corner, I say, "I'm sorry. I'm sorry. I'm sorry." Hard barriers begin releasing.

Tapping under my left eye, the point for fear and neediness, as my neighbor later explains, I say almost reluctantly, "I surrender, I surrender, I surrender." And then I get it, I'm surrendering to process, to life, to reality, to what will be, will be. And to the fact that I don't have to run the world. What a relief!

I tap my sternum, "I love you. I love you. I love you." And finally, "Thank you. Thank you. Thank you," I conclude aloud with finger tips touching while my thoughts carry on: *Thank you Thomas for our wonderful years together. Thank you for loving me. Thank you for cups of morning coffee in bed, late night backrubs when I couldn't sleep, financial worries you saved me from. Thank you, Thomas. Oh thank you.*

And Thank you, Princess Ruth, I intone in silent prayer. *Bless you and sleep well. Your ancient wrongs will get a new hearing. I'll do my best to finish your book,* I promise silently and recklessly. *And get your book to people who need to see it.*

My eyes fill again with tears but these are from caring heavenly love, and from simple human kindness.

"The chants and hula, most of which had been passed from generation to generation for centuries, were forbidden; a suppression that would prove catastrophic for the Hawaiians. The chants contained everything a person needed to know about the world; it was a way to worship the gods, to call warriors to battle, to mourn a king, to court a lover, to celebrate the birth of a child. Each successive generation, listening and memorizing learned to be Hawaiian."[131] Everyone was expected to remember ten generations back. The top alii could go back even further.[132]

I keep being surprised at underlying health benefits of ritual Hawaiian practices. This time it's about how healthy chanting is for you.

"Chanting rituals have been part of cultures around the world seemingly forever—from Western churches where worshippers repeat *alleluia* to eastern temples where yogis end their practice with a long exhalation of *ohm.*"[133] This modern author adds that now contemporary medical researchers are demonstrating that even the simplest forms of chanting are remarkably good for our health.

Let me count Robert Gass's ways: 1, chanting boosts levels of nitric acid, which relaxes smooth muscles in arteries and aids in blood flow, including to the brain. This helps bring mental clarity and focus. 2, chanting enhances the flow of cerebrospinal fluid, therefore stimulating the organs and bones as well as the frontal lobes of the brain. 3, chanting can provide cognitive benefits of meditation without the stillness required and 4, chanting can serve as an opportunity to repeat and reinforce affirmations such as *I am at peace* or *Life is good* or whatever has personal meaning to you at the moment.

Robert Gass tells how he used this chanting technique when battling a life-threatening melanoma a number of years ago. Several times each day, every day, he chanted the words *I choose life*, an affirmation that he says helped him endure the rigors of treatment and strengthen his courage.

And keep him alive, I add to myself vowing that the next time Hawaiian chanting is offered by a kumu, I'm going to join the class. Miki, a woman I met at Unity, told me she'd discovered her powerful almost bass voice in chanting. She said chanting was hard to learn but worth it. She behaved like a woman who has found something valuable. Now I see why.

*The people of the islands have no voice in determining
their future, but are virtually relegated to the condition
of the aborigines of the American Continent. An alien
element composed of men of energy and determination
controls all the resources of Honolulu and will employ
them tirelessly to secure their ends.*

Queen Lili'uokalani

CHAPTER TEN

THE WORD PILIKIA (TROUBLE) was on the lips of hundreds
of Hawaiians on the evening of January 16, 1893, as they peeked
from behind doors and around corners, watching American
sailors[134] arrogantly parade two light cannon through the virtually
empty streets of Honolulu. By prearrangement with a small group
of resident Americans, and with the full support of the American
Minister [Henry A. Pierce] to the Independent Kingdom of Hawaii,
the visiting bluejackets were quartered in the vacant building known
as Arion Hall, directly across the street from the government building
and only a short distance from the palace.[135]

The social history author, Fuchs in his 1961 book, stresses that his is an
interpretative history in which he makes observations, not judgments.
Five hundred pages, this Hawaiian history by an impeccably credentialed
academic man has enough detail to drown in or take the rest of your life to
understand. Now I better understand my impatience: too much to learn
about Hawaii and too little time.

Fuchs' beginning of his book, though, is quite clear. The title of his
Prologue that begins this chapter is, *A Kingdom Passes*:

Queen Liliuokalani protested the landing, but the American occupation of Hawaii was beyond her control. Early the next afternoon, the local revolutionaries [mostly missionary connected] seized the government building, demanded the Queen's abdication, and declared martial law. The United States government, through its Minister, gave immediate diplomatic recognition to the rebel group, which then proclaimed the abrogation of the monarchy, forced the resignation of the sorrowful but dignified Queen, and launched the American flag where the Hawaiian pennant had flown.

The rebel leaders believed they had wrested political power from an extravagant and autocratic native government. But to the overwhelming majority of Hawaiians, from the Queen to the commoner in the taro patch, a black cloud had descended over the Islands: their birthright had been stolen.

American control over the life of the Islands had been extensive for many years.[136]

It is documented again and again; the U.S. simply stole the Hawaiian Islands. And we continue the occupation today with about a quarter of the land of the islands occupied by our military forces. The U.S. needs to clean up its act, acknowledge what we've done, and make restoration, make *pono*, make right. Or at least make as right as we can for of course, problems are unbelievably complex with land ownership at the heart of them. Who and how and with what legal right?

Every once in a while I just have to laugh at myself, that I'm so serious about solving old problems in Hawaii, as if I could. I'm having hard enough time even defining the problems! So I should lighten up a bit, and recognize that there are lots of opposite opinions.

Today's *The Garden Island*, in fact, has a *Letter to the Editor* reiterating how lucky we are to be Americans living in Hawaii. Countries have overtaken other countries since history began, the writer observed, and so it's inevitable that might makes right. Our Hawaiian take-over just happened, he says; the aggressor could have been Great Brittan, or Russia—and aren't we lucky it wasn't. I sigh believing the luckiness of the take-over is in the eye of the beholder. I bet Hawaiians get really sick of hearing how *lucky* they are to be Americans. And here I am stuck trying to understand Hawaiian and American history, even if I can't!

Once again Hanapepe library holds a treasure. If you really want to do as this video suggests and see Hawaiian history through Hawaiian eyes try *Act of War: The Overthrow of the Hawaiian Nation*[137]—a one-hour presentation of the events surrounding the overthrow of the Kingdom of Hawaii in 1892. This video also manages to let us know that the 1848 Mehele, land distribution of Hawaii, was run by the Land Commission run by [you know it] the missionaries. The back cover says:

> In mid-January, 1893, armed troop from the U.S.S. Boston landed at Honolulu in support of a coup d'etat against the constitutional sovereign of the nation of Hawaii, Queen Liliuokalani. The event marked the culmination of a century of foreign intervention in our islands and was described by U.S. President Grover Cleveland as "an act of war." Today, after another century of dispossession, we the real people of Hawaii, the Kanaka Maoli, are asserting our right to self determination.[138]

Most effectively included is a short history of the Hawaiian Islands and in particular are interspersed data showing the dramatic decline of Hawaiian population such as falling from one million at contact with Captain Cook to an estimated 40,000 in 1982. The video tells how the missionaries misled, possibly without intention, by telling Hawaiians that the reason you're dying like crazy is because you don't believe in their one god, Jesus Christ. *Believe and you'll live forever*. The missionaries meant after you're dead; Hawaiians thought it meant now.

Scratch the surface of a different Hawaiian book and a whole new back story emerges. Tava and Keale,[139] a daughter and son of the forbidden island of Niihau, off the coast of Kauai, have a different take from the usual idyllic picture. And once again census figures tell a tale: in 1778 there were

10,000 kanaka (common people) listed on Niihau but in 1868, not even 100 years later, census figures show only 300.

"The decline of the Hawaiian population was compounded by fundamental changes in land tenure. Niihau was originally monarchy land except for some small parcels. Following the Great Mahele of 1848, when the lands of the Hawaiian Kingdom were divided into royal government and common lands, the Niihauans tried to purchase or lease their property."[140] Two natives did get leases but in 1858 "a new government agent raised the leases to unheard-of prices, making it necessary for natives to move to Kauai."

"Kamehameha V issued the following statement when Niihau was deeded to the new *haole kings*[141] [Sinclairs]:

> The natives are yours and you are the new chief, and they will work and serve you according to the laws and customs of the King of Hawaii. They are subject to this rule only—if it does not interfere with the people's rights of a grant of a little land to plant food, a place for a home, firewood and the right to fish their waters.[142]

The natives wrote letters of protest[143] as King Kamehameha Four had promised they could buy their land. But the Sinclairs (now the Robinsons) were deeded the land anyway by Kamehameha Five. Another reason people left was that the Sinclairs—turning the island into a cattle and sheep ranch—ordered all the people's dogs killed to protect their flocks. Not a very happy outcome I should imagine as people love their pets and people left the island to protect them.

These authors remind us that in older times Niihau people wove makaloa (a native sedge) sleeping mats, which were the finest in the Hawaiian islands. Niihau shell leis, now prized and expensive, are one of the few ways Niihau natives earn money.

I still wonder where the "forbidden" came from? And what is the legal basis to exempt the Hawaiian island of Niihau from rules and laws that supposedly apply to all Hawaiian shoreline? Is this tested in court or simply long, long use?[144] And does that long use become law after a while? Question beyond me.

Still we keep reading, as recently as 2010, "He was immediately greeted by a Hawaiian man with a rifle and a woman with a camera," says a swimmer with an escort boat going from Barking Sands on Kauai and coming ashore on Niihau.[145] And the hassle goes on with a Front page headline, "Kaua'i firemen caught fishing off Ni'ihau," complete with pictures.[146] And a Letter to the Editor: "The ocean around the state belongs to Hawaii and the U.S.A, not the Robinsons. Haven't they taken enough from the Hawaiian people. They live on stolen land from the Hawaiians and now they want the ocean too."[147]

I'm adjusting my diet to eat more local produce. This diet and health change brings a bedrock of sureness, of pleasure, of *rightness*. To try and keep some balance, I'm reading about *beauty* in *Deep Nutrition: Why Your Genes Need Traditional Food,* written by a local physician, Catherine and her chef husband, Luke Shanahan. I'm understanding how a *correctness* in human ethical affairs also brings this sense of correctness, rightness, symmetry, beauty, *pono*—where everything goes as it should and life lives itself. All serious disruptions of life events are made right, are made pono. One person or group of people is not pulling the fabric of human affairs out of symmetry—not taking more than their fair share, doing actual wrong, or imposing their will on others by force.

I see this in early Hawaiian history. Even though the so-called lower class lived under rules of *Kapu*—certain things and places being strictly forbidden, or taboo—one's idea of an unfair harshness to an ordinary Hawaiian person modifies upon learning that over-seeing this kapu system is the mitigating festival of *Makahiki* when all kapu rules are relaxed. Wars are also forbidden during *Makahiki*.

Alii rulers walk their fiefdom checking things, fixing the broken, setting affairs back in their best order, judging disputes—making everything *pono*. Extraordinary for modern sensibilities, *Makahiki*, this time of clean-up holiday and celebration in honor of the god Lono (agriculture, music), lasts four months from October or November to

February or March, depending on celestial calculations. Celebration for everyone lasts for four months! What a way to live. Who but the most wealthy among us could even contemplate a holiday lasting four months?[148]

What were daily lives like in Princess Ruth's time? Practices of solitude and stillness, use of breath? What were their beliefs? How did they pursue spiritual development? I had supposed all women were oppressed—yet here is Princess Ruth, governing the Big Island and inheriting huge wealth. And Queen K effectively ruled the islands. What is the *Aloha* way? How do I find it uncorrupted after all these years?

No sooner do I pose my questions than I receive an answer:

> Mana (spiritual power) is a part of all aspects of creation. Care must be taken to respect the *mana* of the land, the plants, the animals, the *akua* [soul], and other humans. One's own *mana* is not to be neglected or misused.
>
> *Malama* (caring) is the means by which we protect the *mana* inherent in all things. Conversation practices, spiritual devotion, caring for all aspects of our health and careful regard for others are some of the ways we *malama* our relationships. When we are successful in doing so, those relationships nurture us in turn. The land that is cared for feeds us; the body and spirit we treat properly serves us so we can persevere; the person who is respected and cherished meets his obligations to our relationship in return.
>
> When we successfully *malama* all our relationships so that the *mana* inherent in them is undisturbed we achieve a state called *pono* (righteousness). To be *pono* is to be in balance with the rest of creation, to meet our obligations. As in all human societies this ideal state is not easily achieved or maintained. While the formal system of *kapu* that once reinforced *pono* behavior ceased to exist in 1819, Native Hawaiians today continue striving to perpetuate the spiritual values, beliefs and practices that define who we are.[149]

If we wanted to make things right in Hawaii, how could the process happen?

We could begin conversation. We could ask: What is redress and restoration to the Hawaiian people? Who are the Hawaiian people? Why is restitution needed, who needs it and how can it be achieved?

Maybe nothing can be done, but consider this. On the bike path in Wailua Beach on Kauai, after Native Hawaiian protest, the Kauai mayor of Portuguese ancestry, changed plans and decided against building the path over iwi kupuna (bones of ancestors). Still currently left in place is the Planning Commission and Planning Department continuing to allow Joe Brescia to build over known iwi kupuna as he'd built a home over and around the graves of at least 30 Native Hawaiians. Except just today is an update; the trial against Native Hawaiians arrested for trespassing, conspiracy and slander-of-title was ended with a $1 settlement. The Hawaiians claim victory.

Consider also that we truly live in, and are ourselves creating, a different world. In this new world those old secrets and dreadful behaviors come to life. And we begin understanding at deeper levels that we're not supposed to take advantage of others to live a life of ease, or get rich off the oppressed backs of others. There's hoopla now over cheap-priced goods made with oppressed labor. We're getting it that *I win and you lose* behaviors are not-nice at best and down-right selfish and miserable at worst. Just as we're ponying up for healthy organic food, more and more of us are willing to pay fairly for our goods and services. This new world trots out to light-of-day information some would rather keep hidden.

We could look at exactly how the State Council of Hawaiian Congregational Churches' apology and restoration in the form of actual money from the church came about. And if we wished, for example, to right U.S. wrongs in Hawaii—most especially the *stealing of land*, the abrogation of monarchy—how would the pono process be defined and actually begin?

As it turns out, some Hawaiians work on these concerns. Wool has not been pulled over their eyes. It's called the sovereignty movement.

What makes one morning like glue, sad, unmoving while the next day brings uplift and joy, hope, expectation. We *know* this day will bring something great. Yesterday began under a cloud but I put on Ray Charles's instrumental *Sweet 16 Bars,* danced to further work on messes of papers, then cleaned and ordered the house, and ended by feeling fine.

This morning holds joy. My heart sings with the mourning dove calling so urgently outside my window. Barbara gave me a tiny blue egg shell saying, "These doves are not too bright; they drop their eggs just anywhere." Perhaps now the doves cry over misplaced blue eggs.

In thinking about Hawaiians, I believe their indigenous culture is what makes these islands so special. We—all who come later—benefit on their backs. It's time we paid back. First in a couple of understandings. We arrive, lucky in this time of heavy pollution, into an atmosphere steeped in incredible beauty, a paradise on earth. Hawaii presents us with a bedrock of nature and human nature:

> Two outstanding qualities of the Hawaiian are their tolerance and racial pride. One drop of Hawaiian blood and they call themselves, proudly, Hawaiian. But, along with this racial pride, Hawaiians have an immeasurable quality of tolerance for all other races. We who live here in these islands and are the beneficiaries of this quality called the "aloha-spirit" feel that, in creating it, the Hawaiian race has made a contribution to mankind as definite as that of other races who have excelled in economic achievements.[150]

Put in different language: feelings of *superiority* are beyond outworn. Instead we could recognize the real superiority of aloha, sophisticated personal relationships, and the desirability of beauty and peace over competition, war, selfishness and false ownership.

I enjoy my early morning visit to Salt Pond. Incredible to realize that not a few miles from here destruction happens amid a different but equally idyllic-looking scene. I need to feel into this loveliness before I deal with what awaits. My work with genetically modified organisms is an explosion waiting to happen. Drowning myself in cold statistics, I haven't truly seen their implications, or what my work actually helps to bring into being.

As a chance to knock over two mynah birds with one lump of lava rock, I'm eager for the Saturday Seed Exchange in Hanapepe. The library, already a frequent visiting spot—their extensive Hawaiian collection a mainstay of my research—is right across from The United Church of Christ, their church hall a Mecca for community events.

The day is perfect: brilliant blue skies graced by accenting low cotton clouds and inviting salt air. Booths spill over into the covered church hall lanai ringed by sitting-level rock walls. I don't have time to wonder if I'll run into Barbara before she taps me on the shoulder. "I've someone for you to meet. Remember, you asked about military presence in Kauai? Well come along. I'll introduce you to someone who knows more than most. Soane Lagmay has a friend with a website, *Island Breath*, a kind of Public Broadcasting, public affairs deal."

Without pause, Barbara darts through a crush of people massed near the entrance, leaving me to follow as best I can and struggling to remember exactly what I'd asked Barbara about. All too soon we're standing before a tall dark-haired man, with dark eyes and bushy dark eyebrows.

"Samantha, meet Soane Lagmay. Soane, Samantha wants to know about military presence on Kauai. I told her you know everything about everything that happens on the Westside."

Soane, smiling broadly, white teeth flashing says, "Not everything. A little." Turning to me, he asks simply, "How can I help?"

"Oh," I stumble, "I've been looking into land use, and wondering who owns Kauai land and who uses how much, and where the land is located? On the Kauai map there's a big hunk colored red, marked off-limits way down in the far West, almost North. It's at the end of the road near the public park, Polihale. Barking Sands, I think it is called. Or something named PMRF."

"I'll leave you two to talk," Barbara says. "There are some new papaya seeds I want to plant. A line of my papayas got contaminated with GMOs."[151] With a sideways look at me, she adds, "We're safe here, no GMO seeds and things are labeled." She's gone before I can react. Soane leads the way to a coffee area where we find seats and surprisingly good coffee.

"Kauai has three military sites. PMRF, or Barking Sands that you mentioned, is the Navy's Pacific Missile Range Facility (PMRF). This base includes Barking Sands, a wonderful old time beach and surfing spot now closed off—the public is only allowed limited access on the Navy's terms.

"Second, up in Kokee Park, on the Makaha Ridge is a super large tracking station. The navy boasts we're a major communication center, set to back up Pearl Harbor.

"The third Navy presence on Kauai is at Port Allen, just up the road from here. Navy ships tie up at the main pier. Local fisherman aren't always too happy as Naval priorities always comes first. We sometimes see nuclear submarines out there off the coastline."

"Wow," I fiddle with my coffee. "The Navy must station a lot of personnel here. But I never see any military people—only a lot of cars on the highway at particular times of the day jamming up traffic. Do they hire locals?"

"People don't realize," Soane looks serious. "The Navy has a few supervisory-type people but most personnel are Manu Kai employees.[152] The Navy now provides the money—well the taxpayers, us—give money to hire Manu Kai contractors to provide security on the base, to run complicated computer tests and practice missile shots for the Navy to shoot down, and probably a lot more that we don't know about. In fact, just about everything is subbed out to Manu Kai and probably others.

"And another thing that doesn't get a lot of publicity is just how extensive and important PMRF is as they coordinate communications over the entire Pacific, millions of miles of ocean. The Navy brags that they've got it covered: below the ocean water with floating golf-ball sized sensors, on the surface of the water, and in the air. Nothing moves in the Pacific but what the Navy knows. Tracks it."

I shudder. "All that power here on our small island. Who knows about this? I never hear anyone talking about Barking Sands except to complain when it's closed to surfing and fishing. Exactly how much land[153] and people and money are we talking about? Is everything classified?" Even though I keep compulsively asking questions, I'm learning frightening facts. "Tell me." I hesitate. "What are you most worried about?"

Soane looks thoughtful. "I guess the water," he says. "Water is right up there in scariness. Before the State of Hawaii leased the land to the Navy— by the way for a dollar an acre—this is Hawaiian land that the military is just taking—the state controlled the testing of the water being pumped off the Mana Plain. The Mana Plain once thrived with water birds of all kinds. Fish in deeper spots. When the area was drained with pumping, the state tested the water. Now the Navy controls the water and any testing that's done. And, get this, the Navy has a cozy connection … excuse me for saying so … with the GMO companies out there. We don't know what pesticides or other crazy stuff is in that water now going into our ocean. Poisoning the reefs. That contaminated wastewater can't be good for the surfers. It's a big unknown."

As Soane sighs and I struggle to understand, Barbara walks up. "There are several kinds of turmerics here to plant," she tells us. "Free for the taking. Turmeric is a king of herbs. So good for you. I eat some fresh every day." After thanking Soane, Barbara and I are off to find turmeric.

At home, Wikipedia[154] jumps to my rescue:

> The Pacific Missile Range Facility (PMRF), at Barking Sands is a U.S. Naval facility and airport located five nautical miles northwest of Kekaha.
>
> PMRF is the world's largest instrumented, multi-dimensional testing and training missile range. US Military and subcontractors favor its relative isolation, ideal year-round tropical climate and encroachment-free environment (see "PMRF Agriculture Preservation

Initiative" below). It is the only range in the world where submarines, surface ships, aircraft, and space vehicles can operate and be tracked simultaneously. There are over 1,100 square miles of instrumented underwater range and over 42,000 square miles of controlled airspace. The base itself covers roughly 2,385 acres.

The base includes a 6,000-foot runway with operations and maintenance facilities. It has roughly 70 housing units and various recreational facilities for those who can access the base.

The base has support facilities at Port Allen, Makaha Ridge, and Kokee State Park.

The base also uses a portion of the nearby island of Niihau for a remotely operated APS-134 surveillance radar, an 1100 acre Test Vehicle Recovery Site, the Perch Electronic Warfare site, multiple EW Portable Simulator sites, and a Helicopter Terrain Flight training course.[155]

Once again I'm learning disturbing information. I think of Princess Ruth and of Bruddah Iz, the incredibly talented, hugely overweight Hawaiian singer making me cry every time with his haunting, *What would they think?* Bruddah Iz (as they pronounce it here) sings on his CD's of Hawaiian elders coming back to see what's been done to their islands. *What would they think? How would they feel?* Evocative and haunting, I never hear Bruddah Iz's song without mentally joining these sorrowing elders surveying their island's desecrated beauty.

To many Hawaiians of my time there was something secretly contemptible in the slick goal of being a winner at the expense of the others in the group.
                    Victoria Nelson, My Time in Hawaii: A Polynesian
                                                            Memoir

CHAPTER ELEVEN

AS IT HAPPENS in one of the caprices of fate, I met an interesting blind woman, Pali Li, at a camping retreat for Quakers. After I learn she is from Oahu, we have several conversations. She tells about her books including the intriguing *Night Rainbow* series. When I mention a new book I'd read about Huna—advertised as Hawaiian spirituality—Pali Lee says that while Huna could be quite helpful, Huna is not Hawaiian. Nor is it based, as is claimed, on ancient Hawaiian teachings. I believe what Pali Li says, especially since I'd already noted the similarity of Huna to Freud's system of ego, id and superego.

Pali Li also tells of receiving an apologetic letter from Charlotte Berney, the author of the book I'd read on Huna that I'd been quite impressed with, *Fundamentals of Hawaiian Mysticism*. Pali Li has since died; John Willis, her Hawaiian husband, much earlier. But Pali Lee and John Willis are quite clear that Huna, and its interpreter Max Freedom Long, are not what they seem.

"… Huna is not, and never was Hawaiian,"[156] these authors say as they document their case with known history and letters from Bishop Museum. "The manuscript and all the correspondence between Theodore Kelsey and Max Long is in the Hawaii State Archives." Pali Li went through Kelsey's journals finding no mention of any meeting between Theodore Kelsey (given as the Huna authority) and Max Long (inventor of Huna).[157]

Pali Lee says, "Today there is no one of Hawaiian blood who does not have Alii blood, and no one that does not have Maka Ainana [commoner] blood, for all was interwoven time and time again."

My favorite is their *bowl of light* story, taught by the kupuna (elders or grandparent) to their moopuna (grandchildren).

> Each child born has at birth, a Bowl of perfect Light. If they tend their Light, it will grow in strength and they can do all things—swim with the shark, fly with the hawk, know and understand all things. If, however, the child becomes envious or jealous they drop a stone into their bowl of Light, and a little of the Light will go out. If they continue to put stones in their Bowl of Light, the Light will go out and they will become a stone. A stone does not grow, nor does it move. If at any time the child tires of being a stone, all they need to do is huli [turn over] the bowl and the stones will all fall away, and the Light will come back and grow once more. [language made generic][158]

Imagine growing up feeling it possible to "swim with the shark, fly with the hawk, know and understand all things?"[159] If we believe that everyone matters, and our choices are important to the whole, we will make more caring and thoughtful choices.

These authors write simply and sincerely that family or ohana was and is the basis of all life. "The Hawaiian family consists of [regular family members] and also the land, the sea, the forests, the flowers, the rainbow, the things in the sea, and the four legged creatures on the land. All these are family. They are to be cared for and loved as a precious child, or an aged grandparent. These are our family.... When elder men of the community passed on, the women were quickly absorbed into the families of the sons. In missionary terms, these were wives, but it was not the same at all for you cared for the family, close or distant. They saw themselves as one."[160]

The following shows the true spirit that has landed the Hawaiians at odds with Western culture and, conversely, what is, perhaps their greatest blessing to offer a needy world.

knew of the French newspaper's exposé about the dangers of MON 863? Who are these people anyway and how are they chosen?

Monsanto apparently was quite clear about what they were doing: *Get this corn (MON 863) out there on the market as quickly as possible; pull the wool over as many eyes as necessary to get the job done.* Monsanto won. We all lost.

Think of the one thousand pages of rat study data. Mention statistical design and analysis and observe how fast people's eyes glaze over. We depend on others to do the right thing. We expect honesty and fairness. And even when we don't get them, scientific methods are clear and precise.

Experimental animal studies are repeatable and accurate or they don't mean diddly-squat. You feed the rats the corn in question. You rigorously test the results: Were the rats damaged in any way? Were baby rats damaged? And their children? We're eating this stuff and feeding it to our kids.[168]

Ninety days? If I'm eating this stuff, putting these new *foods* into my precious body, then I say study and observe them for a couple of years, many generations—and in a lot of animals besides rats! How about some human studies? If the general population—babies and sick people, food animals, me and my loved one—are going to eat these GMOs, then surely they can find some populations somewhere that'll eat this *safe* food—for money, maybe volunteer prison populations? But some people think that, prisoners, like with syphilis experiments, are never volunteers. Or hey, how about those in charge of feeding the GMOs to us? Why don't *they* and *their* loved ones eat MON 863 for two years and then tell us how safe it is?

Maybe GMOs are as harmless and as good for food production as the companies say. If so, why are they so scared of labeling? Tell us what we're eating and let us make the choice to eat GMOs or not.[169]

In my quest to learn more I saw the French movie, *The World According to Monsanto* and this movie is truly horrifying. Money-making at the expense of everything else, death-dealing to our earth, running rough-shod, killing people, *winning*, or so-called success at all costs. So focused on a bottomline goal of money and power that nothing else matters.

Suddenly it's smacked into my mind that I can't do much about Monsanto but I can do something about myself. It's time to root out the bits in one's character that hold one back. What I mean is what holds me back? And, importantly, *What do I want?*

Only just now have I realized I've not asked before, *What do I want?*

I want a clean, joyous earth.

And I want a spiritual partnership I'm surprised to learn. I don't believe I've ever had one. Kevin was the closest and why I've kept hanging on. Hopefully any final futile grasping is quickly passing. I want a spiritual partnership under a banner of spiritual growth, where you support each other, grow, learn, enjoy, do good things with your lives. But do it under a spiritual umbrella: take what you are, where you are and make the intention to move yourself and others forward. What I mean is refining yourselves, being more and more effectively positive for yourselves and your world. Doing right. Pono.

As a woman, a person, how do I grow while protecting myself so I'm not giving away what I need for myself—which I surely have done in the past? How can I best live so I help myself and others? My built-in barometer tells me that *push-push, not enough, not fast enough, not good enough, you're lacking* is itself lacking and that I can replace these negative feelings. The usual American spends most of their thinking time in negativity, I remember reading in *Defy Gravity*. Negativity is the default setting for most people. I'm practicing to spend time in gratitude. Makes me feel immensely better!

I'm working on it but going carefully. I'm not interested in landing in impossible trouble at work. I want my work, need my job. And on a most mundane level, I badly want to stay in bed this cold grey morning and finish my good fun novel—but I'll read more Hawaiian history instead— and later this week visit another special Kauai place. Saw a Holocaust program last night that was fascinating about a Jewish survivor and the daughter of her torturer. A study in contrasts and what a thing to live with. Stays on my mind as I puzzle evil in the world. Is there an ultimate in slaughter of the innocents? Or after a while do we just become numb, the evils blur together? The Hawaiians were and are so taken advantage of.

And another PBS Channel Eleven story of a woman lawyer practicing in Honolulu in the 1940s, Harriet Bouslog,[170] who became a champion of the working class, finally breaking the strangle hold of the plantation system by supporting the strikers.

All those Chinese coolies and other immigrants—desperately poor people brought in to make money for the *Big Five* plantation families who controlled the islands. It's disconcerting: I want to know what happened, then cringe when I find out.

And, it beats at my mind, evil things happening right now: The pesticides and seed and biotech and GMO companies, and the military, going their merry ways disfiguring and polluting our pristine islands, squandering our hard-earned money. How do you get, make, force, cajole, charm, educate people do right?

How many people (not to mention women) get to choose their own lives? Construct them? Own them? Not many, and certainly few who are as ordinary as I am, and as handicapped in so many ways.

I can put past strengths to work again. Figure out the new parameters. For example, pushing like one pointed crazy on a task, as I did in the old days, now gets me high blood pressure. So, what are the new rules and ways to rate myself? To describe success?

My new success has to include decent blood pressure but also joy, pleasure, feeling at peace with myself! I recall a Pen-woman friend from Florida who had her book published (success) and then immediately died of a heart attack (not success).

Set up new guidelines and goals. AND actually I am doing it! I refused the mess of Princess Ruth research all over the place and said ORDER. The beauty of an ordered everyday life now comes before my old 'driving ahead at all costs'. I am doing it! Just figure how to do more and better. And I'm also doing that!

Sad. Sad the world isn't fair. Sad I don't have what I want. Sad that what I want is forever out of reach. My husband Thomas is forever dead and Kevin betrayed me. And besides, *I don't like Kevin anymore.* Kaimana is simply not around. Will he be again?

I could set different tasks for myself. Not old me-first and getting ahead at all costs. But relationships tasks: How can I help you? Be useful to you? What would you like from me?

ASK for help. Who could help me? What do I need and want as balance? My Spiritual Task is unrecompensed teaching, says a recent *I Ching* reading. My writing Princess Ruth's story is becoming my teaching. I get over expecting a reward of any sort. Not money. Not gratitude. I offer something—as my teacher, Lehua, does with her hula. I'm taking hula lessons once a week now and wow is it tough for me. Unlike the natives my hand and body don't glide; they just sort of sit there. I do my best.

And as Lehua does, I also do the best I can with reaching people with my teaching. And that work is the avenue of my new spiritual path, my way of enlarging my character and getting to enlightenment. Simple. Not outside-motivation (fame, money, feeding ego) but inside-motivation. The set-backs are not personal. I do not have to be successful or do everything at once.

But a part I've neglected, could not see, is—everything must move forward at once. And I need to remember that no forward movement is faster than the slowest part, even when I don't know what the slowest part is.

When something hangs up advancement then the hang-up is what needs addressing. I believe that is what I'm doing now as I struggle with Princess Ruth. I'm doing a reintegration of some sort, a re-putting together of myself and the patterns of my life and living it. And especially granting proper time and attention to my tasks and to feelings.

Last night's dream is of Hawaiians. I take part in a hula and chanting ritual. I am off on the left side. Together we, ten or more men and women, reach out to a Spirit of Divine Nature—paying homage, showing gratitude.

Princess Ruth visited with us, and her old Gods. The details aren't clear, but my heart is happy and I wake up smiling.

It is a morning of full moon. Bright, clear, huge, in a cloudless sky, the glorious moon peaks through bordering eucalyptus trees. Rosy sky in the east, day is arriving quietly as if to insist—there will be no problems with me. Nothing but peace, joy and things going right on this day in a beautiful universe.

Too bad I can't float on this sweetness and light into the coming day but I've made a promise to myself. For weeks I've pitched snippets and research into a file labeled *Niihau*, unread mostly, containing lots of contradictory information.

This is the day to pull out the file, read, study between the lines, draw conclusions and, the part that chills my bones—write my feelings. Possibly write conclusions for, let's face it, I hate to come this far in my journey with Princess Ruth without solid results.

I'm also aware that Princess Ruth is at my mental backside poking me forward with her imperative pitchfork: *Time for justice. Pono. Let's make things right.*

Opening the dreaded file, wishing for the millionth time for more confidence and hard knowledge, I plunge into questions about nearby Niihau, the eighth island of Hawaii.

A couple of hard work hours later, I know that if ever a thing is not what it seems, that's mysterious Niihau. What you see is not what you get, not by a long shot.[171]

To unravel mystery, research, and notes I've needed to separate available information into parts:

History & Background. Gay & Robinson and the island of Niihau are two separate deals, a local explains to me. Gay & Robinson is an incorporated company based originally on the two ahupuaa (mountain to shore sections of land) now encompassing about one sixth of the island of Kauai and bought by the Sinclairs and Robinsons around the time of buying Niihau for, who could forget, $10,000 in gold.

Land Ownership. Ownership of Niihau has stayed in a straight inheritance line until now when it's owned by Keith, a bachelor and his brother, Bruce Robinson, married with children to a Niihau woman. Currently, rent from Naval installations on Niihau brings in at least 1.3 million a year. But factual information is hard to come by as money and eccentricity (plus a tad of paranoia) buy tons of privacy. More than one person tells of straying onto private land and ending with an accompanying Chief of Police and a Robinson pistol pointed in their direction or even cocked against their head.

Public views show Keith Robinson as a conservationist and endangered plant protector. Available publicity and videos also paint this appealing portrait.

History of Business of Niihau and of Gay and Robinson. My sources are a Forbes 1995 article. The Robinson Empire, worth half a billion in 1995 now equals—who knows? I asked a financial friend to give me some idea of what half a billion in 1995 would look like today. His answer is to return a list of how he'd spend it!

*In Kauai I could see replacing the oil-fired power plant with solar and wind.

*Build an excellent public library system!

*Build wider single lane roads with special separate bike and walking paths that were paved.

*Buy up as much land as possible to set aside (never to be built upon) for the Nature Conservancy along with an endowment to service it and with a batch of smart lawyers to keep it out of the hands of scoundrels!

*Start forests on the sugar cane land and make parks out of them.

*Build a dual retirement community of the Curmudgeons and Crones (which would be separated but would have socials and visiting rights when ever both sides agreed upon it!)

* To lower the density, pay all Hawaii residents, that agreed with the terms, not to have kids.

*Restrict tourism to manageable levels with sky train transportation (no extra rental cars! I know you would like this one!).

*But then I'm sure I've run out of money quite a few ideas back. Guess I need tens of trillions of dollars! Now did I take your question too literally?

How much would half a billion dollars would be worth now? You didn't put any parameters on it. Is it bearing interest and how much? Just sitting in a bank without interest and you want to know how much inflation has eaten it!? Can't answer your question as stated.

More Land Ownership. How totally fascinating to go wandering through a dry *Surveying the Mahele: Mapping the Hawaiian Land Revolution* and find a short page on the first surveying of Niihau—clouds from the beginning. As noted before, George Norton Wilcox, a missionary son from Kauai, surveyed the recently sold Niihau and missed by some 14,000 acres; George said Niihau was smaller than it is.

"On February 23, 1864, by Royal Patent 2944, it [Niihau] was sold in its entirety by Kamehameha V to James M. and Francis Sinclair. [Here's an example of publicity and "public knowledge" getting it wrong. *Common* knowledge says the matriarch of the New Zealand tribe bought Niihau.] Even before the sale, there was general dissatisfaction among the Hawaiian people with the amount of land that had been sold by Kauikeaouli [Kamehameha III] and his two successors, [Kamehameha Four and Five], Alexander Liholiho and Lot Kamehameha. In this particular transaction, nearly 47,000 (61,000) acres—almost twice the amount granted to all maka ainana [Native Hawaiians] as kuleana awards—was placed in the hands of non-Hawaiians. Just one month before the sale, residents of Niihau petitioned the minister of Interior, G.M. Robertson, to be allowed to purchase the land instead of having it go to foreigners. The sale of Niihau is occasionally cited as one of the reasons for the passage of an act by the legislature on January 3, 1865, that essentially forbade the king from alienating—selling—any additional lands.

Present (including hearsay) My connection is the usual friend of a friend, one who seems honest and sincere as she speaks of relatives by marriage. "My (Cousin Y we'll call her) says Mrs. Robinson is mean."

(This is the Hawaiian wife of Bruce Robinson, currently half owner of the island.) "She orders us around."

A local activist tells me, true or not, "All the natives are on Food Stamps; the school is terrible."

Stewardship: "The U.S. Environmental Protection Agency has ordered Gay & Robinson to pay a fine of $110,000 for its failure to close 40 large-capacity cesspools," according to a press release Wednesday, April 7, 2010. "The federal deadline to close all existing large-capacity cesspools—"waste disposal systems" that serve more than 20 people daily—was April 2005, according to the EPA."[172]

Further on in this press release: "Cesspools discharge raw sewage into the ground, allowing disease-causing pathogens and other contaminants to pollute groundwater, streams and the ocean," said Alexis Strauss, Water Division director of EPA's Pacific Southwest region, in the release. "As five years have passed since the large-capacity cesspool ban took effect, we're working to ensure large-capacity cesspools are closed to protect Hawaii's water resources."

Five years, a grant to pay for fixing the cesspools, and they're still having to fine Gay & Robinson to get the cesspools closed—does this sound like good stewardship to you? Huge hunks of former Gay & Robinson sugar cane land are now leased to GMO companies, including Dow Chemical and Purity, which are pollinating the hell out of it, and sending much of the money they make off-island. What I see is an extreme valuing of bottom-line profits for certain people and not giving a hoot what you do to the environment of Kauai.

Suggested Future of Niihau. Stewardship is more than isolation or attempting to hold off the future. The long enjoyment of Niihau as a private fiefdom needs to come to a finish. Pay the Robinson's their $10,000 in gold (its equivalent perhaps or just consider it rent), thank them hardily for the good they've done for Hawaiians (Preserving native speakers. Preserving culture? For helping Niihau be the only island to stave off Western development) and wave goodbye to all traces of Sinclairs and Robinsons. Hire some of them as consultants if it's deemed useful.

Put it to the native people of Niihau (and possibly relatives off island, their choice) what they want to happen, what they want done with the island. Do they want to make the island into a *Center for Hawaiian Culture and Sovereignty?*—my first suggestion as I believe all Hawaiians have a stake in its evolution, and that, in some form, the island should belong to all Hawaiians and parts leased to only Native Hawaiians. Further—perhaps as some beginning form of restitution to the Hawaiian people—that island affairs be run by their definition of Native Hawaiians.

Well here I am off on another editorial. And this one none of my business and terribly controversial!

I have a history of making decisions very quickly about men. I have always fallen in love fast and without measuring risks. I have a tendency not only to see the best in everyone, but to assume that everyone is emotionally capable of reaching his highest potential. I have fallen in love more times than I care to count with the highest potential of a man, rather than with the man himself, and then I have hung on to the relationship for a long time (sometimes far too long) waiting for the man to ascend to his own greatness.

Elizabeth Gilbert, Eat, Pray, Love: One Woman's
Search for Everything Across Italy, India and Indonesia

CHAPTER TWELVE

MY BREATH IS SOFT. I feel unexpectedly peaceful considering the task before me. I'm almost resigned to my fate. But then Kaimana has that effect. It's an aura he carries. I smile—of course—it's his mana, his personal power. Yet he owns a gentleness I've never known.

We're at Salt Pond, around by the salt-making ponds that give this place its name, the untamed side. Kaimana is swimming and diving over by the rocks. White-water waves dash high on the other side of the coral reef.

For a moment my mind takes over and I want to scream at myself: *What is your problem? Why can't you let well enough alone? Go with the flow like everyone else?*

Then I think *values*. What underlying values run our lives? Since most values hide in the deep blue unconscious we never know they're there until they've wrecked our lives.

A couple of weeks ago, Kaimana went away to take care of a potentially work-threatening procedure that needed doing. That's what he told me and then I was too stressed-out, worried, silly, confused—to return his phone calls. An old injured tendon was acting up. But worse, with strong indications of deep bone infection. And now Kaimana returns, without taking care of his problem. I'm puzzling values and principles and how you deal with them. Kaimana's body is his body of course. He has full unquestioning sovereignty over his body. As we all have—our last refuge being our untouchable minds. I have to talk again with Kaimana. I decide that I'll begin with a confession.

"I was drinking too much," I tell Kaimana twenty minutes later as he lounges beside me in a blue beach chair. "A lost time of my life. A lover (I saw no point in mentioning Kevin by name) had cruelly betrayed me. I simply didn't know how to deal with this betrayal and loss." Keeping my eyes on nearby rocks and further shadows of Niihau island behind them, I dig my toes in the sand. I can't, or won't, look at Kaimana. This is no fun.

"Or, I guess I was self-medicating." I go on. "Dulling the pain. Anyway, on the surface, the alcohol I drank wasn't bothering me. I was cutting lose, feeling no pain, having a grand time for a change. The new man I was involved with had been married to an alcoholic. He'd mentioned my drinking but nothing he'd hinted had slowed my consumption—I will give myself credit—of mostly wine and beer. Then one serious day he says, 'If you don't stop drinking, I'll have to leave you.'"

"Yes," agrees Kaimana, "he had that right. What did you do?"

"I stopped drinking. And was quite surprised at how difficult it was. He'd done me a huge favor by bringing my drinking problem front and center. While it could still be solved fairly easily. I was fast heading for actual physical addiction." The glance I steal at Kaimana shows only love and concern. The bright orange sun approaches the horizon. Niihau is a pale purple silhouette with low clouds hanging to the left. "Still in the heavy drinking stage, I could clean up my act. Later, would be too late. A true alcoholic, I'd never be able to drink again." Taking Kaimana's hand I bring his palm to my mouth and kiss it. Then I turn away from him and continue.

"Plain and simple: I feel you as an ideal mate for this time in my life. Even to finish life with. As past and future come together our possible present expands and expands. *Solve your problem.*" I turn to face him. Against my will I feel my voice going shrilly petulant.

"I see this is really upsetting you." Kaimana's voice is level. He looks concerned. I feel like I'm fighting air. In an abortive conversation when he'd first returned, he'd said something about nagging. That *his* health was *his* problem and *he'd* take care of it. In other words—hands off.

"I don't understand," I say a little desperately. "When we talked before you said you weren't afraid of the operation, of the invasiveness to your body, of being cut. That rather than waiting until you're in real trouble requiring immediate life-saving help, you'd be proactive." I'm thinking that I've gone too far but I'm in too deep now to stop. Talking has costs but so does keeping silent. I can't contain these fears and thoughts by myself. Not expressing concerns will come between us, eat away. Our relationship has two sides. I've harmed myself before by not talking when I should. Whatever else, I won't make that mistake again. I continue.

"*Your* problem impacts *my* life! Listen to this. As I love you more and more, you're asking me to watch, and accept, what I see as your self-defeating behavior." Turning his hand over I kiss each fingertip. "Saying nothing to you is not an option. But neither is becoming a nagging woman. Not my style." Feeling the tension snap in my bones and body, I look around at sea and sky and the far side of the swimming beach. Everything softens in this yellowing evening light. I let this enormous beauty of nature sink into me. Why am I fighting? I'll have to let this situation go. Maybe even Kaimana.

"But on the other side—you are the kindest, most thinking-ahead, considerate man I've ever known. If I'm not head over heels now, I could be in a heartbeat. Does your inaction have reasons I don't know about? Why don't you take care of your injury and let's put it behind us?"

"I decided the operation could be put off." Now it's Kaimana's turn to stare at the ocean. And mine to fall silent while my mind churns: What are deal breakers? Everyone combines good and bad. Can I accept this combination? Is this love? I think so. But what do I know as I've been so wrong so many times. And what difference does love make? Or as the song sings in my head, *what's love got to do with it* anyway? In my experience, love holds pain with little joy and then that joy is swallowed. What are Kaimana's actions telling me? Betrayal sits in my mind pressing down like a stone.

A letter in today's paper points out that Kauai's Tourist Bureau (partly Chamber of Commerce funded) has just spent one million of taxpayer money promoting Kauai for tourists. And how, if you really wanted to help young Hawaiians get better jobs, spend that one million on education— Lord knows education could use it.

The question of tourist or no tourist has no easy answers. On the surface, of course encourage tourism—the tourists pay money that supports local business. This is a prevailing theme along with, tourism creates jobs, jobs, jobs. I am enjoying this fascinating tour through Hawaiian tourism.[173] And how Hawaii has been marketed to appeal to so-called Western tastes. (Not every tourist is an unaware blob and why don't we continue educating them not to be?) Legendary traditions were used to reinforce a tourist-oriented image of Hawaii[174] but what's happening now is "a re-cognition of Hawaii as sustained by indigenous conceptions of place and genre." Using many of Landgraph's[175] photographs emphasizing the power of place, she[176] helps give Hawaii back to Hawaiians. I thought of tourists swarming all over the islands without a clue to what they're seeing and how maybe tourism could use some rethinking—like who truly gains from tourism? And is there a better way to ensure decent living for Hawaiian youth: like education?

We forget how brainwashed we are. George Kanahele[177] reminds us that it was only 1975 when a popular guidebook on Hawaii stated: 'So far there have been no Hawaiian intellectuals. There may never be.' Why? The reason the guidebook gives is because Hawaiians are 'allergic to thought.'

.... In our reflecting on our past, I think we should remind ourselves of the important place that the intellectuals occupied in the ancient Hawaiian elite. They were, after all, the Kahuna, the scholar-priests. Since there was no written language, everything had to be recorded in the memory banks of these intellectual giants. The old Hawaiians, therefore, must have had enormous respect for the human mind, and for those who were gifted in its use. How good it is to see us rediscovering this traditional value.[178]

I like Kanahele's description of a model outstanding Hawaiian businessperson of the year: "has a good balance sheet, but who also exhibits the spirit of aloha. Successful yet still is generous, warm, considerate and caring."

Those cesspools of Gay and Robinson[179] wallow across my mind and I wonder if they're fixed yet. Being fined by the day has got to get somebody moving. And I think of people doing right, being pono, and other people making money at all costs.

Powerful and immediate connections, synchronicity, become more commonplace. I mention to Kaimana that my left arm itches like crazy and nothing I put on my skin helps.

Kaimana lifts my sleeve exposing an angry patch of skin. His eyes become brown lasers intensely focused on my arm. Moving his right palm he holds his hand about two inches over my skin. It's probably my imagination but already I feel better.

"If you like we can visit my friend, Levon Ohai, over in Kapaa. I think he's home. He teaches classes in plant medicine at the University in Honolulu. Levon is old time *kahu laau lapaau*—a kupuna or teacher expert who uses plants in the practice of medicine. Trained by his Grandfather. Calls plants that he uses in his healing, *warriors*. What do you think?"

"Yes." *Chicken skin*, they call it here. Chill bumps raise the hair on the back of my neck. I'm thrilled. And a tiny bit scared, but I know I'm in for something special. Just what I've wanted: a chance to get closer to the heart of Kauai and local life and people.

I know he's a grandfather himself but Levon is attractive, vital, dressed in black trousers and black and grey striped T-shirt. Kaimana has introduced us and disappeared. Levon and I share a square table, sitting next to each other, but at right angles so we can look ahead or turn easily to face the other. Energy and good will surround him like a mantle. I've read of *naau* (deep inner feeling) and today I open to experience their effect finding that *naau* becomes guiding intuition.

And it's okay that I find tears welling up as the healer reassures me about my life and my ability to fulfill my purpose—a purpose I wasn't even sure I could fulfill, but which gains strength. Gratitude floods me that someone, a person, this person takes the time to beam love and healing and understanding to a stranger, even if I am a friend of a friend.

Levon answers as I've asked about health and healing. "Environment, and the life style you make for yourself: smoking, over drinking, sweets and other death foods. When we examine the history of patients, a form of hoopono, what environment did you grow up in? Like a plant did you have all you needed: space, soil, fertilizer, water, sun. Or did you grow up starved, not enough but still you survived? You are strong, a survivor. Plants and people: many similarities."

"I think I understand," I say. "With hoopono you search out root causes. You go to the heart of the matter."

"Beyond that," agrees Levon. "It's the root cause within an environment. How to make restoration? Grow a healthy individual? Supply what is lacking no matter what it is. For some people, illness is their occupation. Or they can search and not find. Picture this: a woman came to me. High blood pressure. Nothing she tried worked for her. She told of her gardening. How she'd worked and worked to eradicate a particular plant. But try as she might, the plant was totally insistent as it kept returning no matter how she pulled it up or doused it with harsh chemicals.

"That plant you call a weed," I told her, "is used to treat high blood pressure. You pray for healing," I said, "and your environment answers by insisting on growing for you the plant you need."

"You use everything." I am deeply impressed feeling the power of Levon's intention focused on me. I've read that Hawaiians have no weeds, and remember the lantana with its beautiful blossoms of orange and red, pink and yellow, that I'd tried vainly to eradicate from my yard in Florida.

Someone told me lantana was a weed, and I wasn't yet able to see past the name. I have changed. Now I see more beauty in nature, see it everywhere in sky and mountains and ocean.

"I startled my Healing Herb class at the University the first day by asking the students to write the answer to: 'What is worse than rape?'"

My mind runs away. Levon's question is unexpected, shocking. I can think of nothing worse than rape. That intimate invasion of your body. Being helpless, unprotected, overpowered against your will.

"Remember, Julius Caesar?" Levon asks. "How he ended?"

"Yes," my mouth dry, I spit out some words, "Caesar was killed."

"Caesar was stabbed to death. By supposed friends, Brutus for one. His best friend. A man he'd been through the campaigns of war with, shared his life with. Betrayed to death. 'Et tu, Brutus. Even you?'"

Betrayal, the theme of my book about Princess Ruth and Hawaii. How I'd felt stabbed through the heart at Kevin's betrayal, my life over, an essential innocence betrayed. Betrayal, a theme of my life. Even Thomas in a weird way betraying me by dying. How did Levon know? How had he plucked this theme from thin air? I am almost shaking, my skin growing cold.

Levon reaches a warm strong hand to grasp mine. His hand pours strength into me. My shaking stops. "Betrayal is the worst," Levon says as if he knew my secrets. "And yet, and yet we must forgive the wrongdoers. Go on with our life."

"Skin," I intone almost randomly, "how do you treat skin rashes, skin problems?"

"Put your urine on the rash." I didn't even flinch. "Urine is like blood, a bodily product. It should be clear if you drink enough water. Keep your body alkaline and you'll never get cancer."

"Kaimana told me you offer classes here on Kauai in herbal healing. If you'll let me know when and where, I'd like to attend."

Later, on our way home as I talk excitedly about Levon, Kaimana hands me a *Garden Island* article that fills in a few blanks:

There are ways of healing the sick other than prescription drugs, surgery, radiation and chemotherapy.... The difference between medical science today and *laau lapaau* is that in medical science, there is no love, no healing—it's think and then do—it's an unbalanced profession. But in *laau lapaau*, we believe in treating the whole person.

"We do not treat only the symptoms, we treat the cause and it's the treatment as a whole, as a total program which goes into several phases, and when completed, you're healed or cured."[180]

I'll put urine on my skin rash and I've vowed to eat more fresh turmeric which Levon says is a foundation herb.[181]

Earlier I've told of my personal loss of 'reasons for living' while bemoaning the unrootedness of our U.S. materialistic culture. Down to bedrock, after losing my husband, life had lost its savor and structure. This is surely a reason I've latched on so hard to Princess Ruth. The Princess offers connection, meaning, different ways of looking at things. I'd thought Kaimana was my answer but if he won't take care of his health, what future have we?

Something strange happens to me sometimes with food and books. I just don't want to deal with them. I won't eat the food, good for me or not. Excellent as the particular dish no doubt is, I don't want it. Sometimes I keep the food around for a long time and then pitch it. Lately I'm learning. *Oh,* I shrug to myself, *it's one of those,* and I give it away quick to someone saying, "As far as I know there's nothing wrong with this food. It's just not right for me now." The books also I tend to keep around until the library's due date, or past, and then I return them barely read, if at all.

Speaking of which, I notice my study lately is focused, without conscious planning, on myth, legends, and stories of old Hawaii. I'll check out books of myths from the library, not find what I look for—even if I don't know what that is—and return the books.[182]

I think of all the negative information out there about King Kalakaua (This is Burns' *The Last King of Paradise*) how he's criticized again and again in Hawaiian history and then King Kalakaua's own incredible book, *The Legends and Myths of Hawaii* springs to my notice.[183]

Also speaking to me, I find this in a more modern book of Hawaiian myths:

> The need to find renewal and rebirth is equally urgent for those of us who are not Hawaiian. Most of us have lost our bearings. We have lost connection with our own life force and with the instinctual tie to the earth upon which we live. We have lost our relationship to the world of nature and to the world of the spirit, as well as our connections with each other. Our human nature is in jeopardy as we balance on the sheer cliff that is the terrain of contemporary life. Most of us have no social structure like an ohana to provide support, so we each must find our relationships with one another and with whatever we may call our aumakua.[184]

Ohana is family (whatever form that family takes), an interwoven unit offering predictable mutual support and encouragement. *Aumakua* is likewise a form of mutual support from our ancestors, our Gods, nature, spirits, however we define something larger than ourselves.

What I feel from Hawaii is an overwhelming connection with nature, with life, with creativity, spirit, with belonging.

But talk about ohana! Our U.S. culture offers such a limited concept of family:

> When I [George Kahumoku, Jr.] was 27 years old, I woke up one morning and I couldn't walk, my legs were just numb.... The doctor had a look at me and decided to do a surgical biopsy.... When I woke up it was around 10 o'clock the next morning ... and my whole family was there in the room. My wife was there, my mom, my aunties, and all my hanai [foster] kids. Their eyes were all full of tears but no one wanted to say anything.... the tests confirmed the worst—I had cancer of the testicle. Even worse, all of my lymph nodes

were cancerous …. most times people with my condition live less than six months. I was 27 years old and my son was eight years old….And I was going to be dead before the year was out.

At this point my tutu (grandmother) entered the picture. She had already saved my life once, when I was six weeks old. She was like a family healer in a way…. She called everybody and said, 'Look, we're going to do something called kukulu kumahana, which is where you join the life forces. Everybody's going to fast and pray together'… This is called hooke ai…. By the end of the fifth day there were probably 2,000 to 3,000 people fasting, my whole family, aunties, uncles, cousins, my brothers—wherever they were. My mom said that Nappy Pulawa and the Hawaiians in jail at McNeil Island Penitentiary in Tacoma, Washington were praying for me too.[185]

Tutu interprets a dream of George's: What he throws in a fire in his dream is what of the past he wants to be rid of, "What you're going to keep and what you're going to forget about our past. You must choose and take the best of two worlds, from Western culture and from our Hawaiian culture." And tutu told George he'd be cured in six weeks!

George did the Hawaiian stuff (herbs tutu gave him, whatever) and the Western surgery and chemotherapy and radiation. Six weeks to the day, George's x-rays were clear and he was told to get out of the hospital!

"Even today," George says, "I still choose the best from each culture, Western and Hawaiian. I believe that they can compliment each other, as Auntie Edith Kanakaole and my tutus taught me. I'm sure glad that when I had cancer I didn't have to do one without the other."

Of my search through Hawaiian myth I must say George Kahumoku, Jr's *A Hawaiian Life* is fascinating, holding my interest throughout his short book. Now I'll have to hear some of his music.

Can companies do well by doing good? .... Companies that simply do everything they can to boost profits will end up increasing social welfare. In circumstances in which profits and social welfare are in direct opposition, an appeal to corporate social responsibility will almost always be ineffective. In the end, social responsibility is a financial calculation for executives, just like any other aspect of their business. The only sure way to influence corporate decision-making is to impose an unacceptable cost—regulatory mandates, taxes, punitive fines, public embarrassment—on socially unacceptable behavior.

Aneel Karnani in MIT Sloan Management Review,
The Week, October 8, 2010

It is not the strongest of the species that survive, or the most intelligent, but the one most responsive to change.

Charles Darwin[186]

Chapter Thirteen

KAUAI POURS NATURE'S BEAUTIES upon me, three times as if I needed these reminders—which I sometimes do.

First, to banish a low mood I take myself, as usual, to Salt Pond beach. I drive in by the small airport, off the asphalt, straight down a red rocky terrible road whose saving grace is its short ten yards. Parking my pickup by large rocks to the right fencing off the salt pans, I grab a towel, hold onto my keys as I lock the truck, kick off my *Big Save* black and white flip-flops and head like a lemming across yielding sand to the sea. Peeling off my red velour cover-up, dropping keys, towel and flip-flops, I continue my headlong dash into the sea. So scrumptiously beautiful—clear blue skies with some accenting low white clouds, the ocean water today is the palest clear green. Floating on my back, I wonder whether life gets any better than this?

A bit down the beach, a parked pickup is backed into the sand with a couple of kids wading under the watchful eyes of their father and mother back under the shade. White cascades of water splash against the reef as I flip my wet body over to watch. The water is cool velvet against my skin. I play and float watching my toes and the sky and far land rising to the mountains. After a time I paddle lazily into shore.

Sand is coarse under my feet as I follow my plan to wander left down deserted raw beach that looks undisturbed since forever. I walk as close to the rising reef as possible skirting tide pools and marveling at the sea's striated rock and reef leavings. *There's not another living soul around*, as the song says. I am Robinson Crusoe alone with a borning universe. As the reef flattens, the sea, close to high tide, covers usual long low stretches of coral rock. Previously at low tide I've ventured far out. Now I walk along watching breakers in the distance and then interesting shells under my feet—some of my best finds are from Salt Pond—and coral and rocks, in tiny tide pools. My mind is somewhere. This is all pure enjoyment.

Suddenly, to my left toward scrub land there is a dark shadow on the beach which shouldn't be here. Instantly aware I stop and look. It's a monk seal, almost at my feet. Eyes closed, its head is tilted up; the seal is asleep. These are wild animals, endangered and federally protected, I remember. You're not supposed to get close and I'm between the seal and the sea. Looking at its whiskers and darling little cat face, I feel the animal's exhaustion; it sleeps so deeply. I watch the seal, not a large one, with several metal markers on its back flippers and turn to look at the long low reef it has traversed to get here. No wonder the small seal is tired; I think of its journey slithering over this reef.

When I tire of looking, I back away, my bare feet unavoidably crunching on sand and small bits of coral. The seal stirs, opens huge brown eyes as it watches me watching it. The seal isn't afraid and neither am I. We are equals, as the only visible living things around. I yearn to bend down and pet the monk seal, but I know better and satisfy myself by telling the seal, mentally, how beautiful it is, before backing away slowly, holding our gaze until I'm far enough to continue down the beach as it makes a left turn, waves rattling over loose stones. When I look back the seal is invisible behind a low rise of sand. And when I check the spot on my return journey, the seal is still there, sleeping.

The next day I'm running to Lihue town for errands. A strange rain is coming down. Blue skies to my back and overhead the sun shines. Still a slight rain drops down. I get to the pickup without getting very wet but immediately *remember* that I don't have my eyeglasses. Can't see small print without them. Blessing fate that I remember my glasses before I'm trying to read what will be invisible print without them, I run back to my rented cottage. Then, not finding my glasses where they're supposed to be, I quickly conclude the glasses are in my purse, in the truck. Running back through misty rain, I find my glasses just where they're supposed to be. I shrug, sometimes things are as they are.

Then just before Lawai valley, in the relatively high spot of Kalaheo, a rainbow marches from side to side, all seven colors so vivid and distinct I can't believe it. As I drive along as slowly as I dare, I experience this magic rainbow as it *moves* down the valley ahead of me. The sun is shining and I watch the sunbeams shine through the rainbow's end so close I can almost reach out and touch the shimmering light. Even after the rainbow has jumped ahead, shining light remains to mark the rainbow's former place. How glorious. A marvel of nature. And after my false return for my glasses, I've arrived at the perfect time to see this rainbow that I continue to watch as it shines its magic whenever the trees allow. *Thank you*, I whisper. *Thank you.*

The third event follows a day or so later. I've called to visit a Bed and Breakfast I've read about in Anahola—which I've since learned the locals pronounce *Ah-na-ho-la* and not *An-a-ho-la*. As I hold directions in my left hand, it's fun driving all the way to the end of the mostly deserted road, beach houses and ocean on my right. At the true end of the narrow, washed out one-lane road I turn around and go back to my designated place across from the canoes on the beach. No one is around but one man sitting in a white lawn chair between the B & B and the next door house.

"They've gone to the doctor," he tells me, "should be back soon."

I say, "I'll take a walk on the beach and check if they're back when I return."

A small river cuts the beach as I turn left at the sea. Except for a young Hawaiian woman surf fishing, the shoreline is deserted, clean and beautifully quiet—only the low constant drumming of a further-out coral reef. Striding along I decide to walk to the one-lane bridge I've passed on the way here.

The sea is the sea, always there, constant, a heart-beating reminder of eternal nature. The shore-side is a different matter. Beach houses line this stretch of beach I walk, with back gardens of individual choices. Several are small islands of comfort and joy: two easy beach chairs with a table between; I can visualize a happy twosome savoring the view and themselves at their leisure. A couple of back gardens are wild jungles of plants dripping down to the ocean, branches touching the water. I have to get wet to get around an especially low-riding batch of low bushes. These owners are surely breaking the law by using their cultivated plants as barriers to casual beach walkers like me. I can't help but wonder how Native Hawaiians who live here feel about these false barriers; I see these owners as guarded, suspicious. Selfish actually with closed hearts thinking their puny human selves can own limitless beauty of blue sky, turquoise sea and golden sand.

As I walk and think and tell stories to myself, the rhythm of time settles into timelessness. The back gardens now are all beautiful. Ahead is my targeted one-lane bridge with low rocks on the ocean side perfect for sitting. I spend time finding a volcanic rock that speaks to me with a special view to match the day and then I sit. I am one grain of sand in the universe. And yet I am this universe's center for without me to appreciate, this now-universe doesn't exist. We are co-creators. I sit until I am part rock, part sand, part sky and sea water.

After a time, I walk back along the car-deserted highway. My B & B people have not returned. I leave a note and drive home perfectly content with my day and its treasures.

In Waimea I turn right just past the movie theater up toward the hospital and deep purple mountains of Kokee. As the main parking lot by the community center is full, I park on the street with my truck tilted toward the mountains.

Following a woman pushing a wheeled cooler, I pause. The large room is buzzing. I've seen my 'friend of a friend's' white van with distinctive black Hawaiian petroglyphs out front; I know Leilani is here. Awkwardly I pause at the door looking around. I'm probably not supposed to be here but I need first-hand experience. These are local people meeting together— ordinary citizens who are *sick and tired,* as Leilani told me, *of dangerous chemicals being indiscriminately sprayed on their land and especially around their children.*

With no foreboding that my future is about to change forever, I spy Leilani and head straight over toward the front of one of six or seven long tables set with metal chairs. Two casually dressed men in their thirties sit at a smaller table facing the long tables, while an intent man on the left works a camera on a tripod.

I've just greeted Leilani and, thankfully, a couple of other people I've at least seen before, when a young woman appears. She's one of Hawaii's beautiful mixture of races, probably Hawaiian with Chinese and Caucasian thrown in for good measure. She isn't smiling as she holds out a sign-up book. "This is a closed meeting," she says meaning, *Who the devil are you?* Not too surprised as I've expected some version of this suspicious attitude, I put on my non-threatening open-smiling face, and eagerly take the sign-up book as Leilani quickly says, "She's okay," gesturing to me. And the acquaintance across the table nods in agreement over the papers she's stapling, "I know her." *Wow,* I think, *these people mean business. This is serious.*

Almost immediately Jayson Burns introduces himself (later I take a card) and his fellow attorney from Las Vegas. This group has met before and Jayson immediately recaps: "This is a community organizational meeting against the indiscriminate use of pesticides by Pioneer (Dupont Chemical) here on the Westside. These are banned pesticides. Pesticides kill. Pesticides are designed to annihilate weeds and pests. Pesticides kill organisms. All living organism. Kids are especially susceptible. These chemicals come over the fence on the wind causing incidences of rashes, flue-like symptoms, headaches, asthma. Certain pesticides cause increasing cancer rates as ample scientific evidence clearly shows.

"Pioneer knows what it is doing. These chemicals—atrazine and lorban—are clearly labeled **Hazardous to Humans and Environment**. Each bag of chemicals is individually labeled. These pesticides are banned by law wherever children gather: schools, homes, playgrounds, churches. Dust clouds off our extensive GMO fields laden with pesticides come through the air covering your homes and schools, filling the air we breathe."

I can't help but think of the Mexican nationals we've got working at Purity. The ones suited up and running the spraying machines. They probably can't even read the labels. Maybe this is why we don't hire locals for this work; some Hawaiians would refuse to spray banned chemicals on their beloved ohana and land.

The woman across the table raises her hand high and speaks so all can hear: "Excuse me," she says, "I can't stay for the entire meeting and I have questions." I'm watching her and miss the lawyer's affirmative nod as she continues, "I talked with Earth Justice and they said we should get clear a few things—like who agrees to the settlement, if we do continue with a class-action lawsuit. And who pays for all the medical testing you'll need? And suppose some people settle for a certain amount of money. But they don't follow through that Pioneer has to cease and desist." Pausing she is emphatic and determined, "I want Pioneer out of here."

"The disclosure form includes three things," says Jayson. He and the other lawyer have been taking turns talking. "Number one is people's health. Number two is prices of their homes—after all when you're next to a source of pesticide contamination, the value of your home goes down. When we won our recent case in Honolulu, where the golf club was spraying pesticides, the people won a settlement for the loss in value of their homes. The third part of Disclosure includes an injunction that means Stop. The court mandates or orders that the pesticide spraying be stopped.

"For your other question, the cancer cases will be tried separately. I think there're twenty-three cases of cancer so far who have come forward. Those are each separate cases."

"Remember, there is no cost to you. Ever," says the other lawyer. "When we take this on, we pay all charges of testing and expert witnesses. We're interested in helping you in large part because it's the right thing to do. We want Pioneer to pay for the harm they've done."

A woman near the front with her T-shirt hiked up so her extensive tattoos show, says forcefully, "Someone has to stand up," and then she asks a question I don't hear. But the lawyer says, "We all have to work together if you decide you want us to represent you. We'll need medical screening, lab work. We'll need you to keep your eyes and ears open and your mouths shut. The worst thing we can do now is trumpet our intentions. We want Pioneer carrying on as usual," he pauses dramatically, "not spraying those fields at three in the morning with nobody around."

My mind again goes immediately to the Mexican nationals that my company hires to run the spraying machines. Who knows what they're spraying; when I ask Kevin he mentions fertilizer. And how Purity's fertilizer is chemically matched to this soil and that Purity gets three and more crops a year in Hawaii as our climate is so special and pure.

People around me are laughing about the 'keeping your mouth shut' remark and the tension level drops. Westsiders are notoriously complacent. Scared of making waves, losing their jobs. Leilani even stands up and says, "Purity people are probably here tonight so it's important not to demonize them. We all need jobs." While the attorneys agree with Leilani, I notice they mention secrecy again. But when papers are handed out for signing nearly everyone signs up for the class-action suit.

From the beginning, as the community meeting progresses, I shrink further into myself. More and more pure ugliness about GMO companies is surfacing that I don't want to see or acknowledge. My relentless mind has concluded that if Pioneer is causing this reckless damage to people and environment, then it's for sure that so is my Purity Corporation. There's no running away and no place to hide. I'm helping to enable this rape of an—until now—helpless island community. I'm on the wrong side.

Odd how quickly and thoroughly change happens. Like a silver bullet meant only for me, I know I'll have to resign my job at Purity. My conscience will no longer let me support any part of GMOs. In spite of my rushing fear, what I feel is vast relief, since I also know how I can help. On Kevin's desk I've seen complete schedules for spraying the fields. I'm certain the content of those sprays is also included. My resolution is sudden and diamond hard. I don't know how I'll do it, but I'm getting those schedules and chemical lists to these two attorneys.

The morning is enchantment. Rosy dawn light peaks around dark clouds as I walk for the newspaper. A thin moon is delicate over clouds as it holds up its edges to catch fading starlight. Over to the left is another mass of dark clouds. The fragile moon and dawning light soaring above are so hopeful my heart lifts. Beauty catches in my throat.

Gathering up the newspaper I slip back inside to set my timer for my usual fifteen minutes of meditation. As is my practice I run through a quick focus on my chakras, crown to root, a few deep relaxing breaths and the world goes away. With my eyes closed I open my inner eyes to float on swirling purple light that clarifies into an eye, then an elephant eye, then faces, anonymous faces. The eyes and faces are nothing new; I try not to pay too much attention as attention knocks me out of the floating pleasure of disengagement of thought. I yearn toward something; I don't know what. This joyful melting is why I meditate. My thinking will surrenders to what *is*, to the experiences washing through me. From the left corner of my vision a small swirl of blue grows, takes center view, while edges of silver intersperse this deepening slow spiraling blue-purple. Disembodied sound floats in the air, a hard distant drumming.

Then, like watching a dream, Princess Ruth chants and it's as if I am chanting with her. Potent low tones rumble. The mana of Princess Ruth pulls me with her. We entreat, approach and join awesome unseen forces. There are no clear words until Princess Ruth speaks—aloha love shining through her beautiful face. *Mahalo*, she intones to me. *Thank you.* I don't hear words. Thoughts float like plumeria blossoms that I'll understand later: *Blessings for caring for my Hawaiian people. Blessings on your truth telling.*

Love, oneness washes me like a rising tide over coral. Love is all there is. A tiny cell in the oneness of creation, I don't hear a voice, only glimpsing a thought as the Princess fades into a deep blue nexus moving into diffuse light. From time being endless, time now rushes too fast. *Sovereignty*, I catch the Princess's last word understanding this is a direction I must take. The Princess wants me to learn more about sovereignty.

And loud and clear my heart is speaking. What this moment comes down to is: if I don't want to become part of the same mess as the oppressors, that is, the missionaries, their descendants, the 'out for a quick buck' businessmen, unthinking military, GMO seed companies and despoilers in general, then I've got to investigate and support the best sovereignty I can find. Support native Hawaiian causes. Support right and fair government. Support sustainability.

"Don't get me started," she says. I've run into Leilani, almost literally, outside Hanapepe library. A pleasure of living in a small town is finding friends when you're running errands, takes the edge off. I've asked Lalani how the class-action suit against Pioneer is progressing.

"Why not tell me?" I persist. "Last thing I heard Pioneer was to give warning before they sprayed pesticides."

"Those warnings are useless." Leilani is disgusted. "Pioneer says they'll spray every day and if they don't then an amended email does. Do you realize those companies are spraying 35 to 40 hours each and every week? Somebody told me the bugs are eating them alive. With all that poison spray they're probably mutating insects as big as gophers."

"Not much help from the notices," I agree.

"And," Leilani is getting more upset by the second, "have you seen that warning on all the spray notifications? I have a copy right here. Look at this:

> This communication is for use by the intended recipient and contains information that may be Privileged, confidential or copyrighted under applicable law. If you are not the intended recipient, you are hereby formally notified that any use, copying or distribution of this e-mail, in whole or in part, is strictly prohibited. Please notify the sender by return e-mail and delete this e-mail from your system. Unless explicitly and conspicuously designated as "E-Contract Intended", this e-mail does not constitute a contract offer, a contract amendment, or an acceptance of a contract offer. This e-mail does not constitute a consent to the use of sender's contact information for direct marketing purposes or for transfers of data to third parties.
> Francais Deutsch Italiano Espanol Portugues Japanese Chinese Korean http://www.DuPont.com/corp/email_disclaimer.html[187]

"Well that's pretty interesting," I say. "What do you think it means?"

"It means that we on the West side have a heavy-duty problem with pesticides[188] and pollution[189] in addition to GMOs."

"There is one huge ray of good hope," I say, "Did you see in this morning's *Garden Island* that the county is taking action against the seed companies?"

"You don't mean it."

"Right on the front page. Dow Agro and Pioneer are being cited for 'unpermitted grubbing violations.'"

"What's *grubbing?*"

"You'll have to read the article[190] but I think *grubbing* is runoff into the ocean that impacts the reefs and fishing."

"That is good news, indeed." Leilani is smiling. "Say, did you get that email from Diana about hemp? She tells of many healthy uses for hemp[191] and how perfect that old sugar cane land would be for growing it. Makes sense to me. Wish we could talk more, but I've got to run. Nice to see you."

I go to the public hearing on our Kekaha shrimp farm, held in the Waimea Theatre. The shrimp farm wants a permit to dump 30,000 gallons of shrimp waste water into the ocean off Barking Sands. Quoting from today's *Letter to the Editor*: "This waste water comes from the middle of shallow shrimp growth ponds and contains shrimp fecal matter, leftover shrimp food, and small pieces of dead shrimp. This water is discharged untreated into Kinikini ditch and empties across the beach at Kinikini reef.

"Many surfers, fishermen and beach users experienced smelly polluted water due to this discharge when the previous shrimp farm was in operation. Also noticed was an increase in sharks at Kinikini due to the chumming effect of the discharge." And the writer goes on.

The six o'clock meeting is both interesting and boring, boring. The meeting is quite well attended. People are called to give their testimony before the State Department of Health hearing officer,[192] for and against. A company man gives his spiel harping on jobs for the locals. Surfers speak passionately of 'the best surf spot on the island, why would you do this? and sharks, sharks and how would you like to swim with the shrimp-feeding sharks?' A former superferry protest leader asks the moderator, "Does this hearing matter? Have you already made your decision in Honolulu? We've been to meetings before which are already a done deal." Dressed in shirt, shorts and flip-flops, a former policeman, he is impressive as he closes with something like, "Steps will be taken if you allow this polluted dumping in our clean ocean water. We want weekly testing. And we want it on the liquid coming directly out of the farm and into a drainage ditch. That ditch leads to the popular Kinikini surf spot near Kehaha Beach Park. Testing 6,000 feet away in the ocean won't cut it." He sits down to applause. Another talks of not wanting his kids swimming in polluted water and when another surfer speaks of swimming in shrimp do-do, there's a lot of laughter.

Then an old Hawaiian, in halting English, gives the history of the shrimp farm area saying, "Look up the origins of that shrimp farm land. They got no business there. That's crown or ceded lands. Are they paying us rent?"

And on and on, passionate people with vastly different stances, including an articulate man who suggests the shrimp farm sell its shrimp waste to farmers for fertilizer. Seems like a great idea to me; I wonder if it is? Another speaker seeks to bring compromise, praising the shrimp farm for bringing sustainable jobs, and protein food to our area, "These are the kind of jobs we want," he says, "and the way things are going, we may need that source of local protein. And the shrimp farm needs to do right by cleaning up that discharge water before sending it to the ocean."

Even one of the new owners of the shrimp farm gives testimony. I can't hear him, his voice is so soft, but he gets a round of applause from this discerning audience.

I drive home slowly, pondering. If what I see is real, this is local action at its best. But if all these statements are running straight to the wastebasket in Honolulu then what I've seen is an exercise in futility.

Then again, how do you make and/or encourage companies to do right? As the opening quote to this chapter says, "The only sure way to influence corporate decision-making is to impose an unacceptable cost—regulatory mandates, taxes, punitive fines, public embarrassment—on socially unacceptable behavior." From what I've seen tonight, we've got two shots: regulatory mandates (if our government in Honolulu does what they should) and public embarrassment—many local people watching like hawks. And prepared to speak out, take further action.

I will follow this shrimp farm federal permit process because I want to see what happens.

So many great books about Hawaii. I could spend my life reading. Sometimes I'm tempted to drown in a particular era or get lost in learning about ancient customs. One such book is by an anonymous author writing a daily serial in a Hawaiian language newspaper of 1905 and 1906 (*Ka*

Nai Aupuni) now translated into English. It's a chant-story (at least 40 known versions) of the younger sister of Pele (Woman of the Sunrise: Lightning-skirted Beauty of Halemaumau),[193] Pele, and a man of course— this handsome one is from Kauai and speaks:

> This seems the kind of beauty
> Whose slightest glance
> Stirs the sacred ancestral repository
> Alluring beyond compare.[194]

Page thirteen begins *Pele Recites the Winds* and Pele continues reciting winds connected with Kauai place names through page twenty-five. Imagine, simply imagine having that many names for wind, and then one person reciting—from memory of course since they didn't have writing— just this part of the chant. What an achievement! Now realize this book (chant) has 440 pages!

With lyrical writing, footnotes, original language (translated to English), and evocative paintings this is a real find I'll come back to.

Follow up on our shrimp farm permit is persuasive. All four of today's *Letters to the Editor*, over a week later, pertain to the shrimp farm and are unanimous in their desire for keeping our sea water clean. In the first letter, Robert A. Zelkovsky writes:

"The first sentence of the article written by Paul Curtis appearing in the November 26th *The Garden Island* answers all questions concerning the shrimp farm ("Kekaha farm owner has plans for much more than shrimp") Paul writes, "Blessed with some of the purest sea water in the world." Well, then don't turn around and use it as your dumping ground!"[195]

Varieties of delicious bananas were a pleasant find in Hawaiian markets: tiny sweet finger bananas, apple bananas, a general banana with real ripeness and taste, even red ones and ever so often, a new variety to try. Plantains were also an experience: cook them green or allow the fruit to ripen into sweet-tart, sliced delights.

I knew people who mindlessly bought large, often half-green Costco bananas from South America but I happily gave them up, and with never a thought of GMOs and bananas. My enlightenment arrives unexpectedly via a *New Yorker* article,[196] a fascinating capsule of the history of bananas— including a current banana blight which may well spell the end of Costco-type bananas. The article takes note of Australian private and government supported GMO research into, hopefully, a blight-resistant commercial banana.

As I read this article it sneaked up on me: realization that GMOs can (notice *can* not necessarily *have*) a positive side. It's partly relooking over George Kahumoku, Jr[197] saying—after a life-transforming illness— that he's aiming to take the best from the two cultures of Hawaiian and American. This doesn't mean one runs roughshod over the other but deep respect, deep listening, deep discernment for what each has to offer.

> From a biological perspective, I love genetic diversity. That's what makes the world safe, what makes it thrive. It means that everything is terribly healthy. And when you see the narrowing of genetic culture, that's when you know things are going to die.[198]

Here is James Dale, a GMO banana researcher operating with full transparency, with government guidelines, with private and Australian government support and with biological awareness and knowledge. He currently works on a GMO blight-resistant banana— which he will offer to the world. (It seems money isn't James Dale's only goal.)

I suddenly understand that from the beginning, GMO-promoting Monsanto has acted like a stupid bully: *my way or the highway. And I don't care what it costs you, or the world.*

Anyone with respect for human life wishes to protect our precious human species. We are all we have. First Principle: *Do No Harm*. Of course we (our scientists and watchdogs) must err on the side of the precautionary principle. Science is open, proverbially redo-able or it isn't true science— it's being a bully, which is how I see Monsanto.

The question becomes "How long do aware people and those in the way of harm go on letting wrongs be committed: indiscriminate spraying of pesticides, suing farmers and monopoly practices, cloaked open-field experiments?"

Wrong is wrong, no matter how many government officials or ignorant judges say it is right. The truth will out. All we have to do is make it so.

Healing is an ancient practice. It is also a major integrated view of the world and its components, on the premise that there is a common life force in the universe which connects all living things, and that this 'life energy' can be channeled as a healing force between people, between all living beings. When the flow of life energy is low or blocked in someone they feel sick or depressed, 'lifeless.' There are many techniques from different sources by which we can learn to heighten and channel our energy, our healing powers. Healing is the process of doing this in order to help ourselves or each other. Basic to the concept of healing are the concepts of balance and truth. Unearthing the true natures of ourselves as women today is healing in itself because we can then understand and function congruently with our energies. Seeking to correct the imbalance of women's position in society and their personal lives is also a healing process which helps everyone to be more in touch with themselves.

Anica Vesel Mander & Anne Kent Rush,
Feminism as Therapy

CHAPTER FOURTEEN

"SHE WAS ONE of the strong women of our community, the ones who took up the slack, who cared for the wasted and the wounded.... At any given moment, you'd find them out there."[199] We all know women like this: civilizers, caretakers of their traditions, families, communities and foreigners.[200]

The history of women in our society is a long one of course. Some histories tell the truth. And that singing truth sparkles. As I work on *Princess Ruth* a vague uneasiness tells me I miss, or don't see, important Hawaiian history. Then I find what's lacking as I dive into *Shaping Hawaii: The Voices of Women.*[201]

Immigration information is absolutely key to understanding current Hawaii. Like slow-motion flowers opening, I gain a new picture of how present-day Hawaii has come to be. Population figures help a lot.[202] And I'd have paid even more attention if I'd known how important I'd soon find immigration knowledge.

Amazingly author Joyce Lebra manages to convey effects of both large (effect of successive waves of immigration) and small (individual women leading individual and group lives).[203]

In 1853 the Caucasian population of Hawai'i numbered only 1,687. "Within a generation or two, their descendants became the directors of the pineapple and sugar enterprises, the banks, and the railroads. They formed a *haole* elite that controlled the *Big Five* corporations. Some of these firms and their successors still operate today."

Lebra says *Haole* originally meant *stranger* in Hawaiian or, more literally, one without a voice, without knowledge of culture. At first it was used for all visitors, though today it is used only for Caucasians.

A good part of these 1,687 Caucasians are missionary connected. And about the missionaries, part of me wants to jump up and down and yell, *"Yeah, I knew it all along—that many missionary sons stole Hawaiian land right and left."*

Still I'm shocked: "The land commission (composed of missionaries) recommended in 1851 that every missionary who had served eight years in Hawaii and did not own 560 acres of land be allowed to purchase that amount at a reduced rate.[204] This became law, and several individuals, including non-missionary Charles R. Bishop— the originator with his wife Pauahi [Bernice] of the Island-wide Bishop Estate—purchased large tracts of land. The list of missionary purchasers includes names such as Judd, Alexander, Baldwin, Dole, and Gulick.

Later, "in 1895 a Homestead Act was passed that limited the amount of land that could be sold in a single parcel to one thousand acres. Many of the *homesteaders* were straw buyers for planters or leased land to plantations. These practices enabled the sugar planters to divert homestead lands to their own use, to accumulate enormous tracts, and to vitiate [gut] the purpose of the homestead legislation, which was to encourage independent farming and return Hawaiians to the soil." Lebra notes there are some good missionaries but she doesn't name any!

Here's Lebra's version of how the land moved away from the Hawaiians:

> By ancient tradition, all land belonged to the king. In 1848 King Kamehameha III instituted the Great *Mahele*, through which a portion of royal lands was allotted to the *alii* (nobility) and a portion to commoners. Titles were settled by the payment of fees. Once in private ownership, the lands could be resold, and by 1850 aliens could purchase the Mahele land directly. Some of the new owners, in fact, sold land to *haole* in exchange for services. The government in 1846 offered land for sale in Manoa and Makawao at $1 per acre. Aliens were able to buy land for fee simple [outright ownership], and the production of sugar accelerated the *haole* demand for land. Some missionaries were granted land in exchange for services rendered to kings or *ali'i*. Some also purchased large tracts of land after the *Mahele*. When, in addition, the 1850 Masters' and Servants' Act established a Bureau of Immigration to import labor to work on the plantations, the plantation economy controlled by the *haole* began to boom. *Haole* also engineered the downfall of the Hawaiian monarchy and the annexation of Hawaii to the United States in 1898. The *haole*, although fewer than 5 percent of the population, controlled the land, enterprise, labor and finally the politics in Hawaii, though with annexation, native Hawaiians all became U.S. citizens with the right to vote and they [haoles] dominated politics for generations.[205]

I'm intrigued that the first sugar cane plantation was started on this island in 1835 by William Hooper of Boston, who was sent to Koloa,

Kauai, by Ladd and Company, a mercantile trading house in Honolulu. The company leased 980 acres of land from Kamehameha III and hired his Hawaiian workers, for which a tax was paid to the king. Workers didn't get money but scrip. Hawaiians weren't happy and the manager suggested they import Chinese (very poor Chinese males who would take whatever was dished out). Pay was discriminatory based on race.[206] There were lots of strikes over the years because the plantation owners treated their workers so badly.[207]

By 1900 the number of Chinese imported immigrants (mostly male) reached 25,767. Today the most common Hawaiian ethnic mixture is Chinese-Hawaiian. Incidentally, I can't recall exactly but somewhere there's a note in my research that leprosy, so devastating to native Hawaiians, traveled to Hawaii with the poverty-stricken Chinese immigrants.[208]

Next came Portuguese immigrants and by 1910 people of Portuguese descent were more than the Chinese (25,767). Portuguese were favored because they brought their wives and settled permanently but Portuguese were, conveniently, not regarded as haole.

Then came Japanese, more than 60,000 by 1900. And by 1900, 40 percent of the Hawaiian population was Japanese, twice as much as anybody else including Hawaiians. "During the years between 1907 and 1924, Japanese women came in by the shipload as the famous *picture brides*. By 1924 there were 200,000 Japanese in Hawaii."

"The last major ethnic group[209] to be imported by the planters as contract labor were the Filipinos, 120,000 of whom arrived between 1907 and 1913."[210]

Attitudes toward subsequent ethnic groups were: "For the kama aina [old-timer] haole, the goal was to control; for the Hawaiians, to recapture the past [get their land and way of life back]; for the Portuguese, to be considered haole; for the Chinese, to win economic independence; for the Japanese, to be accepted; for the Filipinos, to return to their home in the Philippines."[211]

From a current perspective, these massive numbers of imported immigrants (what amounted to poor indentured servants and plantation workers) simply boggles my mind and sensibilities.

First you take the Hawaiian people's land. Then you bring in huge numbers of foreigners, pay them dirt wages, steal traditional Hawaiian water for your crops, and make tons of money for yourself and your friends. Then you tell everybody how great you are. And how inferior everyone else is, especially native Hawaiians, while you create a privileged existence for you, your family and friends.

It's beyond boggling the mind, where are criminal charges?

I fall. A visitor drowns on the South shore. What is the connection?

Coming home from a Sierra Club walk, tired, I slip on rocks and fall on my tailbone—a painful injury. But one I've since blessed for healing time allows reflection. After asking myself how I could be so careless, I receive answers that surprise me.

First, beauty is everywhere you look: rocks, mountains, flowering trees, turquoise sea.

Second, beauty is benign. Beauty is welcoming, safe, harmless and so we feel, perhaps unconsciously, that nothing unpleasant can happen to us.

Third, beauty is all good things—but beauty has a dark side. And we're lucky when we realize this penetrating fact early in our acquaintance with Hawaii. Those beautiful ocean waves can knock us down, knock us into rocks, grab us in a riptide and carry us away so far we never make it back. Rogue waves descend without warning into placid tide pools. Walk far out on a coral reef on giant-wave days and risk being swept away. One careless step and you fall twenty-five feet or a hundred or more.

"Look or walk," a knowledgeable friend warns on a mountain hike. "Walk or talk," he advises.

Fourth, beauty can carry us away to death, to falling, to drowning. Remember the dark side.

After exploring Joyce Lebra's large picture of the populating of Hawaii, and completely unaware of how immigration will impact my future, I continue by looking at some individual women's stories.

In native Hawaiian culture, kupuna (grandparents) frequently raised the children. "Grandmothers were social engineers of the ohana (home), preservers of aspects of tradition and harmony within the family. When discord threatened the domestic peace, it was the grandmother (sometimes the grandfather) who presided over the hooponopono, a structured mechanism for conflict resolution through discussion, prayer, and forgiveness. 'We were taught in the family never to go to bed angry with our brothers and sisters,' said one respondent.'"[212]

Lebra tells of Japanese women workers returning to their crowded quarters after ten hours in the fields, the "women had to cook, wash, clean, and care for children. If a woman had a second child, she often had to stop working in the fields because she had to take care of her children. Without plantation wages, many turned to sewing, to operating boardinghouses or bathhouses, or to taking in laundry for bachelors to supplement the family income, as did women of other ethnic groups." They (Japanese) were the only community in Hawaii that did not intermarry with other ethnic groups before World War II.

It's interesting that around 1900, before full-fledged strikes began, "the planters hired Hawaiian, Portuguese, and Chinese strikebreakers at $1.50 a day, compared with the 69 cents they paid regular workers. Some reasons for all immigration and especially Japanese and Okinawan-Japanese immigrations were to escape poverty, population pressure, the lack of jobs, and military conscription.

Continuing with immigration, Lebra says, "The arrival of the first Koreans on the plantations in 1902 pleased the Hawaiian Sugar Planters' Association (HSPA). One report to the HSPA noted that the immigrants had been in a starving condition in Korea and 'seem to be just what our plantations need.' This total was approximately 7,500 and was about ten men to one woman.

Then the HSPA saw Japanese as giving trouble (too many and strikers were organizing) and started importing Filipinos. *Did anybody's conscience ever bother them; did they consider any ramifications of what they were doing?*[213]

For incredible stories of immigrant women, "The most extreme case was the Filipina who, besides raising her own sixteen children, took in laundry and ironing and prepared lunches for Filipino bachelors in her camp. She averaged, by her account, not more than two hours' sleep a night and did so without becoming ill, even without complaint. Although her case was extreme, many other respondents reported rising at 3:30 or 4:00 in the morning to start an arduous round of chores. It was not possible for husbands to help with these domestic tasks—even had it occurred to them to do so—since the men had their own heavy workloads in the fields."

Lebra concludes that in the first generation, "all women (including missionary wives) were faced with the common problems of survival in a strange land, initially without basic necessities, such as food, housing, and essential language skills. By the second generation and beyond, haole women had solved these critical problems in survival and enjoyed the economic and social advantages of their elite status, not the least of which were attending private schools and employing servants from more recently arrived ethnic groups."

Education was, and remains, a critical issue for women.

For a contemporary view of what's going on at the time, Isabella L. Bird,[214] traveling for her health in Hawaii, writes letters home to her sister in the 1870s.

"I was unfavorably impressed in both lectures by the way in which the natives [Hawaiians] and their interests were quietly ignored, or as quietly subordinated to the sugar interest." Bird is writing of the islands being annexed and the *reciprocity treaty* where the U.S. gets Pearl Harbor and the sugar plantations don't have to pay tariffs. And what do the Hawaiian people gain here except to lose Pearl Harbor to the U.S. military?

Bird's description of her boat ride over to Kauai from Honolulu illustrates that the 'good old days' are not always good: "The heat and suffocation were nearly intolerable, the black flies swarming, the mosquitoes countless and vicious, the fleas agile beyond anything, and the cockroaches gigantic. Some of the finer cargo was in the cabin and large rats, only too visible by the light of a swinging lamp, were assailing it, and one with a portentous tail ran over my berth more than once, producing a stampede among the cockroaches each time. I have seldom spent a more miserable night."[215]

Bird closes her book with a wish which has so far remained unfilled in its entirety ".. that the extinction which threatens the nation may be averted, and that under a gracious Divine Providence, Hawaii may still remain the inheritance of the Hawaiians."

This charming book also includes black and white pictures of the time, including an unobstructed Diamond Head and a familiar awful one of the older Princess Ruth.

Fresh air in Hawaii takes on new meaning. Air is purified across 2,000 plus miles of open sea—sunlight blazing through clouds and water. You've got to work hard to mess up this environment. Not that companies aren't giving it a good try. GMO fields for sure come to mind and Kekaha shrimp farm wanting a permit to dump 30,000 gallons of polluted shrimp waste water into the pure ocean.

Kona (south) winds also have a role in a seldom recurring task, the last time was ten years ago. *The Garden Island* has a lead article: *Tombolo returns to Poipu Beach*. Of course I'd been to Poipu Beach which has a habit of being named Number One U.S. Best Beach. The place is gorgeous.

With Barbara I drive my truck, beach gear thrown in back (this convenience is why I own a pick-up truck) past beach parking by Brennecke's, turn right, drive to the end and park in the last row facing the Marriott Hotel and condos. This is "public parking."

We're loaded with gear today: beach umbrella, picnic cooler, snorkeling mesh bags and low beach chairs. Wearing our bathing suits under cover-ups, loaded to the max, we pick our way over the sand far to the right.

As Barbara digs the tent pole back and forth in the sand to anchor our bright blue umbrella, I gaze around. How did I live so long unaware of this splendid beauty? Waves pour at my feet and low volcanic rock further right guards the outdoor hotel bar. Ahead a few people swim and snorkel, further out are the surfers. To the left the beach curves around in a slow circle. Men, women and children—many bursting out of their skimpy bathing suits—feather the cream-colored sand. Tourists are thinking *Nobody knows me here. I'm free to take chances, be risqué in my apparel.*

I examine the beach just beyond the outdoor showers. When I was last here, beach alapaka grew far down toward the sand; today the beach is cleared up to an attractive fence leaving a lot more space for sun and sea bathers. Momentarily I'm grateful for the local men I read about who decided to take matters into their own hands and reclaimed this beach from the rich vacation house behind it.[216] I could almost feel sorry for the occupants' loss of privacy, but not really. They took a chance building so close to the beach and probably gambled on the vacant land next door staying vacant, not becoming a booming Sheraton Hotel and condos.

Dark movement in the ocean ahead captures my attention.

"It's a turtle," enthuses Barbara, the umbrella up and advancing with me to get a closer look. The rising and falling sea is clean pale green where the sunlight shines through. The surfers far out in front of the Sheraton ride a big wave. The turtle stays close to shore and then we spot a foot-long baby beside the mother. As the waves recede, mother, only for a moment, sticks her prehistoric head clear of the water.

Barbara and I lounge under our blue umbrella, nibbling on cheese and crackers digging out curry hummus with celery and drinking Perrier from green glass bottles as touristy as anybody. I don't think I'll go in the ocean today but this is a favorite snorkeling place. I can walk out on sloping sand to easily put on flippers and fish come right up and nibble your toes.

How could anyone want to spoil this? I think. *It is heaven* and I gaze at people walking to the low island barely connected to the land—that low strip of connecting sand is the tombolo. As waves rush in, people dash across the narrow strip of sand to the safety of land on either side. Because

I'd never heard the word, I'd looked up *tombolo*—an island attached to the main shore by a narrow piece of land such as a spit or bar.[217]

Visiting the same Kauai beaches at different times I marvel at changes: high sand banks or none, a wide or narrow beach, lots of debris or clean and sparkling. Today I decide to walk over the tombolo to the small island; I have to run across as waves crash from both sides. The island is rocky with many small tide pools and high breaking waves coming from the sea.

"You know I just don't understand," I say quickly voicing a nagging concern. "How could the same people who are doing such a short-sighted job of running our publicly-owned electric company—how could these incumbents keep getting re-elected? I just don't get it."

Barbara's glance is almost pitying. "In the first place, people don't vote. Engrossed in their own lives, people just don't vote. I always tell friends, 'Be sure and vote; you're voting for four or five others who won't bother.'"

"So you could say people get what they deserve," I say. "Only problem is the disinterested take the rest of us along with them. Have you heard the latest? Damming the sacred Wailua river for electrical power[218] and outsourcing the entire thing to a mainland company … only interested, as usual, in bottom line profits to them. We don't need any enemies," I say bitterly, "we already have them running our electrical company and planning board. Or whoever gives those terrible permits. And, you can see," I continue while having to laugh at myself. "I complain but I don't even know the process!"

"Well," Barbara temporizes, "there is always left-over plantation mentality and stick-togetherness. It's natural for immigrant groups to feel loyalty, to vote for their own. And county workers are the largest voting block. Someone told me the mayor makes them support him, even give him contributions and when they don't contribute, they get fired."

"What," I exclaim. "Can this really be true? In this day and age?"

"You want to get elected to public office on this island, you better have one of the large immigrant groups behind you." Barbara's tones are emphatic as she adds, handing me a covered plate, "Try this new cheese. And I think there's some wine in here somewhere." She's poking around in the cooler. "I could use some; how about you?"

My mind is twirling. Which immigrant groups?   What is the composition of this island population anyway? But before I can gather my thoughts, Barbara has moved on to talk about her farm. As she brings me up-to-date I relax into the day. The beach is breath-takingly beautiful. It is a happy satisfied tired as Barbara and I pack up our beach stuff, stop to wash the sand off our feet and head for home.

I feel much too good to write in my Journal and ordinarily I would not. Today it's necessary if I don't want to forget. Too many experiences pile up: The Botanical Garden, The Farm and the lovely chocolate tour, and the tsunami. Oh, and I stayed up most of last night reading Kaylie Jones' memoir: *Lies My Mother Never Told Me*. I'm glad for the new information but her book leaves a bad taste. Such a mess. Poor Jones [James Jones,[219] her father, my friend, author of *From Here to Eternity*]; I have more sympathy for him now. But did he really *save* Kaylie as he hoped to do?

I like to think I'm repaid for my reading by Jones' quote from *The Book of the Samurai* which lays out a peril and the dilemma of my work with Princess Ruth. "To hate injustice and stand on righteousness is a difficult thing. Furthermore, to think that being righteous is the best one can do and to do one's utmost to be righteous will, on the contrary, bring many mistakes. The Way [Taoism] is in a higher place than righteousness.

This is very difficult to discover, but it is the highest wisdom." I'm still working on this one.

The tsunami never came; the monstrous earthquake off Japan generates only loud early warnings which petered into four or so inches of sea rise here in Kauai. It could have been worse of course. Somehow the weight of sea water traveling at major speeds, hitting our beaches, lifting all in its path: it's disquieting. I load my computers into the car, Journals, cheese, bread, lots of water and head to elevated ground at the Golf course in Kalaheo out by the pavilion, high and overlooking the wide ocean. I expect to see sea waves and salt water suck out, out, and the ocean rush to cover empty beach shore and then surging sea water return up and up—who knew how high the waves and water?

A hundred people and I wait amid news reports and warnings while the day grows more beautiful and nothing happens. Then the all-clear comes and at varying intervals people fold their lawn chairs, pick up their empty bottles, and drift away. End of tsunami.

Tiny fears lurk as reminders. From the corners of my eyes I sense the sea *could* burst its boundaries, creep in the night, catch me asleep in bed, no place to hide. I dislike thinking this about myself, but I fear that some trusting security of peaceful sleep has fled with the tsunami. Although, come to think of it, all those years in Florida, even time in the heart of several hurricanes, and I don't *fear* hurricanes, I respect them. *Prepare, bless early warning systems, and go about your day*, I tell myself. From the way those early sirens blasted today, I'd be a volcanic rock to sleep unaware until a tsunami actually hits. *My fate is different*, I think until, unless—why does my retentive little mind do this?—unless that marked hunk of the Big Island breaks into the sea and we're all done for. I saw a break like that in the earth in Southern California, a San Andreas fault line showing itself in a 810 mile line of disturbed earth eerily like that marking line in the dirt on the Big Island.

The chocolate farm tour starts auspiciously with a *Cup of Gold*. Someone has trimmed this usual vine into a blossom-laden bush at the front of the low building where our tour starts and finishes. The flower cups are metallic-looking gold and gorgeous. It's a usual lovely day as our casual young-woman guide leads our group wandering through a grassy plant walkway going down and then meandering along babbling water. We see fruiting trees of lychee, starfruit, soursop, apple bananas and other exotic plants planted among bee hives. Later I'll buy and enjoy a jar of their pure light honey. Loving care and good maintenance are conspicuous. Our guide tells us this is a teaching farm and talks of "sustainable diversified agriculture for Kauai's future," as we linger past creaking timber bamboo, another future farm product.

After a bit we arrive before the chocolate plants which are tall and thin, almost scraggly. But I think it's because of their large leaves and the spaces on the trunk where chocolate pods grow. Strange to see fruit (chocolate pods) growing from trunks and not on the usual ends of limbs. The pods are deep rich orange, paler orange, some green and all shades in between. The pods are elongated coming to points at either end and have slow ridges on their skins.

With permission, I've taken a pod home from the Botanical Garden and cut it open to find seeds enclosed in a gelatinous mass which is rather sweet in contrast to the bitter taste of the chocolate seed inside. Still, I like chomping down on separate sticky-sweet chocolate beans thinking how terribly healthy it must be to eat them this way. I'd then scooped out the seeds, frozen and eaten them one at a time over days.

A bit later, under vanilla orchids growing in shading trees we learn each orchid is hand-pollinated to yield high-priced vanilla beans. At the chocolate tent, out on the grounds, we taste small pieces of chocolate and rate them for amount of cacao—the part that's so good for you. With paper and pen we try out names for the chocolate we're tasting. I'm delighted of course when my two favorites are the highest in cacao. But then I've been a chocolate connoisseur for years.[220]

Hawaiian elders have described Kauai as the crown of the archipelago. *Anahola: Kauai's Mystic Hawaiian Village* [221] is a fabulous peach of a coffee table book. Lots of love went into the making of this gem (and I've later learned 11 years of work); aloha shines from every page and photograph. "Nowhere on Earth is such a paradise," quotes Auntie Emmaline White.

Hawaiian to the core, this author offers an opening Prayer: (*Pule*)

> *My Prayer. May this book inspire you to treasure & preserve all that is precious to Anahola. For all who live here may it fortify your knowledge, appreciation and love for this place we call home. May it remind you of your cultural roots. For those who can only rest here for a short while may this book uplift your spirits and take you back to your Hawaiian paradise on earth. May our divine Source, the giver of life and death, bless all who read this book. 'Amene* (Hawaiian for Amen).[222]

Here at last is an antidote to GMO horror—life and love. Ironically, fertile and sustainable Anahola is almost directly opposite on the island from Hanapepe to Waimea, hotbeds of GMOs and pesticides.

As a special bonus for reading *Anahola*, I finally gain names for sharp mountain features that have long intrigued me. *Anahola Peaks* is the easy name, part of the Kalalea Mountain around mile marker 13 but visible for miles. "Anahola, although it appears small, is the most densely populated Hawaiian stronghold on the island of Kauai and is second only to Waianae, on Oahu, in the State of Hawaii. Over 7,000 Native Hawaiians and their descendants live in this area.... Anahola is truly a magnificent ahupuaa [section of land from mountain to sea] that is totally self-sustainable.... This eco-system was cared for wisely so that it would sustain the people forever. It was a bond of nature and spirit, blended together with man and woman to meet their every need."[223]

In addition to stunning photographs, I find confirmation of my kumu hula Lehua's teachings with almost her exact wording that *Kaona* is a special way to convey a true or secret meaning of something by using another word in its place. "The word *pua*, she tells us, "literally means *flower*, but its kaona (secret) word would actually mean *sweetheart* or *a loved one*— or even the female private anatomy." Hawaiians had fun and kept things private. I am deeply touched and tears of appreciation come with reading that *Leialoha*, the Hawaiian name Kumu Lehua gave me, means lei of love. "We have been raised and immersed in aloha. We are the pua, the flowers, the children in leialoha, the lei of love."[224]

Another bonus for reading *Anahola* is the mystical history and presence of this place. Friends told me of Polihale as a jumping off point for spirits leaving the earth and that the Dalai Lama had asked to visit two places in Hawaii, both in Kauai: Polihale and Anahola. Departed souls jump off at Polihale. Arriving souls come through a cave (natural hole in the mountain) or portal in those peaks that so intrigue: Konanae and Kikoo with the hole in the mountain (cave or portal) at the bottom of Kikoo along the mountain ridge.

Enthralled by the *Elder Spirit of Wisdom* section and interviews and stories about Anahola residents, I realize this is a book I'll ask Ed and

Cynthia at *Talk Story Bookstore* in Hanapepe to track. I'd like to own my own copy of this inspiring, joyful and beautiful book.

Astonishing how quickly I've put down roots in Kauai and how possessive I am of my little rented home-place. It isn't fancy, but for now, this house and island are personal charges to guard. Yet, equally and I've never felt this before, Kauai guards, protects and educates me. How extraordinary—or maybe only marvelous for me as several local friends go into great detail relating how they've lived past lives on Kauai and how they respond at certain locations with Polihale and the North Shore heading the list.

Certain places fit certain people. What sends me into outer space are sparkling back-lighted late-evening eucalyptus leaves. Especially when there is wind, I *feel* visitors, spirits if you use your imagination. I feel I'm not alone. Drawn into these moving green leaves and dark branches, I have no problem joining Hawaiians to believe in nature's awesome powers and to believe in things beyond normal comprehension. The beach, sea, and the mountains and sky and flowers and waterfalls are so special.

What can we do to fit in as haoles who've chosen, even been chosen, to make Hawaii their home?

First thing: Get rid of any arrogance whatsoever. Or any idea you've done anyone except yourself a favor by moving here.

Next consider: How will you pay your fair share for the blessings you accrue automatically by moving to these Islands? As you acquire consciousness about what wrongs our haole ancestors have done, and continue doing—what congressperson will you write? What will you say? How will you spend time and energy and self-education challenging the status quo? As I ponder, I suppose a bottom line question is: How do you make your share of restitution?

As I consider Hawaiian-ness, and myself as a single individual lucky enough to *choose,* and be able to choose, to live in this special corner of the world, I accept my challenge: How do I justify my life, my existence?

How lucky I am. Princess Ruth gives me enough reason-for-my-existence to last forever and a day!

Yet still I puzzle at the door of Hawaiian-ness. In my heart I am kama aina (long time resident). I live and belong here. Perhaps for now this is sufficient.

Two enjoyable weekend days and nights, and I've easily acquired badly needed education on modern Hawaii—but Oahu style. I'm also reinforced in my belief that quantitative differences exists between Honolulu on Oahu and the other islands. Still it's such a gift to be greatly entertained and taught so much. The author John Griffin is a master teacher; I envy his ability to distill essences into fascinating characters as he picks up major underlying Hawaiian motifs.

> Most Hawaiians are still here, struggling to survive in what used to be their own country. Some serve as political front men for the haoles in the Big Five, just like some Irish served the English.... In Hawaii, people didn't say *Japs*, but they muttered about the Japanese being clannish and bound by tradition. Chinese were often considered tight and wily, like Jews. Hawaiians undependable and lazy. Koreans crude. Haoles were arrogant and insensitive. Filipinos simple but sometimes violent. Portuguese were like the Poles on the mainland. ...
>
> Behind the muttering, nicknames and jokes, the intermarriage rate goes up, and we haven't had race violence for a long time.[225]

One of Griffin's Hawaiian characters, in jail, says that Hawaiians have to make it any way they can against haoles and the Japanese. Others comment that Honolulu is so screwed up, especially for Hawaiians, and that "some Hawaiians are calling me a coconut—brown on the surface, white inside." Griffin gives a great picture of inside workings of mixed-nationality families, homosexual men and lesbians and how they evolve over time. He writes his family sagas from the inside of running a company, over time, over education, over choices and deaths. Along the way his haole gives a farewell talk:

Some of you know how much I have been bothered by Hawaii's unreached potential, its stalled political revolution that's become a perpetuating dynasty, its economy strapped to fading plantations, military spending and endless tourism growth, and our growing provincialism in the middle of the Pacific. Look at the concrete jungle of Waikiki, look at the rush hour smog—the Hawaii I see here today, a rainbow of races, flowers on the trade winds, the beauty of the mountains, valleys, surf and shores, and what it means to live on an island with its mixture of limits and endless horizons.[226]

I puzzle over *perpetuating dynasty*. I'd love to ask John Griffin if he means Hawaii's long time Japanese Senators and Representatives in Congress? Or perhaps the legal corporative, Bishop Estate that Charles Bishop instigated?

I'm sitting alone in the empty lunch room area at work, devastated. Drinking lousy coffee that's only fit to pitch out the door.

I know better than most how life throws nasty tricks. By all that's expected, I'd still be living my married dream life in California. Yet here I am on a quiet small island in the middle of the Pacific Ocean, with a new life, severe money problems, an unexpected set of male companions and crazy puzzles at work. And I don't want to deal with any of it.

We count on our friends being there for us: alive and healthy. Fascinated (at least somewhat) to talk and share joys, happenings and concerns. Barbara's been out of work for ten days now. I miss her and our increasing friendship. Barbara is ill, very sick and none of the doctors know why. Or how to help her. She's in ICU at Wilcox hospital in Lihue, our largest town.

As I look up from my coffee, Agatha comes in, hesitates a step, and then sits down with me. Thoughts of Agatha's father weave across my mind. How his sacred birthright was interrupted. How ancient Hawaiian healing practices and power (mana) weren't passed on to next generations. As I privately hope, and am sure, that at least some Hawaiian healing knowledge got passed on anyway, Kaimana's story of missionaries at Wailua throwing sacred healing stones into the sea crosses my mind. We can surely use all varieties of healing information as strange illnesses and happenings multiply all over the world, especially on the mainland. Imagine—bedbugs in the Empire State building. The internet tells of whole US cities infested with bedbugs, now immune to chemicals that used to kill them deader than doornails as the cliché says.

"No change for Barbara," Agatha answers my unasked question. "I just called the hospital. No visitors allowed. No change. The doctors do say her immune system is weaker."

"We're talking about healing, aren't we?" As Agatha takes out her water jar, I sip my terrible coffee, adding, "Ancient Chinese had it right—the healer-physician only got paid when his client was well; if his patient became sick, the doctor didn't get paid."

"Sounds like a winner to me," Agatha agrees as she pulls out a bottle of capsules and selects two which she takes with water.

"Is that Noni?" I ask curious.

Agatha pushes the bottle toward me.

"Yes," I say. "This is exactly what my naturopath ordered for me, *Maui Noni*. 'To build up my immune system,' she said, 'and to kill a mild fungal infection.' Tell me," I'm still curious, "is this the small greenish-yellow fruit I see growing along Hawaii's beaches and sand and in forest areas? The one that smells so bad?"

Agatha laughs. "You're right about the smell. When I was growing up we made our own Noni juice—lots of Hawaiians still do. We took the concoction with lemon and whatever we could find to cut the smell and taste. My tutu made juice from fresh Noni she'd push through a sieve and, surprisingly, there is no smell with the fresh. You know," there's a lilt in her voice, "I hear they're doing clinical medical trials with Noni at the University of Hawaii.

"Listen," she takes out a *Maui Noni* advertisement: "Noni contains the world's richest source of cellular rejuvenating enzymes. And in traditional Polynesian herbal medicine and native Hawaiian cultures, the

Noni fruit is widely praised for its life-extending properties, including supporting immune functions, aiding digestive health, and promoting well-being."

"Wow," I say. "I know the stuff is strong and works fast. My doctor had me order three bottles, but I only needed one. I heard that legislator Rep. Helene Hale testified that a heated-up Noni leaf healed her black eye in one day. Too bad we can't slip some Noni to Barbara but I'll bet if we carried Noni to the hospital, the doctors wouldn't let us within a mile of her."

As Agatha agrees I ponder how to ask another question. There are two I've been dying to ask but the last thing I want is to be insulting to my Hawaiian friend. Or to ask something she would think was none of my haole business. "Agatha," I take a chance, "I'm confused. Do *Kahuna* and *Huna* mean the same thing: wise elders and teachers?"

"The simple answer," Agatha says after some thought, "is Yes. A more complicated one is that Kahuna includes what you'd call black and white magic. White magic being healing. Black including ancient skills of laying spells, even praying someone to death."[227]

Taking a deep breath—I knew she was trusting me to understand—she adds, "Huna Hawaii has room for the unexplained. Nature is powerful here—not yet entirely paved over. The beauty opens your mind. Huna is considered by many to be *healer* only and some people get mighty upset when you mix up the titles of *Kahuna* and *Huna*."

"Thank you." I am sincere. "That's nice of you to tell me. And for a reward," I grin feeling better in spite of my coffee now thankfully gone, "Can I ask another question?"

"Ask away. I'll help if I can."

Before I open my mouth, the door bursts open. Kevin makes straight for our table. "They've got a diagnosis," he says loudly. "The hospital just called. Barbara has Rose Gardener's disease or sporotrichosis."

As soon as I'm home I look up *sporotrichosis* and find it's a fungal disease and "usually affects the skin, although other rare forms can affect the lungs, joints, bones, and even the brain. Because roses can spread the disease, it is one of a few diseases referred to as rose-thorn or rose-gardeners' disease."[228]

And then the most salient fact: "Serious complications can also develop in patients who have a compromised immune system"[229] Barbara always works so hard with her two jobs, here and on her organic farm. I'm sure she's run down and with a weak immune system. I'm worried.

*With over half our U.S. budget now going to the military—
isn't it way past time to find better ways to operate in the
world than invasion and occupation by our military?*

*The United States spends over 487 billion conducting
a war in Iraq while the United Nations estimates that for
less than half that amount we could provide clean water,
adequate diets, sanitation services, and basic education
to every person on the planet.*

John Perkins, Confessions of An Economic Hit Man

*This is what they do: they scarify country, they shred its
people and its dreams to satisfy their own appetites. To
feed their avarice. They've been doing it for a hundred
years, and it's just like Jet said: they change their faces
and colours, they rearrange the disguise. But underneath
they're all the same, and they never change....*

You let the past imprison you, you'll die in that jail.

Adrian Hyland, Gunshot Road

CHAPTER FIFTEEN

TWICE TODAY I'VE HEARD someone call my name. No one at the door
when I look. An odd noise in the attic. A spooky day.

The name keeps dodging my thoughts. I can almost reach out and
touch the book I want to find, but every time I almost get the name, like
a mirage, it is gone again. Am I dreaming the whole thing? Has it really
happened as I dimly remember? The basic deadly plot is here; I remember
the story. The Royal Chief's School in the mid 1850s is involved. Around
that time, deliberately, haole foreigners hatch a deal among themselves

pledging to marry high-born native Hawaiian women. As I almost recall, the men parceled out the women—you take this one; I'll go for that one. Then following customs and actual laws of that time in the U.S. and England, the haole men will be in charge. Effectively, Hawaiian land and riches will be under foreign control. I struggle to remember when I'd read the book, where? Nothing comes clear.

The air is heavy; the night dark and stormy and ominous. High trees blow in the wind shaking like they'll fall in the next minute. Wind whistles and shrieks as I've never heard before. Rare lightning brightens skies streaking with fire and crashing thunder. I can't sleep, restless. For no reason I feel an impending doom. Old ghosts of long ago troubles shiver in my thoughts just below the surface. I walk the floor. Back and forth to the kitchen, I fix cup after cup of hot tea. Let the cups of tea get cold.

Scared to work on the computer, I've unplugged it. I'm afraid of lightening strikes as my computer is manually plugged into electricity. I decide to read, to ignore the storm. Snatching at random from my stack of research books, I'm soon engrossed. The bookmark opens to Charles Bishop and his fictional wooing[230] of Bernice or Pauahi Paki at the missionary run Royal Chief's School.

Charles Bishop's name is familiar of course; he's a major player in Hawaii's early fate with missionary white men. Charles Reed Bishop was a businessman.[231] Born in Glenn Falls, New York, he sailed to Hawaii in 1846 at the age of 24. On May 4, 1850 (he's 28, she's 15 or 16 and engaged to Prince Lot, Princess Ruth's half-brother who is slated to be a next King of Hawaii) Charles marries Bernice Pauhi Paki, descendant of the royal House of Kamehameha, despite the objections of her parents. A private ceremony in the Royal Chief's School is not attended by her family.[232]

Charles Bishop, who started with nothing but good looks if you don't mind eyes that are too narrow, and an 8th grade education—with the help of his friends and new wife's family quickly works his way up the business ladder in Hawaii. Among other things he founds Hawaii's first successful bank, now known as First Hawaiian Bank. Bishop lived out his life in San Francisco following his wife's death about six months after she'd inherited Princess Ruth's vast wealth. Bernice died of breast cancer.

The storm outside is soon forgotten as I return to Rosemary Patterson's novel.[233] I'm fascinated.

"Hawaiians didn't worship the idols like the westerners thought. They just used them as representations to channel higher energy through." Patterson's observation makes sense to me and reinforces my notion that—in a total reversal—common Hawaiian culture is quite advanced spiritually over the haole missionaries of that time.

Remember the pure cruelty of the missionary Cookes telling these captive children at the Chief's School that it is the will of God that the Hawaiian race is dying out? These are the kid's relatives, for heaven's sake. And these are missionaries supposed to bring enlightenment. The situation is almost beyond belief. I'm reminded of those Milgram experiments on people following orders from an authority figure to raise the magnitude of electricity they are shooting to a subject who is screaming and yelling for them to stop. Amazing that so many poor experimental souls follow-the-orders-from-an-authority figure and they just keep on raising the electricity rate, even after there is only an ominous silence from the supposed experimental victim, who is actually a confederate of the experimenter.

Dragging my attention back, I have a hard time processing what I'm reading. This following section has gone back in time to just after Charles Bishop meets Bernice:

> "Adieu, sweet Princess," Bishop addressed her back. [She's already told him she's engaged and is going to the kitchen to get away.] "We'll meet again, I promise you. You're right, Reverend Damon. She's just as virtuous as she's beautiful and rich."
>
> "That young lady will inherit a king's fortune in land from Abner and Konia Paki, Bishop ... You'll notice doors open magically to you if you marry her."
>
> "Perhaps you're right. My mother and other relatives in America will be horrified at a marriage to someone of dark skin. But if it will boost my business chances it might be worth the sacrifice, I suppose."
>
> "That princess would be a wise choice."

"Tell me, honestly, will you, what you think about the financial opportunities in this pagan land? ...."

"The financial opportunities, here, Bishop are unlimited." I listened, astounded [this is the narrator speaking] as the reverend gave Charles Bishop a lecture on the prospects in Hawaii. He assured Bishop that one of his associates, Dr. Gerritt Judd, the former doctor of the American mission, had cultivated the present King [Kamehameha III] during one of his bouts of illness and had become his close advisor. The Reverend assured Bishop that Dr. Judd had convinced the king to allow private sale and ownership of land to westerners. He added that this was much to the joy of the members of the mission as they were recently instructed that funding was being discontinued for them from the Board For Foreign Missions in the States."[234]

I almost jump out of my skin when my reading light flickers, goes out, and stays out. The time is 1:30 a.m. when I last looked. I'm wide awake but should get to bed. Lightning and thunder have ceased somewhat and the wind died down. High time I am asleep since I can't see beyond the candle I've prudently left burning. I can hardly wait to read more of this captivating story about Bishop and his wife Bernice. Bernice is cousin and dear friend of Princess Ruth. I've a feeling Princess Ruth fits in this story, but how?

Several hours later. Sleep, trance, dream? The past come back full force? Hawaiian Nightwalkers returned to settle ancient wrongs? Surely Princess Ruth brings this dream event that I watch spellbound.

It's a forceful Charles Bishop, young in years and before he's the husband of school girl, Bernice Pauhi Paki.

Charles is laying down the law to Isaac Davis, not yet the second husband of Princess Ruth.

"You fool," Charles shouts at Isaac. "You indolent idiot." Isaac shrinks his six foot two as small as his body will go. "You got Princess Ruth to deal with because you're the only one tall enough for that wild heathen." A dream Charles tightens his hands together and takes a controlled breath while he continues his tirade to Isaac. "Look. I'm going to be plain and simple with you. Of course the Princess is trouble. A pain. What did you expect? The richest woman of them all! You idiot," Charles is yelling again.

Isaac just shakes his head. "You don't know Princess Ruth. A hardhead. That woman won't even listen to me talk. Just laughs that loud Kamehameha roar. So undignified. You wouldn't believe. Refuses to let me even give advice to her."

"You have to figure out what will work. Manipulate events." Charles turns even more icy. "How do you think I felt getting close to Bernice? At least she's hapa haole, half white. A silly romantic schoolgirl. And those Cookes who run the Chief's School? I had to sit in their parlor hour after stupid hour. Flattering them. Encouraging their religious nonsense. Asking their opinion as if I mean it. You must," a dream Charles actually shakes his fist, "keep your eyes on the goal. On our plans. Don't come whining to me again. It's not good for us to be seen together right now."

Charles is growing dimmer. "We all agreed to do our part. Your part is Princess Ruth. See to it without delay."

I wake to the reverberating noise of a large crash. Where am I? Reorienting myself takes a moment. I'm in bed waking from a dream. I listen intently straining my ears. There's no more sound. Perhaps the crash was only a part of my dream. I flip on the light. Four a.m. I switch off the lamp while giving thanks the island electricity is back on.

I settle back to sleep hoping I'll dream again. Whether he is rich or not, I've got a bad taste in my mouth that Charles Bishop is a calculating rat. Out for himself only and heaven help any native Hawaiians who get in his way.

I'm half asleep, in that dreaming space where the unreal is real and the real takes on gauzy raiments' of long ago ghosts. Suddenly my dream arrives.

It's Princess Ruth. We're inside a long grass hut which I somehow understand is her home on the Big Island that I've seen in pictures. She's young and beautiful. Spectacular in her passion, only a thrown cloth over her shoulders to cover her nakedness. "No. No." She stands toe to toe with Isaac, fully dressed, who looks completely exasperated. "I," she points to herself, "I … will … not … sell … any … aina." Princess Ruth beats both fists on her chest. Isaac looks like he's trapped in front of a tiger, his frown getting darker and deeper.

"I … sign … no … papers." Princess Ruth throws off her covering cloth. "Get it," she yells. "No papers selling any land to nobody."

The Princess is magnificent. I want to cheer her on. Placing both hands on her hips, she lifts her chin." I am the Governor of this island. What I say is final." The Princess is provocative. How Isaac keeps his hands off her, I don't understand. *Looks like a clear invitation to bed*, I quickly think. This woman is both infuriating and gorgeous, true royalty from head to toe.

With absolutely no warning—the dream Princess Ruth didn't see it coming and neither do I—Isaac hauls back his right hand into a fist. Hits the woman as hard as he can. Dead center in the face. The woman's nose squirts rich red blood. The beautiful woman's hands instinctively cover her face. Blood pours. Isaac turns 180 degrees on his heels. Leaves.

I'm shaking as I wake in the night opening my eyes to darkness. My heart is beating so fast I don't know if I can stand it. Pity and horror tear through my breath and blood. "Thank you, Princess Ruth," I breathe aloud in the darkness. "Thank you for letting me see how it was for you." Using the sheet I wipe away tears, grope for a Kleenex. "I'm so sorry your nose didn't heal right. Got infected. I'm so awfully sorry."

I know in my heart that this is what uncivilized men do—escalate to physical violence when they don't get their own way. My heart goes out. I am Princess Ruth's sister—both of us damaged by ignorant thoughtless men. But Princess Ruth doomed to carry her burden of a deformed face out in the open. For the rest of her life. Made ugly to the thoughtless for the entire rest of her life. Betrayed by the man in her life. Betrayed body and soul by her lawfully wedded husband.

What worse can you do to a beautiful woman? Let me count the ways.

I walk outside to get the paper. I walk from darkness behind me into the beginning of light. Huge dark clouds, high and towering, obscure where the sun will be. But a birthing pink new-day insists, for there over in the corner, hangs a small lacy pink cloud. Day will come. I'm given this day, given life that I might appreciate and feel the glory, that I might be useful and enjoy all the tasks and opportunities of this day. How lucky I am.

And my Hawaiian research continues for I use every spare moment.

Mahele, that great partitioning of Hawaiian lands, ironically means *to share*. *Surveying the Mahele* is loaded with fascinating tidbits and some weaseling about, or making excuses:

> One fact is virtually uncontested: Little of the land of Hawaii is still in the possession of those people who are largely of Hawaiian ancestry. There is no question that the *mahele* did more than provide for the transition to private ownership of land; it resulted in non-Hawaiians quickly gaining possession of large tracts of land and ultimately acquiring much of the most valuable land, other than that retained by the government. The *mahele* even proved a failure in that last regard, because the crown and government lands were lost to Hawaiians after the overthrow of the monarchy.[235]

Lost sounds careless, like it's the Hawaiian's fault their crown and government lands moved out of their control—how about stolen? Which is what really happened. We won't lose sight of these *crown* and *government* lands. But take a look below and remember that *Surveying the Mahele* writes of surveyors like George Norton Wilcox who missed surveying Niihau by 14,000 acres claiming 47,000 when Niihau was really 61,000 acres:

> Missionaries who acted as surveyors and land agents seem to have done so partly because they felt such duties were consistent with their chosen work, and partly because they felt the need to give their families financial security or benefits that could not otherwise be obtained. The fact that descendants of missionary families ended up controlling a significant portion of the land in Hawaii is not in itself an indication that the missionaries themselves had planned to wrest control of the country from the people they came to help.[236]

Well maybe not. But what do you think? And, shouldn't these wrongs be rectified? Here's another tidbit from *Surveying the Mahele* that as a resident of Kauai, fascinated me: "Interestingly, this was the only ahupuaa [Kalihikai: a section of land from mountain to shore] on Kauai that was given to an alii native to the island [Keliiahonui, the son of Kaumualii or King K], the rest being given to alii born and raised on the other islands." Given, and isn't that interesting—you just up and give the land where native people live and have always lived—to, effectively, strangers from other islands.

Wilcox Hospital is imposing, cold and impersonal. It's hard not to be intimidated as I'm coming to see Barbara, now well enough to have visitors. Then I laugh to myself remembering the horse ridden up these steps to visit its owner. The friend thought seeing his horse would cheer him up. I'll bet hospital officials weren't amused.

I'm still smiling as I search out Barbara's room down corridors quiet in mid-afternoon lull. Barbara, propped in bed, dim light, sips water in her private room. At first glance she's white and drawn until a radiant welcome.

"How are you?" I grin holding up my bouquet of pink ginger.

"I'm good. Much better. There's a vase for those flowers." She points. "Just add them to those birds-of-paradise."

"You had us all mighty worried." I follow flower instructions, then pull up a chair. The air feels slightly antiseptic and I'm slightly uneasy as always in hospitals with their heavy reminders of illness and death just out of sight.

As if she catches my wariness, Barbara looks hard into my face. "I need help," she says simply. "It's my farm. It's a big worry. I could lose my farm." Her smile and radiant look gone, she's again white and drawn and looks years older than I remember.

"Oh Barbara," I say, my heart going out to my friend, "tell me what I can do?"

The relief on Barbara's face is palpable. Taking a deep breath, she sighs as if releasing a worry to the wind. "I need boots on the ground," she says borrowing military terminology. "When I got ill, my farm-partner left. Maybe she thought I was contagious." Barbara tries to smile. "She just picked up her suitcases and actually vacated the island. I never dreamed such a thing. The doctors tell me I'm lucky. But I'll be stuck here for a while. They don't know how long."

"It's okay," I say. "I'll go to your farm right now. Check things out for you. Give me directions. And tell me, which is the neighbor who called you? I'll talk with them and report back. See what they think."

As I squeeze Barbara's hand and leave, my mind catches on a wild idea. Barbara needs farm help. I'll be out of a job as I do my whistle-blowing and leave or get fired. Perhaps against all odds, this is a win-win situation in cocoon.

Achieving the impossible requires that you outwit your voice of reason and access the whimsical part of your nature that inherently delights in the possibilities of the imagination.

Consider that we are living at a major turning point in the history of humanity, a time of great crisis and great opportunity. It may be unreasonable to imagine that you can make a difference to a world in crisis based on how you undertake your own healing, yet I believe this to be true. It makes no sense to our logical minds that as we heal, the whole of life heals. Yet the power of one mustard seed can move a mountain; the power of one clear light does illuminate the darkness; the power of a person devoted to truth becomes a channel for healing grace that benefits all humanity.

Carolyn Myss, Defy Gravity:
Healing Beyond the Bounds of Reason

CHAPTER SIXTEEN

ALICE WALKER SAYS that we are pioneering. "Deep inside us is the longing for rebirth as women powerful enough to make a difference in the saving of the world. The Grandmother self is hungering to be born—not as someone small and destined for Alzheimer's or a nursing home, but intense, concentrated, her true size, focused on the truth of our situation as human beings who have lost our way."[237]

I think it's the Chinese who observed—*if you save a life then you're responsible for that life.* Information from *Aloha Niihau: Oral Histories*[238] brings disquiet. On Niihau, who is saving who from what?

This uneasiness starts as intrigue: three sweet women's faces on the cover. And that *Aloha Niihau* is written in Hawaiian with questions for students and that all is translated into English is fitting. At first glance, life on Niihau is idyllic: no locked doors, children always safe, always family and neighbors to watch over them, no rent, beaches, fishing, pig hunting, community gatherings where everyone takes part. Some schooling. And then I notice there's church, church and more church.

One of the authors and her family moved to Kauai when she was thirteen. Her brother with heart problems needed to be near a hospital; Niihau has neither hospital nor physician:

> Now we live here on Kauai and we continue those things that we learned from our parents as they did them on Niihau: morning family devotional, evening family devotional and weekday services. [Weekday services are Monday, Wednesday and Saturday.] You can go to weekday services after church, but sometimes it is not possible. But you can have devotional at home. Some families are not able to make services at the church, but they hold services at home. You can have weekday services at home. You can have morning and evening family devotional at home and then on Sundays, you go to church.[239]

My atheist father, a snatched away at twelve altar-boy Catholic, yells gleefully in my ear, *Religion is the opiate of the masses.*

Disquiet rolls upon me. All that church. All that indoctrination that started with the Sinclairs and Robinsons buying the island. All that, *Do unto others.* All that isolation. Leave Niihau and you can't come back. Isolation. Inbreeding. Isolation. Cut off from their kin and kind. Hawaiians are family; old Hawaiians didn't isolate themselves.

It's disquieting. Something feels not right on Niihau.

I awake with Princess Ruth urgent in my thoughts. She wants me to do something but I don't know what. The dream is pleasant. Princess Ruth is happy sitting in the midst of flowing Wailua river water, high upstream where it's shallow. Not my choice of fish but she munches on a raw mullet like a carefree maiden. Beautiful. The banks of the murmuring river are lush green. A vine hangs over where happy people wait to swing out and drop laughing into the river. Joy and happiness.

Still Princess Ruth has a message for me. *Move on*, I can swear I hear the words. *You can't stay still. Move on*. In the dream, she looks at me expectedly, slightly smiling. *It's time for the next thing.*

I come awake wondering, *What can we do? What is the next thing?*

My mind fills immediately with recent reading and I know there are good people to help. "The business rule of thumb in the last century—cheaper is better—is being supplemented by a new mantra for success: sustainable is better, healthier is better, and humane is better, too."[240]

Radical transparency lets us know true facts so we can vote with our shopping dollars. So, like with Wikileaks, we learn the truth behind the lies and equivocating.

Ecological Intelligence[241] tells us what many already know, that customers are no longer lone individuals, isolated and voiceless. Sharing information freely creates a collective awareness that can trigger a coordinated reaction. "Consumers can talk back to business in a far more powerful way than ever, en masse and synchronized."[242]

Eighty thousand nurses and Trans fat are an *Ecological Intelligence* real life example of what can happen when *true labeling* is followed.

Trans fat (hydrogenated oils) was patented by chemist Wilhelm Normann in1902 and soon were giving cakes, cookies, and the like a longer shelf life. A first hint of official trouble (almost a hundred years later; keep that in mind about GMOs and pesticides) was a 1993 British medical journal *The Lancet* reporting data from more than eighty thousand nurses, noticing that women whose diets were high in trans fats had a higher likelihood of heart attacks.

By 1997, 939 nurses had already died from heart disease. The researchers knew what was going on with trans fat, but the rest of us danced in ignorance. By 2000 the FDA released a study estimating that removing trans fat from U.S. foods could save about seven thousand lives a year. If you labeled trans fat then consumers could make healthy choices.

In 2001 *The Institute of Medicine* concluded: there is no *safe* level of trans fat in food.

Interestingly, companies vowing they couldn't cut trans fat found that—when competitors cut the fat, labeled their products, and customers bought them by the droves—yes, these companies can get rid of trans fat (hydrogenated oils) and were soon proudly labeling their products as "trans fat free."

The federal government never banned hydrogenated oils. The crucial shift was in the *information available* to consumers. The public (is anybody surprised) wants health. And, if necessary, is willing to pay more for it.

Here's a powerful GMO solution. Make the companies label the stuff and watch people stay away in droves. Get accurate information to the public about GMOs—and the companies who push them—and watch what happens.

Aware and concerned consumers are already learning how ratty, politically-driven, and plain out-of-date our U.S testing for toxicology is when compared with Europe's REACH (Registration, Evaluation, and Authorization of Chemicals).[243]

When we know the hidden impacts of our choices, we make better choices. Simple as that. And we need to support good-choice companies. Full transparency about the impacts of what we buy "allows shoppers to vote with their dollars for more ecologically intelligent technologies, ingredients, and design—and so shifts market share toward them—commerce will reform itself, not just in the name of responsibility but in pursuit of profit."[244] We decide for ourselves: will we pay more for ethically made and labeled products? Go to the necessary trouble to search them out? Remember, with every purchase we are voting with our dollars.

For the moment Barbara and I sit quietly. With slight color in her cheeks and animation she's looking more like her old self. Staying in bed in the hospital and being inactive, especially after her farm-working lifestyle, has brought her unaccustomed aches and pains. I'm telling her about Kaimana and a healing method he uses to control pain.

"I was so worried," I tell Barbara. "Kaimana had a chronic health problem that he refused to take care of. First he told me he would have an operation when the doctors said he should, and then he refused. He simply announced he'd changed his mind."

"That was a shock, I'll bet," Barbara observes.

"Yes, I came close to leaving him because of it. Then after some thought I began understanding what it's like dealing with an addicted person. I got it that you don't interact with a person, you deal with an addiction because the addiction always comes first!"

"Never thought about it like that, but I imagine you're right. Think of the gyrations people go through to get their hands on cigarettes, or alcohol, drugs. So, after a while you're an idiot to get upset when the addicted one does it again—whatever it is. They're just being an addict, always putting their addiction first," Barbara says thoughtfully.

"Yes," I agree. "I thought Kaimana had a serious problem that he was refusing to take care of. Ever. Well," I shrug and feel my lips go up in a smile, "I was wrong. Kaimana was taking care of his problem, only outside of conventional paths. He wanted things private until he knew the healing would work. He was in a program with his friend Levon, doing a deep hooponopono. Kaimana's descriptions are graphic. I almost see them happening. All the old negativity stored in his body, sucking energy, is released by prayer, forgiveness, knowledge.

"And new knowledge is gained. Kaimana tells of going toward pain instead of our usual scrambling away as fast as we can, blocking out the pain. And he used chakra points in the center of his hands to laser-point and focus his healing force ... mana, I suppose ... to needed places."

I learn forward taking her hand. "Barbara, listen to this—you may want to try it: in your thoughts, reach out to the pain. Take a deep breath and open your mind to experience all the pain you can. Hold the pain. Feel the pain. Become the pain. Let pain saturate your universe. Breathe the pain and stay holding the pain as long as you can. I tried this for myself with hurts and small pains and it works."[245]

"What have I got to lose? I'll try it."

"If it is disgraceful for a single individual to steal, it is no less disgraceful for a nation, an aggregate of individuals, to steal." Walter Gresham, U.S. Secretary of state, 1893-1895[246]

I've got my head in my hands, sighing loudly, close to feeling put-upon—the Princess wants me to learn more about sovereignty, about Hawaii being a separate independent nation. As a newcomer, I feel as welcome as a tornado. Sovereignty, now my task, has a **Keep Away** sign around its neck for many dedicated women and men put lives at risk, spend great energy and thought on these questions.

For good reason I've skated around—*What To Do Now About Sovereignty*. Sovereignty is too complicated, too long ago, and what could I do anyway? Excellent reasons for continuing to dig my head in the sand, and as helpful. Creeping past my resistance with the enthusiasm of a snail, I finally get it: Princess Ruth hasn't brought me this far so I'd pussyfoot away from the difficult.

Then as usual when I become serious, sovereignty percolates in surprising places. Amazed, I find this in a contemporary novel about quilts:

[Should Hawaii leave the U.S.?] Nani didn't believe that was a practical goal. She wanted reparations for stolen lands, government support for the preservation of native culture, and a formal apology from the United States government—and as a botanist, she also wanted a strong federal commitment to protect the islands' native ecology....

Nani also didn't want reparations limited to native Hawaiians alone, but to the descendants of all people of all ethnicities who had pledged their loyalty to the Kingdom of Hawaii before the overthrow—Hawaiian, Asian, and European alike. This put her at odds with others who believed only native Hawaiians deserved compensation. You have to understand, the Hawaiian sovereignty movement was and still is fractured. Different people with different ideas of what is right and what should be done, sometimes so busy arguing among themselves that little good is accomplished…. Nani knew that unless the different factions could unite, or at least cooperate, they would never make any real progress…. She met with leaders of various groups to help them find common ground, certain principles that they could all stand behind. She hoped that if they could achieve even one small goal by working together, they would see the wisdom in putting aside their differences and forming a lasting alliance.[247]

"Hawaiians need to learn to work together." I make my pronouncement as if I know what I'm talking about—I've just read a novel about quilts and I'm definite. *Hawaiians will never get sovereignty until they learn to work together.* Meaning: Hawaiians will never get justice, fairness, redress until they come together and learn to speak as one voice.

"That's a cop-out." Strong, without anger, the middle-aged Hawaiian man with white hair in a pony tail sits across the table. It's his and his wife Grace's petroglyph-marked table. Michael and Grace have graciously come to sit with me at their Bed and Breakfast across from the rolling ocean in Anahola where I've come to check out staying here. "Look at your Democrats and Republicans. Do they agree? Look at our county council. Look at any group of people. Every single person alive has their own opinion."

Instantly I'm brought to a new reality. The matter of Hawaiian sovereignty is as difficult a problem as I've ever seen. And, truth to tell, I took the easy way out: Hawaiians need to learn to work together.

Well hell—don't we all? Need to learn to work together for the good of all. Learn to do right? Care for our Brothers and Sisters? Et cetera. *Get real,* I tell myself. *Get some common sense. Don't talk about things you know nothing about.*

And especially not to people who've been right there on the front lines— gone to jail for their beliefs in the famous Anahola14[248] case in 1991. Get some respect.

Grace, a sweet woman who seems good to the bone, has managed to give me the Kama aina rate for staying here. I get the phone number again knowing I will return. Michael and Grace are relieved as we uncover mutual friends. "Nice women," is the agreement and I'm approved by association.

Michael and Grace have power, mana. Their place has mana power. The unseen twin Anahola mountains pull like a magnet. I want to be here. This is the portal of birth that the Dalai Lama was intent on visiting. Sovereignty born here? A new sovereignty? I could believe it.

Now to study *Wahine Noa: for the life of my country.* This is Keahi Felix's twenty-year personal story of her engagement with sovereignty—a book handed me yesterday by a friend in a synchronicity that makes me appreciate anew Princess Ruth and the tasks she gives me.

I'm captured from the opening page: *Five Ways This Book May Lead You To Appreciate Hawaiians and Hawaii In A New Way.*[249] "So you think we in Hawaii have a host culture? Think again. Hosts are the owners of the house where the party is held."

My capsule of Keahi Felix's story is that the Graces in Anahola took matters into their own hands and three times built a community center and home upon vacant land listed as Homestead Lands. The State of Hawaii sent police to decimate the first buildings; hurricane Iniki got the second rebuilding and, after the third rebuilding, the police destroyed the buildings and also carted away the Graces and twelve friends, including the author, to jail for their audacity. The Graces and their friends were making a point—Homelands[250] for the native Hawaiians are a tragic joke:

> After 70 years, the Advisory committee finds that the homesteading program has provided very few tangible benefits for beneficiaries of the trust. Only 17.5 percent of available lands are being homesteaded. At the same time, over 62 percent of the lands are being used by non-natives, often for minimal compensation. Especially egregious is the continued questionable use of valuable homelands by the United States Government, with virtually no compensation to the trust. These

include some of the most suitable lands for development of homes. With a waiting list of over 20,000 applicants, it is unconscionable that the United States should continue to so blatantly and arrogantly defy the interests of the Native Hawaiian community, whose rights it should be aggressively defending. The Advisory Committee solicits the help of the United States Commission on Civil Rights in Requiring the return of these improperly held lands, or an exchange of lands at least equally suited for homesteading.[251]

Sovereignty takes on a different flavor:

> What I want Hawaiians to gain most of all is what I call sovereignty of spirit—a combination of culture pride, discipline and drive. That is more important than all the money and land. No Great White Father, no Uncle Tats can give you that. You must want it, and find it, yourselves—and until you do, Hawaii will not be complete for any of us … End of sermon. Thank you and aloha from my heart.[252]

Several friends have joined pro-sovereignty *The Hawaiian Kingdom Government*;[253] they've given up their U.S. passports for those issued by the Kingdom. I haven't yet taken this step but I'm following with intense interest the court actions of Dr. David Keanu Sai[254] as he seeks redress in international court "against the United States of America concerning the prolonged occupation of the Hawaiian Kingdom, which was filed with the United Nations Security Council on July 5, 2001."[255]

I'm living a Judy Chicago story. This artist found the subject matter of her holocaust paintings so depressing that she had to force herself to run every morning before she could summon the energy to actually begin painting.

I feel so small. And the task is huge. Living now is perilous and momentous as never before. *Overwhelmed* is what I mostly feel. How can I—a haole newcomer hope to understand these complex Hawaiian islands with their fascinating sinned-against and wronged people?

Yet I also begin to understand my current intersection between a perceived future that leads to total human extinction and my growing conviction that I must do all I can—right or wrong—to change the course of a dismal future. And how insane is that? One person against the world. This behavior gets you locked up, makes you crazy, or take drugs, or make a mess of your life and of those around you. Or to simply waste your existence on this planet.

Alternatives. Tell your truth as sanely as you can. Seek alliances and support where you can find them. I think we're back to what I've told and retold myself over the years: *I do what I can.* I don't have to be brilliant. Or perfect. Or get it done tomorrow. My task is simply to do what I can. To follow Princess Ruth's directions. Which means in this case to beam my version of truth-light on Hawaiian history as this history has shared itself with me in all its myriad fascinations. It's truth and lies and betrayal. And including a past Hawaiian history that extends into this present.

How to write it and live it and understand it? An impossible task except for the most brilliant and I'm not! I never set out to save the world; saving myself is a full time occupation.

Still things happen. Small understandings arrive. Then I'll learn why those particular puzzling events happened. And their meaning, for as present events become clearer, future paths gain definition and appeal.

I always knew things were wrong with the way our government and institutions ran things. In the first place they were run entirely by white men with a few token women and minorities scattered among the powerful white. A lot of those powerful men weren't fair and didn't play fair. They said one thing and did another. They lied and did their best to convince us their lies were truth. They won, that is, they made money, exercised power and most of them cared less than nothing about the rest of us. Increasingly, bottom line immediate profit was all.

As for myself, I joined the winning side when I could and mostly kept my mouth shut, my eyes down, and tried to figure things out. What rules did we play by today? To get along as best I could for myself and those I cared for. Normal. Like most people. Win some, lose some. Take care of yourself.

And then along come a couple of books that knock me into a change of consciousness. First, *John Perkins, Confessions of An Economic Hit Man* with his[256] "The United States spends over 487 billion conducting a war in Iraq while the United Nations estimates that for less than half that amount we could provide clean water, adequate diets, sanitation services, and basic education to every person on the planet."[257] This is from his introduction in 2004.

Powerful men have taken over the blatant running of the world and unchecked men and multinational corporations (many American) are taking all of us into extinction. The human race is heading, purely and simply, into the death of our world. And for what? So a very few can make so-called profit and money. And hold power beyond belief.

Money and power rule. Those in charge don't care how they get the power and money or who or what is damaged or killed in the process. Everything comes down to an immediate bottom line. An expert who has been there writes:

> … this imperialist drive has been and continues to be the cause of most wars, pollution, starvation, species extinctions, and genocides. And it has always taken a serious toll on the conscience and well-being of the citizens of those empires, contributing to social malaise and resulting in a situation where the wealthiest cultures in human history are plagued with the highest rates of suicide, drug abuse, and violence.[258]

I will only become more shrill if I go on. You'll have to read his book.

In John Perkins' newer book: *The Secret History of the American Empire: The Truth About Economic Hit Men, Jackals, and How to Change the World,* Perkins covers our world from an American Empire insider's chilling viewpoint. Beginning with Jakarta in Asia, through Latin America, the

Middle East and ending in Africa we learn who and where the bodies and countries are harmed and buried and who did it. Along with Judy Chicago (running to build energy before painting the holocaust), I'll need to run around the world to assimilate this one!

Yet Perkins is hopeful. He tells of RAN [259]who is changing corporation policies and practices for the better. And other reformer groups uniting under: "We commit to creating a stable, sustainable, and peaceful world for all people everywhere." No one, even in the depths of their poverty is left out. Perkins closes with, "Today is the day for us to begin to truly change the world."[260]

Speaking of changing the world, I've given my world a nice jolt. With my heart in my mouth (now I know what that means) I march into Kevin's office, bold as if I belonged there. I knew he was out of town. I'd scouted and also knew his secretary was late from lunch and likely to be later still as an old boyfriend was implicated.

Nervously, my over the shoulder purse held my digital camera, I walked into Kevin's office as if I belonged, found latest records in his in-box, photographed them and some letters from home-office that I photographed unread. Snooping around a bit, I found more old pesticide records and took pictures of them.

Then I got out of the office trying not to wonder how this would end, but not hesitating at all to put everything on a disk file and mail it off to the class-action lawyer. My relief is immense. At long last I am on the right side.

The headline of the *Garden & Grinds* (food) section of *The Garden Island* grabs my attention: *Judge Orders Removal of Sugar Beet Seed Plants.*[261] Last I remember those GMO beets were on full throttle straight for our dinner table. "In his order Tuesday, [Judge Jeffrey] White wrote that the environmental groups had shown that the genetically modified sugar beets could contaminate other crops, including through cross-pollination.

'The likely environmental harm … is irreparable,' White wrote."

Judge White had earlier ruled to put on hold a permit to plant sugar beet plants to grow seeds to grow tons more sugar beets. The judge just stopped that GMO permit process in its usually well-oiled process by our U.S. Department of Agriculture's Animal and Plant Health Inspection Services. Anyway the judge told this part of the Ag Department, No. And they gave the permit anyway. Now the judge says, in effect, *Too bad you didn't follow my directions and do an environmental study. I'm still saying No until you do.*

This article makes me think first, that something concrete is finally being done to regulate GMO food from the bottom up—as GMOs should have been subjected to peer and scientific study in the first place. And then I remember Michael Taylor (former Monsanto lawyer) and how he's recycled back and forth between Monsanto—in some views, the most evil company in the world—and our government quite often.

This current GMO contest is probably only beginning. Which side of the debate do you think Michael Taylor's going to come down on: Powerfully and influentially, and knowing where-all-the rule-bending-spaces-to-promote-and-protect GMOs are? Let us guess!

"We need to talk." Kaimana is quietly serious his dark eyes intent but loving.

Was I hearing right? A man who actually wants to talk. "What?" I ask brilliantly.

"Pack for a camping weekend. Something warm. We'll leave at four tomorrow. Be in Maui in an hour."

I search Kaimana's face looking for I know not what. "Yes," I say as inevitable as rain. "We do need to talk."

And so Kaimana takes me to Maui. I am dazzled as I'm meant to be. Maui. An island. Romance in the Pacific. Pearl Harbor. James Michener. And my past of course swimming underwater, haunting the cozy moon, dodging shadow clouds at night. Adventure you can drive to—if you know where and Kaimana had been to Maui before.

He was shot in Iraq leading some troops where he shouldn't have been. Recuperating took a long time. He had an old buddy, half Hawaiian, half Japanese in Lahaina who'd showed him this place.

'Why did you do it?' I ask. Kaimana had gone in an open door first and been hit in the low back—a dangerous wound.

"I was the leader," he said simply. "My responsibility."

He blotted the stars and the wind and the rain when it came. Our hidden place was on a cliff overlooking rocks and the ocean. Nothing between us and Alaska, he said, but thousands of miles of open blue water, a few whales, some tuna and various unseen sea creatures. We'd pitched our tent under Australian pines, notorious tall weed-trees, noxious and prone to break.

Wind whipped the branches as we lost our thinking minds. Or set them aside. Separately (we spoke of it later), we considered the danger and dismissed it. For what we held in our arms was the rarest of jewels. Hearts long-starved found shelter. Storm and death were nothing to us. We'd already been there. But this, this was new.

How love makes the world narrow and expand at once while you own both spaces. Only the lover exists, yet the new world is immense creating itself.

We're in the womb of time (I thought the next morning) as we skirted volcanic rock to the tide pools. The dawn was clear with a setting full moon. The air glowed sort of yellow, pearly, luminous, a thing apart. Magic. Anything could happen.

We spoke not a word. I watched the rocks, the volcanic boulders as we descended to the sea. Old coral had risen over the millennium to the surface broken by storms too immense to imagine. Kaimana watched me. I felt him drink my face, skim off emotion like foam as it arose. Fiercely vulnerable, I brushed away all the jealous ghosts from the past. We were alive. The ghosts were dead having had their chances.

So close to the tide pools now, empty crab shells splattered the encircling rock rising like a Hollywood set behind us. Then a yellow butterfly here by the sea, two white terns. Life and death walking hand in hand. In the first shallow tide pool, tiny darting fish. Beauty being born time out of mind. Creation began here, all life. All was shadows then darkness came to bask in the open, primitive life crawling from the sea. So long ago time has no meaning, primitive, elemental, no humans but us.

We were frail containers. Emotion beat through my skin punching holes in all I had been. I closed my eyes and simply felt this new world. I was the restless ocean so patient and fierce. I was this enduring rock, contorted in marvelous ways. In one million years one pound of sand would be created. Each grain was a birth, a joy, a step up evolution's ladder.

A blow hole gulped behind me, noisy breathing, straining for air, a monster driving me forward.

Our eyes fastened on the towels. We laid them on top of each other where the moss, moistened by sea water, grew between the tide pools. I stepped out of myself with my bathing suit dismissed at my feet. Only his eyes wide as the wind. Only his hands steady, silent, the reality of statues, stone come to life. Tears slid down my cheeks. He cradled my face as tender as feathers. What was me? What was sea? What was him? Wrapped in dreams of all I'd ever wanted, I didn't know or care.

When happiness comes, take it. Take it, I exulted. No reality but this. And this is forever. How could I not love Kaimana? How could I ever stop? Creation and destruction. Love and war. Dare I say he showed me heaven? And the essence of nature on earth.

It used to amaze me when love-making was done nothing was left. Those intense feelings, that merging should leave residue like sparkling stars, some glitter. And odd how memories catch on certain happenings: a remark, a look on a face, a gesture, a slim body in a particular light, a zipper going down on brown corduroy slacks, two bodies together, how one touches a bare back on a gold couch and the other jumps. How a woman lies on a bed eyes closed. A man enters, watches, bends and gently kisses her foot—mouth and hands lingering as she opens her eyes.

I love you. The times it's said and means nothing.

I love you. The times it's not said and means everything.

I love you. The times it's not spoken nor needs to be.

What a marvelous thing to own a body. What a toy. A plaything. An instrument. A joy. "What do you do," Kaimana asks, "when you've done everything—kissed, loved, held as tight as you can—and still you want more?"

"You do what we're doing," I said. "You talk, you move in their mind. You crawl in their heart." I lick the edge of his mouth. "You try not to spoil it," I said.

"You make promises and you hold to them." After a long pause, gazing deep into my eyes, Kaimana adds. "What was two is now one."

Princess Ruth pushes me but I don't know what she wants. A vague uneasiness settles and I'm usually driven to do something. Anything. With too much to feel and think about—Kaimana has changed my entire life and I know it—the internet is a perfect match for my mood—a splendid way to waste time and not think about things.

After a couple hours on the internet chasing FDA and USDA, Michael Taylor and Monsanto, I am discouraged with our government and its impartiality. But gaining access to inner workings lifts my mood—this of the USDA and the FDA:

> The Food and Drug Administration (FDA) and the United States Department of Agriculture (USDA) work in conjunction to protect the American people on issues related to the safety of the food and medicines we consume ...
>
> The FDA is an agency consisting of a number of centers and offices dealing with specific topics. It is part of the U.S. Department of Health and Human Services and is responsible for protecting the public health by assuring the safety and efficacy of drugs, biological products, medical devices, cosmetics, products that emit radiation and the nation's food supply ...
>
> The USDA is a full federal government department headed by a cabinet member, the Secretary of Agriculture ... The FDA and

USDA work toward maintaining the safety of the food chain and its consumers. ...

The FDA is involved in regulating drugs, medical products and potential health risks that are not in scope for the USDA. This can at times cause friction between the two agencies and their policies toward certain groups or businesses. One prime example would be tobacco products.[262]

My reading on friction between the FDA and USDA is that the FDA wants tobacco products out of here as tobacco addicts, maims and kills people. The USDA says it must protect farmers (read big tobacco companies) instead of telling farmers and big tobacco to get real, that their products kill, cause billions in health care costs (as if they didn't know) and to find something else to grow. And to do it right now.

Michael Taylor and Monsanto: These are so intertwined it's sickening.[263]

And here's another view of Monsanto's Michael Taylor;[264] is this really true?

USDA oversees everything we put into our body. We are getting a representative of a company I would say is the most evil in the world. Yes, even more so than Halliburton and Exxon, and that is saying something.

Michael Taylor Esq is a Washington D.C. attorney who once represented Monsanto in that regard. He replaced Clarence Thomas. Taylor also used his powerful connections to be named as an FDA and USDA undersecretary, where he wrote the guidelines for the *future* approval of genetically engineered organisms, thereby serving his true master, Monsanto.

Taylor performed a key role by paving the way for the approval of Monsanto's genetically engineered organisms for our food supply.[265]

It is early morning. I sense the coming day still wrapped in darkness like my dreaming state, not yet ready to release. The drums let me know I am in a place of the Hawaiians. I'm in a canoe on the pale brown Wailua River looking over to shore into a Hawaiian settlement. The huge heiau is directly above on the pali cliff, invisible through hau bushes.

Princess Ruth beckons and through the magic of dreams I am at her side in a glade of red and pink ginger flowers. I am sitting on a coconut stool; she's regal on a throne-like affair I notice without registering as I'm focused on her face and manner. Princess Ruth has a message and I notice that we don't use words only speak with our minds.

"I will always be with you," she tells my brain cells. "I am an ancestor. You can call on me. When you need me … ask for help."

I am rocked in deep oceans of no-nonsense love as long lines of strong ancestor women fade into the distance. As the drums grow softer I feel myself moving through layers of time.

Coming awake, emerging into today's awareness, I muse on what is required to step into this field of love. This Circle of Grace. This wisdom and beauty of everyday life, of doing the best you can? What is needed for transformation? I think of owing allegiance to something larger than yourself—having a pure heart and sincere intention to act for the good of all. Idly I wonder what it could be like to be part of a Council of Women with power, internally and out in the world.

"Oh Barbara," I call from the door as I dance into her hospital room. "You won't believe it. So many problems solved just like that. When Kaimana and I came back from Maui, we already knew. We're going to move in together. Kaimana wants us married first." Barbara and I beam at each other. She looks as happy as I feel. "And I guess I want a commitment too," I admit.

"So much to tell, Barbara, You won't believe it." I remember to take a deep breath. "I was going through my stuff again, thinking about moving … when I found that Chinese box of Thomas's childhood things. It was under blankets in the back of the closet. I didn't even hesitate but opened the box ready to face whatever I'd find. Barbara, it's wonderful. Bonds. Canadian bonds. First thing when I opened the box, bonds."

"What an incredible gift." Barbara's joy for me lights up her face. "I'm so glad. I know you've been worried about money and now you don't have to be. What a gift he's given you."

"Thomas left a note. He was worried about the economy, concerned about our savings, our future." I'm feeling both happy and sad as I take a chair. "Thomas planned to give me the note and the bonds. And then he died before he could. All this time and he's been looking out for me. I'm so sorry for doubting him, doubting his love. He knew the bonds would make me feel safe. Thomas was an extraordinary man. He knew me so well. And loved me. Now I can rest in that assurance. I feel a completion.

"And that's not all." I take her hand. "My lawyer says there's enough to do whatever I want. And what I want," I pause to calm myself and remember to breathe, "is to buy half your farm. I know you've been looking for a new partner. Kaimana and I talked it over and agreed to ask you about creating a partnership for the three of us. Isn't it wonderful? Everything is wonderful."

As if to join our party, a smiling nurse enters wheeling trays of medication.

"And how are you feeling today?" she asks Barbara with an aside to me, "We were all watching her carefully. She's much improved now."

"I can see that," I say. "Thank you for your concern and care."

Barbara has her temperature taken, swallows pills and the nurse wheels away.

"I've so much to tell you. I keep remembering and then forgetting." My beating heart takes up a faster rhythm. "Such an exciting time."

I find out all this horrible stuff, become involved and then almost forget why I delved into background facts in the first place. It's so I can better understand the where, how and why of genetically modified organisms (GMOs). I learn GMOs have been questionable right from the start, that chemical and pesticide companies, masquerading as healthy seed and food producers, have lied and cheated their way to vast wealth for themselves and deleterious health for the rest of us.

Now for some local connections. And how fascinating to realize that here's exactly where Princess Ruth has been leading me all along!

It's those 3400 acres of prime former sugar cane land here on the Westside. The toxic acres from Hanapepe to Waimea that Bobby's *Letter to the Editor* wrote about. That 3400 acres recently leased to Dow AgroSciences (Dow Chemical) by Gay & Robinson, the corporation and not the direct owners of Niihau. The kicker here is that these 3400 acres are supposed to be, and will remain, *farm* land. But farm land that's sliced and diced and pesticided to death by any chemical or GMO company that leases it. Is this insecticide treatment of precious Hawaiian land *farming*? I don't think so. Is this conservation, sustainable practices? I don't think so. Is it neighborly to fence everything so people can't get to the beach—leaving only one not-so-good road? What are they hiding?

Is this carrying on the rape, the stealing of Kauai, of Hawaii? Perpetuating wrongs, poisonings done to the people, to the land, to Hawaii? Yes. Yes. Yes.

The truth will set people free, Princess Ruth informs me. Her voice in my head is emphatically loud.

"Samantha, I don't understand but I need to tell you a dream."

Kaimana and I sit side by side slightly turned toward each other in low beach chairs. It is that magic time when day yields to night but not quite yet as the air is still luminously yellow with a recently set sun.

I am relaxed and happy and unconcerned as I say, "Tell me."

"Princess Ruth came to me," he says simply.

No longer relaxed, I draw a sharp breathe but say nothing. Waiting.

"She wore a purple gown—looked like velvet—and was so royal I felt like kneeling but there wasn't time. The Princess looked straight at me. Then she smiled graciously … the entire dream only lasted a moment. Princess Ruth moved a hand toward me and said—she was as clear as could be, "You must help Samantha. Her next task. But …" Kaimana is perplexed

... "But, somehow, it was like we'd do this *obligation* together. Samantha," Kaimana takes my hand. "What does this mean?"

I open my mouth but never get a chance to say a word for the light breeze blowing behind us surges into a strong wind like a wall of water that picks up a light scarf I had thrown over my hair. The wind is so sudden I grab my hair but my scarf is already gone.

As Kaimana and I watch the wind dances my pale purple scarf high in the air and out over ocean. Silhouetted against the light, the scarf hangs for long seconds, then dips sharply and comes back to me like a blessing.

We are a small island set in far reaches of a turquoise sea. Yet we have the seeds of greatness. Sustainability is within our grasp. Feeding all our people—and more than just food. Fairness for all. Social justice. Happy lives useful for themselves and inspirations for others.

We can take charge, design, and put in place a new social system. With real liberty and justice for all. Why not?

Use hooponopono to bring justice and to lay ancient problems to final rest. Mitigate and settle differences by employing that magnificent Hawaiian human interaction tool of hooponopono, a healing method developed by Hawaiian ancestors. Kick out the bad guys. Expose them. Make their lives so miserable they can't wait to leave. Why not?

Have contests for great ideas, and superior people to implement them. Meld the best of all cultures past and present. Why not?

Have each town or community set goals, each organization, island-wide. Why not? We, on Kauai, in the islands, live in physical paradise on earth. Why not make the island a paradise indeed, a model, a pattern, a living breathing natural, never before seen on earth, paradise for all?

I think we can, as the conscious among us unite.

"Barbara, it makes no sense. I can't explain. Logic has nothing to do with it." I look at Barbara knowing my face holds equal expressions of puzzlement and strong purpose. "It was like dominoes," I say. "One after one, after one—dreams of Princess Ruth, Kaimana and even Leilani urging me, reminding me I have the money to spend."

Sitting outside the covers, blooming health, Barbara watches intently waiting for me to continue talking.

"What is this?" I burst out. "All these huge messes I've survived: Thomas' death, moving to Kauai, finding the money he left me, the GMOs, getting fired—text message, no less, so typical of Kevin I can't even get angry.

"And then Kaimana and me, like a dream and yet I know it is real. And you, Barbara. You've got your health back. Home to your farm tomorrow. How wonderful is that!"

"Okay Samantha. Slow down." Barbara lifts her right hand in a smoothing gesture. "Take a deep breath. We have plenty of time ... all afternoon. Don't worry. Besides, how bad can it be? You've even said you feel completed with Princess Ruth and your study of Hawaiian history."

As I breathe deeply I feel into the texture of this day. It is all good. I draw another breath as far down into my lungs as I can, let it out slowly.

"I want to run for Mayor of Kauai in the next election."

(Endnotes)

1 *The High Chiefess: Ruth Keelikolani* by Kristin Zambucka
2 I took literary license.
3 Deborah Kent, author of *Hawaii*, a 2008 Scholastic book.
4 *No Mana'o loha O Kaho'olawe* (The Many Feelings of Love For Kaho'olawe) by Walter Ritte Jr. and Richard Sawyer
5 Yet if history stops. What then? We destroy ourselves. We create monster contamination—like GMO's or that deep-water oil hole blown in the Gulf—except if these new contamination threats are fatal to all people, then history can no longer bring eventual justice. Or, cynically, history continues grinding away; we just may not be happy with its results as we become just another extinct species!
6 *E Na Hulu Kupuna Na Puna Ola Maoli No* by Anne Kapulani Landgraf (supported by Hawaiian Affairs and Kamehameha Schools)
7 Juan Wilson, "Down with King Corn," March 2, 2008, The Garden Island (TGI). "On Sunday, Feb. 3, TGI reported"…shortly after 6 p.m. in Hanapepe, a 40-foot shipping container carried by the rain-swollen Hanapepe River struck the bridge …. Eyewitnesses claim the floating container broke open when it hit the main highway bridge and some say they smelled pesticides and saw warning labels on packaging. This container continued out into Hanapepe Bay."
8 *greenpeace.org/gmo*
9 **From:** "Dr. Betty Martini,D.Hum." <bettym19@mindspring.com>
Date: December 9, 2009 10:03:56 AM PST
To: "Ban-GEF-lists.txinfinet.com" <Ban-GEF@lists.txinfinet.com>
Subject: Bayer Loses in Court ---Admits GMO Contamination is Out of Control

Date: Wed, 9 Dec 2009 09:24:25 -0800

Subject: Bayer Loses in Court ---Admits GMO Contamination is Out of
    Control

Bayer Admits GMO Contamination is Out of Control

* Greenpeace International, Dec 8, 2009

* <http://www.greenpeace.org/>Straight to the Source

Bayer has admitted it has been unable to control the spread of its
    genetically-engineered organisms despite 'the best practices [to stop
    contamination]'(1). It shows that all outdoors field trials or commercial
    growing of GE crops must be stopped before our crops are irreversibly
    contaminated.

$2 million US dollar verdict against Bayer confirms company's liability for
    an uncontrollable technology

Greenpeace welcomes the United States federal jury ruling on 4 December
    2009 that Bayer CropScience LP must pay $2 million US dollars to
    two Missouri farmers after their rice crop was contaminated with an
    experimental variety of rice that the company was testing in 2006.

This verdict confirms that the responsibility for the consequences of GE
    (genetic engineering) contamination rests with the company that
    releases GE crops.

Bayer has admitted it has been unable to control the spread of its
    genetically-engineered organisms despite 'the best practices [to stop
    contamination]'(1). It shows that all outdoors field trials or commercial
    growing of GE crops must be stopped before our crops are irreversibly
    contaminated.

A report prepared for Greenpeace International concluded that the total
    costs incurred throughout the world as a result of the contamination
    are estimated to range from $741 million to $1.285 billion US dollars.
    (2) The verdict indicates that Bayer is liable for what could turn out to
    be a large proportion of these costs, as it awards damages in the first
    two of more than 1,000 currently pending lawsuits. The decision must
    be used to support all claims for losses incurred by other US farmers
    whose crops have suffered from GE contamination.

(1) Bayers Defense lawyer, Mark Ferguson as reported in Harris, A. 2009. Bayer Blamed at Trial for Crops 'Contaminated' by Modified Rice. Bloomberg News 4th November 2009, available at:

<http://www.bloomberg.com/apps/news?pid=newsarchive&s id=aT1kD1GOt0N0>http://www.bloomberg.com/apps/ news?pid=newsarchive&sid=aT...

(2) E.N. Blue (2007) Risky Business. Economic and regulatory impacts from the unintended release of genetically engineered rice varieties into the rice merchandising system of the US. Report prepared for Greenpeace International, available online at <http://www.greenpeace. org/raw/content/international/press/reports/risky-business.pdf>http:// www.greenpeace.org/raw/content/international/press....

10 http://www.zimbio.com/Kauai+Hawaii/articles/64/ The+Mystical+Menehune

11 *E Na Hulu Kupuna Na Puna Ola Maoli No* by Anne Kapulani Landgraf

12 *The SuperFerry Chronicles: Hawaii's Uprising Against Militarism, Commercialism and the Desecration of the Earth* by Koohan Paik & Jerry Mander

13 *Honolulu* by Anan Brennert

14 ibid

15 Adrienne Rich, a feminist poet

16 *Diving Deep and Surfacing* by Carol Christ.

17 80 percent by the following account.

18 www.archives.gov/education/lessons/hawaii-petition/

19 This system went on for hundreds of years. Old chief dies peacefully, or is killed probably in war, and new chief takes control of what the old chief had. Common people simply changed their allegiance. Or if they wished, they moved on as people were not serfs or tied to the land. The ruling chief does a good job or people vote with their feet and leave. Fewer people on a chief's land equals fewer people to work and less prestige, and beside everyone knows they left because he—did whatever. The Hawaiians had very cleverly built in checks and balances. The new king, chief, alii (different names for same function) now has the power. Or when the old chief dies, sometimes the question of who will be the

new chief is settled by subordinate chiefs and spiritual leaders getting together and collectively selecting the best person to be their new chief. Hereditary spiritual leaders, advisors to the chief, for example, *kahuna lapaau* are highborn Hawaiians trained in herbal healing. More later about kahunas.

20 Taro and poi (pounded kalo) are a means of survival for the Hawaii people. By eating taro as poi, one at a time as a ritual around the poi bowl *umeke* at the center of the diners, the protocol of Hawaii is maintained. This is a ceremony of life that brings people together and supports a relationship of ohana (family) and of appreciation with the aumakua (ancestors). One-finger poi is thick, three-finger is thin and two-finger is just right. In the old days a person might eat up to five pounds a day.

21 My notes on taro (kalo) combine words from Agnes Keaolani Marti-Kini's *Anahola*, Wikipedia and random reading.

22 Another source says there are well over 100.

23 Vastly simplified, **Lono** presided over fertility, agriculture, rainfall, and music.

    Kane, considered the highest of the four major Hawaiian deities, represented the god of procreation and was worshipped as ancestor of chiefs and commoners. Kane is the creator and gives life and is associated with dawn, sun and sky. No human sacrifice or laborious ritual was needed in the worship of Kane.

    However, **Ku**, brought over by the Tahitians was a war god, reportedly requiring animal and human sacrifices.

    Kanaloa was god of the Underworld and a teacher of magic, according to some. *Kana* means light and *Loa* means far away. According to W.S. Merwin in *The Folding Cliffs* Kanaloa was the God of the West, the Ocean and Death. I've a friend who walks the Kalalau trail on full moon nights and he tells me he feels the presence of Kanaloa, of Nightmarchers. You're supposed to lie down in the dirt off the path until they pass, he tells me and that he doesn't do this but is always careful to be respectful. He says he's felt and heard Nightmarchers clear as anything.

24 *E Na Hulu Kupuna Na Puna Ola Maoli No* by Anne Kapulani Landgraf. When giving a Hawaiian name, Ikiikiikapoliopele, to always give the complete name, a bit tough for the non-native. I can barely get through the pronunciation when I speak slowly. Pele is easier. I cannot think of Princess Ruth as separate from Hawaii as she is embedded in these islands. I feel her mana is founded in nature, in the power of land, trees, mountains, sea and in her alii training and belief's, her self-discipline in spiritual matters.

25 *The Garden Island*, published an article about Princess Ruth and her connection with Kauai. The local historian, Hank Soboleski sent me an email of his article.

26 Deborah Kent, author of *Hawaii*, a 2008 Scholastic book.

27 *The Last King of Paradise* by Eugene Burns.

28 www.canoeplants.com/hau.html

29 *The High Chiefess Ruth Keelikolani* by Kristin Zambucka.

30 Victoria Heckman, *K.O.'D in the Rift*. "In a lease-hold condo or home, the building might be yours, but the land it sat on wasn't. Owners of the dwelling paid rent to the owner of the land. It made for interesting evictions—having to remove your whole house if the owner of the land booted you off."

31 *The Last King of Paradise* by Eugene Burns.

32 *The High Chiefess Ruth Keelikolani* by Kristin Zambucka.

33 ibid. "But U.S. Commissioner Gregg's dispatch to the U.S. Secretary of State, dated July 30, 1857, indicates that Pierce may have had a friendlier association with the Kamehameha family at one time. The dispatch states that Bernice Pauahi Bishop was "...commonly reputed to be the daughter of H.A. Pierce, and there are substantial reasons for believing it."

34 *The Descendants* by Kaui Hart Hemmings.

35 With over half our U.S. budget now going to the military—it's way past time to find better ways to operate in the world than invasion and occupation by our military.

36 *The Last King of Paradise* by Eugene Burns.

37 *Pregnant Darkness* by Monika Wikman.

38 "There were around 84,000 military personnel stationed in Hawaii when Pearl Harbor happened." *The Garden Island*, January 18, 2011, A7. Found in this article about the death of the man who announced the attack. Why so many U.S. soldiers?

39 Claire Hope Cummings, *Food for Everyone*, Yes!, Spring 2009. Claire Hope Cummings is an environmental lawyer, journalist, and the author of *Uncertain Peril: Genetic Engineering and the Future of Seeds*. This book is published in 2008 by Beacon Press, which is Unitarian-Universalist based, a good sign I thought, and then realized, *there I go trusting religion again.*

40 ibid

41 U.S. scientist Amanda Chakrabarty

42 It's also interesting to note that in 1992, "Michael Taylor was appointed FDA's Deputy Commissioner for Policy, a role created to expedite governmental approval process for genetically engineered foods. Prior to his appointment, Taylor was an attorney for Monsanto. Taylor then went on to become Monsanto's Vice-President," a 1992 *Food Democracy* article about Taylor.

43 *Dave Sulkin Cares* by Fletcher Knebel (of *Seven Days in May* fame).

44 Or how about this: "Bones of past indiscretions lay buried in the back yards of most of Kauai's politicians and businessmen, and it was Garcia's [wants to build the resort] unfailing memory as to the location of the burial plots that gave him his clout."

    Or getting to the heart of it: "I call to order the committee's public hearing on the proposal to rezone two square miles of west-side Kauai, popularly known as Menehune Beach [Kekaha in disguise], to permit commercial resort structures. I know plenty of you people, both the construction folks who need jobs and the environmentalists who sometimes want to preserve wild parts of the island at all costs, think this hearing will determine our future for years to come."

Or there's a recent example in Koloa where mall-makers couldn't wait to destroy 100-year-old huge shading monkey-pod trees. Now with the economic down-turn it's three years later and they can't afford to build their shopping center—but historic monkey-pod trees are gone forever.

45 **Here I go again**. I no sooner gain some notion of farmer/GMO interaction than up pops *The Future of Food*. While reading is always my preferred method of learning and entertainment, I admit these documentary films come close to changing my mind. This one is immediate, informative, graphic and beautiful as the film ranges from individual canola farmers in Saskatchewan, Canada to the fields of Oaxaca, Mexico telling the story of corn. I can almost feel my hair curling in horror. How have these companies been allowed to range so far out of control and decency? Can't someone do something about this? Cover information:

> *The Future of Food* offers an in-depth investigation into the disturbing truth behind the unlabeled, patented, genetically engineered foods that have quietly filled U.S. grocery store shelves for the past decade…. The health implications, government policies and push towards globalization are all part of the reason why many people are alarmed about the introduction of genetically altered crops into our food supply…. changing what we eat as huge multinational corporations seek to control the world's food system. The film also explores alternatives to large-scale industrial agriculture, placing organic and sustainable agriculture as real solutions to the farm crisis today.

46 *Kauai: The Separate Kingdom* by Edward Joesting

47 As an aside for those following my Hawaiian history journey, in the following endnote I'll be explaining ancient Kauaian history for myself—not everyone's cup of choice.

48 Let's go back to 1796, before Kamehameha One unites the islands. In July 1796 Kaumualii (King K), 16 years old, is ruler of Kauai and naturally wants his people, and himself I'm sure, to remain free of Kamehameha rule.

"Kaumualii (King K) probably possessed the highest lineage of any chief in all the Islands," states Edward Joesting in his *Kauai: The Separate Kingdom.*

Kamehameha begins his invasion of Kauai with close to 1500 canoes and 10,000 soldiers, half of them armed with muskets—from the U.S. Halfway across the 60-mile wide Kaieie Waho Channel, a huge wind materializes. When the lead canoes capsize, the other canoes sink like dominoes and Kamehameha has to order the remaining canoes to turn back.

However, stories told in Kauai reveal that some warriors made it to Kauai and were defeated and killed, and that invader skulls, after heavy storms, still turn up on Kauai beaches.

"The powerful prayer possessed by King K's mother would put fear and uncertainty in the heart of any mortal. Moreover, throughout the Islands Kauai was noted for the religious nature of its people often referred to as Kauai *pule oo*, Kauai of strong prayers. Certainly these things weighed on Kamehameha's mind, yet he remained determined that Kauai should come under his control."

Kamehameha tried a second time to invade Kauai with even larger forces but, before he set sail, a virulent pestilence struck. It was so bad that people died before they could even get home. Kamehameha caught the horrible disease and survived but all thoughts of invasion were wiped out.

Time passes as King K uses diplomacy to keep Kauai free of Kamehameha rule. Much later, after Kamehameha I is dead, King K is kidnapped by Kamehameha Two (Lilolilo)—lured aboard his yacht which immediately set sail for Honolulu. Kamehameha Two, surely acting on orders of Queen K who is effectively ruling the islands, takes King K to Oahu where he is married to Queen K—who later also married King K's son, George. Queen K proceeds to hold the King of Kauai captive and also his son and heir to Kauai, Prince George P. Kaumualii.

Incidentally, Queen K, the childless favorite wife of Kamehameha I, was not his royal wife because her lineage wasn't sufficiently high. Queen K was a big deal in the Hawaiian acceptance of the missionary's religion. After conversion—she got really sick and felt the missionaries saved her life—she kept only King K as her husband. "She traveled and exhorted the people to go to church and to learn to read and write.... She put a kapu (taboo) on the distilling of rum." (Imagine how *no rum* pleased the carousing sailors and whalers who then blamed the missionaries for spoiling their fun.) Queen K also sent envoys to burn and destroy all idols (Hawaiian Gods) throughout the islands. She died in 1832 while King K, the last King of Kauai, had died in 1824.

The famous Hawaiian historian, Samuel Kamakau, reports: "Kaumualii (King K) was a handsome man ... rather slight in build, but he had a good carriage and dressed well. He was gentle of temper, spoke English well, was kind and simple in his ways. It would be well for the nation if there were more chiefs like him." There are lots of good reports of King K and his favorite wife, Deborah Kapule conveniently back on Kauai (he is married to Queen K).

But now King K is dead. And so his Kauai land and power are essentially up for grabs. A couple of different Governors are appointed to govern Kauai but the King's land (Crown land) is not redistributed.

There is a big fight: 1) An uprising led by Prince George P. Kaumualii, son of King K and formerly married to Queen K, to regain Kauai's independence of old against 2) Other chiefs (mostly on Oahu and Maui) who remain loyal to the Kamehameha line. These outside chiefs are (surprise, surprise) supported by King K's favorite wife Deborah Kapule who had remained on Kauai (while he was kidnapped and married to Queen K.; I don't think Deborah Kapule is Prince George's mother.) Prince George, leader of the Kauai revolt, is reportedly not a good guy and the Deborah Kapule-supported forces of Kamehameha win the uprising. Which means that Kamehameha forces are in charge. Kauai is now ruled by off-island non-Kauaians.

Here's an eyewitness account after the big battle between George (King K's son) and Kamehameha forces: "The hill is still held in bitter remembrance, as being one of the many spots, where sets of wanton cruelty were perpetuated on the prisoners taken in the last rebellion."

The disaffected chiefs and their tenants [of Kauai] were distributed among the other islands where it would be impossible for them to combine in another conspiracy. Their lands [Kauai] were divided among the loyal favorites and chiefs, who filled the minor offices with their creatures. The poor serfs [ordinary people] were looked upon in the contemptuous light of conquered rebels; and for many years groaned under the heavy exactions of their new lords.

This is a sad time for Kauai. All the other island chiefs who've ever had grudges and felt vindictive against Kauai come out of the woodwork; they finagle grants of Kauai land from the Kamehameha rulers. These off-island new chiefs basically don't give a hoot for Kauai's people; they dispossess native people, make them work like slaves, and the entire social order of hundreds of years is disturbed.

A condensed view reveals: "In 1821 Kaumualii [King K] was taken prisoner by Liholiho, Kamehameha II, and placed in exile on Oahu. The following year *alii* from Oahu and other islands arrived to rule Kauai. Kaumualii died in Honolulu in 1824 and Kauai's lands were given to these newcomer alii. This takeover was unsuccessfully opposed by a ragtag group of fighters led by Humehume. This event marked the end of Kauai as an independent kingdom and made it part of the Hawaiian Kingdom."

What Joesting doesn't make clear is that Humehume is another name for Prince George who is the son of Kaumualii [King K] and, of course, the hereditary ruler of Kauai. Also left out is the rather tragic back story of Prince George. His father, King K, had sent his son to the mainland to get educated. Somehow Prince George's funds didn't travel with him and Prince George went through hard times. He tried for three years to get home to Kauai and never forgot that the blood of chiefs flowed in his veins. By now Prince George is in a missionary-type school (still in the U.S.) with classmates also from Hawaii. But Kanui, Hopa and Honolu, the sons of commoners, were pious while Prince George, in the missionary's view, is not. Prince George could never understand why anyone could favor commoners over a King's son. Missionaries however gained quick favor with King K on Kauai when the missionaries brought back Prince George, who the king had feared was dead.

In any case, back to the unification of the Hawaiian islands, remember that as soon as he controls all the islands, Kamehameha One has outlawed war. So, theoretically at least, Kauai deserves this harsh treatment for its rebellion. Or look at it another way—in trying to hold on to its freedom, Kauai got smashed and the winners wrote new rules.

49 *In A Hawaiian Valley* by Kathleen Mellen.

50 Farmers Markets are all over Kauai; I usually go to Kekaha, Hanapepe or Waimea. Sometimes to Kalaheo, Koloa, Kapaa, depending on the day, or the large Saturday morning one at the community college, especially if I want goat cheese.

51 A while ago a local goat farmer got sick of it and outed four restaurants to the light of truth. Started with her *Letter to the Editor* and ended with a front page article in the Sunday paper, complete with a charming close-up of a black and white goat. [*The Garden Island*, Sunday, February 13, 2011, Front page] These restaurants, advertising themselves as serving local goat cheese, weren't buying local cheese at all. Probably *local* from Costco. Admittedly cheaper but definitely not local, and definitely not as tasty as I've tried both.

52 "Crop genetic diversity is critical to the continuing development of varieties resistant to new pests, diseases, and changing climatic and environmental conditions. In this way, diversity is essential for global food security. The lack of genetic diversity, in fact, can be linked to many of the major crop epidemics in human history. Biological diversity must be protected and respected...."

53 Greenpeace.org/gmo

54 Jeffrey Smith, in *HealthKeeprs Magazine.*

55 Eugene Burns, *The Last King of Paradise.*

56 Princess Regent Liliuokalani is Hawaii's last Hawaiian ruler who will later be disposed as Hawaii is taken over by the U.S. military and haole businessmen. In 1881 she is acting as ruler while her brother King David is traveling.

57 ibid

58 Taupouri Tangaro: *Lele Kawa: Fire Rituals of Pele.* Pure poetry. Purely wonderful. Amazing mele, chant, hula dedicated to Pele, handed down by oral tradition, this mele chant is reinterpreted by a current hula, chant practitioner. Included especially for its highly sophisticated *life dedicated for the furtherance of life is the payment for being healed.* Princess Ruth chants and prays and asks to save her people.

> Ia ulu kini o ke akua lā
> Ulu mai ʻo Kāne, ʻo Kanaloa
> ʻO Hiʻiaka, kaula mana ia e
> Nāna i hōʻuluʻulu i nā maʻi
> A ʻaʻe a ulu a noho i kou kuahu
> Eia ka wai lā, he wai ola e
> E ola hoʻi e
> [NBE: 141]

> O rise, you many forms of heightened awareness
> Consciousness and unconscious take your station
> For Hiʻiaka is the cord, the seer who is endowed
> For she alone will gather all ailment
> Rise and tread upon your station.
> Mount your shrine that I am
> For I bring you water, the liquid transport of life
> Live!

"The equitable exchange for healing spiritual imbalance is the actual life of the patient. Here the water of life refers to the water contained in the body of the patient. Life dedicated for the furtherance of life is the payment for being healed."

59 A federal judge has ruled that the government failed to adequately assess the environmental impacts of genetically engineered sugar beets before approving the crop for cultivation in the United States. The decision could lead to a ban on the planting of the beets, which have been widely adopted by farmers.

.... How has it happened that our US Department of Agriculture, instead of doing its mandated job of protecting our food supply, is now being sued, so far successfully, by the *Center for Food Safety*, the *Sierra Club*, the *Organic Seed Alliance,* and *High Mowing Organic Seeds*, a small seed company?

The beets contain a bacterial gene licensed by Monsanto that renders them impervious to glyphosate, an herbicide that Monsanto sells as *Roundup*. That allows the herbicide to kill weeds without harming the crop," according to the article.

I see what's happening here. Monsanto sells the new sugar beet seeds to farmers, then Monsanto sells the farmers their chemical pesticide, *Roundup. Roundup* will kill ordinary beets but it won't kill these genetically modified sugar beets.

Roundup sounds like old-fashioned Western country.

Words can be deceiving. Instead of rounding up baby calves, the new *Roundup*, rounds up and kills weeds. This still sounds fine, even sort of pleasant, certainly innocuous.

Roundup is the brand name of a systemic, broad-spectrum herbicide produced by the U.S. company Monsanto, which contains the active ingredient glyphosate. Glyphosate, is classed by the European Union as "dangerous for the environment" and "toxic for aquatic organisms", says Wikipedia, adding that in January 2007, Monsanto was convicted of false advertising in France with the results being confirmed in 2009.

Monsanto developed and patented the glyphosate molecule in the 1970s, and has marketed *Roundup* from 1973. The main active ingredient of *Roundup* is the isopropylamine salt of glyphosant. Another important ingredient is the surfactant POEA (polyethoxylated tallow amine)—known for its toxicity in wildlife and increasing herbicide penetration in plant cells.

And something truly horrifying: a friend recently told me that our Costco here on Kauai is now selling 50 pound bags of *Roundup*. It's enough to curdle your blood. People all over our small island buying 50 pounds of this poison and using it liberally. What strange plants will we mutate here on our small dot in the Pacific? How many extra of ourselves will we kill with various cancers?

To bring this back to sugar beets, Monsanto also produces seeds which grow into plants genetically engineered to be tolerant to glyphosate, which are known as *Roundup Ready* crops. The genes contained in these seeds are patented. Such crops allow farmers to use glyphosate as a post-emergence herbicide against most broadleaf and cereal weeds. Soy was the first Roundup Ready crop. Now we also have corn. And who knows what other food crops. I continue reading about the sugar beets:

> The *Non-Genetically Modified (GM) Beet Sugar Registry* is worried about a lack of knowledge about the long-term health and environmental impacts of GMO beet sugar. They want to give consumers a choice about whether they eat foods containing GMO sugar in the absence of mandatory labeling for GMO foods.
>
> Jeffrey Smith, director of the *Institute for Responsible Technology*—one of a dozen sponsors of the registry—said: *We need to avoid the all-too-common situation of finding out a product is harmful after it has been approved and widely distributed. Requiring that GMO foods be labeled is the only protection consumers have if they want to avoid eating GMO foods.*
>
> "*The Center for Food Safety* (CFS) said the *US Environmental Protection Agency* increased allowable levels of herbicide residue on GMO sugar beet roots "at the request of Monsanto."

CFS has also said that the recent mercury contamination of high fructose corn syrup has made companies particularly nervous about the introduction of unlabeled GMO beet sugar to the US food supply.

It said: "The registry shows the food industry's increasing apprehension about the government's ability to adequately regulate food production technologies."

Tom Stearns, president of *High Mowing Organic Seeds*, which has also sponsored the registry, expressed concern that GMO sugar beets would cross-pollinate with related crops such as chard and table beets, meaning that the issue could affect other foods and food ingredients.

"Overseas markets have already rejected other GMO products, so the economic future of many of our nation's farmers is being needlessly risked," he said.

The registry has been signed by 73 grocery chains and food producers so far, documenting a pledge to "seek wherever possible to avoid using GMO beet sugar in our products" and urging the sugar beet industry to avoid using GMO beets.

60 Michael J. Crumb, "Agriculture experts: Contamination from GM alfalfa certain," *The Garden Island*, February 16, 2011.
61 Author and lecturer, from her 1935 autobiography.
62 And a sexual one I picked up from Burns, *The Last King of Paradise*—with details from Paul Pearsall's *Partners in Pleasure: Sharing Success, Creating Joy, Fulfilling Dreams—Together*: "The *kane* [man] would go and find just a little powder or pollen from the *hinano*, the male blossom of the pandarus tree. He would put some pollen on his fingertip and blow it very gently onto the *'o'i'o* [clitoris] of his lover." The *kupuna* winked at her husband and they laughed together as he added without embarrassment, "It was our secret and my lover knew its power."

To become partners in pleasure along the lines of the seventh prescription, our relationships might want to take some clues from these Hawaiian ways of enjoying anticipation, teasing, and fun in sexual intimacy. A little less foreplay and a little more playing together might add a new dose of delight to your sexual intimacy.

63 *And Then There Were None* video by Elizabeth Kapu'uwailane Lindsey

64 An award-winning documentary created by the second great-granddaughter of Hawaiian high chiefs and English sea farers. This video is 26 minutes. Check your library or Amazon.com. If you only see one film about Hawaii, I suggest *Then There Were None*.

65 **Decisions to spoil** or destroy beauty are made by a person. *Cut down that tree. Build a dump there. Throw your Budweiser can out the window. Pitch your MacDonald plastic coffee cup.* Big decisions. Little decisions. Someone in the military (we'll never know who) was willing to choose the Hawaiian island of Kahoolawe and bomb it in naval training missions from World War II until 1990. Reverberations would actually shake Maui seven miles away. These kinds of decisions continue to be made. Our newspaper tells of a Japanese-ancestry judge blithely ruling that it's quite okay to build a road over sacred Hawaiian ancestral bones. Where is the righteousness in this outcome? If I feel sick at a miscarriage of justice, how must native Hawaiians feel?

    If you wanted to raise consciousness of our true debt to Native Hawaiians, how would you do it? Questions way too large for me.

66 http://www.huffingtonpost.com/

67 *Amelia: A Novel of Mid-nineteenth Century Hawaii* by Juliet Rice Wichman, a missionary granddaughter. is published by the Kauai Museum Association.

68 ibid

69 *Reminiscences of a Life in the Islands* by Helen Kapililani Sanborn Davis

70 Told me by someone I respect who knows, but who doesn't wish to be named

71 From a 1979 *National Geographic* article. "The Bishop Estate is the largest private landowner in Hawaii with 55,000 acres. "Estate revenues help educate children of Hawaiian ancestry. The land was bequeathed for that use in the late 1800's by Princess Bernice Pauahi Bishop and her husband, Charles." Bishop Estate and 38 other private landowners,

own 45 percent of Hawaii's 4.1 million acres which is 88 percent when government land is excluded.

Charles Bishop seems such a conniver, I don't trust his motivation on anything. And, truth to tell, especially that sacred cow in Hawaii, Kamehameha Schools. To my way of thinking if these trustees, currently making one million bucks a year each in salary, had any heart, during the Hawaiian school crises these last years with mandatory furlough days from an already much too short school year, the Kamehameha trustees would have ponyed up some cash and help for the rest of Hawaiian school children. Instead of reserving all their money-attention for themselves and for Kamehameha Schools, terrific as they surely are.

"They skim the cream off the intellectual top," someone explains to me, "educate the students to their way of thinking and congratulate themselves on their jobs well done—basically increasing the wealth of Bishop Estates. And too frequently," my friend gossips, "lining their own pockets. Or their friends."

So much was stolen from the almost-numb early Native Hawaiians that Kamehameha schools gained unfair advantage which is probably the way Bishop set them up. Who pays one million each, a year, to five trustees? Except as payoff of a kind. "Hawaii has hundreds of qualified good-hearted people who would happily and gladly take on these trustee jobs for a dollar a year," my friend explains.

Billie Beamer, author and former Hawaiian Home Commission chairperson and our jump-off point for Hawaiian history: "These Hawaiians believe that the overthrow in 1893 of our last monarch—Queen Liliuokalani—was illegal. After she was forced to abdicate and was put in prison, the businessmen who organized that move [Bishop was part of this] took more than 900,000 acres of crown land, which ended up as government property. The Hawaiians want it back, plus damages."

It's a tricky business, stealing land. Look at Honolulu yellow pages and you'll find umpteen listings of attorneys. Most are engaged in converting leasehold land into fee-simple ownership, or arranging new leases. Remember fee simple, never mind how you got here, you own the land outright and have clear title to sell it—American style. Leasehold means that someone else can own the land under your building.

"Politics, too, makes headlines in Honolulu. Hawaii became a United States territory in 1900, a state in 1959. For the first half of this century, the Republican Party ruled. Then came the "revolution of 1954. Backed by the International Longshoremen's and Warehousemen's Union and many AJA's (Americans of Japanese Ancestry) a Democratic regime began." And lasted with what has become politics as usual. Your cronies get the plums while ordinary people get the pits. Or they're tossed a second-class plum every so often to keep down major revolt.

And in the meantime we've got ordinary people in Hawaii trying to lead ordinary lives.

72 *Under God with liberty and justice for all.* But turns out only if you're a white male, and a rich and/or powerful one is the top of this heap. I'm realizing the rest of us must struggle not to be totally influenced by only *their* values and rules. An endemic problem? Peruse this quote from novelist Victoria Sullivan: "Subtle cues from the white male hierarchy are supposed to be recognized and illicit responses that reassure it remains in power. Since she wasn't male or white, any response she gave was viewed as a threat. At least she'd stopped thinking that the "misunderstandings" were her failure. In lighter moments, she had remarked to David that secret information was genetically coded on the Y chromosome," states Victoria I. Sullivan in *Adoption.*

73 *The I Who Speaks Is Not I* by Jo Ann Lordahl

74 Olana Ai, one of the younger kumu hula, quoted by Elizbeth Buck in *Paradise Remade.*

75 Ka'a'awa; a novel about Hawaii in the 1850s by O. A. Bushnell.

76 This is one of the sources: *The Hawaiian Chiefs' Children's School 1839-1850, A Record Compiled from the Diary and Letters of Amos Starr Cooke and Juliette Montague Cooke* by their granddaughter Mary Atherton Richards

77 Sympathetic and knowledgeable tutors could have worked wonders with these royal children. Hawaii could still be a sovereign nation, self governing, free.

78 There's a scene in Rosemary Patterson's novel about this school, *Kula Keiki Aliʻi* (Chief Children School) of the two remaining brothers, Lot and Alexander, talking over Moses' coffin about how, being the oldest, Moses often took the blame, and the beatings, for the others.

79 *Ancient Hawaii* by Herbert Kawainui Kane

80 *Hotel Honolulu* by Paul Theroux

81 *Ancient Hawaiian Civilization* by Handy, Emory, Bryan, Buck, Wise and Others, with an introduction by the 1933 President of Kamehameha Schools, the premiere educational institute for native Hawaiians funded by the Bishop trust, which got five sixth of its money and land from Princess Ruth. Princess Ruth and Bernice had talked of how best to help their Hawaiian people.

82 Wikipedia, the free encyclopedia.

83 "But no one's going to sell you real medicine for a couple of bucks, and they're never going to share the real thing anyway, because they're Indians and you're white, and until you make good on all the treaties you broke, they're not giving you anything."

"I had nothing to do with that," John said.

"But you're still reaping the benefits of what your forefathers stole from us."

John shook his head. "There's nothing I can do. I can't give you back your lands, or whatever it is that you want."

"You can't write to your congressman?" *The Mystery of Grace* by Charles De Lint.

84 This Prince became a politician in the Territory of Hawaii as delegate to the United States Congress, and as such is the first native Hawaiian and only person ever elected to that body who was born a royal.

85 More Prince Kuhio from Kauai and land information follows: Rosemary Patterson in *Kuhina Nui*, tells it like this.

"This is Waimanalo," Kiana replied. This section is part of the Hawaiian Homes Land. In 1922, Prince Kuhio, the Territorial Delegate To Congress managed to get one million acres of very poor agricultural land placed into homesteads to be awarded to native Hawaiians. This was in exchange for changes to the Organic Act that allowed twenty-six thousand acres of perfect agricultural land to remain in the hands of the Sugar Plantation owners. Hawaiians who live here now just lease the land. And when they die they can only turn the homes over to relatives if they have fifty percent Hawaiian blood.

Remember the 50% Hawaiian blood that Elizabeth Kapu'uwailane Lindsey spoke of in her documentary *And Then There Were None*? Lindsey tells how her over 50 percent Hawaiian blood mother waited her whole life for Homestead government land. How her mother died still waiting. And how, now, none of her daughters can apply for or inherit Homestead government land claims because the daughters don't have the necessary 50 percent Hawaiian blood.

Wrongs that keep being perpetuated. Wait long enough, as Lindsey so eloquently points out, and there'll be no pure-blooded Hawaiians. Or even fifty percent ones.

Briefly, here's how Rosemary Patterson tells this tale of how made-their-own-luck rich missionaries come to own Hawaii, while native Hawaiians become landless and continue to struggle. Patterson puts hard information into conversation that I've cherry-picked:

"One of the big estates [probably Bishop] that owns much of the land on Oahu evicted their tenants so the land could be sold for subdivision. It's the same all over.... In the late 1840's Kamehameha III was convinced by his advisor, Dr. Gerrit Judd, one of the former members of the mission, to allow private ownership of land in Hawaii.... Kamehameha III changed the way land was held in Hawaii. In 1850 he gave one third of the crown lands to the chiefs, kept one third of the land to himself for government, and gave some supposedly to commoners who could prove they were working it, providing they made a legal claim....

Most of the land was purchased from the Chiefs and the commoners, who did not understand private ownership, by missionaries, their descendants and other foreigners for very little and transferred into enormous sugar plantations. In 1893 the land supposedly belonging to the Monarch was grabbed by the Provisional Government along with other so-called government lands and ceded to the U.S. in 1898 when, Hawaii was annexed. Native Hawaiians would like some of this land back or at least some benefit from the revenues produced from it. Right now there are twenty-five thousand native Hawaiians on waiting lists for Homestead land while only a small amount of native Hawaiian families have obtained the leases to Hawaiian Homes Land they were promised in 1921.

Rosemary Patterson shares an attitude from native Hawaiians:

My ex-fiancé, Keolo, says that many Hawaiians do not want to join the western rat race. They are deeply alienated from western ways. Their way of life has long been ridiculed by westerners and their ancestral lands have been taken from them. Keolo says that at the very least native Hawaiians should be given a choice. Some lands should remain in native Hawaiian hands so that those who chose to do so can live a subsistence lifestyle .... Keolo says that until very recently natives were only educated to be servants and plantation workers. Local foreigners' descendants were educated on the mainland and the professional jobs were given to them or others like themselves who came to Hawaii.

I finish reading Rosemary Patterson around midnight thoroughly awake and upset.

I start off prejudiced against Prince Kuhio (Jonah Kuhio Kalanianaole from Kauai) and I've never quite gotten over it. My prejudice is built on a snatch of information that his Act, when he is a Representative to Congress from Hawaii—supposedly of great benefit to the Hawaiian people of securing land for them—was really a great concession to the haole sugar plantation owners of that time. If anything could change my mind it would be a biography of Prince Kuhio. Prince Kuhio is a charming man, of great support apparently to his aunt Queen Liliuokalani, the last ruler of a free Hawaii. Here, as is so often the case with Hawaiian history, I find mixed messages:

> During Kuhio's career as Delegate, the political scene was not always pleasant or friendly.... The prince was a full-blooded Hawaiian and a strongly independent person... yet, the plantation owners were one of the largest group of his supporters .... Toward the latter part of 1911, Kuhio received many letters in Washington from homesteaders and those who were trying to get homesteads. Those seeking a holding were complaining that the plantation owners were trying to discourage them by cutting off their water supply. Those who had homesteads, were also having difficulty with the plantations. They tried to close-in the farmers, so their cost of transporting produce to market would be so high they could not make a living from it.
>
> When leases on government lands expired, any group of six or more citizens could petition for homesteading rights. The sugar planters were bitterly opposed to this as they were often using the land for the cultivation of sugar, and did not want to give it up.

But here's the killer:

> On April 15, 1920, Kuhio's argument in Congress was that the common people had been omitted in the Great Mahele of 1848. He explained to his colleagues, that after the king and chiefs acquired 1,619,000 acres of land, the local government received 1,505,460

acres. The remaining 948,000 acres that should have been conveyed to the common people, reverted to the crown instead.

[What's not made clear here is that *the crown* is really the government—effectively our U.S. controlled government.]

Kuhio was extremely critical of this injustice to the commoners. His criticism carried on to the gaining of the land by the missionaries. Cupid (Kuhio) related that <u>33 missionary families received 41,000 acres, while at the same time, 3,000 Hawaiian families obtained only 28,000 acres</u>.... Today the great majority of the Hawaiian people own no land. [Underlining mine]

86 "Broken Promise: Hawaiians Wait in Vain for Their Land" by Susan Faludi, *The Wall Street Journal*, Monday, September 9, 1991

87 Abraham Fornander's *An Account of the Polynesian Race: Its Origin and Migrations, and the Ancient History of the Hawaiian People to the Times of Kamehameha.*

88 [Judge] Fornander married Pinao Alanakapu, an alii, or female chief, from Molokai. She was familiar with many of the old Polynesian traditions, as well as the genealogies, chants, and *meles* of her own family. From her he leaned to speak and write Hawaiian and to appreciate the splendid old culture of her people—a culture that was rapidly dying. He avidly collected legends, chants, and genealogies, writing them in Hawaiian and being extremely careful to use the original wording.... His aptitude for languages helped him ... as he not only read and wrote in Hawaiian and Swedish but knew English, German, and French, as well. He had also studied Hebrew, Latin, and Greek and in *An Account of the Polynesian Race* makes comparisons among words of forty different languages.

89 The missionaries arrive on the Big Island to find:

Kamehameha was dead.... The old religion had been swept away, its priesthood dispersed, its temples demolished, its taboos shattered, its cruelties forbidden. There had been rebellion and bloodshed, but now there was peace.

The way lay open for the Mission! ....

By his fast-sailing vessel, the *Neo*, the king [Kamehameha Two] had sent a message to Governor Boki [his brother on Oahu]: "This is my command. Furnish the *haoles* with land and houses and with provisions. Let them dwell in Honolulu for one year, if they do not make any trouble." ....

The missionaries saw their job as teaching everyone their version of Christian values and making the nation literate—kings to half-caste children. And so the whaling and sea captains and traders nodded in agreement in May 5, 1820 that education was okay.

"No one remembered then," comments Albertine Loomis, "that Christianity is really a radical doctrine and education a very yeasty brew. No one foresaw that a people's expanding sense of their own worth could rock a social structure or rend an economic pattern."

The Mission was on trial. It had been grudgingly admitted to the Islands and was still watched from some quarters with suspicion and from others with enmity. Hawaii was less than a year from its latest civil war....What the impetuous king approved one day might anger him the next and on the third might look to him like intrigue with an ambitious underling....

For the blind and the aged, the sick and the insane, the Hawaiians showed no pity; they taunted them and drove them away, left them to starve or buried them alive in pit or stone-pile. They mated so casually, killed so calmly their unwanted infants, gave away so readily their children to other households that those who had come from America to *save* them thought at first they had no hearts at all....

When the old religion was shattered, the idols destroyed and the priesthood abolished, the hula master hid away his god, the *akua hulahula*, dispersed his musicians and his dancers and then fell ill and died. After that the chants were heard only when a group gathered of their own accord, perhaps to hail the birth of a child....

No man could build in Hawaii so much as a grass shack without royal leave…. Everywhere nature smiled, benign and sparkling; everywhere humans were gaunt, wizened, desolate…. "Twenty thousand human beings," he [Elisha] wrote, "wretched and ignorant …. Have no encouragement to work or acquire property, as everything they possess lies at the disposal of the chiefs and is liable to be taken away by them at their pleasure … to give them the light of science and revelation, and all the blessings of civilization and christianity is … our appointed work. But who is sufficient for these things?" [The old kapu system keeping things in place was earlier destroyed. Hawaiians are sick and dying; whalers and seaman run rampant.]

This next bit I paraphrased from missionary Loomis shows differences: There was trouble about ships the royalty had ordered which were late arriving and royalty, no longer wanting them, had to be persuaded which took months and the chiefs still didn't pay actual cash money.

King K of Kauai purchased a very inferior Brig and Cargo of Captain Suter, for more than six times the brig's cost in America. The traders knew what they were doing. The missionaries, pushing their religion, called it as they saw it: 'taking unfair advantage of the natives'. "These were not pleasant things to hear and see if you were in Hawaii to collect old debts or to sell new goods for ten times their worth." It galled the chiefs to owe thousands for such vessels; they felt tricked and cheated. Which they were. "Every agent knew that as long as a fresh supply of goods came to market, it would be next to impossible to collect the old accounts. But every Yankee wanted his share of the cream while the skimming was good."

Meanwhile "on the Big Island where Queen K had lately traveled with her retinue, she had seized and destroyed images by the hundreds. From caves and dens and the thatch of commoners' houses her men brought them forth … they were flung down in the royal enclosure at Kailua and kindled…. And watching the smoke puff upward, Queen

K saw completed the work of destruction begun in 1819 when she had encouraged Liholiho [Kamehameha Two] to break with idolatry." (They broke Kapu rule by publicly eating together, men and women.)

> Queen K had known then that the taboos, bearing so heavily on women, were a curb to her power. She had seen how the overthrow of superstition would strengthen her. She had hinted to Liholiho that the old ways were foolish and pointed out that prayers and sacrifices to the gods had not saved Kamehameha [One] from death....

Liholiho [Kamehameha II], irked by the ceremonial restraints and priestly bans on his indulgences, had wavered, then consented [to breaking the kapu rule].

American traders are still trying to collect their inflated debts when the American naval *Dolphin* comes to port, an eighty-eight-foot, twelve-gun schooner. The captain meets the chiefs in council to thrash out the matter of the debts. This much the alii acknowledged—though Liholiho [Kamehameha II and Kaumualii (King K, the last King of Kauai)] were dead, their pledges must still be paid ... and the chiefs reminded the lieutenant bitterly that an American firm [not named] had owed a vast sum to the Hawaiians since the days of Kamehameha [One]. If the debt of Liholiho [Kamehameha Two] became the debt of his successors, they asked, why didn't the claim of Kamehameha [One] become the claim of the present government? Incidentally I never found out anymore about the vast American company debt; how much, and was it ever paid?

The chiefs make an excellent point: We, the Hawaiians have to pay our debts; the Americans don't have to pay their debts to us, and can also blatantly cheat us.

However, as Loomis tells the tale, in 1826 the chiefs called the people together: "As a nation we have a great debt to the men of America. Fifteen thousand piculs of sandalwood we must bring now from the forests and deliver to these men."

A contemporary note is that Hawaii's precious sandalwood forests are no more. Sandalwood was harvested to death. As was koa, a beautiful wood like black walnut, used for furniture, guitars. In long ago times highly prized koa wood forests used to cover Kauai, now the few large trees that are left grow almost entirely on restricted lands.

Albertine Loomis ends her novel: "But always through the wonderful, quiet efficacy of printed words, there would stand the record of what true, peace-loving men, white and brown, had agreed together on a day in 1826, that the "life of the land" might endure in righteousness." [These are handed-down purported words of Kamehameha Three—very young at the time.]

90 And remember, we start this missionary story after much encroachment, death and wrongs already done to the Hawaiian people. These are the original missionaries, not their descendants about whom we're learning differently.

91 [Letter continued] In those camps massive flocks of chickens during the day and cats at night destroy gardens and flower beds. Every morning when I pick up the newspaper in the driveway I smell some kind of –cide in the air.

My grandson was on the front page of *TGI* helping up his friend of Waimea Canyon School when they were hit twice and I removed my son from St. Theresa Kekaha before they were hit.

The chemical supervisor at the GMO in Waimea had previously put six G&R sugar employees in the clinic. This same person was spraying Roundup from the air instead of Polaris. Was atrazine used, a widely used herbicide? Moreover, is that now in Kaumakani/Pakala drinking water?

The state DOH and DOW does not test our well water. So who does? Surfrider Foundation? They cannot even put a trash can for all the broken glass that litters one mile east and west from the Pakala surf spot. By the way, my rent was raised to pay for the EPA suit.

Whatever happen to the $300,000 from the county? Shouldn't somebody in the G&R accounting or administration department do some jail time before rent was raised? People on the Westside should be concerned.

When their field trucks use the road they drop mud and dirt on the road which you take home in your fenders. Is Fido or Fluffy sick? Any sores on the kids? And what about the dust? I got more dust now then when sugar was here because we did not harrow up wind after 9 or 10. Also we never used the highway but at two junctions where a water truck was stationed. The drift on the dust and chemicals is two miles.

Fred Dente is right again when he says: "Even though many of the jobs go to non-union workers on temporary work permits from Micronesia and other places, and even though most of the profits these companies make go off to corporate headquarters overseas, they have the nerve to justify their existence here by telling us how many hundreds of millions of dollars they generate in their diabolical experiments."

Out of 300 employees at G&R only 60 were hired, of that 30 were former supervisors. You know, the guys that can wear the same clothes for two months without getting dirty, never seen a callous on their hands, and drive around all day and never get out their trucks. Yeah, the same guys that milked and broke Lihue's, McBride, Olokele and finally G&R.

92 Ansel Adams (photographer), and Edward Joesting in *An Introduction to Hawaii*, written in 1964.

93 Haunani-Kay Trask, *From A Native Daughter: Colonialism and Sovereignty in Hawaii.*

94 365 Tao: Daily Meditations by Deng Ming-Da

95 *Memoirs* by Pablo Neruda

96 Anthony Sommer's *KPD Blue: A Decade of Racism, Sexism, and Political Corruption in (and all around) the Kauai Police Department.*

97 "The county's strategy was to hope the plaintiffs would give up in frustration or from lack of money to pay lawyers or they would simply die of old age waiting for a trial date. The county has plenty of money to pay lawyers and lots of patience," asserts *KPD Blue* which adds "There is a gaggle of activists who show up at every Kauai County Council

meeting to complain, usually quite correctly how inept and unethical most [Kauai] county agencies are.

98 "Forty years after the enactment of the Civil Rights Act, it's hard for people from the mainland United States—even people in other parts of Hawaii—to realize that, on Kauai at least, it's always all about race....

It is impossible to overstate how important it is in Kauai culture to be a native of the island. Anyone who comes from the outside is considered by locals to be taking a job that should have gone to a native Kauaian (even if no one from Kauai is qualified for the job)....

Kauai was the only county in Hawaii without a homeless shelter. The Kauai Humane Society boasted a dog pound that cost $3 million donated mostly by Princeville haoles to build but there was nothing for people without homes. Rich haoles love dogs, not poor people...."

And here's a bit on how much of our taxes on Kauai are paid out in settling lawsuits: "As usual, the trial never took place. Kauai County was willing to pay a lot of taxpayer dollars to keep its dirty laundry from public view. "More than a year later, in May 2007, Kauai County settles the lawsuit and paid Tokashiki $325,000." She's suing for whistleblowing legal protection for telling the truth or blowing the whistle on illegal behavior and being fired. And *KDP Blue* delineates several more of these! All involving the spending of large sums of our taxpayer money.

99 *KPD Blue*

100 Quaker minister, women's rights leader, abolitionist, peace activist, humanitarian.

101 Hawaiian University professor and activist.

102 And the disrespect goes on. "Work continues after bones, artifacts unearthed." Front page, *The Garden Island*, April 29, 2011. The/our government is digging next to the Wailua River. "Again, another septic system/leach field on another Hawaiian graveyard," said Kaiulani Edens, who got arrested along with James Alalem. "What are we, the toilet? We kanakas are the toilet. Our sacred sites are toilets."

103 And, come to think of it, local people. Why doesn't somebody do something! But there I go again, drumming up causes. What I would do, were I moneybags Queen for a Year, is consult Native Hawaiians using their hooponopono methods, tear down the sorry place and, if they thought it a good idea, begin a park or a Center of Native Hawaiian Culture.

104 And our brilliant public electric company that isn't public but currently run by autocrats, is publicly considering damming this magnificent stream higher up. These are the outstanding folks that spend our public money on a glossy magazine (monthly I think) telling how great they are with actual recipes for island dishes; what century do they live in?

105 ibid

106 *Night Is a Sharkskin Drum* by Haunani-Kay Trask

107 Vastly condensed, somewhat repetitious, and in little snippets some of what I find follows: *Celebrating Advocacy* (CA) says there's no evidence for Menehune (the famed ancient little people). That Menehunes were *common, skilled, hard working Hawaiians.*

Proponents for Menehune point to an 1820 census of Kauai, by Kaumualii (King K), the ruling Alii Aimoku of the island, which listed 65 people as Menehune.

CA carefully defines a Hawaiian church: "One with historical Hawaiian roots where services were conducted, totally or partially, in Hawaiian, where programs were traditionally Hawaiian in style and mode; and whose members and leadership were predominantly Hawaiian."

"The Hawai'i mission is regarded as a great accomplishment of the American Board, perhaps its greatest ever—an entire Nation was converted." But today these churches are smaller and few conduct services in Hawaiian.

CA says of early history: "Information passed on in chants and archaeological and linguistic evidence point to the Marqueesans as the first to arrive in Hawai'i in the period 300-500 A.D." Communal in character, the Marqueesans created a society with no distinction in status. Ability carried you to leadership. Things rocked along nicely. Hawaiians learned to be Hawaiians.

Ancient Hawaiians believed that all things possessed a soul: animals, trees, stones, stars and clouds, as well as humans. "Religion and mythology were interwoven in the culture. The gods of Ancient Hawaii were like great chiefs from far lands who visited among the people, at times appearing as humans or animals and sometimes residing in stone or wooden images."

Then, CA states, around 1000-1200 the Tahitians came bringing a stratified society composed of the Alii (the Chiefs), the Maka ainana (ordinary people), the Kaua (the outcasts or slaves), and an adjunct class of Priests, the Kahuna, who were advisors to the Chiefs. "Bigger in stature than the first inhabitants, the Tahitians dominated ... power to rule was based on bloodline."

"There were powerful nature gods ... and lesser gods ... over crafts and professions. Entwined with the religion and culture was the kapu system that actually ruled all aspects of every day living including ali'i, kahuna [priests, leaders, elders], maki ainana [commoners] and kaua [slaves]. Kahuna [priests] conducted rituals to keep the kapu intact."

After 1820 as foreigners, traders, opportunists poured in, the kapu system was weakened as "natives saw that foreigners suffered no repercussions as they ignored the ... taboos" and, at the same time, strange diseases were killing Hawaiians right and left.

Queen K, as you'll remember, was Kamehameha One's widow and regent of new King Kamehameha Two (Liholiho). They formally broke the Kapu system by dining together with Keouolani, a fellow wife of Kamehameha One, who was also was the mother of Kamehameha Two and Three and step-mother of Princess Ruth. Queen K was co-ruler and Queen Regent from 1819 until her death in June 5, 1832.

When the first missionaries arrived in Kona on the Big Island in April 4, 1820, Liholiho (Kamehameha Two) said, "We have just gotten rid of one religion, I am not sure we are quite ready for another." But the King sent the missionaries on to Oahu.

Earlier there was a big fight on Oahu as Kamehameha Two's cousin tried to restore the ancient Kapu system, but when he and his wife were killed in battle, the missionaries' task was made possible and much easier.

"All told, 12 companies of Missionaries would eventually reach Hawaii's shores." The alii trusted the missionaries. Alii rulers needed all the help they could find with a demoralized population—carousing sailors and whalers and alcohol—and Hawaiians dying in huge numbers.

The missionaries, quickly realizing the necessity, soon learned the Hawaiian language. They translated and printed "a spelling book, texts, and the Bible…. As early as 1824, the Regent [Kamehameha Three who is twelve years old, Kamehameha Two and his wife having died of measles in London] and the Council of Chiefs ordered the establishment of schools throughout the islands, made attendance compulsory," and the government paid for this. Hawaii became a literate nation.

The missionaries caught a big break early on when Queen K (she's remained the co-ruler of Hawaii) made "a declaration that Christianity was the new Kapu" (rule).

"Until 1838, the Hawaiian Kingdom was governed without legal enactment, based on a system of common-law consisting of the ancient kapu and practices of the celebrated Chiefs. It was passed down by tradition."

Kamehameha Three (by now 26; Queen K is dead; she'd probably have had more sense) relinquishing absolute powers, promulgated the Constitution of 1840 which transformed the ancient ruling system into a Constitutional Monarchy. Not much help for the native Hawaiians, but this did get Hawaii recognized by other countries.

108   Most Hawaiians were maka'ainana. "Aina" means land and the maka'ainana were people who lived on the land. They were fishermen, farmers and craftsmen.

109 *Okay*, I sigh, sleep long gone and I'm still too shaken and scared to even try, *let's look this one up on Wikipedia.* Which I soon do, quickly learning this was not a brilliant idea as there are pictures of hairy crawly creatures (fifty varieties!) and I'm trying to forget mine. Information also tells how harmful the bites are, that the bigger the insect the more poison, and here's what to do should you be bitten. Mainly get help.

   Still I find a couple of encouraging things: there are indoor and outdoor centipedes. Indoor ones are an inch and half long while the outdoor are one to six inches. Mine is clearly outdoor; I've never even seen an indoor one. My neighbor is right; centipedes come indoors when it rains and, here's a part I like, the outdoor centipedes soon die inside.

110 www.HealthierEating.org and www.responsibletechnology.org.

111 *Celebrating Advocacy: Past, Present & Future* compiled and edited by Aletha Kaohi ... [et al.].

112 ibid

113 ibid

114 The State Council administers Endowments and Funds for the churches and without operating funds to slant its actions, "Reconciliation is the State Council's direction for the foreseeable future. .... [The State Council] aims to enlighten, enliven, and uplift Hawaiians."

115 *Behold Kauai: Modern Days – Ancient Ways* by Dawn Fraser Kawahara, who has lived in Kauai over 25 years.

116 Robert Mann, biochemist, University of Auckland. Quoted in *Genetic Roulette: The Documented Health Risks of Genetically Engineered Foods*, by Jeffrey M. Smith. On page 32: "Sheep died after grazing in *Bt* cotton fields. (*Bt* is a pesticide gene artificially added to the cotton.) 1. After the cotton harvest in parts of India, sheep herds grazed continuously on *Bt* cotton plants. 2. Reports from four villages revealed that abut 25% of the sheep died within a week. 3. Post mortem studies suggest a toxic reaction."

117 *Genetic Roulette* quote by Jeremy Rifkin, president, *Foundation on Economic Trends* and a big deal person.

118 *Genetic Roulette* quote, Page 144 Ricarda A. Steinbrecher, molecular geneticist, says in *Econexus*.

119 Gerrit P. Judd in *Hawaii: An Informal History.* This is after Kamehameha Five (her half-brother) dies and Princess Ruth is next in line for the throne.

120 Another source says she did not attend this school but did read and write.

121 *The Royal Mausoleum of Hawai'i*, Pamphlet, April 1997, Received from William Kaihe'ekai Maioho, curator.

122 http://en.wikipedia.org/wiki/Lunalilo

123 This research is from geobiologist Hope Jahren of the University of Hawaii at Manoa's School of Ocean and Earth Science and Technology and is reported in a November 12, 2008 article by David Biello in *Scientific American.*

124 Ibid

125 "Corn tends to have more of this 13C than other plants. That telltale signature persists as the corn travels through the complex system that turns it into feed, which is consumed and processed by cattle to grow tissue. It continues after the animals are slaughtered and the meat is cooked. The result: 93 percent of the tissue that comprised the hamburger meat was derived from corn."

   "Corn has been criticized as being unsustainable based on the unusual amount of fertilizer, water and machinery required to bring it to harvest," says geobiologist Hope Jahren of the University of Hawaii at Manoa's School of Ocean and Earth Science and Technology, who led the research. I recommend the article. www.scientificamerican. com/article.cfm?id=that-burger-youre-eating-is-mostly-corn.

126 "Genetically Modified Hawaii: New varieties of genetically engineered crops thrive in the world's most isolated landmass" by Robynne Boyd, Scientific American, December 8, 2008.

127 "I pass these corn fields every day when I go to the beach to go swimming," says Marty Kuala, 68, a 36-year resident of the town

Koloa who worked in a plant nursery (that grew native plants such as naupaka, aalii, and naio) in 2005. "It's kind of a new thing that we're starting to see these fields [of genetically modified or engineered crops] all over the place. GMOs [genetically modified organisms] are growing in the Mahaulepu area on Kauai's south shore and even in the large populated areas of Lihue, our biggest town."

This year, only 1.67 million tons of raw sugar were produced, nearly one million tons less than just a decade earlier; only 13,900 acres (5,625 hectares) in the state were set aside for pineapples in 2006 [the latest year for which pineapple stats are available) compared with a whopping 76,700 acres (31,039 hectares) in 1991.

The other crops vying for state land: flowers and nursery plants, macadamia nuts, coffee, milk, algae, tomatoes, bananas and papaya.

Genetically modified food has been a source of debate since hitting the market in 1994. The E.U. had banned the imports of GM crops for 20 years, however in 2006 the World Trade Organization (WTO) ruled that the ban violated international trade rules. The U.S. Food and Drug Administration (FDA) has deemed it safe and has so far declined to limit or block the burgeoning industry.

128 ibid
129 E. Victoria Shook, *Ho'oponopono: Contemporary Uses of a Hawaiian Problem-Solving Process.*
130 http://blog.mrfire.com/dr-hew-lens-hooponopono/
131 *I Myself Have Seen It: The Myth of Hawai'i* by Susanna Moore
132 *Voices of Wisdom: Hawaiian Elders Speak* by M. J. Harden
133 *Chanting: Discovering Spirit in Sound* by Robert Gass
134 Many sources call them marines.
135 *Hawaii Pono: A Social History* by Lawrence Fuchs, a 1961 book.
136 ibid
137 *Act of War: The Overthrow of the Hawaiian Nation,* Video by University of Hawaii
138 ibid
139 Niihau: The Traditions of an Hawaiian Island by Rerioterai Tava and Moses K. Keale Sr.

140 ibid

141 Someone told me the Sinclairs (and Robinsons), until recently, actually called themselves the *Kings of Niihau*. (And Queens, I suppose; I can't resist!)

142 ibid

143 ibid. See their appendix.

144 "Robinson family may sell Niihau, leave Hawaii," by Trish Moore, Star Bulletin, April 17, 1996.

145 Ron Mizutant, "An Unforgettable Swim to Niihau," *MidWeek*, September 29, 2010.

146 Article by Leo Azambuja, September 28, 2010.

147 James Silva, in *The Garden Island*, September 29, 2010

148 *Wikipedia* reports that:

> The Makahiki season was the Ancient Hawaiian New Year festival, in honor of the god Lono.... Thus it might be thought of as including the equivalent of modern Thanksgiving and Christmas traditions. Many religious ceremonies happened during this period. The people stopped work, made offerings to the chief or alii, and then spent their time practicing sports, feasting, dancing and having a good time. War during those four months was kapu (forbidden).
>
> The Makahiki festival was celebrated in three phases. The first phase was a time of spiritual cleansing and making hookupu, offerings to the gods. The Konohiki, a class of royalty that at this time of year provided the service of tax collector, collected agricultural and aquacultural products such as pigs, taro, sweet potatoes, dry fish, kapa and mats. Some hookupu also were in the form of forest products such as feathers. The Hawaiian people had no money or other similar medium of exchange. These hookupu were offered on the altars of Lono at heiau – temples - in each district around the island. Offerings also were made at the ahupuaa, stone altars set up at the boundary lines of each community. [Ahupuaa are sections of land with borders running from mountain to sea.]

All war was outlawed to allow unimpeded passage of the image of Lono. The festival proceeded in a clockwise circle around the island as the image of Lono (Akua Loa, a long pole with a strip of tapa and other embellishments attached) was carried by the priests. At each ahupuaa (each community also is called an ahupuaa) the caretakers of that community presented hookupu to the Lono image, a fertility god who caused things to grow and who gave plenty of prosperity to the islands.

The second phase was a time of celebration: of hula dancing, of sports (boxing, wrestling, sliding on sleds, javelin marksmanship, bowling, surfing, canoe races, relays, and swimming), of singing and of feasting. One of the best preserved lava sled courses is the Keauhou Holua National Historic Landmark.

In the third phase, the waaauhau - tax canoe - was loaded with hookupu and taken out to sea where it was set adrift as a gift to Lono. At the end of the Makahiki festival, the chief would go off shore in a canoe. When he came back in he stepped on shore and a group of warriors threw spears at him. He had to deflect or parry the spears to prove his worthiness to continue to rule.

Too bad we don't have some version of this method of choosing our leaders. You like the chief, you don't aim too diligently. You think your leader does a lousy job, you do your best to take him out!

149 Browsing, I found the above in *Native Hawaiian Spirituality*, an article by Alberta Pualani Hopkins, in a 2000, *First Peoples Theology Journal*. Browsing finished, I sit at a library table and try to pick up my thinking where I left off.

150 Kathleen Mellen writing *In A Hawaiian Valley* in 1943 (I've made her language inclusive).

151 *Papaya: The Failure of GE (GMO) Papaya in Hawaii*, Greenpeace, May 2006 page 10 "The GE (GMO) papaya has not been a success in Hawaii—an assessment based on USDA data actually proves that the introduction and cultivation of GE papaya in Hawaii has been a disaster. All major statistical indicators of the health of the Hawaiian

papaya industry have declined since the GE fruit's introduction. The industry is getting smaller. Prices are down. Production of fresh papayas is at its lowest level in more than a generation. The Hawaiian papaya industry has already lost export markets and, if present trends continue, it will shrink to the point of being only for the local market. If that comes to pass, GE papaya promoters will have only themselves to blame for the decline of their industry.

It seems clear that GE papaya is more devastating than the virus—the papaya industry was in better shape during the 'virus attack' than it has been ever since the introduction of GE papaya. While the virus can harm papayas, and can make conventional papaya growing difficult, it does not pose a serious problem for organic papaya farmers.

See also *Hawaiian Papaya: GMO Contaminated* by Melanie Bondera & Mark Query, 2006. I've also heard from a reliable source that GMO papaya is more susceptible to root rot.

152 Manu Kai, LLC in Honolulu, HI is a private company categorized under Computer Facilities Management. Our records show it was established in 2006 and incorporated in Hawaii. Current estimates show this company has an annual revenue of 6,100,000 and employs a staff of approximately 99.

153 "PMRF lease, buffer zone approved," Front page, Paul C. Curtis, *The Garden Island*, May 25, 2004. "The state Board of Land and Natural Resources yesterday approved a lease and easements allowing … expansion of the U.S. Navy's Pacific Missile Range Facility at Barking Sands…. unanimously approved a 200-acre land lease, and an agricultural preservation initiative that covers over 5,000 acres of the north end of the Mana Plain."

154 Wikipedia, http://en.wikipedia.org/wiki/Pacific_Missile_Range_Facility

155 ibid

156 *Ho'opono* and *Tales from the Night Rainbow* and *The Story of a Woman, a People, and an Island* were written with Pali Lee's Hawaiian husband,

Koko (John) Willis, with the intent to share and to keep alive for their Molokai family their real Hawaiian history.

157 **An example of** a closer to home vocabulary of Hawaiian spirituality than Huna, is from Terry Shintani's 1997 *Hawaii Diet*:

Ancient Principles of the Hawaii Diet

* *Kumu* - The Source. *Nana i ke kumu* (Look to the source or Look to the teacher). Get to the root cause of a problem

* *Lokahi* – Oneness. Wholeness. Unity. Consensus. Harmony. Each part is related to the whole.

* *Pono* – Justice. Righteousness. Proper balance of all aspects in nature. All is related - eat too much meat (kill animals) it comes back to get us! When we harm the world, the world harms us.

* *Aloha* - Universal Love. Joining of heaven and earth - also face to face and *ha*, breath of life. Spirit of aloha is to give and to give endlessly. Give and it is returned, even if spiritually.

* *Mana* - Life Force. Spirit. In China, *chi*. In India, *prana*. Hawaiian rulers had *mana* and were judged on how they used it.

* *Ano Ano* - The Seed of All Things. Plant a seed of thought and help create a reality. Nurture the thought into a physical reality. Visualization.

Although purportedly based in ancient Hawaiian practices, note the similarities to current New Age thinking in these following *Steps to translate a thought into reality*: (And here I am with my suspicious mind; I don't know enough to know if the following is truly Hawaiian or only another foreigner attempting to rip off Hawaii! But I do know someone I can ask and I will!)

* Sit quietly and search your soul, see truly what it is you desire, and then make sure it is in harmony with God's plan. Pray, and if it is in God's plan, he will give you what you ask.

*Ask for guidance to ensure that what you want is good for all involved.

*State clearly, in detail, the condition that you want with words, numbers, data. Be specific about what you want. Remember that words have power.

*See this end result in full detail with color, sound, and action. Remember, "Faith is the assurance of things hoped for, the conviction of things not seen" (Hebrews 11:1).

*Feel what it will be like to have this desired result come to fruition.

*Do not tell others except those who are absolutely committed to your success about the seed you have planted.

*Pray for the results each day with the words you have chosen and give gratitude as you see and feel this result being accomplished.

158 *Ho'opono* and *Tales from the Night Rainbow* and *The Story of a Woman, a People, and an Island* were written with Pali Lee's Hawaiian husband, Koko (John) Willis, with the intent to share and to keep alive for their Molokai family their real Hawaiian history.

159 ibid

160 ibid

161 ibid

162 This bit is from Chris McKinney's *Mililani Mauka*.

163 "Broken Promise: Hawaiians Wait in Vain for Their Land" by Susan Faludi, *The Wall Street Journal*, Monday, September 9, 1991.

164 The United States deeply wronged the owners of this Hawaiian land when we got here and the missionaries began taking over. The Hawaiian people, like the Blacks in the old south, the Indians in the U.S., the colonized and despoiled everywhere, are suffering the inevitable results of our wrongs. Wrongs that still continue. Wrongs that of course, just to make things interesting, have a few rights tossed among them.

165 http//www.greenpeace.org/international/press/reports/mon863-chronicle-of-deception

166 http:www.ncbi.nim.nih.gov/pubmed/21338670

167 Highlights from the six page Greenpeace review: **August 13, 2002**: The Monsanto company submits to the German authorities an application to import genetically engineered MON863 maize into the EU [European Union]. This submission contains a 90-day rat feeding study.

Five entries later: In the conclusions of the rat feeding study provided by Monsanto is a disturbing fact, namely that the feeding study was performed by a third company (Covance Laboratories), but the statistical analysis of the data was made by Monsanto itself.

November 10, 2003, a French group sues to obtain complete rat feeding data.

After a lot of gyrations: April 23, 2004: They get the rat feeding data and the French newspaper *Le Monde* exposes the MON863 scandal. The newspaper covers the significant changes in the blood of rats, which were fed with MON863 and reveals that the CGB's experts had expressed safety concerns.

May 2004: Greenpeace requests the data from the rat feeding study with MON863 from the German authorities.

Finally after a lot of jockeying back and forth June 9, 2005: The Cologne administrative court decides that Monsanto has to give their rat feeding study data to Greenpeace.

June 20, 2005: The German high court reaffirms that the data from the rat feeding study shall be given to Greenpeace. Greenpeace publishes the complete rat feeding study (more than 1000 pages) on the internet.

September 15, 2005: An independent expert on biostatistics from the University of Hamburg makes a written statement to Greenpeace on the statistical design of Monsanto's rat feeding study. The expert states, "Significant differences were indeed found in the study, and afterwards were classified as irrelevant. (This is as if a marksman had shot at a wall and the rings of a target were drawn around where the shot had made a hole, and it was then maintained he had hit the target dead centre.)" [Isn't this fascinating!]

January 13, 2006: Despite the concerns raised by EU member states, members of the EU parliament and 10,000 cyberactivists alerted by Greenpeace, the EU Commission authorizes the placing on the market of foods and food ingredients derived from MON863 maize.

168   These are toxic unknown substances we're dealing with. MON 863 is not food as usual. This is not a nature-made, tested over millennium

in our living-earth laboratory, but a man-made construct. Patented and making money for Monsanto.

169 http://www.greenpeace.org/intrnational/prss/releases/seralini-study-MON863 - This follow up article reveals the following:

> Berlin, Germany – Laboratory rats, fed with a genetically engineered (GE) [or MON863] maize produced by Monsanto, have shown signs of toxicity in kidney and liver, according to a new study.(1) This is the first time that a GE product which has been cleared for use as food for humans and animals has shown signs of toxic effects on internal organs…. The data shows that MON863 has significant health risks associated with it; nonetheless, the European Commission granted licenses to market the maize for consumption by both humans and animals. (3).… In a joint press conference with Greenpeace at Berlin, Professor Seralini said, "Monsanto's analyses do not stand up to rigorous scrutiny – to begin with, their statistical protocols are highly questionable. Worse, the company failed to run a sufficient analysis of the differences in animal weight. Crucial data from urine tests were concealed in the company's own publications."
>
> …. Greenpeace is demanding the complete and immediate withdrawal of Monsanto's MON 863 maize from the global market and is calling upon governments to undertake an urgent reassessment of all other authorized GE [GMO] products and a strict review of current testing methods. "This is the final nail in the coffin for the credibility of the current authorization system for GE [GMO] products. Once it's known that a system designed to protect human and animal health has approved a high-risk product despite clear evidence of its dangers, we need to start strip-searching *all* GE products on the market, and immediately abort this flawed approval procedure," said Christopher Then, Genetic Engineer campaigner, *Greenpeace International.*

170 www.hawaii.edu/biograph/biohi/biographies.html

171 Almost everyone I talk with explains to me that the *Robinsons are land rich and cash poor*. One even tells of being in a K-Mart parking lot when Keith asks to borrow 20 bucks to buy dog food, apparently not having the cash. Or credit?

The story sticks in my mind about John Paul Getty installing pay phones in his English mansion because he was tired of guests making long distant calls and leaving him (one of the richest men in the world) to pay for them. And a rich cousin told me that anytime people talked *poor* to her, she talked *poorer*. What most people do when they get in trouble with lack of money is sell something they have—like incredible amounts of land. But, then, as a Surfrider person tells me, they plan to sue because they don't believe Robinsons have proper title to the land. As you can observe, rumors abound!

172 4-8-10, *Front Page of The Garden Island*, "EPA Fines Gay & Robinson for Cesspools," by Coco Zickos.

173 *Legendary Hawai'i and the Politics of Place: Tradition, Translation, and Tourism* by Cristina Bacchilega

174 Learn more from Rosemary I. Patterson's *Aloha and Mai Tais: A novel About Hawaii In The 1930s and 1940s*. Westerns "reinterpret rewrite Hawaiian music. Their music is another nail in the coffin of Hawaiian culture. Their lyrics are insulting to Hawaiians … and their dance routines take our sacred hula and oral history and transform them into a Hollywood plot and chorus line."

175 *E Na Hulu Kupuna Na Puna Ola Maoli No* by Anne Kapulani Landgraf

176 *Legendary Hawai'i and the Politics of Place: Tradition, Translation, and Tourism* by Cristina Bacchilega

177 George Kanahele and his 1982, *Hawaiian Renaissance* point out: "We should all be elated that a once rich culture threatened with extinction has been able to survive and now appears to be thriving in spite of the odds against it." And that consciously or unconsciously, everyone who claims or wants Hawaii to be home, wants to share in its Hawaiianness. To the extent that this is true, then, we're all part of the Hawaiian Renaissance—bringing Hawaiian culture and values to the forefront.

178 ibid

179 4-8-10, Front page of *The Garden Island*.

180 Newspaper article by Anne O'Malley with pictures and quotes from Levon - Article appeared in June 11, 2008 edition of KAUA`I PEOPLE.

181 Turmeric is a smaller pungent cousin to my favorite ginger I use in tea every day.

182 William Hyde Rice's, *Hawaiian Legends*, published by Bishop Museum Press, in 1923 & 1977 is one such book. I thought it would be a treasure trove. But the information is wrong for me. The black and white pictures though are stunning. It's gratuitous but Kauai's *Hawaiian Legends* was one book that just didn't ring true. Interested though I am in legends, I could not read it. Someone obviously put a lot of work into this book but I never found the heart.

183 His five hundred and twenty-two page book of Hawaiian history and legends is first published in 1888 by Charles Tuttle and then forgotten for about a hundred years. The contrast between this and Rice's book is simply amazing. If I didn't know better I'd think they wrote of different countries. And maybe they do!

184 Rita Knipe, *The Water of Life: A Jungian Journey Through Hawaiian Myth*.

185 *A Hawaiian Life* by George Kahumoku, Jr

186 Quoted in Kathy E. Magliato's *Healing Hearts: A Memoir of a Female Heart Surgeon*.

187 Email received April, 10, 2010.

188 [Editor's note from http://islandbreath.blogspot.com: Dow is the corporation that brought us Napalm and Agent Orange used to burn and deforest Vietnam, Laos and Cambodia. It is the company that created the dioxin that turned the Love Canal neighborhood of New York into a ghost town. It's the company that bought out Union Carbide, the outfit that produced the Bohpal, India, chemical catastrophe. Dow is the company that's probably come to Kauai to produce pesticide resistant, genetically altered, patented seed corn.

For more info on Dow, see The Truth about Dow.] http://islandbreath.
blogspot.com/2010/06/message-from-dow-gmo.html

189   [2nd Editor's note from http://islandbreath.blogspot.com: We
      attempted to contact Dow's Kauai office (808-335-5081) listed in the
      phone book. There was no answer or message at the number. What
      we've learned from other GMO operations leads us to believe that
      what Dow AgroScience will not do is help free food production from
      the petro-chemical industry we are addicted to. They will not help
      feed the world or even feed Kauai. Kauai's sugarcane lands have been
      deforested and the topsoil has been destroyed and contaminated. We
      need to restore our soil, grasslands and forests. We need to produce
      ten times as much local food as we do today to survive here after
      petro-collapse. We do not want Dow on Kauai. Dow is a chemical
      company, not a food producer.] http://islandbreath.blogspot.
      com/2010/06/message-from-dow-gmo.html

190   "County takes legal action against seed companies: Dow Agro,
      Pioneer addressing unpermitted grubbing violations," by Vanessa
      Van Voorhis, *The Garden Island*, May 4, 2011.

191   Cathrine Pearson, "Hemp For Your Health: 7 Uses," *The Huffingtonn
      Post*, May 6, 2011

192   Steven Jacobson

193   *The Epic Tale of Hiiakaikapoliopele:* Woman of the sunrise, lightning-
      skirted beauty by Ho'oulumahiehie, translated by Paukea Nogelmeier

194   ibid

195   Letter to the Editor- March 28, 2011 from Carl Berg of Surfrider
      Foundation.

      So now the mainland owners of the shrimp farm (Integrated
      Aquaculture) have extorted $250,000 from the County [the shrimp
      farm deliberately choose a bad location next to a long-time waste site]
      and have been issued a permit from the Department of Health that
      allows them to discharge 20 million gallons a day of nutrient and
      bacteria laden waste water. The shrimp farm was required to test for
      more pollutants, but very infrequently, and only once a year if they
      only discharge into the ditch.

The community of Kekaha should carefully watch the operations at the shrimp farm. If you see dead fish or shrimp, smell rotten stuff, or feel slimy shrimp water, then immediately email or call Gary I. Gill, the new Deputy Director for Environmental Health in Honolulu and let him know. His email address is gary.gill@doh.hawaii.gov and his telephone number is 808-586-4424. He will make sure the shrimp farm meets the permit requirements.

196 Mike Peed, "We Have No Bananas: Can scientists defeat a devastating blight?" *The New Yorker*, January 10, 2011, pp 28-34.

197 *A Hawaiian Life* by George Kahumoku, Jr

198 James Dale, a professor at Queensland University of Technology, in Brisbane, who experiments with genetically modified crops. In 1994 he produced one of the first genetically transformed Cavendishes. Quoted in Mike Peed, "We Have No Bananas: Can scientists defeat a devastating blight?" *The New Yorker*, January 10, 2011, pp 28-34.

199 Adrian Hyland, in *Gunshot Road*

200 Women's histories and lives are different from men's. Every woman is a leader; we're all leaders of our own lives. And the sooner we come to consciousness of our own self, the more useful and enjoyable we can make our life and influence.

Every women is the leader of her family; she has that power of being the center of home life in any but the most oppressive family and society. True, some families and societies oppress and denigrate; women are little more than chattels.

Education is always a way out, offering better survival and possible transformation. We see these graphic changes as women in undeveloped countries like India and Africa use small personal loans to transform their traditional poverty and ignorance into improved lives for themselves and their families. Educate a woman and we educate a family as my mother used to say. Educate enough families and we transform communities and, hopefully, societies, our world.

Closer to home we've got our problems. The US Paycheck Fairness Act was passed by the House in 2009 but still languishes in the Senate. Federal studies show women still earn roughly 80 cents for every dollar earned by men. The Paycheck Act would protect employees who share salary information with co-workers and would require employers to show that wage differences are job-related, not gender-based. It's now the end of 2010 and our country is still hanging around with this discrimination and unfairness.

201 *Shaping Hawaii: The Voices of Women: Oral Histories of the Islands' First Settlers* by Joyce Lebra.

202 And if you are Native Hawaiian, or even kama' aina like me and love this paradise, you'll probably read this history and break your heart one more time. Or maybe even start getting furious enough to do something about rank injustice.

203 Following quotes and information are from Lebra.

204 Fivehundred and sixty acres of land in Hawaii!!

205 *Shaping Hawaii: The Voices of Women: Oral Histories of the Islands' First Settlers* by Joyce Lebra

206 Sugar companies subverted the Homestead law (passed for the benefit of Hawaiians) by using fake homesteaders to buy land which made their plantations larger and pushed more Hawaiians off their land.

207 "Many Hawaiians lost land in the decade following the Great Mahele. They were driven off by alien concepts of sale and purchase, by requirements that they present claims to land on which they had always lived. It was not only the loss of land but also an alien social system that made them in many respects strangers in their own land. Instances of loss of land through deceit were legion."

208 For this grievous story see John Tayman, *The Colony*, 2006

209 Before them came 6,000 Puerto Ricans arriving in 1900-1901; 8,000 Koreans and 8,000 Spaniards arrived between 1907 and 1913. Lebra says that after immigrating 2,869 men and boys over the age of twelve from Puerto Rico, in October 14, 1901 the cold-blooded trustees of the Hawaiian Sugar Planters' Association (HSPA) decided to discontinue that immigration (Their original plan was to import 5,000), and the first phase of immigration was concluded.

210 ibid

211 ibid

212 Another says that Goddess Pele was important to her family. Each family had a totemic protector (aumakua) which also guided the soul to its final resting place after a family member's death. Another woman told of the Menehune (small people) who lived in caves on Kauai and Oahu, planted taro and sweet potatoes, enjoyed sports and games, and could even control the weather.

213 "During the decade following both annexations, 109,928 Filipino workers and families immigrated to Hawaii. The exodus of labor from the Philippines was so great that in 1915 the Philippine government passed laws restricting and regulating labor recruitment. [Still in] 1926 over half the sugar plantation labor in Hawaii was Filipino and as the most recently arrived ethnic group, the Filipinos were incorporated at the bottom of the socioeconomic plantation structure." With lots more men than women, women married early which cut off their education and helped keep them downtrodden at the low end of the totem pole.

214 Isabella L. Bird, *Six Months in the Sandwich Islands*

215 ibid

216 "Volunteers triple size of Poipu beach," Paul C. Curtis, *The Garden Island*, July 14, 2010.

217 Wikipedia says the act of a spit reaching out to an island is far from random. By looking at the geomorphology of tombolos it is possible to understand how they are made. Tombolos are known to form by wave refraction. As waves near an island they are slowed down by the shallow water surrounding it. These waves then refract or *bend* around the island to the opposite side as they approached. In other words, the waves sweep sediment together from both sides. Eventually, when enough sediment has built up the beach shoreline, known as a spit, will connect with an island and form a tombolo. Tombolos help us understand the sensitivity of shorelines. A small piece of land, such as an island, can change the way the waves are moving which then leads to different deposits of sand.

218 In an act of either ignorance or audacious contempt for water, culture, and recent State court decisions, the KIUC Board of Directors voted on Tuesday, March 29, 2011 to engage the mainland company, Free Flow Power, to secure water rights to develop several hydroelectric projects on Kauai. In fact, these water claims had already been submitted by the Free Flow Power, but the Board decision will make every electrical user on Kauai party to this action. Note that three Board members, Carol Bain, Ben Sullivan, and Jan Tenbruggencate voted against this action. Email from Ken Taylor 4-1-11

219 Prototype for my novel *Secrets*.

220 To find something that tastes so good is so good for you—how excellent is that!

"Cacao beans, the base of chocolate, contain flavonoids (antioxidant-containing plant pigments) that make the antioxidants in dark chocolate nearly eight times as abundant as those in strawberries, which are themselves considered an excellent source." And then we learn that "cacao beans help lower blood pressure and LDL (bad) cholesterol and that cacao increases levels of serotonin, a natural antidepressant, as well," adds the internet.

But there's chocolate and then there's chocolate. The only way to be sure you are getting a reasonable amount of flavonoids in chocolate is to select those containing at least 70% cacao and white chocolate isn't really chocolate and all chocolate contains lots of calories along with the flavonoids—an average is 150 calories per ounce so best not stuff yourself. (Source: Joy Bauer, a weight specialist.)

221 *Anahola: Kauai's Mystic Hawaiian Village* by Agnes Keaolani Marti-Kini, 2009.

222 ibid

223 ibid

224 Quoting Esther Kaleialoha talking about sovereignty.

225 *Halfway to Asia* by John Griffin

226 ibid

227 "Kahuna were priests believed to possess special powers, including the most notorious—the ability to pray a person to death or to health.

There were several schools of Kahuna, and the power was passed from father to son. To succeed in his lethal prayers, the kahuna needed to obtain something connected with the intended victim—a lock of hair or nail parings, for example. These omens left at the doorstep inspired such fear that the targeted victims often, in fact, died. In 1850, during the reign of Kamehameha II, a law was passed against the practice, but it continued surreptitiously until long after. I recall one instance that occurred during my childhood in the 1930s.

Some kahuna dealt with healing rather than death, and these healing kahuna were often women. Kahuna were also consulted before new ventures were undertaken." Joyce Lebra, *Shaping Hawaii: The Voices of Women: Oral Histories of the Islands' First Settlers.*

228 I further learn from Wikipedia that the disease usually affects farmers, gardeners, and agricultural workers entering through small cuts and abrasions in the skin to cause the infection. And interestingly that Sporotrichosis can also be acquired from handling cats with the disease and is an occupational hazard for veterinarians.

229 http://en.wikipedia.org/wiki/Immune_system

230 Rosemary Patterson's *Kula Keiki Alii: A Novel Partially Based On The Effect of The Chief's Children's School on Hawaii's Monarchs* (yes, this is the complete title)

231 Wikipedia notes.

232 *Pauahi: The Kamehameha Legacy* by George Kanahele

233 Rosemary Patterson's *Kula Keiki Alii: A Novel Partially Based On The Effect of The Chief's Children's School on Hawaii's Monarchs* (yes, this is the complete title)

234 ibid

235 *Surveying the Mahele: Mapping the Hawaiian Land Revolution* by Riley M. Moffat & Gary L. Fitzpatrick

236 ibid

237 Alice Walker, *Now Is The Time To Open Your Heart*

238 *Aloha Niihau: Oral Histories* by Emalia Licayan, Virginia Nizo, and Elama Kanahee

239 ibid

240 Daniel Goleman in *Ecological Intelligence.*

241 ibid

242 A telling example of consumer action concerns farmers in India in 2004 near a Coca-Cola plant. The farmers were given sludge, a bottling plant by-product, for their fields. When analyzed, this sludge showed heavy metals and when these findings were posted on web pages, media throughout India and the world took notice. The court ordered a shutdown of that bottling plant resulting in a drop in Coke sales throughout India. With bottom line profits affected, Coke got busy and fixed the problems including looking at water use at their factories world-wide.

243 Help with finding safe products is there if you hunt for it. The average American woman applies one to two dozen personal care products daily. *Skin Deep*, www.cosmeticsdatabase.com tells us which of these contain chemicals harmful to our body's biggest organ, the skin.

244 Daniel Goleman in *Ecological Intelligence*

245 *Reconnecting the Healing Circle* http://www.joannlordahl.com/Items/ Item.php?ThisId=Reconnecting

246 *Wahine Noa: for the life of my country* written by Keahi Felix

247 *The Aloha Quilt* by Jennifer Chiaverini

248 *Wahine Noa: for the life of my country* written by Keahi Felix

249 1. It will give you information that amplifies what you already know

2. It will change your mind about what you think you know

3. It will peel your skin and heighten your sensitivities before you get totally sunburnt by prevailing American propaganda

4. It will show you why Hawaii is a nation in search of itself and, therefore, why achieving solidarity of viewpoint among Hawaiian activists is an inch-by-inch process. It will reveal why all residents of the Hawaiian Islands are implicated and invited to enter the process of restoration of the original country. It will pull from 19th century records why a number of other countries are stakeholders too in that restoration

5. It will enable you to interpret the following metaphor – Hawaii's destiny is to be the fire in the rainbow.

250 "Broken Promise: Hawaiians Wait in Vain for Their Land" by Susan Faludi, *The Wall Street Journal*, Monday, September 9, 1991.

251 Quoted from Felix. Hawaii Advisory Committee to the U. S. Commission on Civil Rights, Letter of Transmittal, *A Broken Trust: the Hawaiian Homelands Program: Seventy Years of Failure of the Federal and State Governments to Protect the Civil Rights of Native Hawaiians*, U.S. Government Printing Office: 1991 – 617-651/41065.

252 John Griffin, *Web of Islands: A Hawaii-Pacific Novel* & *Halfway to Asia*

253 http://www.hawaiiankingdom.org

254 ibid

255 http://www2.hawaii.edu/~anu/

256 You've seen this before.

257 *John Perkins, Confessions of An Economic Hit Man*

258 ibid

259 RAN (Rainforest Action Network www.ran.org)

260 John Perkins, *The Secret History of the American Empire: The Truth About Economic Hit Men, Jackals, and How to Change the World*

261 This Associated Press article by Michael J Crumb in early December, 2010 goes on and on giving both sides. I'm only reporting one.

"This is the first time ever a federal court ordered an illegal biotech crop destroyed," said George Kimbrell, an attorney for the Centers for Food Safety. And Paul Atchitoff of Earthjustice said, White's ruling is, "an indication that the government needs to start doing its job. The USDA needs to stop ignoring the environmental laws regarding genetically modified crops."

262 For fuller information go to Robert Agar at www.ehow.com/about_5453728_fda-vs-usda]

263 Isabelia Kenfield's article in the Organic Consumers Association in August 2009. "Michael R. Taylor's appointment by the Obama administration to the Food and Drug Administration (FDA) on

July 7th sparked immediate debate and even outrage among many food and agriculture researchers and activists. The Vice President for Public Policy at Monsanto Corp. from 1998 until 2001, Taylor exemplifies the revolving door between the food industry and the government agencies that regulate it. He is reviled for shaping and implementing the government's favorable agricultural biotechnology [GMO] policies during the Clinton administration."

This interesting article goes on to note, carefully of course, that Taylor's real job is probably to push sales of GMO seeds and pesticides (read Monsanto) in Africa and he's already enlisting powerful help.

Several articles call Michael Taylor a Food Czar; he is recently appointed as a senior adviser to the FDA Commissioner on food safety. An FDA news release:

> Michael R. Taylor, J.D., a nationally recognized food safety expert and research professor at George Washington University's School of Public Health and Health Services, will return to the U.S. Food and Drug Administration to serve as senior advisor to the commissioner.
>
> 'I am pleased to welcome Mike Taylor back to the FDA,' Commissioner of Food and Drugs Margaret A. Hamburg, M.D., said in announcing Taylor's appointment. 'His expertise and leadership on food safety issues will help the agency to develop and implement the prevention based strategy we need to ensure the safety of the food we eat.'

264 Currently he is Obama's Food Security Tzar
265 www.blackjew.net/2009/01/michael-taylor
266 *The Royal Torch* by Billie F. Beamer; *Celebrating Advocacy: Past, Present & Future*: compiled and edited by Aletha Kaohi ... [et al.] and "The Royal Mausoleum of Hawai'i," Pamphlet, April 1997, received from William Kaihe'ekai Maioho, curator.
267 http://en.wikipedia.org/wiki/Kamehameha_II

268 http://en.wikipedia.org/wiki/Kamehameha_III

269 http://en.wikipedia.org/wiki/Sugar_plantations_in_Hawaii

270 http://en.wikipedia.org/wiki/Kamehameha_IV

271 http://en.wikipedia.org/wiki/Kamehameha_V

272 http://en.wikipedia.org/wiki/Kalākaua

273 Is this basic outline of Hawaiian history simple—yes. Is this history complete—no. Accurate—no. The problem occurs again and again: A point of view, or the writer's bias carries and informs purported facts. In this case of Beamer's, the bias is that the Tahitian chiefs and their descendants are evil. And perpetuating their evil, yea until current days. A simplistic point of view and what could we do about that history anyway? The past is over and done and too long ago. Now we'll just blame the victims, say they deserved everything they got, and let the past go as missionary-history, self-justified that. Not our fight, not our responsibility. Nothing to do with us now living our comfortable, already complicated-enough lives. We're too busy to bother with all that past stuff.

But I'm stuck. I can't run and neither can I fully accept this take on Hawaiian history. Besides, it's incomplete. Perhaps a path now is my filling in some blanks in Beamer's list of Island Rulers, which I have begun. (And here I am giving my gathered up version of Hawaiian history; both true and untrue of course. But only I know how much work I've put into this history, as if that matters, and that something solid to follow and to hang speculation upon is better than nothing!)

Book List

A Chronicle and Flora of Niihau by Juliet Rice Wichman and Harold St. John

A Hawaiian Life by George Kahumoku, Jr

Act of War: The Overthrow of the Hawaiian Nation, Video by University of Hawaii

Adoption by Victoria I. Sullivan

Aloha and Mai Tais: A novel About Hawaii In The 1930s and 1940s by Rosemary I. Patterson

Aloha, Kauai: A Childhood by Waimea Williams

Aloha Niihau: Oral Histories by Emalia Licayan, Virginia Nizo, and Eama Kanahele

The Aloha Quilt by Jennifer Chiaverini

Amelia: A Novel of Mid-nineteenth Century Hawaii by Juliet Rice Wichman

Ancient Hawaii by Herbert Kawainui Kane

Ano Ano = The Seed by Kristin Zambucka

An Account of the Polynesian Race: Its Origin and Migrations, and the Ancient History of the Hawaiian People to the Times of Kamehameha by Abraham Fornander

An Introduction to Hawaii by Ansel Adams (photographer), and Edward Joesting

An Island in the Turquoise Sea: Stories of Kauai by Carl F. Heintze

Anahola: Kauai's Mystic Hawaiian Village by Agnes Keaolani Marti-Kini

Ancient Hawaiian Civilization by Handy, Emory, Bryan, Buck, Wise and Others

And Then There Were None video by Elizabeth Kapu'uwailane Lindsey

Behold Kaua'i: Modern Days – Ancient Ways by Dawn Fraser Kawahara

Between the Deep Blue Sea and Me by Lurline Wailana McGregor

The Bone Hook, by Ian MacMillan

"Broken Promise: Hawaiians Wait in Vain for Their Land" by Susan Faludi, *The Wall Street Journal*, Monday, September 9, 1991

Celebrating Advocacy: Past, Present & Future compiled and edited by Aletha Kaohi ... [et al.]

Chanting: Discovering Spirit in Sound by Robert Gass

Collapse: How Societies Choose to Fail or Succeed by Jared Diamond

Confessions of An Economic Hit Man by John Perkins

Conquest of Hawaii, History Channel & article by Charles K. Maxwell, *Maui News*, October 21, 2003

Deep Nutrition: Why Your Genes Need Traditional Food, by Catherine and Luke Shanahan

Defy Gravity: Healing Beyond the Bounds of Reason by Caroline Myss

The Descendants by Kaui Hart Hemmings

Dismembering Lahui: A History of the Hawaiian Nation to 1887 by Jonathan Kay Kamakawiwo'ole Osorio

Diving Deep and Surfacing by Carol Christ

E Na Hulu Kupuna Na Puna Ola Maoli No by Anne Kapulani Landgraf

Eat, Pray, Love: One Woman's Search for Everything Across Italy, India and Indonesia by Elizabeth Gilbert

Ecological Intelligence by Daniel Goleman

Emma: Hawaii's Remarkable Queen by George S. Kanahele

The Empty Throne by Lori Kamae

The Epic Tale of Hiiakaikapoliopele: Woman of the sunrise, lightning-skirted beauty by Ho'oulumahiehie, translated by Paukea Nogelmeier

Exposed: The Toxic Chemistry of Everyday Products and What's at Stake for American Power by Mark Schapiro.

Facing Hawaii's Future: Harvesting Essential Information about GMO's by A Project of Hawaii SEED, www.hawaiiseed.org, a non-profit, most informative organization

Feminism as Therapy by Anica Vesel Mander & Anne Kent Rush

First Peoples Theology Journal, "Native Hawaiian Spirituality," by Alberta Pualani Hopkins

Fragments of Hawaiian History by John Papa Ii

From a Native Daughter: Colonialism and Sovereignty in Hawai'i by Hunani-Kay Trask

Genetic Roulette: The Documented Health Risks of Genetically Engineered Foods by Jeffrey M. Smith

The Future of Food, CD by Lily Films

"Genetically Modified Hawaii: New varieties of genetically engineered crops thrive in the world's most isolated landmass," *Scientific American* by Robynne Boyd

"Getting to Know Ruth: The princess defied Western ways and paid for it by being ignored by historians until now," by John Berger, jberger@starbulletin.com

Grapes of Canaan by Albertine Loomis

Halfway to Asia by John Griffin

Hawaii by Deborah Kent, a 2008 Scholastic book.

Hawaii Pono: A Social History by Lawrence Fuchs

Hawaii's Story by Hawaii's Queen Liliuokalani

Hawaiian Antiquities, David Malo (Incredible source of ancient Hawaiian knowledge.)

The Hawaiian Chiefs' Children's School 1839-1850, A Record Compiled from the Diary and Letters of Amos Starr Cooke and Juliette Montague Cooke by their granddaughter Mary Atherton Richards

"Hawaiian Nation – Part One & Part Two," www.islandbreath.org by Juan Wilson

The Hawaiian Revolution: Tomorrow is Too Late by William Andrew Fritz

Hawaiian Values by Dr. George S. Kanahele, Editor

The Heart of Being Hawaiian, by Sally-jo Keala-o-Anuenue

"High Chief Ruth Keelikolani and Her Acquaintance with Kauai," by Hank Soboleski

The High Chiefess: Ruth Keelikolani by Kristin Zambucka

Honolulu by Anan Brennert

Ho'oponopono: Contemporary Uses of a Hawaiian Problem-Solving Process by E. Victoria Shook.

Ho'oulumahiehie. Ka mo'olelo hiwahiwa o Kawelo, edited by Hiapokeikikane Kichie Perreira

I Myself Have Seen It: The Myth of Hawai'i by Susanna Moore

Images of America: Kauai by Stormy Cozad

In A Hawaiian Valley by Kathleen Mellen

Ka'a'awa; a novel about Hawaii in the 1850s by O. A. Bushnell

Kauai: Now & Then, video by Terrence Moeller Production (A beautiful 55 minute documentary with gorgeous scenery and Kauaian people around the island telling their story. Lovely and representative of the times of their memories and of the now and then changes.)

Kauai: The Separate Kingdom by Edward Joesting

K.O.'D in the Rift by Victoria Heckman

Kuhina Nui by Rosemary Patterson

Kuleana by The Ho'ulu Hou Project: Stories Told By Us

The Kumuliph: An Hawaiian Creation Myth or *An Account of The Creation of the World According to Hawaiian Tradition* by Liliuokalani of Hawaii

The Last King of Paradise by Eugene Burns

"Last Will and Testament of the Late Hon. Ruth Keelikolani." January 24, 1883 by www.hawaiialive.org

Legendary Hawai'i and the Politics of Place: Tradition, Translation, and Tourism by Cristina Bacchilega

The Legends and Myths of Hawaii by His Hawaiian Majesty Kalakaua

Lele Kawa: Fire Rituals of Pele by Taupouri Tangaro

The Lost Art of Gratitude, by Alexander McCall Smith

Making Peace: Ho'oponopono Then & Now, Stories contributed by Samuel M. Kamakau and Grace Cora Oness and Retold in Hawaiian and English by Malcolm Naea Chun

Memoirs by Pablo Neruda

Mililani Mauka by Chris McKinney

The Mystery of Grace by Charles De Lint

My Time in Hawaii: A Polynesian Memoir by Victoria Nelson

Night Is a Sharkskin Drum by Haunani-Kay Trask

Niihau: The Traditions of an Hawaiian Island by Rerioterai Tava and Moses K. Keale Sr.

No Mana'o loha O Kaho'olawe (The Many Feelings of Love For Kaho'olawe) by Walter Ritte Jr. and Richard Sawyer

Now Is The Time To Open Your Heart, by Alice Walker

"Old Pain, New Hope", *Yes,* by Sheldon Ito

Paradise Remade: The Politics of Culture and History in Hawai'i by Elizbeth Buck

Partners in Pleasure: Sharing Success, Creating Joy, Fulfilling Dreans—Together by Paul Pearsall.

Pauahi: The Kamehameha Legacy by George Kanahele

"Princess Ruth Keelikolani, Hawaiian Alii," by Kalena Silva in *Biography Hawaii: Five Lives, A Series of Public Remembrances,* A television documentary

Queen Emma and Lawai by David Forbes, pamplet

Reminiscences of a Life in the Islands by Helen Kapililani Sanborn Davis

Resource Units in Hawaiian Culture: revised edition by Donald D. Kilolani Mitchell

"Robinson family may sell Niihau, leave Hawaii," by Trish Moore, *Star Bulletin*, April 17, 1996.

The Royal Mausoleum of Hawai'i, Pamphlet, April 1997, Received from William Kaihe'ekai Maioho, curator.

The Royal Torch by Billie F. Beamer

"Ruta Keanololani Kamuolaulani Keelikolani Kanahoahoa: A View from Her Time," by Puakea Nogelmeier

The Secret History of the American Empire: The Truth About Economic Hit Men, Jackals, and How to Change the World by John Perkins

Seeds of Deception: Exposing Industry and Government Lies About the Safety of the Genetically Engineered Foods You're Eating by Jeffrey M. Smith

Shaping Hawaii: The Voices of Women: Oral Histories of the Islands' First Settlers by Joyce Lebra

Shark Dialogues by Kiana Davenport

So You Want to Live in Hawaii by Toni Polancy

Song of the Exile, by Kiana Davenport

"Spell for a Traveler" by Lisel Mueller, quoted in Monika Wikman, *Pregnant Darkness: Alchemy and the Rebirth of Consciousness*

The SuperFerry Chronicles: Hawaii's Uprising Against Miltarism, Commercialism and the Desecration of the Earth by Koohan Paik & Jerry Mander

Surveying the Mahele: Mapping the Hawaiian Land Revolution by Riley M. Moffat & Gary L. Fitzpatrick

Tales from the Night Rainbow by Koko Willis & Pali Jae Lee

365 Tao: Daily Meditations by Deng Ming-Dao

Uncertain Peril: Genetic Engineering and the Future of Seeds by Claire Hope Cummings

Voices of Wisdom: Hawaiian Elders Speak by M. J. Harden

Wahine Noa: for the life of my country by Keahi Felix

Web of Islands: A Hawaii-Pacific Novel by John Griffin

Words Earth Aloha: The Source of Hawaiian Music, Documentary by Eddie & Myrna Kamae

The Water of Life: A Jungian Journey Through Hawaiian Myth by Rita Knipe

Wise Secrets of Aloha by Kahuna Harry Uhane Jim & Garnette Arledge.

Who Owns the Crown Lands of Hawai'i? by Jon M. Van Dyke

The World According to Monsanto: Pollution, Corruption, And the Control of Our Food Supply by Marie-Monique Robin

Backpiece: A Chronology of Hawaiian Rulers, including Princess Ruth dates.

Beamer's Island Rulers[266]
[Princess Ruth lived from 1826-1883]

AD 400   First Migration to Hawaii from Marguesas

1100   Tahitian chiefs and warriors conquer agricultural natives

1100-   Tribal wars between six chiefdoms,

1795   human sacrifices rampant practice [How true is this? I'm skeptical.]

1778   Captain Cook comes upon the isolated islands

1805   Merchant ships bring new technology and plague, half or more of the Hawaiian population dies

1810   With western arms, Kamehameha is King, centralizes land and control -

King Kaumualii (King K) is the last independent King of Kauai 1780 to1824 – accepts Kamehameha rule but remains as King on Kauai in 1810.

1819   King Kamehameha One appoints his young son Liholiho (lee-ho-lee-ho), age 22 as King (Kamehameha Two,[267] and Queen Kaahumanu (Queen K) his favorite to be spiritual leader and advisor to the king. Kamehameha One dies, rigid taboo system disbanded. Chaos reigns. Queen K is co-regent with Kamehameha Two.

1820   Seven protestant missionaries arrive, Catholics follow in 1828 [Actually 14 missionaries arrived counting the wives who played major roles.]

1821   The new young King Kamehameha II (at Queen K's instigation) comes to Kauai, invites King K aboard and sails away to Honolulu where King K, is forced to marry Queen K, to ensure the island chain's union.

1824   Kamehameha Two dies

1825   Kamehameha Three[268] is King [Became king at eleven; tries to modernize Hawaii]

1826   Princess Ruth Born

1840   First constitution for islands, foreign advisors for so-called primitive Kings

1850   Plantations gain power – Big Five - Sugar[269]

1854   Kamehameha Three dies

1855   Kamehameha Four[270] is King Alexander Liholiho [Princess Ruth's half brother, traveled – went to Chief's Children School]

1863   Kamehameha Four dies

1863   Kamehameha Five[271] is King Lot [Princess Ruth's half brother, went to Chief's Children School]

1871   Kamehameha Five dies

1873	Kamehameha Six – Lunalilo - Last Kamehameha king of the Kingdom of Hawaii
1874	Ruled from January 8, 1873 until February 3, 1874 when he dies.
1874	David Kalakaua[272] becomes King of Hawaii. (Not a Kamehameha) Merrie Monarch. Brings back traditional Hawaii. He builds Iolani palace which inspires Princess Ruth to build her more elaborate Keoua Hale Palace
1881	Princess Ruth stops volcano in Hilo
1883	Princess Ruth Died
1891	David Kalakaua died on January 20, 1891
1891	David Kalakaua's sister, Queen Liliuokalani, assumes throne by vote after King David dies.
1893	Overthrow of Monarchy, Queen Liliuokalani deposed
1898-	Hawaii annexed to United States
1900	Granted Territorial status
1941	Pearl Harbor attacked by Japan
1959	Hawaii granted Statehood[273]

Made in the USA
Charleston, SC
11 June 2013